Praise for *New York Times* bestselling author
Lynsay Sands and the Argeneau Vampire series

'Sands writes books that keep readers coming back
for more . . . clever, steamy, with a deliciously wicked
sense of humour that readers will gobble up'
Katie MacAlister

'Inventive, sexy, and fun'
Angela Knight

'Delightful and full of interesting characters
and romance'
Romantic Times

'Vampire lovers will find themselves laughing throughout.
Sands' trademark humour and genuine characters keep
her series fresh and her readers hooked'
Publishers Weekly

The Accidental Vampire

LYNSAY SANDS

Published by arrangement with HarperCollins Publishers,
New York, New York USA

First published in Great Britain in 2012 by
Gollancz
An imprint of the Orion Publishing Group
Orion House, 5 Upper St Martin's Lane, London WC2H 9EA
An Hachette UK Company

3 5 7 9 10 8 6 4 2

A CIP catalogue record for this book is available
from the British Library

ISBN 978 0 575 11071 7

Printed in Great Britain by Clays Ltd, St Ives plc

The Orion Publishing Group's policy is to use papers that are
natural, renewable and recyclable products and made from wood
grown in sustainable forests. The logging and manufacturing
processes are expected to conform to the environmental regulations
of the country of origin.

www.lynsaysands.net
www.orionbooks.co.uk

For Mike, Karen, and Owen,
for letting me turn Day into Knight

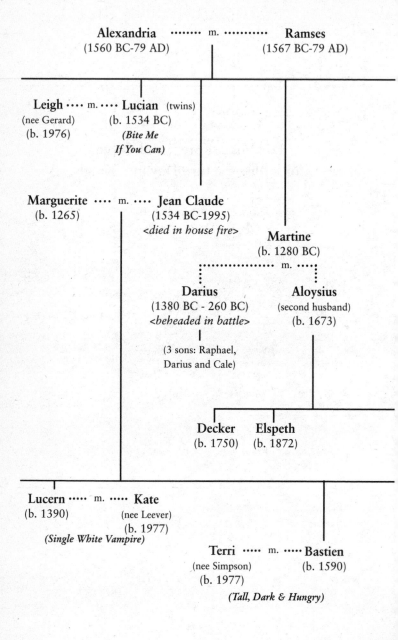

Argeneau Family Tree

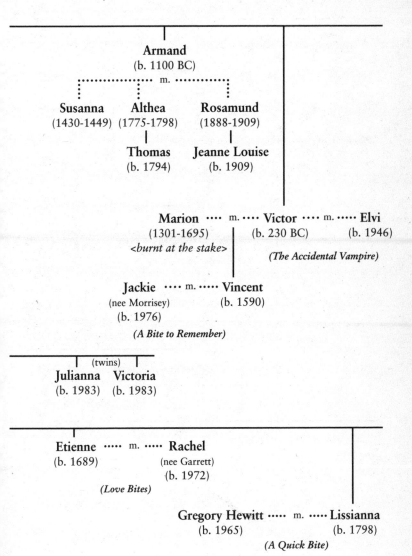

Armand
(b. 1100 BC)
·········· m. ··········

Susanna   **Althea**   **Rosamund**
(1430-1449)   (1775-1798)   (1888-1909)

Thomas   **Jeanne Louise**
(b. 1794)   (b. 1909)

Marion ···· m. ···· **Victor** ···· m. ····· **Elvi**
(1301-1695)   (b. 230 BC)   (b. 1946)
<burnt at the stake>

(The Accidental Vampire)

Jackie ···· m. ····· **Vincent**
(nee Morrisey)   (b. 1590)
(b. 1976)

(A Bite to Remember)

(twins)
Julianna   **Victoria**
(b. 1983)   (b. 1983)

Etienne ····· m. ····· **Rachel**
(b. 1689)   (nee Garrett)
(b. 1972)

(Love Bites)

Gregory Hewitt ····· m. ····· **Lissianna**
(b. 1965)   (b. 1798)

(A Quick Bite)

One

It was a high-pitched scream that woke Elvi. Piercing and full of terror, it ripped her from sleep and had her moving before she was quite awake. She started up abruptly only to curse and drop back down when her head slammed into the wooden lid of the coffin.

Groaning at the pain vibrating through her skull, Elvi closed her eyes against the stars dancing before them and pressed a hand against her forehead. She'd really cracked herself good and would have liked to clasp her head in both hands and roll around in agony for a moment, but the casket wouldn't allow it.

And then a second terrified shriek reminded her of why she was awake.

She reached out with the hand not holding her head and gave the coffin lid a shove that sent it flying open. She then had to release her head to get up. Climbing out of a coffin was a two-handed job, and ridiculously strenuous first thing in the morning. Especially before her first bag of blood.

Elvi cursed her way out of the contraption, her bare feet slapping on the hardwood floor as she hurried out of her room without even bothering to grab a robe to cover the white cotton nightgown she wore. Another scream cut the air as she raced up the hall. A fourth was being issued just as she burst into Mabel's room. Elvi slammed the door open, uncaring that it crashed into the wall and probably left a lovely hole.

She spotted Mabel at once, standing on the bed in her robe, backed against the wall, silver hair a chaotic mass around her head and eyes wide with panic. The woman was waving a body brush wildly in the air at a bat that was swooping just as wildly around the room near the ceiling. She was also, apparently, screeching every time the winged animal came anywhere near her. Elvi watched as the bat swerved to avoid hitting the far wall and swooped back toward Mabel, setting off another shriek.

Veering to the side to avoid the waving shower brush, the bat swept through the open bathroom door and briefly out of sight. Elvi rushed over and slammed the door closed, trapping it inside.

"Oh!" Mabel collapsed on the bed, hugging the shower brush to her chest. "Oh, thank God."

Elvi propped her hands on her hips and scowled at her housemate. "You opened your windows last night."

Mabel sighed at the accusation in her voice. "I had to open the windows. It was hot, Elvi."

"I know it was hot, Mabel. I live here too."

"But your windows have screens on them. The ones in your bedroom, at least."

"I sleep in a coffin," she pointed out in dry tones. "There are no windows in a coffin. Trust me, I *know* it was hot. But you can't open your windows until the replacement screens are in."

"Well, when the hell are they going to put them in already?" Mabel asked impatiently. "It's been two weeks now."

"They had to be specially made and shipped from the manufacturer," Elvi reminded her.

"Yes, because every damned window in this place is a different size," Mabel muttered.

Elvi's mouth quirked with amusement at her disgust. "Welcome to the world of Victorian houses. Ain't it great?"

"Ha!" Mabel snarled, and then sat up with alarm when Elvi moved toward the door to the hall. "Hey! Where are you going?"

"Back to my coffin."

"But what about the bat?" she asked with dismay, scrambling off the bed as quickly as her sixty-two-year-old body would allow and hurrying after her.

"What about it?" she asked, continuing up the hall.

"Well, aren't you going to get it out of my bathroom?"

"Do I look stupid to you?" Elvi asked with disbelief. "I'm not going near that thing. Call Animal Control."

"Animal Control? They won't be open now."

"They must have someone on call for emergencies. Call and find out," Elvi said firmly over her shoulder.

"But that could take hours," Mabel protested. "Can't you just get it out? I mean, you should have some sort of affinity with it."

Elvi paused at the door to her own room and turned on her in amazement. "Do I look like a flying rat to you?"

"No, of course not," Mabel said quickly, then added, "but you're a vampire and it's a bat . . . There should be some empathy or understanding or . . . *something*. Maybe if you tried you could talk to it."

"Right, and by that reasoning we should all be able to talk to monkeys. Let's try that the next time we're near a zoo," Elvi snorted, then repeated, "call Animal Control."

"Elvi!" Mabel cried and stomped her foot when Elvi turned to continue on into her room. "I can't take a shower with that thing in there."

"Mabel, there are six bathrooms in this house with showers and tubs. Use one of the others."

"But—"

Elvi closed the door on her further protest and moved toward the coffin, but paused when her eye caught the time on the digital clock on her dresser. Whipping back around, she yanked her door open and scowled at Mabel's retreating back. "It's nine o'clock!"

"So?" Mabel sounded miffed and kept walking.

"So why didn't you wake me up at eight o'clock like I asked?"

"Because you haven't been sleeping well, and you're exhausted, and I decided to let you sleep in . . . rather kindly in my opinion, but then I'm a kind considerate person . . . unlike some people who won't even try to talk to a bat for a dear faithful friend."

Elvi scowled over the attempt to put her on a guilt trip, and then ground out, "Mabel, it's Owen's birthday today. I have to make a cake and see to the decorations, and—"

Heaving out a long-suffering sigh, Mabel paused and turned to face her. "I saw to the decorating earlier and then came home for a shower for the festivities. I was going to wake you after I'd showered. As for the cake . . ." She shrugged. "They'll wait. The party can't start without you."

When Elvi just stood glaring at her, Mabel waved her away. "Go on. Go take your shower. I'll get dressed and then come help you get ready since *I* can't shower."

"Call Animal Control," Elvi growled, refusing to feel guilty, then slammed her door shut.

"I just can't believe it. An immortal advertising in the Wanted Items ads in the *Toronto Star*! Unbelievable."

Victor threw DJ a glance tinged with irritation. If the younger immortal hadn't been driving the BMW they were both in, he would have cuffed him in the head. As it was, all he could do was mutter in response, "I gathered that the first time you said it, DJ . . . which was two hours and over a hundred repeats ago. I get it. Stop saying it."

"Sorry, but . . ." DJ Benoit shook his head, sending his shoulder-length, sandy-colored hair flying as he repeated, "I just can't believe it."

Rolling his eyes, Victor turned to peer out the tinted car window at the passing night. They were speeding down the highway on the last leg of a two-and-a-half-hour journey, flying past the bright lights of vehicle after vehicle, leaving them behind with little concern for getting a ticket. Victor didn't protest or criticize. Time obviously still held the younger man in its thrall, making him impatient and eager to get the journey over with. Given more time, DJ would realize there was no need to rush; time was not an adversary to be beaten by their kind.

"I mean, in the *Wanted Items ads*," DJ said, drawing his attention again. "Like a male vampire was a bike you could buy or something. What was she hoping to gain from it?"

"Presumably, a lifemate," Victor said dryly.

"You can't find a lifemate like that," DJ protested at once, then added uncertainly, "can you?"

Victor shrugged. "Stranger things have happened."

"Yeah, but . . . Surely she must have realized she'd draw the ire of the council. *Advertising* for God's sake! That's a major faux pas. We're not supposed to draw attention to our people."

"Hmm," Victor grunted. "Our best hope is that any mortals who saw it will think it's a joke or that the ad was purchased by some unfortunate soul with a twisted mind."

"A whackjob," DJ muttered, and then nodded firmly. "That's probably what she is too. She has to be. I mean, come on. None of our kind would be this stupid."

Victor refrained from pointing out that the man had believed it just moments ago and spent the last two hours bemoaning the fact that one of their kind had advertised in the newspaper. He simply let him change his tune as he liked. For himself, Victor's mind wasn't made up. He was content to wait until he met the woman.

"What do you think?"

"About what?" Victor asked.

"Is she for real?" DJ asked, apparently still on the fence about what they were dealing with here.

"How would I know?" he asked with irritation. "I don't know a thing about her. You're the one who answered the ad and has been sending letters to her for the last three weeks."

"E-mails," DJ corrected. "We really have to drag you into the twenty-first century, Argeneau. If you'd had a computer and knew how to use it, you could have done the e-mailing rather than have me do it."

"Which is precisely why I don't intend to get one," Victor announced pointedly. "So, as you are the one who corresponded with her, you tell me. What do you think? Are we on a wild goose chase? Will we find a wannabe Goth baby playing at being a vamp?"

DJ frowned as he considered the matter. "I'm not sure. We exchanged a dozen or so e-mails, but I didn't really learn a thing about the woman. She was irritatingly evasive about everything." He scowled at the road and then added, "In fact, her e-mails were mostly full of questions. She seemed most concerned with verifying that you truly are what you claim to be."

"About *you* and what *you* claimed to be," Victor corrected, thinking it a verbal slip. "I haven't even read the e-mails."

"No, but I was answering them in your name, so used your e-mail account and gave her answers about you."

"What?" Victor turned on him sharply. "I don't have an e-mail account."

"You do now," DJ informed him. "OneHotArgeneau@hotmail.com."

Before Vincent could blast him, DJ hurried on saying, "Well, you did say to answer the ad and try to get her interest so we could find out more about her." He shrugged. "I figured we had a better chance to get her interest if you were the one answering. You're more interesting than me."

"How do you figure that?" he asked with amazement.

"You're rich," DJ answered promptly. "And the

brother of the most powerful immortal on this continent, not to mention a member of one of the oldest families. Chicks go in for that sort of thing. Money, power
. . . It doesn't hurt that you're good-looking either."

"She could hardly have any idea what I look like,"
Victor pointed out with a scowl.

"I e-mailed her a picture," DJ announced. When Victor turned on him, he said defensively, "Well, she asked
for one. So, I sent her the only one I had. The one of
you and Lucian at Lissianna's wedding. Of course," he
added, casting Victor's shoulder-length dark hair and
black jeans and T-shirt a glance. "Your hair was much
shorter then and you were in a suit. You don't look
much like that now."

Victor glowered, and then forced himself to relax
back in the passenger seat. "And what did you receive
in return for this picture and information about my
bloodlines?"

DJ made a face. "Not as much as I'd hoped. A brief
synopsis of her life and a photo."

Removing one hand from the steering wheel, he
reached blindly into the backseat and picked up a file
he'd set there when they got in the car. He handed it to
Victor. "It's in there on one of the e-mails."

Victor opened the file. A photocopy of the newspaper
ad was on top.

*Wanted: Male vampire for attractive and self-
supporting female vampire. Seeking compan-
ionship and a possible love connection. Must
be willing to relocate. Only real vampires need
apply.*

Shaking his head, he continued to leaf through the papers as DJ recounted what he'd learned.

"She's a widow, and part owner with a friend in a Mexican restaurant as well as a bed-and-breakfast. I can't remember the friend's name. Both businesses are in Port Henry. She's lived there her whole life."

Victor grunted at this rundown as he found the picture. It showed a beautiful woman with long dark hair, large dark eyes and full red lips. The name on the back said Elvi.

Victor slid the photo back in the file after the briefest look. She was a beautiful woman, but beauty rarely affected him. He'd seen much of it over his lifetime, enough that it no longer impressed him. It was his experience that beauty was the best way to distract one from, and/or hide, an unbearable ugliness. The devil surely wouldn't show up to tempt covered in warts and slime.

"So?" DJ queried when Victor set the file back on the backseat. "What do you think?"

"I think I can't tell anything from a picture and that little bit of information you managed to get," Victor said, then spotted the sign for the exit they wanted, and added, "but we'll find out soon enough."

DJ made a *tsk* of disgust. "This is probably all a huge waste of time. She didn't seem impressed by the name Argeneau. If she was one of us, she'd have been impressed."

Victor shrugged. "We aren't the only old, powerful family. Maybe she comes from one herself so isn't impressed. Or maybe she's just moved over from Europe. The Argeneau name doesn't carry as much weight over there as it did before we moved. There are a lot of old, powerful families there. Whatever the case, she still has to be checked out."

"Right," DJ said on an exhalation, and then cheered up and added, "On the bright side, if she turns out to be a whacko wannabe, we can get in the car and head straight back to Toronto. We'd be back home by midnight, easy."

Victor smiled faintly, but didn't comment as he watched the rural road they'd exited onto slowly morph into an urban area with first farmhouses and barns appearing out of the darkness, then houses. These quickly gave way to businesses; a gas station, the requisite doughnut shop, secondhand stores, and banks.

"We're meeting her at her restaurant?" Victor asked glancing over the signs on the storefronts they were passing.

"Yes. Bella Black's," DJ said. "It's supposed to be on Main Street. She said it was on the left, halfway between the second and third set of lights."

"This is the second set of lights," Victor pointed out as they stopped at the red light. They both glanced along the road, reading the signs.

"Bella Black's," DJ said aloud even as Victor spotted the building in question. Port Henry was obviously one of the older towns in Ontario. Most of the storefronts on the street were Victorian in design. Bella Black's was no exception, but the sign was large and colorful and the large front window had a painted mural of a sleek green iguana amidst a bower of flowers.

Victor contemplated the odd choice of design, and then turned his gaze back to the road as a car reversed into the very last available parking spot. A couple got out and crossed to the restaurant.

The light changed then and DJ eased their own car forward, passing Bella Black's as the couple reached the entrance and pulled the door open. They were treated to a brief view of light and color and milling people, then the door closed behind the couple, leaving the street silent once more.

"Busy," DJ commented. "It looks like every car parked on this road could belong to just the clients of the restaurant."

"Hmm," Victor grunted. "Turn here."

They found a spot on the side street and Victor quickly got out. He took the opportunity to stretch his arms and legs, relieved to be out of the car. Somewhat claustrophobic, he'd always felt trapped inside closed vehicles. Victor actually preferred motorcycles, but this was business not pleasure and needs must.

"So," DJ commented as he joined Victor on the sidewalk. "I guess it doesn't matter that you don't much look like your photo anymore. She'll no doubt know you by the very fact that she doesn't know you."

Victor scowled with confusion. "What the hell are you on about?"

DJ shrugged. "Well, there are . . . what? five hundred people in this town? She probably knows everyone who lives here. We'll stand out like sore thumbs."

"Right," Victor snapped, moving a little more quickly as he approached the door. He just wanted to get this over with and find out if the woman was an immortal or not. If she wasn't, they could leave and head home. However, if she was . . .

Victor's mouth tightened.

If Elvi Black was an immortal, he had to find out all he could about her and take her back to the council for judgment. As DJ had said, drawing attention to herself with this ad was considered a major faux pas. He had to find out what other faux pas she was committing. Judging by the fact that there were also certain rumors circulating around the Toronto club scene that a female vampire was living in one of the small southern towns, advertising wasn't her only mistake.

DJ opened the restaurant door and Victor paused as a rush of heat and sound rolled over them, coming through the opening on a wave of delectable scents. The glimpse they'd had earlier of the restaurant really hadn't told the whole tale; the place wasn't just busy, it was packed. People filled every chair and stool and nearly as many were standing around the open bar at the front of the restaurant . . . and every single one of these people went silent and turned to peer their way as they entered, including the mariachi band that had been strolling between the crowded tables.

"Have you ever been to Mexico?"

Victor answered DJ's hushed question with a shake of the head.

"Neither have I," DJ admitted. "But I think I might like it."

Victor's mouth twisted dubiously at this claim as he ignored the rudely staring people and slid his gaze over the colorful décor of the restaurant. The walls were a pale cream broken by splash after splash of color, a blue and gold sombrero hanging on the wall, a huge bright green statue of an iguana and its young on a shelf, a string of clay pots filled with sunflowers as well as several color prints, most of them by Diego Rivera. And on top of all that there were colorful streamers, balloons, and a huge *Happy Birthday* banner.

Even without the celebratory décor, it was too much color and excitement for Victor. He preferred soothing blues and cool whites. This was . . . loud and almost blinding to his senses.

"Can I help you, boys?"

Victor glanced down at the man who had approached. Five foot eleven or there about, the man was a good six inches shorter than Victor himself, and three or four inches shorter than DJ. He carried himself with the authority that his badge and uniform afforded him, obviously the local police. Possibly the only one, Victor guessed. It was a small town after all.

"Well?" The officer demanded, his voice and expression going hard in response to Victor's silent examination.

"No," he answered simply and started to move past him, pausing abruptly when he found his arm caught in a firm grip.

"This is a private party," the officer said grimly, and Victor understood why their entrance had drawn attention.

"I was invited," Victor announced. The answer seemed to echo in the room, making him realize just how quiet the restaurant had become now that the talking and music had stopped. Suddenly uncomfortable, he shifted as the officer studied him more closely.

"Victor Argeneau?" he finally asked, his voice uncertain.

Victor nodded, wondering how the man knew his name. He had a brief horrible memory of a T-shirt his computer geek nephew Etienne had favored for a while. It had been plain white with the words "I'm the teenage nympho you've been talking to on-line" or something of that ilk. For one moment he feared this was Elvi Black, but then the man smiled faintly and said, "You don't look much like that picture Mabel showed me. Your hair was shorter and you were wearing a suit and tie."

Victor had no idea who Mabel was and didn't care, but the picture in question was the one DJ had said he'd e-mailed to Elvi Black.

"And you brought a friend," the officer went on, his gaze turning to DJ with an appraising quality. If Victor looked scruffy compared to his photo, DJ just plain looked scruffy. He had developed something of an allergy to shaving about a year earlier and now resembled a young grizzly Adams. He too wore jeans and a T-shirt, but his jeans were blue and his T-shirt bore the name Alexander Keith's and a logo for the popular brand of beer. DJ wasn't much into fashion.

"He drove me," Victor said as explanation, and was immediately annoyed that he offered one.

"Don't you have a car, son?" the officer asked suspiciously.

Victor's mouth tightened. It was always seen as a bit less respectable not to have a car in Canada.

"I have several. I don't like to drive cars," Victor answered shortly and then asked, "Where is Elvi?"

"She isn't here yet. I'm supposed to keep you company for a bit."

When Victor raised an eyebrow in question, the man shook his head and held out his hand. "I'm forgetting my manners. Teddy Brunswick, police captain of Port Henry, at your service."

Victor accepted the hand and shook it, his attention on the wide grin now on Captain Teddy Brunswick's face. The expression made him look like the sheriff from an old black-and-white series he used to watch. It made him wonder if there wasn't some goofy, geeky idiot deputy running around somewhere. Victor was a big television buff and had no problem imagining a grinning idiot Don Knotts–type following this more intelligent, mellow man around. He managed to refrain from asking.

"Captain Brunswick." Victor gave a nod, then, since the man already knew his name, simply turned to gesture to his younger companion and said, "DJ."

"DJ what?" the officer asked bluntly.

The question made the younger immortal smile. "DJ Benoit. Gonna run me through the system and see if anything pops up?"

"Yes," Officer Brunswick said unapologetically.

DJ actually laughed, then glanced to Victor and announced, "I like him."

"He just insulted you," Victor pointed out with amusement. The lad often made him smile, which was a rarity. Little made him smile these last three centuries, but he found working with DJ similar to working with an overexuberant puppy. Victor actually enjoyed him for a partner more than the many morose men he'd worked with before, and was growing rather attached to the lad. Still, the day the boy peed on someone's carpet, he'd be asking for a new partner.

"You shouldn't really be insulted," Captain Brunswick told DJ. "I've already checked out Argeneau and the names of the others coming here looking to date our Elvi."

Victor decided then that Captain Brunswick was a man who needed his memory wiped. So would this Mabel by the sounds of it. And then what he'd said registered and Victor frowned. "The others coming here?" he echoed, scowling at DJ. "There are others coming?"

DJ shrugged, silently saying he knew nothing about it. It was Brunswick who answered. Smiling with amusement, he asked, "You didn't think you were the only one to answer the ad, did you?" Before Victor could respond, he added, "There are six men coming tonight. You're the first to arrive."

Victor wasn't pleased at this news, but was more concerned with the displeasure now on Brunswick's face.

"I hope they all don't bring friends or the house is going to be crowded," the officer commented, and then shook his head and said, "Come, I've kept you standing here long enough. I'll show you to your table."

When Officer Brunswick turned to lead the way through the crowded restaurant, DJ started to follow, but Victor caught his arm to hold him back and asked, "What does he mean by *'the house will be crowded'*?"

"I told you Elvi invited us down for the week," DJ reminded him.

"Yes," he acknowledged impatiently. "But I expected we'd be staying at a hotel, not someone's house."

"It's a bed-and-breakfast. Casey Cottage. Elvi owns it," DJ murmured. "It'll be fine."

"Are you boys coming or has the thought of competition scared you off?"

Victor stiffened. Captain Brunswick had paused at an empty booth halfway up the right-hand side of the restaurant, one Victor was sure hadn't been empty when they entered. No one had left the restaurant, however, so he supposed whoever had been seated there when they'd entered, had now joined the crowd milling around the bar at the front of the restaurant.

"This job is looking more and more interesting by the minute," DJ commented under his breath as they moved forward to join Brunswick.

Victor's only response was a grunt. To him, the situation seemed to be growing more complicated by the minute, and more troublesome.

"Here we are." Captain Brunswick stood blocking the far side of the booth, obviously expecting them to squeeze into the nearer side together.

Victor immediately stepped aside and gestured DJ in. Claustrophobic as he found cars, there was no way he was going to be trapped on the inside of a booth.

Making a face, DJ slipped quickly along the seat, scrunching himself up in the corner. Victor settled next to him, ignoring the way the younger immortal proceeded to mutter and shift about with discomfort. The booth was really far too small for two grown men to sit side by side; especially two grown men well over six feet tall and half as wide. They were both built like warriors of old, which was handy when it came to hunting. Size intimidated and any advantage was useful.

"Mabel will join us as soon as she and Elvi arrive," Brunswick commented as the conversations in the room began again. The mariachi band was apparently taking a break, but the patrons were at least no longer silent, though they were still staring and Victor suspected the conversations being held around the room were mostly about him and DJ.

Victor ignored the glances cast their way and nodded in response to Brunswick's comment, but still had no idea who Mabel was and still didn't care. His only interest in Port Henry was to meet this Elvi so he could sort out if she truly was one of them or they could get in the car and head home.

Victor used to enjoy his work. However, he'd found himself growing weary of late. He was, in effect, a hunter tired of the hunt. Rather useless he supposed. On the other hand, Victor acknowledged to himself, he had no special desire to be at home either. He didn't seem to be satisfied or at peace anywhere anymore, but then he never really had been since his wife, Marion's, death. He also found himself tired a lot of the time, his dissatisfaction increasing. It was something he tried not to think about too often. He may be bored and weary with life right now, but had no wish to go rogue as many other of his kind had gone at this stage.

"Mabel!" DJ said suddenly, apparently just placing the name. "She's Elvi's friend and the co-owner of the restaurant, and the bed-and-breakfast. Right?"

Brunswick nodded. "Her best friend. If Mabel doesn't like you, you can forget about Elvi. Those two have been thick as thieves since they were kids. She's—"

He paused abruptly when the room suddenly quieted again. Leaning sideways, Brunswick peered toward the front door and then got abruptly to his feet. "Another one's arrived. Excuse me."

Two

Elvi was blow-drying her hair when Mabel knocked at the door and shouted something. Frowning, she turned off the hair dryer and called, "What?"

"Are you almost ready?" the woman said impatiently.

"Yes, yes, I'm coming." Elvi quickly began to wrap the cord around the dryer, her gaze sliding longingly over the tub as she did. She'd taken a shower but would have preferred a bath. Elvi loved her tub. It was a large, spa tub with water jets. She'd spared no expense in purchasing it, figuring she deserved it. After all, she'd had to give up her lovely, king-sized bed for a coffin; a luxurious bath seemed only fair.

At the time, Mabel hadn't been at all sure if she should be bathing *or* showering. After all, there was never any mention of Dracula ever bathing. However, after a life-time of good hygiene, Elvi refused to go without, dead or not. If her skin began to slough off when wet, then so be it. At least it would be clean dead skin.

Fortunately, that hadn't happened. Elvi had been showering and bathing for five years without any unusual repercussions that she could see. Thank God.

"We're running late," Mabel called out.

Rolling her eyes, Elvi set the hair dryer in the cupboard, crossed to the door, and opened it.

"Of course we're running late. You let me sleep in," she pointed out testily, stepping into the bedroom with just a large bath sheet wrapped around her.

"That's gratitude for you," Mabel muttered, shoving a glass of blood into her hand. "Drink this and then get dressed. I laid out the new dress on your bed."

Elvi raised her eyebrows as she gulped down half the cold, thick liquid, then lowered the glass to point out "I don't have a bed, Mabel. I have a coffin. I only *wish* I had a bed."

Making a face, Mabel took away the half-empty glass and gave her a push to get her moving. "Dress."

Elvi moved toward the casket in the center of her large, nearly empty room, her shoulders slumping miserably. God, she missed her bed. A king-sized, deluxe model, she and Harry had picked it out together shortly before his death. It had been like sleeping on a cloud. Now she slept in a crate.

Elvi scowled at the dark, walnut casket as she paused beside it.

Catching her expression Mabel said, "Maybe Brendan can do something with your coffin to make it more comfortable."

Her scowl deepened. She'd already put a bedcover in it. Anything else would make it so she didn't fit, or nearly, and she found it claustrophobic enough without making the interior smaller.

"I doubt there's anything he could do," she said, not wanting Mabel to bother the local funeral home director. The man had already gone to great trouble, layering the bottom with dirt from both Mexico and her garden, and then installing a special liner so that the smell and dirt didn't seep through the satin. She didn't want to trouble him further. Elvi hated to be a bother.

She pulled on the dress Mabel had set out, tugged it into place, then peered down at herself and grimaced. It was new, but very much like all her other work dresses. Long, black, and sleek, it had a low neckline and was form-fitting all the way down to her knees where a slit started, allowing some movement. It would restrict every step she took and flash a good deal of lower leg as well.

This was another of her pet peeves. The wardrobe of the undead. It just didn't suit her style at all.

"I wish I didn't have to wear these stupid dresses," she muttered, reaching back to do up the zipper.

"Everyone gets a kick out of them." Mabel brushed her hands aside to take over the task. "It's what they expect."

"Hmm," Elvi murmured. "Would they ever be disappointed to see me running around here in jogging pants and T-shirts."

"You can't do that this week," Mabel told her firmly. "We have a full house of guests."

"Do we?" she asked with surprise. After that fateful trip that had ended Elvi's life, she and Mabel had gone into business together, starting a Mexican restaurant they'd called Bella Black's. The name had been Mabel's idea. It had also been Mabel's idea to sell the house she'd once shared with her deceased husband and move in with Elvi, who lived just three very short blocks from the restaurant. It had made things much easier for both of them. Still, with just the two of them, the house had echoed with emptiness and soon Mabel was suggesting they turn the old Victorian mansion into a bed-and-breakfast as a second income in case the restaurant floundered and failed.

Not that such an event was likely. Bella's was busy every night of the week, thanks to Elvi's status as a sort of town mascot. Still, Elvi had spent the better part of her marriage as a housewife. She enjoyed cooking and looking after others. She might not be able to eat anymore, but Elvi could still cook and did so every chance she got. She loved to touch and smell the food she could no longer consume, and watching others enjoy her efforts was as close as she could get to enjoying them herself. So, they'd renovated the old, Victorian manor, finishing the attic and putting in three bedrooms with en suite bathrooms there, and then named it Casey Cottage after Elvi's daughter.

The only trouble was that most of the guests were locals who stayed at the bed-and-breakfast simply to be able to say they'd slept in the home of a vampire. They had certain expectations as to what a vampire should look like and how they should behave, thanks to shows such as *Elvira, Mistress of the Dark* and so on, so she was forced to wear these ridiculous outfits at the restaurant as well as when they had guests at the bed-and-breakfast. Which was most of the time. The Mistress of the Dark had a lot to answer for, in Elvi's mind. Including the fact that everyone now called her Elvi rather than Ellen, the name she'd been born with, or even Ellie, which was what most of her friends had called her before she died.

"Here, don't forget your bells."

Elvi grimaced as she took the anklet laced with bells. They'd been a gift from Mabel right after her turning. She'd claimed she thought they were charming, but Elvi knew the truth was they kept her from sneaking up on the other woman and startling her. Mabel had never admitted it, but Elvi knew she had been somewhat frightened of her after her death. If not for their long friendship and her loyalty, Elvi might have been lost. So she'd worn the silly bells home and continued to wear them as they both adjusted to the changes in her life.

Besides, it was all supposed to fit her image as a sultry vampire. Elvi didn't feel sultry in the getup, she just felt ridiculous. But she donned the item without protest. The townspeople were the only reason she'd survived this cataclysmic change, and their patronage at her restaurant gave her the ability to make a living. If they wished to see her in black gowns and bells, then that's what they'd get.

"Ready?" Mabel asked once Elvi straightened.

"I have to put up my hair," she said.

"Leave it down tonight," Mabel suggested.

"But—"

"It looks better down."

Sighing, Elvi ran her fingers through her hair, wishing she could look in a mirror and be sure it wasn't all wild. But everyone knew vampires didn't have a reflection, although she still had directly after her death. Thinking it must be something that happened gradually and not wishing to see this last proof of the loss of her humanity, Elvi had removed the mirrors from her bedroom and bathroom. Understanding, as always, Mabel had then removed the mirrors in the rest of the house, leaving only the one in her own, and in the guest bathrooms and bedrooms. Elvi had to depend entirely on others to be assured she looked all right.

"Do I need makeup?" she asked.

"You never need makeup," Mabel said dryly. "But put on some of that wine-colored lipstick. It looks good on you."

Elvi moved into the bathroom to do so, sliding the tube along her lips from practice in the absence of a mirror.

"Perfect," Mabel pronounced when she returned to the bedroom. "Come on."

Elvi was silent on the way to the restaurant, her gaze taking in Mabel's pale face and shadowed eyes with concern. The woman had claimed she'd let Elvi sleep in because she'd seemed weary, but Mabel had been looking pale and weary as well lately. The woman was sixty-two years old and should have been easing her workload. Instead, between the restaurant, the bed-and-breakfast, and the daytime chores she did that Elvi couldn't do, she had more to do now than ever before. It worried her.

Mabel wasn't just her friend she was a lifeline. Without her, Elvi was sure she wouldn't have survived what happened to her and constantly fretted over what she'd do when age finally claimed the other woman, an issue that was constantly on her mind lately. They'd already lost both their husbands and several friends to death's grasp. How many more years could Mabel evade the reaper? Elvi was hoping for at least twenty, but that was if they were lucky. If they weren't, she may have much less. The thought depressed her.

"Here we are," Mabel said cheerfully as she parked.

Elvi unbuckled her seat belt and slid out of the car to follow her to the back door of the restaurant, her gaze moving briefly upward. The sky overhead was star studded and clear, without a cloud in sight, and she thought that it must have been just as clear a day, with the sun baking down and warming everything.

The sun was something else Elvi missed terribly. She'd always been a summer person, enjoying the sun and the flowers, trees and grass it encouraged to grow. Now she could only enjoy those flowers and trees by the solar lights that lined her garden. If asked, she couldn't have honestly answered which she missed more, food or sunlight.

Her gaze shot forward as Mabel opened the door and a wave of noise poured over them. It sounded like the diners were right there in the kitchen rather than off in the front of the restaurant. Elvi had never heard it so loud.

Frowning, she slipped past Mabel and crossed the kitchen to step into the small hall between the front and back of the restaurant. She peered with amazement through the beads, stunned at the number of people crammed into the dining room beyond.

"Dear God, this must be some kind of fire hazard," she muttered.

"That's what the fire chief said when I showed his family to their table," Mabel said with amusement. "He warned me the next time we think we'll have such a large turnout, we have to put tables on the sidewalk or something.

Elvi nodded absently, not surprised Mike Knight

hadn't insisted they shut down now. The party was in honor of his son. Mike was the head of the small fire department for the town and the sort of man always happy to lend a hand to friends and neighbors. He was a popular fellow, as was his charming wife, Karen. Their son, Owen, took after them. The number of teenagers present along with the adults attested to that. It looked to Elvi as if nearly half the town was there.

"I know the upper floor isn't done, but maybe we should open it up to make it a little less crowded," Elvi murmured, ignoring the hunger that was rising inside her as her gaze slid over the mass of humanity. Crowded as the dining area and bar was, the air conditioner couldn't keep up with the heat generated. It was hot, people were sweating, and their scent was a wave rolling over her and making her teeth ache. That half-glass of blood hadn't been enough. She should have finished it off, she realized with worry.

"I already did." Mabel leaned closer to gesture up to the balcony running around the upper floor where nearly as many people were milling about.

Elvi stared at them, but her senses were completely attuned to Mabel and she found herself inhaling slowly and savoring the scent. Mabel was a type-II diabetic, her blood always just that tad sweeter than others despite the medication she took, and sweeter blood was yummy blood as Elvi had learned the few times she'd fed from her friend when she'd first turned and had no other recourse. She allowed herself to enjoy the aroma until she felt her teeth shift, then moved quickly away from Mabel with a moan.

"You're hungry." Mabel eyed her with concern. After five years, she recognized the signs. "I should have let you finish the glass of blood I brought you. Should I get you another glass now to tide you over until the cake is ready?"

Elvi considered it, but shook her head. She found biting others somewhat distressing, it made her feel like an animal, but the hungrier she was, the less distressing it was. She could wait and said so.

Mabel nodded, but her gaze moved to the workers in the kitchen, Pedro and Rosita, who did the cooking, and the waitstaff who were bustling back and forth and in and out of the room.

Clapping her hands to get their attention, Mabel said, "Anyone who isn't needed in here, stay out. I want only Elvi, myself, and of course Pedro and Rosita in here." She smiled briefly at the Mexican couple who did the cooking, then added, "I'll put the finished orders on the table in the hall as they come up and you can place the new orders there for me to collect."

Elvi felt herself relax as the waitstaff emptied out and sent a grateful smile Mabel's way. It wasn't the first time she'd ordered everyone but Pedro out of the kitchen. It was a precaution she took on those rare occasions when Elvi was hungry. The gesture was appreciated.

"I'd better get moving on that cake," Elvi murmured, stepping away from the beads and turning to head back into the kitchen. "Maybe I should make two tonight. I don't think one will do for that crowd."

"I was going to suggest it myself," Mabel admitted.

Nodding, Elvi set to work.

"Who is it?" DJ rose up in the booth, craning his head around in an effort to see who had entered the restaurant. He wasn't having any success.

"No one we know," Victor assured him. On the outside of the booth, he merely had to lean to the side to see the tall, thin young man standing by the restaurant entrance.

The boy was glowering at the crowd now eyeing him as curiously as they'd eyed Victor and DJ moments ago. He couldn't have been more than twenty by Victor's guess and was dressed in the Goth fashion with baggy black pants, a billowing black shirt, and studs around his neck and wrists. His hair was long and pure black, obviously dyed. He was also unnaturally pale.

Makeup, Victor thought, noting the black lips and piercings everywhere.

"Is he one of us?" DJ asked as he gave up trying to see and sank back in the booth.

"A wannabe," Victor grunted. Dismissing the youth Brunswick was talking to, he settled back in his own seat. "A Goth costume, makeup and a bad attitude."

"Not surprised," DJ murmured. When Victor raised an eyebrow, he added, "Well, none of our kind is likely to answer a newspaper ad for singles."

"Hmm," Victor murmured noncommittally. It was his opinion that one never knew what others might do. He'd seen stranger things in his life.

"If she really is one of us, she'll spot him for a wannabe right away," DJ said with unconcern. "Of course, she—"

Victor glanced at DJ curiously when the man cut himself off abruptly. Spotting the startled look on his face, he asked, "What is it?"

"I think that iguana just moved," DJ said with a frown.

Following his gaze, Victor peered at the bright green

statue of the family of iguanas. Closer now, he could see that it was actually two adult iguanas with two smaller ones riding on their backs. All of them were stiff and still and Victor shook his head at the other man's moment of whimsy. "Don't be ridiculous, it's a statue."

"No, I'm sure I saw—"

"You can sit here with these two men."

Victor glanced up to see that Brunswick apparently hadn't picked up on the fact the boy wasn't for real and had ushered him to the booth.

"Vlad, this is Victor Argeneau and DJ Benoit," the officer introduced as the younger man slid into the booth. "Gentlemen, this is Vladimir Drake."

"Vladimir Drake?" DJ echoed with a wince, and Victor knew exactly what he was thinking. Being a wannabe was bad enough, but some things just showed poor taste.

"Yeah, you got a problem with that?" the kid asked defensively, then challenged, "Besides, what kind of name is DJ for a vampire?"

"It's short for Dieudonne Jules," DJ said mildly. "It's usually easier for people to use DJ."

"Dieudonne? As in 'God-given'?" Vlad sneered, obviously knowledgeable of some French, but then this was Canada. "And Benoit is short for Benedictine, isn't it? That means blessed." His mouth twisted. "A vampire with the names *given by God* and *blessed*? Yeah right."

DJ glanced to Victor and commented, "I'd think he was a name aficionado and smarter than he looks, but I read his mind."

Victor smiled faintly. He too had read the boy's mind and discovered that while Vlad knew the translation for Dieudonne from years of French in school, and his real name was Benedict. He had looked it up years ago and found the meaning as well as read the diminutives, including Benoit. He'd made everyone call him that for weeks afterward until some other trend had caught his eye.

"Yeah, sure you've read my mind," Vlad said with obvious disbelief. "I bet you two aren't even real vampires."

Victor ignored the challenge, his eyes sliding to Brunswick who still stood to the side of the booth, watching this interaction with interest.

"You show me yours and I'll show you mine," DJ said mildly.

"Show my what?" Vlad asked with a laugh. "You want to see my dick? You're not vampires, you're *gay!*"

Victor reached out to place a hand on DJ's arm as he sensed him stiffening, and then turned slowly to face the boy. He stared at him long and hard until the boy began to squirm on the opposite bench seat, then Victor opened his mouth and let his teeth slide out. He let them stay there briefly, long and sharp and pearly white, then slowly retracted them and closed his mouth.

"Holy shit!" Vlad gasped. He'd gone pale beneath the makeup and was now trembling in his seat. Apparently, for all his posturing, he hadn't been at all prepared to meet a real vampire this night. By Victor's estimation, the boy was seconds away from relieving himself right there in his pants.

"Run along home, little boy," he growled, losing patience. "This is the big league and you're missing more than the balls needed to play here."

Vlad hesitated for barely a heartbeat, then scrambled

out of the booth and hurried toward the exit at nothing short of a run. Victor leaned out to watch him. The minute the wannabe reached the door, he slipped into his thoughts and made him pause while he wiped his mind, replacing his true memories with more mundane ones of a disappointing meeting with an overweight, old wannabe named Elvi.

Satisfied that Vlad wouldn't be running around Toronto screaming about vampires loose in the streets of Port Henry, he mentally urged him out the door and sat back in his seat.

"At least there's one less bed to find," Brunswick commented as he watched the door close behind Vlad. Then he slid into the opposite seat and peered curiously at Victor, "Could you really read his mind?"

Victor raised an eyebrow at the question. If Elvi was truly one of their kind she should have the skill as well, and Brunswick, who claimed to be her friend, should know it. Then again, it could make mortals uncomfortable to know they could be read and controlled. Such knowledge might put a strain on a friendship and she might have kept it to herself.

Before he could decide whether it would cause problems or not to admit he could, another lull hit the conversations in the room and Brunswick glanced toward the door. "Another one. We'll talk later."

Victor watched him slip out of the booth and then leaned to the side again to get a look at the latest arrival. He cursed on spotting the tall, fair-haired man who'd just entered and was now surveying the restaurant.

"Who is it?" DJ shifted in the booth, half raising from his seat again to see, despite it not having worked last time.

"Harpernus Stoyan," Victor answered, his gaze locked on the tall, blond German dressed in cords and a casual shirt.

"Harper?" DJ asked with surprise. "Here? How did he—?"

"The same way we did, I imagine," Victor muttered, settling back in his seat when Brunswick began to lead the man to their table.

"You think he actually answered the ad?" The younger man sounded so amazed that Victor had to roll his eyes. This was another sign of DJ's youth . . . if not in age, then at least in thinking. He himself had long ago learned that once an immortal reached a certain stage, there was little he wouldn't do to find his lifemate. Victor himself wasn't far from that stage. Unfortunately, he'd already found, loved, and lost his lifemate, and didn't hold out much hope that there was another out there for him.

"This is—" Brunswick began as he reached the table. It was as far as he got since Harper had spotted the occupants and recognized them at once.

"Victor! DJ!" he exclaimed. His surprise quickly turned to chagrin and he shook his head. "Fancy meeting the two of you here. It looks like I'll have some competition."

Brunswick's eyebrows rose. "The three of you know each other?"

"We're old friends," Victor admitted as he slid out of the booth to shake hands with Harper.

"Well, I didn't expect that," Brunswick admitted, then glanced past them toward the door and sighed once more. "Number four of six."

Harper and Victor turned to peer at the latest arrival,

both of them scowling when they saw who it was.

"Edward Kenric," DJ muttered, spotting the man as he too got to his feet beside the booth. Unlike the rest of them, Edward had apparently thought a Mexican restaurant meant black tie. He was dressed to impress in a tux, his light hair slicked back from his patrician features.

Brunswick's eyebrows rose at the distaste in DJ's voice. "I take it this is someone else you know?"

"Oh, yes, we know him," DJ admitted, then added under his breath, "the pompous prick."

Brunswick smiled faintly, but merely asked, "Is he one of you?"

Victor almost said no in hopes the police captain would invite the other immortal to leave. It would be one less complication in this case. However, just as he opened his mouth to answer, he thought to check Brunswick's thoughts first and found that he'd nearly made a very large mistake. The officer had already guessed from their reactions that Edward was one of them; the question wasn't to see if he was, but to see if Victor would answer honestly or take advantage and try to eliminate what Brunswick thought was competition for the hand of the unknown Elvi.

"Yes, he's one of us," Victor answered and then pointed out, "the booth is starting to get a bit crowded. Maybe you should sit him somewhere else."

"Preferably far away," Harper concurred.

"Seating him in the parking lot would be good," DJ suggested.

"The parking lot is full at the moment," Brunswick said with amusement. "I think I'll just sit him here with the three of you. After that we'll have to maybe move to a table, though. That is, if the others are for real as well."

Before anyone could comment, he turned and headed off to greet Edward.

"You should have lied and said Edward wasn't one of us," DJ muttered as they watched Brunswick go. "Now we're going to be stuck with the bastard."

"No, he shouldn't have." Harper settled himself on the far bench seat of the booth as Victor and DJ returned to their side. "It was a test. Brunswick had already guessed Edward is one of us. If Victor had said he wasn't, *he* would have been the one to go," Harper announced, proving he too had read the man's thoughts. He then glanced toward the door, his eyebrows rising. "Isn't that . . . what's his name?" Harper frowned. "Damn . . . Alessandro something."

"Cipriano," Victor muttered, having leaned to the side to see that yet another immortal had entered the restaurant and now joined the conversation between Edward and Brunswick. Like the rest of them, Alessandro had dressed more casually for this meeting. While he wore a billowing white shirt, it was tucked into tight blue jeans.

"Cipriano's all right," DJ commented. "Only one more to go, then. Maybe once he's here, we can finally meet this Elvi."

"There are six of us altogether, then?" Harper asked with interest.

"Five. I'm just Victor's driver on this trip," DJ corrected, then added, "although there was a sixth, but he was just a wannabe and skedaddled pretty quick when Victor showed his fangs."

Harper chuckled, and then something at the door caught his attention again.

"The last has arrived," he announced, eyes narrowing. "He's not one of us, but there's something . . ." He paused, frowning, and then said, "There's something wrong. He's difficult to read, his thoughts are chaotic."

Victor leaned out to peer at the final man. The fellow looked normal enough with brown hair, average looks, and wearing a corduroy jacket over a casual top and dress pants, but when Victor slipped into his mind, he found a miasma of rage and disconnected thoughts. His name was Jason Lerner and Victor had just managed to find his way to Lerner's true intentions in being there when Harper said, "He's quite mad. He's here to stake Elvi, not see if she is his lifemate."

"That *was* his intention," Victor murmured, sifting through the thoughts swirling in the man's head. "But Brunswick has just introduced Edward and Alessandro as immortals and he's thinking they'll do for a target."

"Shit," DJ muttered, rising up in his seat, desperate to see now.

"I don't think Edward or Alessandro have bothered to try to read him," Harper murmured. "Can you control the man, Victor? I can't, but you're older, maybe—"

Harper's voice died as Victor suddenly leapt to his feet and started for the door.

Three

The mortal, Jason Lerner, had just slipped his hand into the inside breast pocket of his jacket when Victor reached the small group and caught him by the wrist.

"Say!" Brunswick protested. "Argeneau, what—?" His question broke off when Victor forced the man's arm sideways, bringing his hand and the stake it held out from beneath the jacket.

"He's not the sort of suitor your Elvi was hoping for. He's a vampire hunter." Victor removed the stake from the man's hand, slid it into his own back pocket, and then glanced to Harper and DJ as they joined them. "We'll take him outside and deal with him."

"Now, just a minute," Brunswick protested. "I'm the law here. I'll—"

"What can you do?" Victor interrupted politely. He could have just slipped into the officer's mind and taken control, but with the entire restaurant watching and listening, persuasion was the better option here.

"I can arrest him," Brunswick answered promptly.

"On what charge? I stopped him before he attacked anyone," Victor pointed out. "And, as far as I know, stakes aren't considered concealed weapons, so you can't charge him with carrying one."

Brunswick frowned. "No, but I can arrest him for being a public nuisance."

"And he shall be back on the streets by morning and hunting your Elvi."

Brunswick's mouth tightened, but he asked, "What can *you* do?"

"We can wipe his mind."

The officer shifted, obviously uncomfortable with the idea. "You won't hurt him?"

"It won't hurt at all. He'll simply forget all about Elvi and this town and vampires," Victor assured him, though, strictly speaking, it wasn't true. Lerner's madness meant they would have to use the three-on-one procedure and there would undoubtedly be damage to his brain. But having been inside his mind, Victor had no problem with that.

Elvi wasn't the first target of Lerner's madness. This mortal had killed women for various imagined reasons. He was a sick individual who had somehow slipped through the cracks and been left to kill various women in his wanderings across the country. If the procedure left him in a fugue state with half his mind destroyed, all women would be safer for it.

"Well, all right," Brunswick said at last. "But just you."

Victor shook his head. "I'll need two of the men. It takes three."

"Alessandro and I will assist you," Edward announced, and then added, "I presume one of us was to be the recipient of the stake he was reaching for? That being the case, it seems only right that we assist in handling the man."

Victor nodded reluctantly and turned the mortal to make him exit the restaurant. Lerner had been docile ever since he'd touched his wrist. Victor was able to control his mind and behavior somewhat so long as he was touching him. He continued to be unresisting as they led him outside.

They dealt with Lerner quickly. Edward, Alessandro, and Victor circled him, each touching his arm or face as they invaded his thoughts and wiped them from his mind. Once finished, the man was unconscious. They moved him, leaning Lerner against the building next door, then Victor took out his cell phone and flipped it open to press a quick-dial number. Edward and Alessandro waited patiently as he called Argeneau Enterprises, explained the situation, and arranged to have the man picked up.

"Do we wait here for them to collect him?" Alessandro asked as Victor flipped his phone closed.

Shaking his head, he pocketed the phone. "He isn't going anywhere and they shouldn't be long. Come on."

He led them back inside.

"All taken care of?" DJ asked as the trio reentered the restaurant. The other men still stood by the door.

Victor nodded and asked, "Do we meet Elvi now?"

"Soon," Brunswick said, and then glanced around. "We'll need a bigger table now that you're all here. I'll see what I can arrange."

"And so there are four of us," Harper said as the officer slipped away.

"You mean five," Alessandro corrected.

"DJ is only here because he drove me," Victor explained.

"Ah." Alessandro nodded, and it was Edward who said, "That's still more competition than I expected."

"No competition at all, really," DJ pointed out. "She can't be the lifemate for all of you."

"That's not entirely true," Harper corrected, and when the other immortals turned to him with surprise, he said, "I had a friend back in Germany in Victorian times. He and his cousin met a woman neither of them could read. She could have been a lifemate to either of them."

DJ's eyebrows drew together. "What happened?"

"They both courted her. She chose his cousin." He glanced away briefly before admitting, "My friend was sure he would never meet another who would suit him so well. Unable to bare the thought of watching his cousin enjoy the happiness he might have had, he destroyed himself."

Silence fell in the group as they absorbed this news and then Brunswick returned.

"I've arranged to switch tables with Jenny Harper and her friends. Follow me, boys." Brunswick didn't wait for agreement, but turned and headed off.

"I have never quite gotten used to being called 'boy' by men who look older, but are really far younger than myself," Harper commented.

Victor merely smiled as he started forward.

"Sit down," Brunswick instructed once they'd reached the table.

"Actually," Harper murmured as the rest of the men sat, "I think I'd like to go thank Ms. Harper and her friends for giving up the table for us. If you'll excuse me."

Without waiting for Brunswick's permission, Harper moved away, slipping through the tables to the booth they'd been at earlier.

Brunswick frowned after him, but then turned back to the table and said, "I need to go in the back and see if Mabel and Elvi have arrived. I shouldn't be long."

He started to turn away, but paused, eyes narrowing at something by the entrance. Victor turned to glance that way, eyebrows rising at the sight of an agitated, gray-haired man in the vestments of a priest rushing toward the officer.

"Teddy Brunswick!" The man was flushed and obviously agitated. "Louise Ascot just told me that you've actually brought half a dozen soulless vampires to Port Henry! What are you thinking?"

"Now, Father," Brunswick caught the priest by the shoulders and turned him back the way he'd come. "There's no call getting all upset over this. Everything's fine."

"Fine?" the man exclaimed, drawing to a halt and turning on him with disbelief. "There is nothing fine about this, Theodore Brunswick. Elvi's one thing, she's a good God-fearing woman even if she doesn't have a soul anymore, but bringing in six more of these beasts?"

"Father, this is neither the time nor the place," Brunswick said firmly, urging him to continue walking. "If you want to talk to me about this, drop by my office in the morning. This is Owen's birthday celebration and I won't have you ruining it for him."

"Owen?" The man looked startled. "Oh, please tell me he isn't going to let Elvi bite him? What if he turns into one too? I won't lose another soul of one of my parishioners. There was nothing we could do about Elvi, but Owen's just a boy. He's . . ."

Victor watched with eyes that were silver ice chips as Brunswick finally urged the man out of the restaurant. There was nothing he hated more than the clergy. It was the church that had condoned his wife's being burnt at the stake. If he could have he would have slaughtered the whole lot of them at the time. But his brother Lucian wouldn't let him. Three hundred years later, Victor's gut still burned at the sight of clergy . . . any clergy. He hated them all.

"Sorry about that," Brunswick murmured, pausing at the table on his way back. "Father O'Flaherty is excitable, but harmless," he assured them, then nodded and turned away. "I'll be right back."

He rushed off to the back of the restaurant, disappearing through a beaded arch on the right side of the back wall. It presumably led to the kitchens. He'd barely gone when Harper returned and claimed his seat.

"Well," DJ said with feigned good cheer, "maybe now we'll finally get to see this Elvi."

"Thank God," Edward said in bored tones. "Then I can read the woman and leave. I hate small towns."

"If you're so sure she won't be your lifemate, why not just leave now?" Victor suggested, and received a scathing look for his trouble.

"I'm not a fool, Argeneau. I'll wait and read her just to be sure rather than waste this long, dull journey."

Victor shrugged with disinterest. The man annoyed him, but hopefully, he wouldn't have to put up with him for long if he couldn't read Elvi.

"Speaking of fools," Edward murmured, spearing Victor with a gaze. "You don't expect us to believe that *you* are here looking for a lifemate?"

Victor was aware of the way DJ stiffened beside him, as well as the fact that the other men were now peering at him with new interest. Alessandro's eyebrows were raised in question. Harper's expression, however, held a tinge of concern. He, as well as the other men, knew Victor was one of the enforcers for the council and was no doubt now considering that if he wasn't there to find a lifemate, he must be there on council business.

"Well, Argeneau?" Edward prompted.

Victor turned an irritated glance toward him, but Brunswick's return prevented his putting the immortal in his place for daring to question him.

"How are we doing here?" Brunswick asked as he settled at the table, then without waiting for an answer, said, "The girls are here and Mabel will be out in just a minute."

"Who is Mabel?" Alessandro asked with confusion. "I am here to meet the Elvi, not Mabel."

"Yes, yes," Brunswick said quickly. "But Mabel is the one in charge of this whole week."

"I thought Elvi was the one in charge." Harper was frowning. "She arranged things with me; the e-mails, the invitation, the directions . . ."

"*Si.* Me also," Alessandro agreed.

"And I." Edward's eyes narrowed on the police captain. It seemed obvious to Victor he was reading his mind and—judging by his expression—was vaguely surprised by what he was learning. Before Victor could slip into the mortal's thoughts, the beads hanging in the door between the restaurant and kitchen jangled, bringing about another abrupt pause to the noise in the room.

Brunswick glanced over his shoulder, and said, "Oh. There she is. I'll be right back." The man was immediately on his feet and rushing away.

"There is who?" Alessandro asked the table at large. "The Mabel or the Elvi?"

"That woman is not an immortal. If she's Elvi, we can get back in the car and head home now," DJ said, but his eyes slid over the woman with something akin to interest as Captain Brunswick led her to their table.

She was in her early sixties by Victor's guess. A tall, trim woman with gray-blond hair and a face with few lines and attractive features that still carried a great deal of the beauty she must have been when younger.

"Mabel, this is Edward Kenric, Harpernus Stoyan, Alessandro Cipriano, Victor Argeneau, and his friend DJ Benoit," Captain Brunswick introduced as he paused at the table. "Gentlemen, this is Mabel Allen."

Victor eyed the woman curiously. This then was the friend who co-owned the restaurant and bed-and-breakfast with Elvi. Brunswick had said her opinion was important to Elvi, but Victor wasn't there to romance a possible lifemate, so merely nodded in greeting.

The other "suitors" showed more interest by actually voicing their hellos. DJ, however, stood and reached to take the woman's hand, saying, *"Enchanté."*

Victor rolled his eyes. DJ usually only resorted to such displays of charm when attempting to pick up women. Generally, they were much younger and melted like soft butter under his efforts. Mabel wasn't so easily impressed. Rather than smile, her mouth tightened and she quickly tugged her hand free.

She then turned her gimlet gaze on Victor. It seemed pretty obvious he didn't meet muster. The woman's mouth turned down with displeasure as she took in his attire and the state of his hair.

"You need a haircut," she announced, and then turned to include DJ in her displeasure. "Both of you do, and a shave."

The comment made Victor run a hand lightly over his chin. He grimaced at the rasp of whiskers. He'd barely woken up when DJ had arrived to collect him that evening. All he'd managed to do before the apartment buzzer had announced his arrival was to drain two bags of blood. With the younger man pacing his living room and poking curiously at everything, Victor had merely jumped in and out of the shower and thrown on his clothes. He'd forgotten to shave or even brush his hair. It had dried the way it laid when he came out of the shower and no doubt looked unkempt.

Having made her displeasure clear, Mabel Allen then turned her attention to the other three men. They faired much better under her critical eye, though a cynical expression crossed her face as she took in Edward's tux. Still, she didn't comment or criticize any of them, but simply nodded as if to say, *"You'll do."* It seemed she preferred their clean-cut presentation to his more relaxed, need-a-comb look.

"Sit down, Mabel," Brunswick suggested. "We can ask the questions you made up."

Victor was just getting irritated at the idea of more grilling when the woman shook her head. "Owen's cake is done. Elvi wants to present it now. She's been awake for a while and is hungry."

"Oh. I guess we'd best get it going, then." Brunswick

frowned and glanced to a table where a couple and two teenage boys sat. His gaze then moved to the back of the restaurant where another family was just leaving the booth nearest the beaded arch. "Maybe we should move the Knights to the booth nearer the kitchen. Those cakes Elvi makes are huge and we don't want her stumbling and dropping it trying to get through this crowd."

"Good idea," Mabel said and the pair moved off.

"The cake is done and she's hungry?" DJ murmured, his eyes trailing the older woman. "This Elvi can't be that old if she still eats cake. If she's young enough it would explain her mistakes."

"Her sire should have taught her such things," Victor responded, watching Brunswick and Mabel speak to one of the teenagers. They then turned to say something to the parents. The quartet rose and started toward the back of the restaurant.

Mabel and Brunswick were at the back of the small group, following the teenager they'd first greeted. The young man wasn't displaying the same eagerness as the others, walking at a much slower pace that soon left them behind the main party. And, Victor noted, while he was smiling, there was a worried edge to his expression. It seemed obvious the boy was nervous and growing more so with every step.

"Will it hurt?" he asked just as they drew level with the table where Victor and the others sat.

The question caught his attention and he narrowed his eyes as Mabel clucked and chided, "Don't be silly, Owen. Of course it won't hurt. Do you think men would be lining up for this if it hurt?"

That response merely made Victor frown with confusion as he tried to sort out what they were talking about. The boy's next question, however, raised alarm bells in his mind.

"I won't turn into one, will I?"

This time there was no clucking and chiding. Mabel and Brunswick exchanged a glance, but the woman merely said, "Now, what would make you ask a question like that? No one else has, have they?"

"That's not a no," the boy pointed out anxiously.

Brunswick and Mabel exchanged another glance, then the woman said firmly, "Don't be silly, Owen. Do you want to do this or not? Because we can just present the cake and skip the rest of it."

There was a brief pause as he glanced toward the booth where the other teenager and his parents were seating themselves, then said quickly, "No, no. I'll do it. Dan would never let me live it down if I backed out."

DJ leaned close and hissed, "They aren't talking about what I think they're talking about, are they?"

Victor's answer was to catch Brunswick's arm as he passed and pull him to a stop. "What's the boy worried about? What is he afraid will hurt?"

"His Birthday Bite," Brunswick answered and would have continued walking, but Victor held him back.

"Birthday Bite?" he queried sharply.

Impatient to get going, Brunswick quickly explained, "On their eighteenth birthday, the boys come here for a special celebratory dinner on the house. They get cake that Elvi makes for them, and then she bites them." He paused, but when there was a deafening silence from the men at the table, he added, "It's sort of a rite of passage from boyhood to manhood."

"A rite of passage?" DJ asked with disbelief.

"The Indians have their rituals, we have ours," Brunswick said with a shrug, then tugged his arm free. "I have to go."

This time, Victor let him escape. This wasn't good. This wasn't good at all.

A sudden hush in the room made them all glance toward the back of the room. Victor's eyes widened as a curvy redhead stepped through the beads separating the restaurant from the kitchen. If this was Elvi, her picture was misleading. For one thing, in the picture, her hair had looked dark rather than the vibrant red it truly was. The photo also hadn't revealed that she was short, no more than five foot three. And she certainly hadn't been wearing the getup she was in now.

His eyes skated over the long, form-fitting gown, lingering over the naked flesh of her lower legs revealed as she walked, then returned to her face. It was the same face and yet now he was noticing the piquant, elfin quality to it, and that her eyes weren't just large, they were huge, and she had the most adorable little nose he'd ever seen. As for her lips—

Victor gave his head a shake. While her picture hadn't impressed him, the real deal somehow robbed him of breath. He found himself staring with fascination, his eyes following as she moved to the table where the boy, Owen, and his family sat.

The faint chime of bells marked her passage and it took a moment for Victor to realize it came from a chain of charms around her ankle. He then found himself staring at that ankle, noting the delicate curve from lower calf to heel.

It wasn't until DJ sucked in a hearty breath that Victor's gaze rose back to the woman herself and he realized she'd reached the table and squeezed herself onto the end of the bench seat with the two teenagers. She was now leaning toward Owen, whispering something in his ear. When the lad swallowed thickly and gave a nervous nod, she chuckled softly. The whole room was silent, everyone seeming to hold their breath.

"Dear God! She's going to bite him right here in front of everyone," DJ gasped with horror.

"She wouldn't dare," Victor breathed with disbelief, but even as he said the words, she leaned in toward the boy again.

"We have to do something!" DJ hissed. "We can't let everyone in here see this."

Victor didn't answer, he was already on his feet, rushing toward the corner booth.

Four

Victor had nearly reached the back booth when Teddy Brunswick suddenly stepped in his way.

"What are you doing, son?" the officer asked grimly.

Victor started to slip into his mind to make him step aside, and then hesitated as he realized another man had moved up behind Brunswick, backing him up . . . And another.

Stiffening, Victor peered slowly around to see that the male patrons seated nearest them were stiff and narrow-eyed, ready to step in should the need arise. It wasn't until DJ spoke that he realized the younger immortal had followed and now had his own back.

"What do we do?" DJ breathed, his voice so low that only Victor could have heard him.

"Son," Brunswick growled before he could answer

DJ. "I asked you a question. What are you doing? You weren't thinking to hurt our Elvi, were you?"

Aware of the sudden shifting around them, Victor glanced about to see that the mortal men were starting to look mean, very much resembling a lynch mob as they closed in. He also noted that Alessandro, Harper, and Edward had moved up to stand behind DJ, offering their support if necessary, but Victor didn't want this to turn into a brawl.

Between their increased strength and their ability to control minds, it would be no problem for the five of them to deal with this crowd, but he didn't want to clean up the mess afterward. The idea of wiping every mind of every patron in the restaurant was wearying, besides it was a risky business. If even one person proved difficult to wipe and managed to retain their memories, they could draw out the memories of the others and it would have been a complete waste of time. He may yet have to wipe the memories of all these people, but would rather avoid it if possible. Victor had no idea what was going on, what these people did or did not know, and didn't want to force such an action until he did.

Taking a deep breath, he lied, "No, of course not. You misunderstood. I had no intention of hurting Elvi. I was just eager to meet her."

"Uh-huh." Brunswick didn't look as if he believed him and Victor understood why when the man asked, "Then why are you clutching Lerner's stake in your hand?"

Victor peered down with surprise at the small wooden stake that he'd apparently pulled from his back pocket as he'd rushed forward. He hadn't been aware he'd done so. Now, he held it out to Brunswick.

"I was bringing it to you . . . as an excuse to come to the table and meet Elvi."

The officer eyed him narrowly for a moment and then allowed his gaze to move over the other three immortals behind them. Apparently none of the "suitors" gave away the game by expression. Brunswick relaxed the tiniest fraction.

"Trying to get the jump on the other men," he suggested.

"Something like that," Victor muttered.

Brunswick nodded slowly, but apparently wasn't totally convinced. He took the stake, but then peered more closely at him. "Show me your teeth again, son. I didn't get a real good look when you were showing them to Vlad."

Victor stiffened. Obviously, the man wished to assure himself he didn't have another vampire hunter on his hands. Victor resented having to prove his status, but suspected he wouldn't get near Elvi if he didn't so opened his mouth and then allowed his incisors to slip down and protrude.

Teddy Brunswick examined them thoroughly, even reaching out to poke at them to ensure they weren't some sort of insert. Seemingly satisfied, he then nodded and relaxed completely.

"Okay, but this is Owen's moment. You can talk to Elvi afterward." Teddy Brunswick gestured to the table where he'd seated the five men earlier. "Go sit down. Mabel and I will join you in a moment."

Victor glanced past Brunswick and saw Elvi glancing curiously their way as she listened distractedly to a smiling, chattering and *unbitten* Owen. Nodding reluctantly, he turned and led the other immortals back to their assigned table.

"So you *are* here on council business," Edward commented as the men reclaimed their seats.

"I was afraid of that," Harper murmured. "I suppose the council wasn't pleased by her advertising in the single's columns."

"Not very, no," Victor admitted.

"I was sure she was going to bite him right there in front of everyone," DJ said apologetically, his gaze shifting back to the birthday booth. His eyes then moved around the crowded restaurant, taking in each patron. "Do you think they all know?"

"How could they not?" Victor asked, following his gaze with a frown. He and DJ might have more on their hands than they'd expected with this case.

"So, what does the council intend to do about Elvi?" Edward asked.

The man's expression was calculating. Victor had no doubt he was considering what this might mean should she turn out to be his lifemate. He glanced at the faces of the other two prospective suitors. All of them were concerned, and with good reason.

"It isn't just the ads," he said finally. "There are rumors running rampant all over the Toronto club scene that there's a female vampire living in one of the small, lakeside towns in southern Ontario."

The three men were silent, only their expressions revealing that they understood the gravity of the matter. There were few laws among their people, but they were important laws and not drawing attention to themselves or the existence of their people was right up there in importance. Another was they weren't allowed to bite a mortal . . . except in cases of an emergency.

His gaze slid to the corner booth again. The woman was laughing at something the teen had said. The boy seemed totally at ease now and he was as lit up as a Christmas tree, apparently his fears had abated. It didn't matter. They weren't allowed to bite because it increased the risk of detection for their people and she apparently intended to bite the boy and, from what Brunswick had said, he wouldn't be the first.

"And she appears to be biting mortals," Alessandro murmured, apparently thinking along the same lines.

Victor didn't comment. He glanced around the restaurant, slipping quickly and easily into various minds. As he'd feared, every single person here knew that Elvi was a vampire . . . and that he and the other men there were too.

Elvi Black was in a great deal of trouble with the council. The kind that could see her staked and left out in the sun all day, then beheaded. He sincerely hoped she wasn't a lifemate to any of the men here.

"Okay."

Victor glanced up with a start to find Brunswick had returned, managing to do so without his hearing or noticing it.

"Okay," Brunswick repeated now that he had everyone's attention. "Mabel and I think it would be best to quickly introduce the bunch of you, and then Elvi will take Owen back to her office for his Birthday Bite. When Mabel goes back to collect the boy, she'll explain what you're doing here, then she can join your table and—"

"What do you mean she'll explain what we're doing here?" Harper interrupted. "She knows. She invited us."

Brunswick grimaced. "Actually, she didn't. Mabel put the ad in the single's column and responded to all your e-mails, then invited you down here for the week. Elvi has no idea about any of this."

"I told you our kind wouldn't be stupid enough to put an ad in a single's column," DJ said with satisfaction.

"No, but your kind are stupid enough to answer it," Brunswick snapped, his face flushed with either embarrassment at being involved in this match-making attempt, or just plain irritation. Possibly, it was both.

"So, she wasn't advertising?" Harper cast a hopeful look Victor's way that seemed to say, *Here's one less sin on her list at least.*

But it was only one, Victor thought, his mouth tightening. He turned his attention back to Brunswick and said, "There are rumors all over the club scene about a beautiful young female vampire residing in a small southern town. Like this one."

"Yes," DJ said, picking up his intent. "Does Elvi go to Toronto and visit the clubs?"

"Well . . ." Brunswick looked slightly embarrassed and glanced away. "She . . . er . . . we . . ."

"Does she?" Victor asked, impatient with his dithering.

"No," Brunswick admitted reluctantly. He ran one hand agitatedly through his hair before explaining, "You see, this is a small town."

No one commented on this obvious statement.

"There's one high school and we all went there together. We're pretty tight because of that, I guess, but over the last five years or so we've lost several of our group. Mabel's husband died six years ago of a heart attack. Elvi's husband and daughter in a car accident a year later, then Elvi turned . . ." He frowned. "It's all been downhill from there. We've lost one or two a year since then, but this year we lost three in a row in a six-month period. We're at that age," he acknowledged solemnly.

Victor remained silent, aware of the discomfort of the other immortals. There was a certain amount of guilt attached to the knowledge that this was not a problem they suffered. Heart attacks, cancer, and so on weren't an issue for them. Victor himself was over two thousand years old. Age wasn't a threat to his kind like it was to mortals.

"We all took the deaths hard," Brunswick went on, "but Elvi seemed to take it worse. She's watching her friends and loved ones die around her and realizes she'll soon be completely alone. Of course, the younger set will step up and befriend her, I'm sure, but it won't be the same. Besides, they'll die soon enough too, and so on." He frowned down at the table and ran his finger around one of the ceramic tiles before admitting, "We don't like the idea of leaving her behind to go through that alone."

Victor's eyes widened at the knowledge that—as they realized their own mortality—these two people, Mabel and Brunswick, were more concerned with their immortal friend being left behind alone, than with how death was creeping up on them. It impressed him and made him curious too.

Victor had always avoided attachments to mortals precisely because they weren't around long in the grand scheme of things. If an average life was sixty-five years, he'd lived more than thirty-four lifetimes. Spending that time watching friends die around you one after another just didn't bear thinking about.

"So . . ." Brunswick straightened. The pink flags in his cheeks announced that he was embarrassed by what he was about to say and his expression was pained. "Barney and I took a couple trips up to Toronto some months ago."

"Barney?" DJ queried lightly.

"My lieutenant."

"Unbelievable," Victor muttered.

"What's that?" Brunswick asked.

"Nothing. Go on. You and Barney made a couple trips to Toronto."

"Yes." He looked uncomfortable again. "We were thinking if there were any vampires in Canada besides Elvi, they'd be in a big city like Toronto. We went looking for some."

This then was how the rumors had started going around the clubs, Victor realized. "You hit the club scene?"

Brunswick nodded. "It was Barney who thought we were more likely to find them at the clubs. He said if there were some, they probably didn't have a town like Port Henry to support and help them get what they needed and he figured they'd probably . . . er . . . hunt at the clubs."

He grimaced apologetically, then admitted, "We were too old for the clubs. The young women thought we were a couple of old perverts. No one would tell us anything. After the third trip with no results, Mabel decided to go the way of the singles ads. She felt sure there must be at least one lonely male vampire out there.

"I thought she was crazy, but . . ." He gestured around the table. "Her way was more successful than our attempts."

The men at the table were silent for a moment, and then DJ stood abruptly. "I need to go to the men's room. Victor?"

Nodding, he stood to follow, knowing the younger immortal wanted to discuss this latest information.

"I thought only girls traveled to the bathroom in packs, but you male vamps do it too, huh? Is it in case someone tries to stake you while you're taking a leak?" Brunswick asked as they moved away from the table, and then added, "You won't have to worry about that here. We're vampire friendly in Port Henry."

Victor ignored him, his mind chewing over what he'd learned as he followed DJ to the washroom and waited as he slipped into the minds of the few men there and made them leave, done with their business or not.

"Well?" DJ said as the door closed behind the last man. "Can we go home now? She didn't put the ad in the paper or spread the rumors around Toronto."

"No," Victor acknowledged. "But she *has* shared the knowledge of her existence with mortals."

DJ waved that away impatiently. "There's no law against that. Marguerite's servants know, and most immortals have one or two mortals in the know. Hell, half of Argeneau Enterprises is made up of mortals who are aware of the secret and sworn to silence on the matter."

"But Brunswick and the other mortals here aren't staying silent on the matter," Victor pointed out.

DJ ran a hand through his hair in agitation. It was obvious that the more they learned about the woman, the more the younger man was feeling sympathy for her.

Victor suspected he was thinking none of this was her fault, but Victor knew the council wouldn't see it that way. Immortals were extremely careful of whom they shared the information with for precisely this reason, and if nothing else, Elvi Black had failed to ensure the people she entrusted the information to were trustworthy. Having a whole town know you were an immortal was hardly being cautious and discreet.

"What if we warn them to silence before we go?" DJ suggested hopefully.

Victor just shook his head and reminded him, "She's biting mortals." Which meant she was on a collision course with the council and it wouldn't be pretty, but it was their job to take care of such matters.

DJ let his breath out on a sigh. "I was hoping you'd forgotten that bit." Scowling, he shook his head. "Who the hell was her sire? He should have told her it was wrong."

"How do you know she *doesn't* know it's wrong?" Victor asked dryly.

"She'd hardly be doing it so openly if she knew the consequences," DJ pointed out. "Using it as a ritual of manhood for all the young men in town is hardly sneaking around and biting boys in the dark. She *can't* know it's against our laws."

"Hmm." Victor supposed that was true. Unless the woman had a death wish and actually wanted her head cut off, she probably didn't know what she was doing was wrong. "Well, it appears that will be our next objective. We need to find out if she is aware of our laws, and who her sire is."

"What does it matter who her sire is?" DJ asked with surprise. "He can't be held responsible for her actions."

"He can if he didn't tell her our laws."

"The only sire likely to turn a mortal and not bother telling them our laws is one who's gone rogue."

"Exactly," Victor agreed.

"Ah." The younger immortal nodded with understanding. "We may have a rogue we don't know about. He might have turned her and left her to her own devices." He nodded again, then asked, "Would the council punish her if she didn't know she was breaking our laws?"

"Ignorance is no excuse, even in mortal court."

DJ sighed and shook his head. "It seems a shame. If she doesn't know any better, there was no intent."

"You sound like a lawyer marshalling his defense," Victor said with a smile.

DJ shrugged. "Maybe I *will* defend her in front of the council. I like her."

"You haven't even met her yet," Victor pointed out with a laugh.

"Well, I like her restaurant, and I read Brunswick's mind," DJ announced. "He thinks she's a 'damned fine woman' always there to help others, and a pillar of the community all her life. She apparently volunteered at everything before she was turned and still does. She's a good woman, Victor. The very fact that her friends would go to all this trouble for her says as much."

"Hmm." He frowned. "Then we'd best find out all we can so that the council can make a fair judgment. Otherwise, I fear she could lose her head."

Mouth tight, DJ nodded and led the way out of the bathroom.

"Are you ready now?" Brunswick asked when they reached the table.

When both men nodded, he heaved out a little breath, and stood. When the other men stood as well, he said, "Now, just remember to keep your traps shut about this ad business and restrict yourself to only saying hello until Mabel has a chance to explain."

"Why not wait to introduce us until after Mabel's explained?" Edward asked dryly. "Surely that makes more sense."

"Not if you know Elvi," Brunswick assured him. "Once she knows what we've done she'll be mad as hell, but she'll also be terribly embarrassed and if she hasn't met you already, she'll no doubt refuse to do so." He shook his head. "No, this is the best way. Now, come on."

As had been the case throughout, the man didn't wait for protests or agreement, but simply gestured for them to follow and turned to head back the way he'd come.

"Well?" Harper asked, glancing to Victor for guidance.

Shrugging, he turned to trail Brunswick, aware that the rest of the men followed suit.

They nearly reached the booth this time. Victor was just walking past the shelf with the statue of the iguana family on it when he noted movement out of the corner of his eye. Then part of the statue separated from the rest and launched itself at him.

And all hell broke loose.

Five

"I told you I saw it move," DJ muttered.

Victor didn't pay him any attention. All his focus was on the petite woman presently fussing over him and pressing a napkin to his ear and neck. Victor's roar when the iguana landed on his neck and shoulder and latched onto his ear had managed to get everyone's attention, but the whole place had erupted in shouts and screams when he'd begun to claw at his neck and spin on the spot.

Shouting for someone named Pedro, Elvi had abandoned the birthday boy and hurried to Victor's side. She'd removed the iguana, passed it off to a little Mexican man who'd come running from the back of the restaurant, and then had snatched up napkins from the nearest table, cooing as she fussed over him.

"I'm so sorry. He's never done anything like this in

the five years we've had the restaurant," she repeated, tugging at his arm to force him to bend over so she didn't have to continue to stand on her tiptoes to see his wound.

Victor grunted and bent obligingly forward, blinking as he found himself peering down the low neckline of her dress at her considerable cleavage.

"Oh dear. We'd best clean this up and put a bandage on it." Her voice sounded shaky as she stepped away from him, removing her bountiful breasts from his view. "You better come with me."

Victor straightened and waited as she excused herself to the birthday boy and his family. He then followed her gyrating hips in the tight skirt as she led the way through the beaded arch and turned into a small office with a desk, two chairs, a small refrigerator, a filing cabinet, and a tall metal cabinet with double doors.

"Have a seat." Elvi gestured to the two chairs in front of the desk. She moved to the metal cabinet and opened one of the doors to reveal shelves stacked neatly with paperwork and various other items including a first-aid kit. Retrieving the small white kit, she set it on the desk and opened it. After a pause, she removed a swatch of cotton, then opened a dark brown bottle and poured some of its contents on the cotton before moving to him.

"This will sting," she warned and set to work cleaning his ear and neck.

Victor sat completely still, hardly noticing the sharp stinging she caused as he inhaled her scent. She smelled of vanilla and spices from the kitchen, a delectable combination that made his mouth water. Tightening his lips, he tried to ignore the smell, but found his nose working to inhale more of it.

"Hmm," Elvi murmured at his side, her breath teasing his ear. "It isn't as bad as I first feared. More blood than damage, thank goodness."

Victor didn't comment. The wound had been quite deep; however his body had started to repair itself at once. This answered one of their questions, however. She couldn't recognize another immortal. It was usually instinctual with their kind. Although, unless taught, they wouldn't recognize the signals their mind and body were sending.

Aware her hands had gone still and hearing her swallow thickly by his ear, he turned to peer at her. Her eyes must have been hazel as a mortal, now the green shone with silver and the brown around the outside glowed gold. She was biting one corner of her lip, a sharp fang poking out as she peered at his still bleeding ear. He wasn't terribly surprised. She was pale and obviously hadn't fed enough. The blood would be tempting to her. He waited curiously to see what she would do.

"Oh." Elvi gave her head a sudden shake and stepped back, one hand coming up to cover her mouth and the fangs he'd glimpsed pushing past her lips. Turning away, she threw the blood-soaked cotton out as if it were on fire. "I'm sure it will heal quickly. Though you might want to let a doctor take a look at it tomorrow."

"There's no need for a doctor," Victor murmured, watching her closely. "Our kind heal quickly and well."

Elvi stilled and turned slowly back.

"Our kind?" she asked uncertainly, still shielding her mouth with one hand.

"Immortals," he said quietly, then used the term Brunswick and Mabel had repeated several times. "Vampires."

Elvi sucked in a breath. "You—You're . . . one too?"

When Victor nodded, her hand fell to her side and she dropped into the opposite chair. She was silent for the longest time, simply staring at him, seemingly at a loss. It was long enough that her teeth withdrew back into their resting place before she finally said, "When I first got back from Mexico, Mabel and I tried to find others, but . . ."

Elvi paused and raised one shaky hand to push the hair back from her face.

"You need to feed," he said mildly.

Nodding reluctantly, she stood and moved to the small refrigerator behind the desk to retrieve a bag of blood. Avoiding his gaze, she grabbed scissors off the desk, clipped off a corner of the bag, and poured half of the blood into a glass on her desk.

Elvi started to raise the glass to her lips at once, then paused and, apparently remembering her manners, held it uncertainly out to Victor. When he shook his head, she lifted it to her lips, and then turned self-consciously away as she drank it. The action seemed one of habit more than anything and Victor watched her curiously. Elvi drank the glass quickly as if knocking back a shot of whiskey. She then poured another glass.

"I thought Owen was to be your meal this night," he commented. "You'll be too full to feed from him."

A small laugh slipped from her lips as she sipped the second glass. "Not likely. I'm pretty sure he's going to chicken out like the rest of them do."

"Chicken out?" Victor asked with interest.

Elvi nodded as she licked her upper lip, then explained, "Most of them do and it's really all just a big bother, but . . ." She shrugged and lifted the glass to her lips.

"If so, then why not forsake this Birthday Bite business?" he asked.

She lowered the glass and peered at him curiously. "You know about that?"

"Your Captain Brunswick was explaining it to me," he admitted.

Something in his tone must have revealed that he wasn't impressed with the whole deal. She nodded and peered down into the glass, then explained, "It all started as a joke. A group of teenagers came in one night. One of the cockier ones was teasing me, trying to get me to bite him. He even went so far as to slice his palm with a pocket knife and hold it out."

Elvi shook her head at the memory. "I wanted to take a switch to his behind. But, of course, I couldn't do that. Instead, I just laughed and said I didn't bite babies." She grimaced. "Foolishly I added, *'Come back when you're a man.'*

Elvi sighed and shrugged. "Two months later he returned. It was his eighteenth birthday. *'I'm a man now, Elvi,' he says. 'Legal. I want my bite.'*"

Her mouth tightened. "I tried to laugh it off, but he wasn't having any of it. He and his friends were causing such a fuss, Mabel finally said, *'He's of age, if he wants it, bite him. It just means one less bag of blood we have to come up with.'*"

"So you bit him," Victor murmured.

She nodded. "Much to his friends' disappointment, I made him come to the back office for it. I wasn't biting him in front of everyone like some freak show. Besides, I—"

"Besides?" Victor prompted when she fell silent.

Elvi shook her head. "It doesn't matter," she mur-

mured, then continued, "a couple weeks later they returned. It was his friend's eighteenth birthday. I could
tell at once that the friend wasn't like the troublemaker.
He didn't really want to be bit; he just didn't want to
look like a sissy in front of his buddy. I brought him
back here, told him he didn't have to do it, and gave
him a bandage for his neck so no one would know.

"I was sorry I'd been so nice about it when I overheard him bragging to his friends about how '*hot*' it had
been." She rolled her eyes. "Of course, with that kind
of press, a couple weeks later another showed up for
his 'Birthday Bite,' then another. It became almost expected. Turning eighteen? Go to Bella's and have Elvi
bite you," she said wryly.

"They all come now, but half of them are only here
because their friends push them into it, while others
want to but are more afraid than they are excited at the
prospect. Then some arrive high or bolstered up by liquid courage and I won't bite any of those. But, they all
come to my office and—bite or no bite—get a bandage
so everyone thinks they went through with it."

She ran her finger around the top of her glass. "I'd
guess one in five actually gets bitten, but they all get a
cake now and a bandage."

"And bragging rights," Victor murmured.

Elvi shrugged. "Boys will be boys."

Victor was silent. This information did affect things.
It might even save her beautiful neck. He wasn't sure.
There was some biting between immortals and their
lovers who were willing and that was mostly ignored
by the council. But while all of these boys were willing, they didn't classify as lovers and the sheer number
of them would upset the council. Then there was the

fact that she wasn't living quietly and trying to avoid detection. Everyone in this town seemed to know what she was.

A knock at the door had Elvi frowning and glancing toward it. She set her glass aside and moved to answer the door, revealing tonight's birthday boy, Owen.

"Mabel said I should come back here," the boy said nervously, his eyes slipping from Elvi to Victor, then away.

"Of course," Elvi murmured, ushering him inside. She then turned to peer at Victor apologetically. "If you'll excuse us?"

Victor hesitated, then stood and left the room. He pulled the door closed, but rather than return to the table, paused and stayed to listen through the door.

Elvi stared at the closed door with regret. She'd never met another vampire and had a million questions she would have liked to ask. She feared she'd missed her opportunity, however. He wasn't a local. Obviously he was just passing through town. She had no idea why he'd stopped at the restaurant. Perhaps those men he'd been with were mortals and had needed to stop for a late dinner. She supposed she'd never know. The man would no doubt return to his friends and leave before she finished with Owen and made her way back out to the dining area.

It was the first time in five years Elvi had met another of her kind and what had she done? Chattered nervously about the Birthday Bite and its origins. It was true he'd asked about it, but if she hadn't been so overset, she might have had the good sense to ask at least one or two of the questions she had. Like what was she? Could she get her soul back? How could she end her existence?

Instead she'd babbled about the biting.

It hadn't just been the fact that he was a vampire that had left her so unsettled. It was the man himself. He was tall and gorgeous and smelled good and Elvi had found him terribly attractive before she'd even found out he was a vampire. That in itself had been disturbing. Elvi hadn't reacted to a man this strongly in years. In her whole life, if she were to be honest with herself. Her husband had been her high school sweetheart. She'd grown up with him and known him all her life. They'd had a comfortable, loving relationship, but she didn't recall ever finding herself responding to his very presence with every fiber of her being as she had to this man's nearness. She'd been so disconcerted by just being near him she hadn't noticed her own reactions to the smell of his blood until her teeth had started to shift, and then her only thought had been to get away from him. While gaining a little distance from him had eased the blood hunger, it hadn't eased her other reactions to him. Elvi had acted like a nervous teenager on her first date, babbling like an idiot about nonsense instead of asking the very important questions she had.

Now she was just feeling confused and torn. Part of her was glad she wouldn't meet him again and be forced to deal with the reactions he caused in her. The other part of her was upset. The idea of another five years passing before happening onto another of her kind and getting the answers she wanted was terribly disheartening.

Sighing, Elvi turned to face Owen.

"So . . ." She eyed him, noting the pallor to his cheeks and his lack of excitement. The boy was staring at the floor, a fine tremor running through his body.

Shaking her head, she said gently, "We don't have to do this, Owen."

He raised his head hopefully, but then his expression and shoulders drooped again just as quickly. "If we don't, my friends will tease me until I die," he said glumly. "We have to do it."

Elvi frowned, thinking that peer pressure sucked. But there was no way she wanted to bite someone who was so obviously terrified of the very idea.

"They don't have to know," she assured him and moved to her desk. Opening the top drawer, she pulled out the box of special bandages for just this sort of occasion. Choosing one with *Happy Birthday* stamped on it in purple, she slid it from the pack and held it up. "Put this on and we'll both just pretend it happened. No one has to know I didn't bite you."

Owen stared at the Band-Aid as if it were a life raft, but asked uncertainly, "What do I say when they ask me what it was like?"

Elvi shrugged. "Just tell them you don't kiss and tell."

His eyes widened with new interest. "There's kissing?"

"No," she said quickly and then chuckled softly at his disappointment. "It's just an old expression that means you won't be indiscreet enough to tell."

"Oh." He sounded disappointed. Apparently if there was no kissing, he wasn't interested. She suspected if she'd said yes, there was kissing, he might have changed his mind and decided to go through with it, but while biting was one thing, she was not going around kissing teenage boys. She might look twenty-five, but Elvi felt every minute of her sixty-two years . . . Which was rather odd when she thought about it.

Before she'd turned, Elvi had always felt like a sixteen-year-old trapped in an old woman's collapsing body. While her body had aged on the outside, gaining wrinkles and weakening with age, she'd never really changed inside. She'd still felt like the same young, hopeful woman she'd been at sixteen, eighteen, and twenty. Now that she'd turned, however, she felt like a sixty-two-year-old fraud hiding in a young woman's body. It seemed she couldn't win for losing.

"Here, put this on your neck." Elvi tossed him the bandage and then moved to her desk to pick up her glass again. She automatically began to gulp it. The flavor had horrified her at first even as she'd craved it. It no longer bothered her, but she wouldn't do anything as crass as savor the flavor in front of Owen. She already knew from Mabel's reactions that it was just gross to actually appear to enjoy the taste of blood, but as it was her only source of nutrition, she couldn't help it.

"What's it taste like?" Owen asked curiously.

Elvi lowered the glass and considered how to answer the question. She finally said, "Surely you've cut a finger or your hand and stuck it in your mouth at some point or other?"

"Yeah," he admitted.

"Well." Elvi shrugged and set the glass down to pour in the rest of the blood. "Then you know what it tastes like."

Owen grimaced. "Doesn't it taste different now that you're a vampire?"

"A bit," she admitted reluctantly. Uncomfortable with the conversation and the fact that it reminded her that she was now something of a freak, Elvi gestured to the door. "You should go eat your cake. I made it myself."

Owen nodded and moved to the door, then paused to glance back.

"Thank you," he offered and ran a finger over the bandage on his neck. "For this."

"You're welcome, Owen. Happy Birthday."

"Thanks," he grinned and reached for the doorknob, adding, "and good luck tonight."

Elvi had started to turn away, but paused and glanced after him with confusion. "What do you mean 'good luck tonight'?"

Owen appeared surprised at the question. "You know . . . the vampire guys that came to town."

"What?" Elvi stared blankly.

Owen frowned at her confusion. "You know . . . that guy who was in here and his friends." When her expression didn't change, he looked worried and murmured, "I know it was supposed to be a secret the last few weeks, but I thought Mabel would have told you by now. I mean they're here. She *has* to tell you."

"Who are here?" Elvi asked, setting her glass down and moving around the desk.

Owen hesitated. Finally, he said, "I don't think I should tell you. I think it's supposed to be a surprise."

"*What's* supposed to be a surprise?" she asked, growing impatient. "I don't like surprises, Owen. Just tell me."

When he continued to hesitate, she shifted impatiently and said, "I won't tell anyone you told me. It will be another secret between us."

A brief struggle took place on his face and then he nodded solemnly. "You should know anyway. And besides, you did this for me."

Elvi's eyes followed the finger he ran over his throat

and she smiled wryly. She hadn't done anything but give him a bandage and supposed he meant the keeping it a secret part.

"All right," Owen shifted his feet and then started back across the room. "I'll tell you."

Elvi settled herself on the corner of her desk and waited patiently for him to begin.

"If you're quite done, I think you should probably return to the table with the others.'"

Victor stiffened at that cold voice. Turning slowly away from the door and the conversation taking place inside, he peered at Mabel, squirming inwardly at being caught eavesdropping. "I was—"

"I know what you were doing," she interrupted dryly.

Victor's gaze narrowed as she slid a hand into her pocket, his alarm bells warning that she may have a weapon there.

"Return to the table please," she insisted, hand still in her pocket.

Victor took in her grim determination and complete lack of fear. She had no clue who she was bossing around. He could have . . . Victor let the *"could haves"* go. He wasn't going to harm the woman and she seemed to know that. Shrugging, he started forward.

Evidently he'd moved closer than she felt comfortable with, and apparently she was also less fearless than he'd thought, for she suddenly whipped a six-inch cross out of her pocket and held it up before her, hissing, "Back."

Victor paused, his expression incredulous as he stared at the cross she was holding up like a shield. This wasn't the weapon he'd expected. He hadn't had one of those flashed at him in centuries. For God's sake, the woman was apparently friends with Elvi; she should know that crosses and other holy relics had no effect on them.

"You can put that away," he said soothingly, hating to see anyone afraid unnecessarily. "It can't harm me and I wasn't going to harm you."

She merely held it out further and narrowed her eyes.

Rolling his own, Victor reached out and closed his hand over the top of the cross, nearly grinning at her wide-eyed look of shock.

"See?" he said after a moment when they both stood frozen. "No hiss of burning flesh, no pain. Religious relics have no effect." Victor released the cross and stepped back to ease her fear at his nearness. "I was listening at the door to see if Elvi would have any trouble with the lad. He seemed frightened and uneager. She handled him beautifully. Now, I shall return to the table to wait with the others."

Dignity restored, Victor continued on out into the dining area.

Six

"What?" Elvi dropped into her desk seat. "They did what?"

Owen swallowed nervously. "They . . . er . . . they put an ad in the paper for a male vampire," he repeated. "And six were supposed to come to the restaurant tonight to meet you. Five of them are already here, I think."

When Elvi stared at him with horror, he shifted uncomfortably, then said, "Well, I'd better get back to the table. Er . . . Thanks . . . for"—he gestured to his neck—"you know."

Elvi heard the door open and close, but just sat there, her mind spinning. She couldn't believe that Mabel and Teddy would . . . Dear God. She didn't know whether to laugh or cry . . . Or throw things. What were they thinking?

The door opened and Mabel stepped into the room.

"I just passed Owen. How are you doing?" Even as she asked the question, her gaze landed on the empty blood bag on the desk. "Chickened out, did he?" Shaking her head, Mabel crossed the room and grabbed the bag to toss it in the garbage, then settled on the corner of Elvi's desk and said, "Listen. I have something to tell you."

"You put an ad in the Toronto paper advertising a single, female vamp looking for a male vamp and picked six to come spend the week in Port Henry," Elvi said dully.

"Ah." Mabel ran her tongue nervously over her lips. "Owen?"

Elvi nodded. "He wished me luck with tonight and then I made him tell me what he was talking about."

"Hmm." Mabel bit her lip and then let out a resigned breath. "Well, it's my own fault. I should have told you earlier, but I was afraid you'd get upset."

"You're damned right I'd have gotten upset!" Elvi snapped, and then asked with disbelief, "What were you thinking?"

"Well—" She hesitated, then said grimly, "I was thinking that I'm sixty-two years old and not going to be around much longer and—"

"Don't say that!" Elvi exclaimed with horror.

"Oh, Elvi." Mabel shook her head sadly. "We've both lost our husbands and several friends the last few years. Three of our set have died in the last six months alone. Who knows how much longer I have here? I don't want to die knowing that you'll be left here alone."

Elvi sat back and stared at her, hating what she was saying, but knowing she was right. Their friends and loved ones were starting to drop like flies and each loss made her feel sad, angry, and just plain guilty because death was something she no longer had to consider.

"This is for the best. If we find you a vampire mate, you'll have someone to help you through . . . everything," Mabel ended lamely rather than mention her own death again.

Elvi was silent. Part of her was tempted by the thought of having someone there for her, someone she didn't have to fear losing. But the other part of her . . .

"I don't think I'm ready to start dating again," she admitted unhappily.

"It's not dating exactly," Mabel assured her, and when Elvi peered at her with open disbelief, she continued, "Look, tons of men responded to the ad. I sorted through them, wrote back and forth and picked the ones I thought might be for real. I didn't do too badly either. It turns out we only had to send two packing. The rest of them are real vampires like you. They're all presentable and seem nice enough . . . well, except that long-haired one Pedro's iguana bit," she added with dislike. "He's a troublemaker that one. That's probably why the lizard jumped on him. Animals sense these things."

Elvi blinked. She'd been so stunned by what Owen had revealed, she hadn't put two and two together and connected her wounded vampire with Mabel and Teddy's plans. Of course, she realized, he wasn't just stopping on his way through town, he was here to meet her . . . because of the single's ad . . . because he thought she was advertising for a man.

"Oh God," she muttered with humiliation.

"No, it will be all right," Mabel assured her quickly as Elvi hunched forward in her chair and covered her flushed face with her hands. "Look, Teddy and I have taken care of everything. All you have to do is spend the week with them at the house and see if you click with one of them. Simple."

Elvi let her hands drop. "They think I'm some desperate old woman who puts ads in the paper."

"Old," Mabel snorted. "If I looked as good as you do, I wouldn't mind being sixty-two. Besides, *they* answered the ad. And *you* didn't put it in. So who's desperate here?"

Elvi muttered, "Oh God. This is so embarrassing."

"It isn't," Mabel insisted. "And it doesn't have to be dating. It will be whatever you want."

When Elvi just shook her head unhappily, Mabel added, "At the very least, you might make friends that you don't have to worry about up and croaking on you. And if we're lucky, they should know other female vamps you can hang out with."

Elvi stopped to ponder that. Perhaps this wasn't as bad as she'd first thought. After all, she'd get to ask all those questions she had. It would be nice not to be so ignorant about what she now was.

"Four out of six, huh?" Elvi asked. "Owen said five were here."

"Oh." Mabel made a face. "The fifth one is a friend of the vampire Pedro's iguana bit." She shook her head. "How immature is that? Needing to bring a friend."

"Oh, I don't know, probably about as mature as a friend having to put an ad in a paper to find you a date," Elvi said dryly.

Mabel stuck out her tongue, then stood and considered her briefly. "You look tired."

"I shouldn't be. You let me sleep late."

"But?" Mabel prompted.

"But I'm weary," Elvi admitted, though she suspected it was a weariness of the soul. The moment she thought that, she felt more depressed. She was a vampire. Dead. Soulless. Spotting the concern on Mabel's face, she forced a smile. "I'm fine."

"You haven't been drinking as much blood as you used to," Mabel pointed out unhappily. "Maybe you're ailing."

"I don't think vampires ail, Mabel."

Mabel nodded, but still looked concerned. "Listen, why don't you just go home and relax? I'll take care of grilling the men."

Elvi's eyebrows rose. "After all the trouble you went to, you're letting me off the hook?"

"Not exactly. I just think it might be better to let you meet them more naturally at the house as you run into them rather than serve you up to them like a roast pig on a platter."

Elvi winced at the imagery. Despite having met one of the men and finding him really quite nice and handsome, her mind presented her with an image of her following Mabel to a table full of Dracula types, all eyeing her speculatively, deciding if she was good enough for them. Shuddering, she shook her head and stood. "I'm not ready for this."

"No," Mabel agreed, slipping an arm around her shoulders and urging her toward the door. "I should have given you a little more warning or something."

"Hmm," Elvi murmured, but didn't think more time would have helped with this. To her it rather felt as if the whole matter was simply emphasizing how different she now was from everyone she'd always known and grown up with. Her difference was something she did her best to avoid acknowledging. A difficult matter considering she slept in a coffin, couldn't look in a mirror, and no longer got to eat food, but Elvi still somehow mostly managed it. She suspected she'd become the *Queen of Denial* these last five years.

"Go home, change into whatever you want, build a fire and pour yourself a glass of w—blood."

Elvi knew Mabel had started out saying wine, but had corrected herself. She wished with all her heart that she could go for the wine. A glass of wine and a fire sounded so relaxing and normal. A glass of blood and a fire just didn't have the same connotation.

"Do you want me to drive you?" Mabel asked as she opened the office door.

Elvi shook her head. "Don't be silly. It's only three blocks."

"All right. Well, you'll have the house to yourself. I'll keep the men here until the restaurant closes."

Victor tapped his fingers impatiently on the table top, his gaze fixed on the arch at the back of the restaurant. Eventually, Elvi had to come out of there, surely? The woman had left them waiting all night while the restaurant slowly emptied and they were grilled by Mabel and Brunswick. An experience to be sure. Used to keeping information about themselves to a minimum with mortals, the five men had sat, shifting uncomfortably and answering as evasively as possible. However, Mabel was a determined sort, asking direct questions such as what they did for a living? Were they married? What were their interests?

Victor had been hard-pressed not to slip into her

mind and make her stop and knew from the glances the men had sent his way, that the others had hoped he would, but hadn't dared themselves with him there. As the oldest, a hunter for the council, and a member of one of the oldest families among their kind, they naturally deferred to him.

Victor hadn't made the woman stop for two simple reasons. One, he felt that if one of the men did turn out to be a lifemate to Elvi Black, then she should have the information Mabel was trying to get for her. The second reason was that he was curious as to how far the woman would go for her friend. It was becoming clear that while their methods were causing Elvi problems with the council, they were done with love and loyalty. These two senior citizens were truly trying to help their Elvi. Being able to present his memories to the council might help the woman when she was finally dragged before them.

Victor's tapping stopped expectantly when the last customer left and Mabel appeared from the kitchen to lock the front door and then moved to their table.

"Right," she said, her gaze moving critically from one to the other.

When the silence began to wear on his nerves, Victor asked, "Are we finally going to get to spend time with Elvi?"

Brunswick glanced at him with surprise. "Elvi went home hours ago. Didn't we mention that?"

"No, you certainly did not," Victor said shortly. "If that is the case, why have we been sitting here for hours watching mortals eat? I thought the whole point of this exercise was to get to know Elvi."

"It is, and you will," Mabel snapped back just as

shortly, then added, "She was tired. I sent her home to relax and get used to the idea of what we've arranged this week."

Understanding immediately flickered through Victor. "You mean she was upset by what you did behind her back."

Mabel scowled, then ignored him and announced, "We're going to the house now. Teddy will take four of you in his car and I'll take the remaining one in mine."

"I'll ride with you," DJ announced getting to his feet.

Victor noted the way Mabel's mouth tightened with displeasure. He too found it difficult to believe DJ would actually volunteer to ride with the old harridan. She'd done nothing but criticize and harass him and DJ all night. The woman most definitely wouldn't have anything good to say about them to Elvi. Not that he cared, but he wondered why DJ would willingly put himself in the woman's company.

"All right, the rest of you are with me, then." Brunswick ushered them to the back of the restaurant.

"What about our car?" DJ asked as they stepped out into the parking lot.

"The house isn't far from here. We're just driving you there so you know where it is. You can come back for your cars later," Mabel answered promptly. She paused beside a red Toyota and opened the driver's door. When DJ started to open the front passenger door, she eyed him narrowly and ordered, "Back seat."

Victor bit his lip to keep from laughing as DJ scowled and got in the back.

"My car's over here," Brunswick announced as he led the way to the only other car in the small lot, a police car parked in the back right corner. Spotting the grill between the front seat and back, Victor moved to the front passenger side door before anyone else could lay claim to it. There was no damned way he was sitting in the caged backseat, squished between two other men.

Mabel hadn't been kidding about the house being close. It was a bare couple of minutes before Brunswick was steering the car into a driveway that curved up behind a large brick Victorian house.

"There are only six bedrooms," Mabel announced as she led them into the front entry. "Elvi's, mine, and four guest bedrooms. That means two of you will have to bunk together." She paused at the foot of a curving staircase to glare at Victor and DJ. "And since you are the one who chose to bring an uninvited friend along, Argeneau, the two of you can be the ones to share."

Victor's mouth tightened, but he didn't comment as she started up the stairs.

"What delightful trim," Edward praised, his gaze slipping over the woodwork above the doors before he turned to follow Mabel. "Victorian?"

"Yes." She actually smiled at Edward, something Victor had almost decided she was incapable of. "The house was built in the 1890s."

"Such fine workmanship." Edward ran his hand lovingly along the curving stair rail. "The Victorians understood the beauty of fine craftsmanship."

"I couldn't agree more." Mabel beamed and slowed so that they were side by side as they continued on.

Victor managed not to gag at the brownie points Edward was racking up. The man was obviously sucking up, somewhat surprising from the pompous Brit.

Once they were on the second floor, Mabel led them

around a corner to the right and along a short hall to a door. "Victor and DJ will sleep here."

She opened the door to show them a large room with a king-sized bed, a sitting area with a couch, chair and table, and a small refrigerator.

Stepping inside, Victor glanced to the right and saw two doors, one leading to a walk-in closet, the other to an en suite bathroom.

"The couch pulls out into a second bed," Brunswick announced, reminding them of his presence. He then shifted and said, "Though, I suppose you won't be needing it. Fortunately, all the rooms are plenty big enough for your coffins."

Victor thought the joke was in poor taste. The fact that none of the other immortals laughed, suggested they agreed. They were all silent as they followed Mabel out of the room and into the hall again.

She led them to the opposite end of the hall and up another curving staircase to the third floor of the house. This level had obviously been recently renovated. The fine woodwork was missing here and everything appeared new. Each room was outfitted with a king-sized bed, a sitting area, its own small refrigerator, and an en suite bathroom.

"I don't know whether you made alternate arrangements, but we stocked up on blood for you," Brunswick announced as Edward stepped over to the refrigerator and opened the door to reveal several bags of blood inside.

"We'd rather you didn't bite the locals," the officer added firmly.

"That won't be a concern," Harper informed him quietly, avoiding Victor's gaze. "It is against our laws to bite mortals unless in case of an emergency."

"It is?" Brunswick frowned, obviously considering that their Elvi was biting mortals. Then he straightened his shoulders and said, "Well, I'm glad to hear it, but I'm the law here in Port Henry. If you have a problem, come see me. If you *are* a problem, you can expect I'll come find you."

As a threat it was effective, Victor thought, or would have been if the man weren't mortal. It seemed obvious that they'd lived so long with their tame Elvi that they now assumed all immortals were as agreeable. The man had a lot to learn. Fortunately for him, Victor had no interest in teaching him.

"I'm going for the car," he growled, turning to head back down.

"Do you want company, Victor?" DJ asked, catching up to him in the second-floor hall, then grinned and added, "I could act as lookout, make sure you don't get caught and get yourself in trouble with Captain Brunswick."

Victor smiled faintly at the teasing offer, not surprised DJ understood he'd feed along the way. He shook his head. "No need."

"Okay. I'm going to grab a bag in our room while you're at it, then," DJ said, continuing on up the hall and around the corner while Victor started lightly down the spiral staircase.

Wondering over the comment about being a look-out to keep Victor from getting in trouble, Elvi started to straighten from the keyhole she'd been peering through, but paused as two more men appeared from the stairs to the third floor. One was a tall fair-haired man. The other was a couple inches shorter and dark-haired. Both were good-looking. She eyed them curiously as they walked past.

"I was not expecting all this," the dark-haired man commented. "The Elvi, she did not mention there would be others here."

"You mean Mabel," the blond corrected and reminded him. "Mabel is the one who wrote the e-mails."

"*Si*. Mabel."

"I didn't expect competition either," the blond now admitted unhappily, and then shrugged. "Such is life."

"Yes," the darker man murmured and then added, "I do not mind Victor or you so much, but Edward, he is a prick."

"Hmm." The blond nodded. "Let's hope he can read her, or that she gives him his walking papers quickly."

The brunette shook his head. "He will be the perfect gentleman in front of her. It is only behind her back he will be shoving his thumb at us. Just look at how he is sucking up to her friend Mabel to get on her good side."

"I think he's slipped into her mind to exert some influence there," the blond said.

"You think?" he asked with surprise. "Well, that's hardly the fair play."

"All's fair in love and lifemates," the blond answered dryly.

Elvi didn't hear the other man's response. The two were out of sight on the stairs and no longer within hearing distance.

"I do love this house. The Victorians had their faults, but architecture wasn't one of them."

Elvi's eyes slid back to the end of the hall as the fifth and final man started up with Mabel and Teddy.

"Oh, I couldn't agree more, Edward," Mabel enthused, and Elvi frowned at the gushing tone to her voice. Mabel never gushed. And this was the Edward the men had mentioned, she realized, eyes narrowing. *"I think he's slipped into her mind and exerted some influence,"* the blond had said. Elvi had no idea what he was talking about, but intended to find out. She wasn't having her friend toyed with.

"I should go get my car," Edward murmured as they passed the door where Elvi crouched, watching through the keyhole.

"Teddy can drive you back to get it," Mabel offered, and Elvi's expression tightened further. It just wasn't like Mabel to volunteer others for a task. If anything, she would have offered to take him herself.

"Uh . . . sure," Teddy agreed, obviously equally surprised at Mabel's volunteering him. "But then I have to head back to the station."

Straightening, Elvi turned away from the door as her mind worked. Was Edward controlling Mabel's mind? And what was this Victor up to that his friend thought he would need a lookout? What the hell had Mabel got them into, inviting these men here? So far the only two who didn't seem to be up to something were the tall, Nordic-looking one and the shorter, Italian chap.

Supposing she wasn't going to find out anything by staying in her room, Elvi straightened her shoulders and moved quickly to the door opposite the one she'd been eavesdropping at. She slipped through the dark sun porch attached to her room and hurried down the stairs to the lower deck.

Seven

"Elvi? Is that you? What are you doing in the bushes?"

Cursing under her breath, Elvi stepped out and crossed to where Teddy stood by his police car. Trying not to sound embarrassed at getting caught lurking, she said, "Hi Teddy."

She tried to decide how to explain her behavior. The truth was, she'd rushed down to the deck and around the house to see what the man called Victor was up to. She'd come around the corner to find him already half a block up the road, headed for Main Street.

Elvi had started to take a step forward to follow, but the blonde and the Italian had come out of the house and she'd ducked into the bushes to avoid being seen. Unfortunately, that was when Teddy had come out heading for the driveway and his car. Of course, he'd spotted her.

"I was, just checking for . . . er . . . aphid damage," she answered lamely.

"Oh." He looked uncertain, and then glanced toward the house when the door opened and Edward, the blonde with the British accent, came out.

Elvi shifted as he approached. She really had no wish to meet him yet.

"Well," she said cheerfully, taking a step back. "I have to check the plants at the side of the house. See you later, Teddy."

Turning abruptly, she hurried around the side of the garage, and then stopped. The street was empty. There was no sign of any of the men anymore. It seemed she wouldn't be following anyone.

"Damn," Elvi muttered as she continued on around the house to the entrance to the lower sun porch and passed through the room to reach the back deck again. A glance toward the driveway showed Teddy and Edward pulling out onto the street.

"Oh, there you are!" Mabel stepped out of the kitchen and smiled. "I wondered where you'd got to. Are you feeling any better?"

"Yes," she lied. The truth was she had a bit of a headache, probably caused by frustration, she thought on a sigh.

Mabel nodded, then glanced upward, taking in the starry night. Her gaze then swung to the yard beyond the large deck and she commented, "I was thinking of having a fire."

"The guests would probably enjoy that," Elvi murmured.

"They're all out, I think," Mabel announced. "Getting their cars."

Elvi was sure the bearded friend of Victor's was still in the house, but didn't say anything and simply followed Mabel to the woodpile to help collect wood.

"Why don't you go get us some drinks while I get the fire started?" Mabel suggested once they'd moved a small pile over to the fire pit.

Elvi turned away and headed to the house. Mabel was better at starting fires anyway. She had finished pouring the drinks and was just trying to open the kitchen door without spilling them when an arm reached past her and pushed the screen door open.

"Allow me."

Elvi paused and turned to glance at the man who'd helped her, the bearded friend of Victor's.

"DJ," he introduced himself with a grin. "And you're Elvi."

She nodded, unable to resist smiling in return despite the blush that rose up on her cheeks. The man's grin was infectious. "What is DJ short for?"

"Dieudonne Jules," he answered promptly.

"Dieudonne?" she echoed, thinking it a beautiful name. "You're the friend, not one of the . . . er . . ."

"Suitors," he supplied gently.

She pulled a face, but nodded.

"Alas, yes, this is true. I'm just here to support a friend," he said, then sniffed delicately and glanced down at the glasses she held.

"Wine?"

"For Mabel," she explained.

"It smells good."

"Yes." She inhaled the scent and sighed with regret that she couldn't have it. "It's the house wine."

"House wine?" he queried.

"We make it ourselves," she explained.

"Really?" His eyebrows rose and he asked, "Am I allowed to have a glass?"

Elvi stared, caught by surprise. She'd thought he was a vampire too, but it seemed he was just a mortal, supporting his vampire friend like Mabel.

She'd barely had that thought, when Elvi recalled that he'd been heading off to grab a bag of blood when Victor had left for the car. Thoroughly confused, she opened her mouth to ask what exactly he was when the door to the garage opened and Victor entered.

Elvi's gaze slid first to his ear and neck, noting the bandage was gone and the wound completely healed, and then her attention slid to the rest of him. She hadn't paid much attention to his looks earlier; she'd been too upset by the iguana attack, and then startled by his being a vampire. Now she took him in properly, and felt herself inhale deeply. The man was gorgeous. Tall, with wide muscular shoulders and sexy as hell with that longish hair and the tight dark jeans and T-shirt he was wearing.

His most striking feature, however, was his eyes, a startling silver blue color she'd never seen before. They were beautiful, big and framed by long lashes. Women would kill to have his eyes.

"Breathe," DJ whispered by her ear as he took the glasses from her suddenly shaking hands.

Elvi flushed and forced herself to look away from Victor. Reminded of DJ, she forced herself to concentrate on him and asked, "You want wine?"

He'd said as much, of course, but she was asking again just to be certain she wasn't misunderstanding anything.

"If it wouldn't be a bother," he said with a nod.

"I'll have one too, if you're offering," Victor announced, moving around the counter to join them.

Elvi blinked, but noticed that DJ also appeared surprised by the request as he glanced at his friend.

Victor shrugged at his amazement. "It smells good."

Elvi wasn't surprised he could smell it from across the room. Her own senses had become extremely strong after the turn. She was confused, however, by the request.

"Elvi?" Mabel opened the screen door. Her gaze slid suspiciously from DJ to Victor as she stepped inside, and she said, "You were taking so long I started to worry."

"I'm fine," Elvi assured her, then turned to glance from one man to the other and repeated carefully, "You want wine?"

When both men nodded, she exchanged a glance with Mabel. The other woman moved closer to her side and both of them crossed their arms over their chests as they eyed the pair.

"So, what's the joke?" Mabel asked grimly.

When the men raised their eyebrows in question, Elvi shifted impatiently and said, "Vampires don't consume anything but blood. You aren't real vampires. So what's this about? You thought it would be fun to—"

Her words died abruptly when DJ suddenly opened his mouth. His teeth looked perfectly normal . . . until his canines slid out and down, becoming long, pointy fangs.

"Oh," she breathed.

"We prefer the term immortals to vampires," Victor announced as DJ retracted his teeth. "And we *can* eat and drink things other than blood, though many of us stop out of boredom after several hundred years."

"We can eat?" Elvi echoed faintly. It was really the only thing he'd said that stuck in her head. "I can *eat*?"

"You didn't know?" DJ asked, his teeth now back in place.

"Dracula never ate," Mabel pointed out, confusion and concern on her face as she peered at Elvi.

"Dracula is a fictional character," Victor said dryly.

"Elvi, are you all right?" Mabel asked worriedly, touching her arm.

Elvi was silent, her head bowed. When she lifted it, she had to blink to see through the tears blurring her eyes. "I can eat."

"Yes, honey, it would seem so." Mabel patted her shoulder.

Elvi closed her eyes, her head spinning. She hadn't eaten a thing in five years and that more than anything else had set her apart from others. It was only after her turning that she'd realized how much people relied on food for social occasions. Birthdays, weddings, showers . . . they were celebrated with feasts, or cakes, or some form of food. Friends even met over coffee or drinks. Every meeting between people somehow revolved around food or drink and that had left her always on the outside. Unable to do either, or so she'd thought, her presence at such functions had often left the others feeling uncomfortable and guilty as they ate or drank in front of her.

That was the emotional side of it. The other side was that Elvi *loved* food. She always had. She loved the smell, the look, the texture, the taste. She loved to cook and she loved to eat. Going without the last five years had been like some sort of torture. Needless torture if what these two men said was true. *She could eat.*

That thought screamed through her head like a banshee, drowning out every other thought in her head with its howling. Elvi suddenly turned to the refrigerator and dragged the door open, only to stare at the contents with dismay.

"Oh, Mabel," she moaned unhappily.

"What?" The woman moved to her side, but seemed to understand the moment her eyes moved over the refrigerator contents. Voice apologetic, she said, "I'm on that diet Dr. Wilburs put me on."

Elvi just stood shaking her head mournfully. Her mind was shrieking cheesecake and the refrigerator held nothing but green things; lettuce, celery, spinach, broccoli. She so wasn't having something green and healthy as her first food in five years.

"I need to go to the grocery store," she decided, slamming the fridge door closed.

"What?" Mabel asked with surprise. "The grocery store is closed at this hour."

"Not A&P," she said, pushing through the trio to hurry around the counter. "It's open twenty-four hours." Stopping at the door to the garage, she whirled around and asked, "Where are the car keys?"

"Just a minute, I'll go with you," Mabel said abruptly. "I just have to find my shoes and purse and—"

"What about the fire?" Elvi asked. She really didn't want to have to wait while Mabel got ready. The woman would insist on changing, and freshening her lipstick, then she wouldn't remember where she'd left her purse and so on, and by the time she was ready to go, Elvi could have been and returned and eaten half a cheesecake.

"Oh, damn. I forgot about the fire," Mabel muttered. "I can't leave it unattended."

"That's okay," Elvi assured her. "I can drive myself. I won't be long."

"You won't be driving your car. The garage door is blocked by my car," Victor announced, moving toward her. "I'll take you. DJ can stay here and help Mabel with the fire."

"I don't need any damned help with the fire," Mabel said with irritation.

"I'm sure you don't," DJ said soothingly, then grinned and added, "but I bet between the two of us, we can make it burn hotter."

Silence fell briefly in the room. Mabel appeared too stunned by the suggestive comment to respond. Victor appeared a bit surprised himself. As for Elvi, while she was a little startled by it as well, the thought of food was on her mind and crowding out everything else. She wasn't going to get into whatever was going on between DJ and Mabel, and she wasn't going to argue about Victor driving her to the store either.

"Let's go," Elvi said abruptly and charged out of the house. She felt absolutely no guilt at abandoning Mabel to DJ's tender mercies. It was Mabel who five years ago had pointed out that vampires don't eat and insisted Elvi not even try because she didn't want to *"hold her head when she vomited it back up."* At that moment, she was blaming Mabel for five years of missed cheesecake, ice cream, and chocolate.

"Cheesecake, ice cream, chocolate," she muttered, charging through the garage and to the side door.

"Is that your grocery list?" Victor asked, sounding amused as he followed her out onto the sidewalk that ran around the garage to the driveway.

"Part of it," Elvi acknowledged, scurrying around to the driveway, only to come to an abrupt halt. The car she supposed must be his was there, a big, silver BMW. But two more cars were presently pulling into the driveway. The Italian and the German were back and blocking in his car.

Victor took one look at Elvi's face and moved past her to the driver's door of the car behind his.

"Harper, don't turn off the engine," he said, pulling the driver's door open. "This is an emergency. We need to get this lady to A&P, but you're blocking my car and I don't think she can wait for you to move it. Will you drive us?"

"Of course." Harper smiled at Elvi through the window and redid the seat belt he'd just undone.

"Thanks." Slamming the door closed, Victor waved Elvi forward and moved to open the back door.

"I'm coming too," the Italian announced as he got out of his own car. She didn't care. They could all come if they wished . . . so long as they didn't slow her down. The very idea of something sweet and silky filling her mouth, coating her taste buds and sliding down her throat to her barren stomach, was threatening to make her drool like a baby.

"What kind of emergency is it?" the Italian asked, slipping into the backseat on the passenger's side even as Elvi climbed in through the opposite door.

"Cheesecake," she answered abruptly, squeezing up against the man to make room as Victor followed her into the backseat.

"Comfy?" Harper asked dryly, peering at them in the rearview mirror from where he sat alone in the front.

Elvi grimaced, but didn't complain or suggest anyone move to the front so Harper wasn't left alone like a chauffeur. She just wanted to get moving.

Harper shrugged and shifted the car into gear, started to reverse, then stopped abruptly as another car pulled in behind them, cutting them off.

"Edward," Victor muttered craning his neck to peer out the back window. He gestured to the man through the window and yelled, "Get out of the way!"

Rather than do as instructed, the man got out of his car.

"Where is everyone going?" he asked politely, eyes sharpening as he peered into the backseat and saw Elvi there.

"We have to get to the A&P," Harper told him. "Move your car so we can get out."

Edward hesitated, and then said, "Wouldn't it be easier just to take my car? It's got larger seats."

"Fine!" Elvi said with exasperation. It would probably be just as quick as waiting for him to get back in the car and back out anyway, she thought. Elvi would have crawled right over Victor to get out of the claustrophobic vehicle if he weren't already heaving a sigh and opening the door. She waited impatiently for him to get out, scrambled out behind him and hurried after him to the vehicle blocking Harper's.

It was a BMW like Vincent's but black. It was also huge and definitely had more seating room. Elvi crawled in, meeting the Italian again as he too climbed into the backseat. Larger though it was, it was still cramped once Victor climbed in and pulled the door closed. These men were big. She still felt a little like a sardine in a can.

Sensing that Alessandro was peering at her, she turned a questioning gaze his way.

"Déjà vu, eh?" he said with a grin, pulling his door closed.

Despite her impatience to get to the grocery store, Elvi found herself grinning in response.

"I am Alessandro Cipriano," he introduced himself, holding out his hand. Once she'd shook it, he gestured to the blond now climbing into the front passenger seat, "and this is Harpernus Stoyan."

"Call me Harper." The man turned to offer his hand as well, in a quick shake, then reached for his seat belt.

"And I am Edward Kenric," their driver announced as he finished with his own seat belt and shifted into reverse.

"I suppose Victor introduced himself properly while you were tending his injury," Harper said, shifting to sit sideways in his seat so he could see her.

"No." Elvi glanced sideways at the man whose lap she was nearly seated on. Dear Lord, all of these men were big. She'd think it was a result of being vampires, but she hadn't suddenly shot up to six feet tall, and gained bigger boobs, so supposed it was purely the result of their gene pool.

"Victor Argeneau," Harper introduced him properly. Elvi and Victor exchanged a nod.

"And you are, I hope, Elvi Black?" Harper said.

"Yes." She blushed, suddenly recalling that all these

men were here to court her. She wanted to blurt that she hadn't posted the ad, but feared they might not believe her.

"Where are we going?" Edward asked.

"Turn left," Elvi instructed, realizing that he'd backed up and turned around and was now paused at the mouth of the driveway unsure which way to go. "We're going to A&P."

"A&P," Edward murmured as he came to a halt at the red light on the corner. "What is the emergency exactly?"

"Cheesecake," Alessandro answered, then shrugged when the British man turned sharp eyes on him. "It's what she said when I asked."

"Turn right here," Elvi muttered with embarrassment. The light was still red, but there was no traffic coming from the sides.

Edward shifted back to face the road and turned as instructed.

"It's straight up this road several blocks," she said. "It's on the left side. I'll warn you when we get close."

Elvi then sat back and tried not to tap her fingers on her knee as Edward Kenric drove up the street at a ridiculously slow speed.

"The speed limit here is fifty kilometers an hour," she informed him when she couldn't stand it any longer.

Kenric cut his eyes to hers in the rearview mirror. He didn't spit out the sharp words she sensed he wanted to, but did pick up speed . . . a little. Elvi could have wept with frustration. She was sure he was only going thirty. She could have run there faster than this . . . carrying one of the men.

Aware that the silence in the car wasn't only her own,

Elvi glanced curiously around at the men. All of them but Edward seemed to be staring at her, though even Edward kept glancing at her in the rearview mirror.

She shifted uncomfortably, then sighed and said, "I didn't put the ad in the paper. Mabel did. I didn't even know what she was up to until tonight."

"We know," Harper informed her gently. "We found that out tonight at the restaurant."

"Oh." She shifted. They were still staring at her, but she hadn't a clue what to say to make them stop . . . short of telling them to, and that seemed rude when they were all rushing to get her to the A&P and cheesecake. Well, all but Edward. He seemed to be a Sunday driver. Why the damned man hadn't just moved his stupid car and let Harper drive, she didn't know. Obviously a control freak, she decided. Good-looking, but he had issues. And he wasn't too bright either. A smart man wouldn't stand between a woman and cheesecake.

A choking sound drew her eyes to the back of Edward's head with alarm. If he had some sort of seizure and delayed her getting to the grocery store . . . *Honestly!*

A chuckle from the Italian made her glance his way and she frowned slightly. "What?"

"Nothing," he said quickly, and then asked, "What do you think of me so far?"

"I don't know you," Elvi said, bewildered by the question.

"No, of course not," he murmured, but watched her almost expectantly.

Shaking her head, Elvi glanced out the front window again to see how far away they were, but now that the man had asked the question, she couldn't seem to help but think about it. What did she think of him?

He seemed all right so far from what she could tell. He was certainly good-looking, and those eyes of his! She'd never seen golden brown eyes before. They were almost as beautiful as Victor's.

Her gaze slid to Harper. He was a handsome man too with his golden hair and silver-green eyes. All four of the men in the car were attractive, but of the four of them she would have said Victor appealed to her the most. She couldn't say why and didn't care to ponder the matter. Besides, they'd reached the grocery store . . . finally.

And Edward was driving past, she realized with horror. Sitting forward, she shrieked, "Here!" Then cried out in surprise as Edward stomped on the brakes and sent everyone slamming backward in their seats.

There was a moment of startled silence in the car, and then Edward turned slowly in his seat and cast a cold glare her way. "Ms. Black. In the future, you might try to avoid screeching in the driver's ear whilst giving directions. It can be quite alarming."

"Sorry," she said meekly. The man could be quite scary when he chose to be.

"She gets the point, Edward. Just pull in here." Victor's voice was harsh and commanding and Edward responded to it, though not before she saw annoyance flicker across his face.

Releasing the breath she'd been holding once he'd stopped glaring at her, Elvi took a cautious breath and offered Victor a grateful smile, then turned to glance questioningly at Alessandro when he tapped her arm.

"You like me, no?" he asked with a grin when she met his gaze.

Elvi stared at him in confusion, and then followed his gaze when he glanced down, realizing only then that when Edward had slammed on the brakes, she'd grabbed the man's knee and was still clutching it for dear life.

A surprised squeak slipped from her lips, and she immediately released his knee, only to realize she was clutching Victor's with her other hand as well. Reclaiming that straying hand too, she crossed her arms over her chest and stared straight ahead at the A&P sign like it was a beacon in the dark.

"Cheesecake, chocolate, ice cream," she muttered under her breath. Nothing else would matter once she had those.

Eight

"She was serious. The emergency is cheesecake?" Edward sounded incredulous as he watched Elvi hover indecisively over the cake counter.

"She hasn't eaten in five years," Victor muttered distractedly as he stood at her side, eyeing the cakes with interest.

"Why not?" Harper asked.

"She didn't know she could," he answered absently.

"What?" Alessandro sounded horrified. "Who is your sire, bella? I would talk to him about this. To leave you in such ignorance . . ."

Elvi ignored him. She had no idea what Alessandro was nattering on about with such outrage. She had no idea what a sire was and couldn't be bothered to sort it out at this point. Didn't he know she needed food?

Elvi had nearly fallen flat on her face in her rush to get

out of the car. Only a steadying hand from Victor had kept her upright. Gasping a *"thank you"* she'd charged for the store, rushing ahead and leaving the men to trail her or not as they liked. It was late enough that the store was nearly empty, which meant lots of carts were all lined up at the front waiting for her.

Elvi had tugged one free and pushed it to the back of the store at a near run, drawing the eye of the few people stacking shelves. They'd glanced her way, and then done a double take when they saw who it was. Elvi had managed a smile for each in passing, knowing that what was startling them was that she was shopping . . . like a real person.

Elvi had arrived at the counter well ahead of the men, but now as they reached her, she still stood hemming and hawing over her choices. This was a serious issue. Her first food in five years. She hoped it tasted the same.

That thought drew her up short. Blood tasted different to her now. What if food did? While she'd lived, blood had been a tinny, nasty thing, but now it was yummy. What if foods that had seemed so yummy when she was alive, now seemed flat and tasteless in death?

A test was necessary, she decided. She wasn't going to drag home food she couldn't even enjoy, but would be left to stare at in mournful depression. She needed to try something and see what it tasted like, but what?

"Elvi?" Victor sounded concerned as he moved to her side. "Are you all right?"

"I need something," she muttered.

"What do you need?" he asked, and she couldn't help but notice Victor sounded rather cautious, as if he were approaching a possibly rabid animal . . . or a mad-woman.

She was too distracted to care. Besides, he obviously didn't understand. She was a woman who hadn't eaten in five years. *Five*. That was one thousand, eight hundred and twenty-five days. That was five thousand, four hundred and seventy-five meals. Actually, more than that since it would be six years this winter. In just a couple months really. How many meals had it been exactly? Elvi wondered and started to do the math and then pushed it aside as unimportant. She hadn't eaten. She wanted food. She was a woman with a mission.

"Can I help you with something, Elvi?"

She glanced to the side and smiled as she recognized the fresh-faced young blonde in the grocery store uniform. Dawn Geoffreys, the granddaughter of a friend.

"Yes, dear," Elvi said brightening. "I need something small to try."

"To try?" Dawn asked with confusion, then her eyes widened with amazement. "You mean like to eat?"

"Yes. These men say I can eat, but I want to try something small first to . . ." Her voice trailed away as her gaze slid past the girl to the older woman approaching.

"Mrs. Ricci," she said with surprise, and then glanced at her wristwatch. It was the middle of the night. Far past the elderly lady's bedtime, she was sure. Leonora Ricci was in her eighties. "What are you doing here so late?"

"I don't sleep very well anymore, dear," Mrs. Ricci answered serenely. "I'm in bed by nine and up by two and looking for something to do. I've found this is the best time to shop. No one shops at this hour . . . Usually," she added with a smile and then glanced at the men surrounding Elvi and asked, "I'm guessing these are your beaus?"

"Oh, yes." Elvi blushed, and quickly introduced them.

Mrs. Ricci greeted each pleasantly and then commented, "Little Teddy was telling me about you boys. I hope you treat our Elvi right. None of that love-them-and-leave-them nonsense kids get into nowadays."

When the men quickly murmured assurances of their good intentions, Mrs. Ricci nodded and turned to Elvi. "I heard you say you wanted something small as I came up. Why not a cookie, dear?"

She gestured to the table behind her stacked with clear boxes of freshly baked cookies and Elvi smiled. A cookie. So simple and perfect! Stepping up to the table, she slid her gaze over the selection: Oatmeal, Chocolate Chip, Double Chocolate Fudge, Hermit Cookies, Shortbread, S'Mores, Butterscotch Chocolate Chip—

"White Chocolate Strawberry cookies?" Elvi read the last selection with interest. "These are new. I don't remember those from when I used to eat."

"Oh, yes." Dawn hurried to her side. "They're new. They're really yummy too."

"Perfect." Elvi slit the seal, opened the container and snatched out a cookie, then hesitated almost afraid to try it. Finally, she raised it cautiously to her nose and sniffed delicately. God, it smelled good! She inhaled more deeply.

"Try it," Mrs. Ricci said. "We are all curious now."

Elvi peered back at the cookie and bit her lip, then said, "But what if food doesn't taste the same anymore? What if it's like dust in my mouth? How disappointing would that be?"

"Oh." Dawn's smile faded, and then she turned to the men. "Will it?"

"No, of course not," Victor snapped impatiently. "It will taste just as good as before. Better even. Your taste buds are more sensitive just like everything else. Didn't your sire teach you anything?"

Elvi had lost interest in his words after the bit about taste buds being more sensitive just like everything else. Her hearing was ten times better, as was her physical strength and speed, but her taste buds too?

"Try it, Elvi," Mrs. Ricci urged again.

Elvi took a breath, then lifted the cookie to her lips, closed her eyes, and took a bite. Her eyes immediately shot open with amazed delight. She was just holding the cookie in her mouth, almost afraid to chew, but it was enough for her taste buds. They went wild. The only way to describe it would be an oral orgasm. After five years of a blood-only diet, this sweet, savory explosion in her mouth made every taste bud stand up, then do somersaults across her tongue.

"Good?" Dawn asked hopefully.

"Mmmmmmmm," Elvi answered on a long moan. "Mmm, mmm, mmmmmmmm."

A chuckle drew her eyes to Alessandro. He was grinning at her with delight. Actually, she saw, all the men were smiling at her indulgently . . . except for Edward.

"If it wouldn't be too much excitement for your senses," Edward said dryly, "perhaps you should try chewing and swallow—"

Elvi shoved the rest of the cookie in his open mouth. She watched him closely as she began to chew her own and reached for another to replace the one Edward was now trying to spit out. Then he paused, his mouth working as his taste buds tasted.

"These are quite good," he said with surprise.

Elvi smiled around the cookie in her own mouth, and then offered the cookie box to Mrs. Ricci.

"Can I try one?" Alessandro asked curiously, and then explained, "I haven't eaten for fifty years, but you seem to enjoy it so much . . ."

"Fifty years!" Mrs. Ricci repeated with dismay. "Someone needs to feed you, son. You come see me if you get hungry. I live across the street from Elvi and I always have something cooking."

Elvi smiled and held the box out to Alessandro, her eyebrows rising when he, Harper, and even Victor immediately reached in to take a cookie each. Seeing the envious expression on Dawn's face, Elvi held the box out to her as well, bringing a smile to the girl's face.

Having finished the half a cookie he'd got, Edward reached for another and frowned at how few were left. "I think we should get more of these."

"Definitely," Harper said with a smile as he finished his own cookie. "These really are quite good."

"Yes, they are," Mrs. Ricci said and moved to the table to collect a box of her own and put it in her basket. She then wished them good evening before continuing on with her own shopping.

The moment she was gone, the men moved to the table, each grabbing a couple of boxes. Elvi grabbed another cookie from the open pack before setting it in the cart, then moved happily back to the cake counter to survey the selection with greedy eyes. Cheesecake, Carrot Cake, a Chocolate Bomb, Black Forest Cake, Lemon Supreme, Cherry Surprise . . . They all looked good to her.

"So?" Alessandro followed and peered at the cakes with interest. "What is good here?"

"I can't decide!" Elvi admitted with dismay. She wanted them all, but couldn't possibly eat it all and so thought choosing two or three would be better, but which two or three?

"You said you wanted cheesecake," Victor reminded her. "Cheesecake, ice cream, and chocolate."

"Yes, but that Caramel Crunch looks yummy too, and which chocolate one? The Chocolate Bomb, the Black Forest cake, or the Fudge Surprise? And look at that carrot cake. It's a masterpiece," she crooned.

Victor surveyed the cakes she'd pointed out with a frown, and then shrugged. "Take them all."

"*All* of them?" she squeaked, torn between hope and horror at the gluttonous thought.

"Why not? You have five years to make up for."

"Victor's right, and we will help you eat them," Harper announced. Stepping forward, he picked up the cheesecake and handed it to Alessandro, then picked up the Chocolate Bomb and Black Forest cake. Victor then picked up the Fudge Surprise and Caramel Crunch.

Elvi surveyed the cakes that were left, then bit her lip and quickly picked up the Cherry Supreme too.

"I like cherries," she said apologetically.

"Ice cream?" Victor asked.

"Oh, yes." Turning, she carefully set her cakes in the cart, and then led the way to the frozen section, pausing abruptly as she passed an end aisle of Mexican food; tacos, seasoning and so on. Elvi absolutely loved Mexican food. She had been cooking it and around it for five years without being able to take even a lick. She stared at the end aisle, her mind in a veritable swoon. She could make tacos, or chimichangas, or, ohhhhhh, fajitas. She'd need steak . . . or maybe chicken. And tomatoes and onions and cheese and—

"I believe we'll be needing another cart," Edward

murmured and turned away to go find one. Elvi hardly noticed his leaving, she was adjusting the grocery list in her head.

"I don't think there is enough room for everything," Alessandro announced with a frown as Edward opened the trunk of the BMW.

"We can put some in the backseat with us, and maybe the front seat too," Elvi suggested, lifting bags out of the first of their three carts. She knew she'd gone a little overboard with the groceries, but really the men hadn't been any help at all, encouraging her as if they were on the Devil's payroll, sent to tempt her into committing the third of the seven deadly sins: gluttony.

Anytime Elvi had debated over two items, they'd simply taken both from her and put them in the cart. And then they'd picked up an item or two themselves, things that caught their eye or interest. Dawn had rung them through her till, her eyes wide the whole time, and Elvi knew this story would be broadcast all over town by breakfast.

As would the fact that when the total had come up, Elvi had reached for her purse only to find that she'd rushed out of the house so quickly, she hadn't brought it with her. Guessing at the problem from her dismayed grasping at the thin air where her purse should have been, four men's hands had suddenly appeared before her, each holding a credit card.

Victor had ended up doing the honors, glaring at the others until they put away their own cards and wallets.

"It's bigger than it looks," Harper said as they fit the last bag into the trunk. "Perhaps I should look into getting one of these."

Elvi didn't comment, but did wonder what these men did. Two owned cars that probably cost more than her house and another was casually considering getting one. Come to think of it, the roadster Alessandro had stepped out of hadn't been cheap either. It seemed Mabel had only picked the wealthier vampires for her.

Elvi's glance caught on a car pulling into the parking lot, and stared, sure she recognized it as it parked under the lights. When the driver opened the door and got out, she caught her breath, and hissed, "Duck!"

Much to her relief, the men paid heed and ducked next to her behind Edward's BMW. All but Victor, Elvi realized when she glanced to her side.

Looking down at where they crouched on the ground, Victor asked, "Is there a problem?"

"No." She grabbed his arm and dragged him down with them. "Just someone I'd rather avoid."

"That wouldn't be Father O'Flaherty, would it?" Victor asked dryly.

Elvi was surprised that he knew who the man was, but said, "He's really a dear old thing, but he hasn't taken my turning as well as the others. It's understandable, I guess."

"Is it?" Victor asked grimly.

"Well, he's a minister and I'm a vampire," she said simply.

Victor muttered something under his breath and straightened.

"Hey," Elvi hissed and stood upright to catch at his arm, then paused when she saw that Father O'Flaherty was entering the grocery store. "Oh . . . I guess we can go."

Elvi spent the ride home trying to figure out what she would eat first. It was a difficult decision, but didn't feel as urgent as her need to get to the grocery store had been. She and the men had eaten six boxes of the cookies as they'd gone through the grocery store. Now Elvi was feeling almost uncomfortably full, both her head and stomach aching. It was just her brain that still wanted more.

"Dear God! What did you do? Buy out the grocery store?" Mabel exclaimed, entering the kitchen from the deck with DJ on her heels as Elvi entered from the garage with the men in tow. All of them were loaded down with grocery bags.

"I couldn't make up my mind," Elvi said with embarrassment as the men began to set down their burdens.

"We'll get the rest," Victor announced and led the men back out through the garage.

"There's more?" Mabel asked with dismay. "Elvi, where are we going to put all this? We only have two refrigerators."

"It's not all perishable," Elvi assured her, grabbing up a bag with ice cream and moving to the freezer. "The rest is mostly boxes and cans. We just brought the cold stuff in first so it wouldn't go bad."

Mabel was shaking her head, but bent to pick up a bag and help.

"I hope you don't intend to eat all of this at once," she said with concern as she began to empty the bag she'd picked up. "You'll make yourself sick."

"No, of course not," Elvi assured her, and was pretty sure it was true. She wanted to eat something, but she really was quite full. She supposed after five years with nothing in it, her stomach had shrunk to the size of a pea and she'd stretched it out with the cookies. Did she really want to stretch it further?

Yes, came the resounding answer in her head. Just a little further. Something small. But what? she wondered as the men returned with the rest of the groceries.

Elvi tried not to feel guilty at the excess of food as they continued unpacking. Instead she concentrated on what she should eat. Where should she start? Cheese-cake? Chocolate? Ice cream? Soft tacos? Spaghetti? Steak? Pepperoni? Knockwurst? Everything was sounding good to her.

"Perhaps a selection of the cheese and crackers," Alessandro murmured, his expression sympathetic as he watched her peer at the groceries with confusion. "That and the nice glass of wine by the fire."

"Cheese," Elvi murmured with relief. That was close to cheesecake, but better for her, wasn't it? But not too healthy . . . And crackers were supposed to be good for settling the stomach.

"Good idea, Alessandro," she said with a smile.

With Mabel and the men helping, it was no time before the bags were empty and the cupboards and refrigerators bursting with food.

"Elvi, you and the men pour yourselves some wine and take it out to sit by the fire," Mabel suggested once they were done. "I'll fix up some cheese and crackers and bring them out."

"I can help," Elvi protested.

"You can help most by going out and sitting with the men and leaving me some room to work," Mabel said firmly, her expression pointed. It was only then that Elvi recalled that she was supposed to be getting to know these men and possibly picking a mate. She'd been so wrapped up in food for the last little bit, she'd quite forgotten that embarrassing little tidbit.

"Here." DJ moved to the wine rack, selected three bottles, and handed them to the men, then fetched wine-glasses and a corkscrew as if he'd lived in the house for a week already. Passing out the various items, he waved them to the door. "Go sit by the fire and get acquainted. I'll help Mabel with the tray."

"I don't need any help," Mabel growled.

Ignoring her, DJ began to herd them toward the door. "Go on."

An odd smile tugging at his lips, Victor took Elvi's arm and steered her to the door. "Shout if you need help."

DJ just grinned as he watched them leave.

"This is nice," Harper commented moments later as they were finally settled around the metal fire pit in the backyard. The fire had been dying out by the time they'd collected chairs from the garage and set them up around the fire. Harper and Alessandro had brought it back to flaming life while Edward, Elvi, and Victor had tended to opening the wine and pouring the glasses.

"Yes," Elvi murmured, staring at the fire through the red wine in her glass.

Mabel and DJ came out moments later with a tray piled with every one of the six cheeses Elvi and the men had picked at the grocery store and at least as many types of crackers piled on a tray. There were also small paper plates for each of them. The group tried the various offerings, commenting on what was good and what was not and various other things.

When the tray was empty, Mabel picked it up and stood.

"I'll get that, Mabel. Sit down," Elvi said as she turned away.

"That's okay. I'm heading off to bed anyway," Mabel said. "You should probably too, soon."

Elvi frowned and glanced at her watch. It was after five A.M. The sun would soon be up, she realized with some surprise, and then acknowledged that she shouldn't be. The restaurant didn't close until two A.M. because of the bar, and then there'd been the house tour, the collecting of cars, and the hour at the grocery store before they'd settled around the fire. The time had seemed to fly by.

Sighing with regret that the first interesting night she'd had in a long time was coming to a close, Elvi collected her wineglass and moved to the fire to dampen it down.

"I'll get that," DJ offered, urging her out of the way.

"Thank you," Elvi murmured, then glanced at the other men to offer a goodnight before slipping away to follow Mabel.

"Well?" the other woman asked as she entered the kitchen.

"They seem nice," she admitted wryly, then laughed and said, "but what did you do, pick the wealthiest and best-looking only?"

"Only the best for my Elvi," Mabel proclaimed.

"What would I do without you?" Elvi asked with a laugh and gave her a hug. "Now, go to bed. It's well past your bedtime."

Nodding, Mabel started out of the room, then paused suddenly and turned back. "I didn't get the chance to tell you . . ."

"What?" Elvi prompted as she opened the dishwasher and bent to place her wineglass inside.

"When we were at the restaurant, that Argeneau fellow touched my cross," Mabel said quietly. "And nothing happened."

"He did?" she asked with amazement. She hadn't dared enter a church or touch anything religious since her turning for fear of bursting into flames or some such thing like in the movies.

Mabel nodded. "You might want to ask him about that tomorrow."

"Yes," Elvi murmured as Mabel continued out of the room.

Closing the dishwasher door, she made her way upstairs. It was late, or early as the case may be, and she knew she should go to bed, but instead found herself wandering through her room to the attached sunroom. Leaving the lights out, she moved to the window and peered down at the half-circle of men around the dying flames. Their voices drifted up to her through the night as Elvi stood watching them. One of them might be a mate for her, she thought with disbelief, and still wasn't sure she was ready for another relationship. It had hurt so much to lose her husband and daughter. . . .

On the bright side, she supposed she wouldn't have to worry about being widowed again with any of these men. They, like her, were already dead.

Grimacing, Elvi moved to sit on the wicker couch. Drawing her feet up under her, she closed her eyes and savored the best day she'd had in five years.

She could eat.

She would no longer feel like an outsider at social functions. If nothing else happened this week, Elvi would be grateful for that.

A tap at the sunroom door made her start and Elvi

glanced over sharply to see Victor standing outside the glass door. Her heart immediately started hammering in her chest and she could actually feel her hands growing sweaty. Squeezing those hands closed, she forced herself to take a deep breath. This reaction to the man was beyond disturbing. She'd like to blame it on some chemical reaction to special pheromones put out by a male vampire, but she didn't seem to have this reaction to the other male vampires now in her home. Elvi almost wished she did. She was too damned old to be acting like a love-struck teenager. Unfortunately, while she was sixty-two years old, she looked twenty-five and he made her feel about sixteen.

Shaking her head at herself, Elvi stood and moved to open the door. She managed what she hoped was a politely inquiring expression and waited for him to speak, afraid that if she opened her mouth it would just be to blurt out something stupid.

"You forgot your ankle bracelet." He held out one hand, opening it to reveal the belled anklet cradled in his fingers. Elvi had taken it off by the fire when the constant jangle had finally got to her. She'd set it on the ground beside her chair and apparently left it there.

"Thank you," she murmured, blushing when she saw the way her fingers were trembling as she took it from him.

As she slid the anklet into her pocket, Victor raised his other hand, revealing two wineglasses and a half-bottle of wine. He had the bottle by the neck and the two delicate goblets by the stems, all caught in the fingers of one hand. "This is all that's left. It seems a shame to waste it. It should be just enough for two glasses, I think."

Elvi almost said no and closed the door to avoid the discomfort she felt in his presence, but there were so many questions she wanted to ask . . . besides, as uncomfortable as she was with her attraction to him, it also made her want to be near him. Relieving him of the two goblets, she moved aside for him to enter.

"This is nice," he murmured, peering around the sunroom.

Elvi followed his gaze over the wicker furniture in the dark. The only light came from the open door to her room, but she expected his eyesight was as sharp as her own. This soft glow was more than enough to see by. She supposed it was how he'd known she was up here.

"How are you feeling?" Victor asked, settling on the couch and holding out a hand for the glasses.

"A little woozy," Elvi admitted quietly as she handed them over. "I haven't had a drop to drink in five years, and it went straight to my head. In fact, I suppose I really shouldn't have any more."

"One more should be all right," he said quietly, pouring the wine. He handed her a glass, picked up the other, and sat back to peer at her.

The silence that filled the room as they sipped their wine seemed to dance along Elvi's nerves. She was terribly aware of his nearness and the delicious male scent of him. She didn't know what aftershave he wore, but she'd like to buy some and sprinkle it in her coffin so she could bury her face in the satin pillow and breathe it in all night long while she slept.

"It seems obvious that you haven't been trained properly in what you can and can't do. Why is that?"

Victor's sudden question sent Elvi's ponderings of his aftershave flying and she stiffened as she took in his words. It was obvious she hadn't been trained? There was *training* for vampires? Like a vampire boot camp or something?

"What do you mean?" she asked finally, and then sat up a little straighter as she realized he was saying she appeared as ignorant as she felt. "What gave me away?"

Victor arched an eyebrow. "For one, you thought you couldn't eat food."

"Oh, yes." Elvi flushed. She supposed that was an obvious giveaway, but really, how was she supposed to know what she could and couldn't do? None of the vampires ever ate or drank anything but blood in the movies and television shows. At least not the ones she and Mabel had seen when Elvi had first turned and they'd done all their research.

"And," Victor added solemnly, drawing her attention back to him, "you obviously don't realize it is against our laws to bite mortals."

Elvi stiffened with alarm. "What? We have laws?"

Victor nodded solemnly.

Elvi sat still, her mind whirling. Laws suggested some form of organization. It also seemed to suggest there were more of their kind than she'd thought. Questions began to whirl through her mind, but were pushed aside in favor of this business of breaking a vampire law. Elvi hadn't ever in her life broken a law. She'd never even so much as jaywalked. It didn't sit well that she'd unknowingly broken one.

"I didn't realize it was against our laws," she said quickly. "In fact, I didn't know there were laws. I wasn't even sure there were others like me."

"I was afraid of that," Victor said, then cursed under his breath.

"You said 'laws.' Plural," she murmured. "What other laws are there?"

Victor opened his mouth, and then shook his head. "There's no sense telling you now. You've been drinking for the first time in years and I'd probably just have to repeat them in the evening when you wake up."

Elvi opened her mouth to protest, but he assured her, "I'll tell you all about them after you've slept."

When she settled back in her seat with resignation, he smiled faintly and added, "Speaking of which, I should probably let you get to bed."

Victor stood and moved to the door. Elvi followed, her gaze dropping of its own accord to his behind. She managed to force it back up as he stepped through the door onto the top step and turned back to say, "Before I go, though, I do need the answer to one question."

"Yes?" she asked curiously.

"Who was your sire?"

Elvi frowned. "What exactly is a sire?" she asked with bewilderment. "Both you and Alessandro have mentioned that word and I haven't a clue what it means."

"It means the one who made you," he explained. "The one who turned you into an immortal."

"Oh," Elvi smiled faintly. She had a feeling she'd heard the phrase before this, probably when she and Mabel had been researching vampires right after their return from Mexico, but as it didn't apply to her, she'd let it slip her mind.

Realizing he was waiting for an answer, Elvi shook her head. "I didn't have a sire."

Victor stared at her nonplussed. "You had to have a sire . . . unless . . ." He paused, then asked doubtfully, "You weren't born an immortal?"

Elvi laughed at the idea. "No, of course not. Five years ago I had gray hair and wrinkles," she assured him. "But no one sired me."

"Someone had to," he insisted.

Elvi peered past him at the lightening sky, her mind automatically going back to the period around her own death. It was a time she didn't like to think about, and in truth was a terrible blur. All she remembered clearly was that she'd bitten Mabel and nearly killed her while out of her head.

"Mabel and I went to Mexico," she said finally. "We were in a car accident and I woke up several days later like this." Elvi forced a smile, shifting uncomfortably when he stared at her with incomprehension. "I guess you could say I'm an accidental vampire."

Forcing a smile, she murmured good night and pulled the door closed before he could say anything more. Elvi didn't like to think about that time in her life and liked even less to talk about it.

Slipping the lock closed, she turned and entered her bedroom, grimacing at the sight of the coffin waiting there. She had a bit of a headache, and her tummy was uncomfortably full, but she was relaxed for the first time in years, thanks to the wine, and she was feeling a little less like a freak with so many of her kind around, yet had to sleep in that blasted thing.

Muttering under her breath, Elvi ignored the dark wooden casket and moved into the bathroom. She wanted a bath before bed, but it was late enough that she'd have to make do with a quick wash. Afraid of collapsing into the semi death that daylight was supposed to bring vampires, Elvi had never risked being out of her coffin after dawn. She wasn't taking the chance tonight either. But tomorrow she would ask Victor what else she could and couldn't do.

Frowning as she rinsed the soap from her face, Elvi realized it hadn't even occurred to her that she could ask her questions of any of the men in her home, that all of them would know the answers. She simply automatically thought to ask Victor. She wasn't sure if that was representative of a comfort level with him she hadn't reached with the others yet, or a simple preference in dealing with him, but suspected it was both. That knowledge was enough to make her suddenly reluctant to ask her questions of him, but it was becoming woefully obvious that despite being a vampire for five years, she was terribly ignorant of what she could and couldn't do. Who knew there were laws and so on? No, she had to ask her questions, and if she was going to ask anyone, it would be Victor.

She'd ask him about coffins first and then move on to things like the ability to slip into others' minds. The conversation she'd overheard between Alessandro and Harper had her curious. Could she read minds and control others as Alessandro had suggested Edward may have done with Mabel?

Mabel had insisted Elvi try to read minds and so on when she'd first changed. After all, Dracula could apparently do it, but Elvi hadn't been able to manage the task and had decided that only he, as the king of vampires, could do it. But if Edward could do it too, maybe she just hadn't tried long enough.

Mabel had also wanted to go to Transylvania and find Dracula, though she'd been sure the name would be different. Mabel had really been into the vampire thing, but then she wasn't the one who'd been turned. She'd wanted to be, at first asking Elvi to turn her as well so they could both be vampires. However, no matter how many times Elvi had bitten her, or how much blood she took, the other woman hadn't turned. Elvi had finally insisted they stop trying when she'd nearly killed her by taking too much blood.

She was glad she'd given it up when two years ago, Mabel had confessed she was really rather glad it hadn't worked. After seeing all that Elvi had lost—food, wine, enjoying the garden in daylight, trips to the beach, barbecues with friends, and so on, she thought perhaps it wasn't such a great deal.

Aside from all those things, Elvi had found herself faced with a myriad of legal problems as well since the change. ID for instance. Passports, driver's licenses, and health cards had to be renewed every so often. All of them had expired within two years of her change. As for replacing them? Forget about it.

According to all her ID she was sixty-two. She didn't look sixty-two. It would have been a problem. Fortunately, she no longer needed a health card, but traveling was out of the question without a passport.

Her driver's license had also lapsed, but Elvi hadn't bothered to renew it even though she could have done so here in town where they knew her and wouldn't question her being sixty-two but looking twenty-five. Renewing it hadn't seemed worth the trouble, however. She could pretty much walk everywhere in Port Henry, but if she needed the car to collect groceries or something, Teddy and Barney wouldn't have given her a hard time. Other than that, she simply didn't drive. The risk was too great should she be pulled over by an out-of-town officer. There was no way she could pass for the sixty-two on her driver's license.

In effect, she was pretty much trapped here in Port Henry. But now that Victor and the others were here she wondered how they dealt with such issues. She had no idea how old they were, but each of them spoke with a certain formality that suggested they were older even than herself.

Except for DJ, she thought, and smiled to herself as she recalled the way he'd been flirting with Mabel all evening. Elvi's friend had obviously found it all rather upsetting and put on her short-tempered, irritated old lady act, but Elvi knew under all the embarrassment the woman was flattered. Mabel was showing her age, but still attractive, and she wondered if DJ might really like her.

Spotting the pink tinge to the sky outside the bathroom window, Elvi rushed through the last of her ablutions. She then scampered into her room and climbed into her coffin with a grimace, wondering when Victor and the others had moved their caskets in. They'd all arrived in cars so must have had them shipped down, she reasoned, as she pulled the lid of her own casket shut.

Nine

"An accidental vampire," Victor muttered to himself as he entered the room he shared with DJ.

"Victor?" The sleepy question came from the far side of the dark room as he closed the door. It was followed by rustling as DJ stirred on the pullout couch. "Did you say something?"

"Yes." Victor snapped on the bedroom light.

DJ sat up, the sheets slipping down to his waist. "I'm up. What's wrong?"

Victor strode across the room, glowering. "Elvi says she's an accidental vampire."

"What?" he asked with confusion.

Victor nodded. "She hasn't learnt any of our laws or rules from her sire because she doesn't think she has one."

"Well, of course she does," DJ said reasonably. "Someone has to have turned her."

"That's what I said," he admitted. "But she says she went to Mexico with Mabel, was in a car accident, and woke up a vampire. She's an *accidental* vampire."

"That's not possible," DJ pointed out. "Maybe the accident is all she remembers. Maybe her sire wiped her memory or something."

"Or *she*," Victor said, and pointed out, "It doesn't have to have been a man."

"Or," DJ said, eyes wide. "Maybe she was injured in the accident and was given contaminated blood by the blood bank."

"No vampire would give blood to a blood bank," Victor said dryly.

"I guess not," he agreed with disappointment, then stiffened and said, "unless they were rogue and looking to contaminate a lot of mortals without exposing themselves to discovery."

Victor gaped at him with disbelief. "You have to stop watching those late-night James Bond marathons."

"Well, it's possible," DJ argued. "It's actually a brilliant plan."

Victor snatched up a pillow from the bed and slammed it into the side of his head. "No it's not brilliant. And it's not what happened here."

"How do you know?" DJ challenged.

"Because, I'm sure even in Mexico they test donated blood before giving it to accident victims. They'd have spotted the nanos right away and pulled the blood to examine further and we'd be exposed by now."

"The immortal could have controlled the minds of

the people who tested it so that they didn't test it at all," DJ suggested.

Victor rolled his eyes. "Then there'd be a hell of a lot of confused new immortals running around Mexico and we'd have heard about it long before now. Elvi was turned five years ago."

"Oh." The idiot looked disappointed at this news. Apparently, he'd been rather excited at the idea of a Goldfinger-type immortal, plotting to take over the world or some such thing by spreading his blood around.

Shaking his head, Victor walked over to the king-sized bed and dropped, sitting on the side to remove his shoes.

"So . . ." DJ said.

When he paused, Victor raised his head to peer at him curiously. "What?"

"Mabel's hot, huh?"

Victor blinked at the change in subject, but acknowledged, "She's an attractive woman." A smile tugged at his lips as he recalled the way DJ had been hanging over her all night. He bent to remove his second shoe.

"I can't read her," DJ blurted.

Victor froze, and then slowly raised his head to stare at the man. He raised one eyebrow in question. "You can't?"

DJ shook his head slowly from side to side. "I tried both at the restaurant and then again when we got back to the house. I can't read her."

Victor let his breath out slowly as he was assaulted by sundry thoughts. The main one was that DJ had met his lifemate.

"That could be a complication," he commented finally.

"Yeah," DJ agreed, then stifled his grin and said solemnly, "I'll try not to let it interfere."

"Right," Victor murmured, but knew that would be impossible. He'd had a lifemate once. He knew the effect she had. The man would be scattered and useless, unable to tear his thoughts from the woman who held his future in her hands like a wee baby bird that could be nurtured to adulthood, or crushed with the barest squeeze.

Sighing, he pushed aside the envy suddenly gnawing at his insides and kicked off his second shoe, then stood and crossed the room to flip off the switch.

"Good night, Victor," DJ said as the darkness dropped over the room again.

"Good night," he said quietly, suddenly terribly, terribly tired.

Elvi woke up late. She suspected it was a result of the alcohol the night before and grimaced over the cotton mouth she was suffering as she stumbled into the bathroom to brush her teeth. She followed that up with a quick shower, then threw on a pair of jeans and a T-shirt and headed for the door, eager to feed.

Both kinds.

She'd have to have blood of course, but would follow that up with real food. Maybe that cheesecake she'd never got to last night. Or ice cream.

Or bacon, Elvi thought as she stepped out of her room and sniffed. Yes, that was definitely bacon she smelled. Cheesecake suddenly went to the bottom of the list of most-desirable foods. It was too sweet for breakfast, despite the fact that it was actually seven o'clock at night.

The delicious scents teasing her nose didn't prepare her for the sight that met her as she entered the kitchen.

Victor stood in front of a pan of spitting, hissing bacon. Harper was at his side, manning the toaster. Alessandro was just closing the coffeepot and turning it on and Edward was squeezing fresh orange juice.

"Good morning," she said brightly, grinning at the sight of so many men working so industriously in her kitchen. Pedro cooked at the restaurant, but Elvi's marriage had been an old-fashioned one with her husband working out of the house and never stepping into her kitchen. This was . . . extraordinary.

All four men turned to look her way as one. They also smiled and greeted her in quadraphonic stereo. "Good morning."

Elvi's grin widened for some reason when she saw that Victor was wearing Mabel's apron. She moved forward, asking, "What can I do to help?"

"Nothing. It's all done," Victor announced. He turned off the burner under the bacon, then grabbed a potholder and opened the oven door to reveal two bowls inside. One held scrambled eggs, the other was full of golden hash browns. Glancing her way, he added, "Sit down."

Elvi hesitated, then defied the order and slid into the kitchen, weaving her way through the men to get to the fridge.

"What are you looking for? I can get it for you." Alessandro moved quickly forward, but Elvi had already opened the door and grabbed a bag of blood. She usually kept some in the refrigerator in her room, but hadn't thought to take any up last night.

"Oh." Alessandro stepped out of the way as she

closed the door. It just put him in front of the shelf of cups, though.

"I need a mug," she said apologetically, lisping slightly around her fangs as just the sight of the bag of blood combined with her hunger to draw them out.

Rather than step out of her way, Alessandro reached up to the open shelf to grab a cup for her.

Before she could take it, though, Victor said, "It takes too long to drink that way. Your breakfast will get cold. Alessandro, show her how to feed from the bag."

"From the bag?" Elvi asked uncertainly, glancing over to see that Victor had placed the eggs and hash browns on the table and was now transferring the bacon from the frying pan to a plate.

"Don't you know how to feed from the bag?" Harper asked with surprise as he carried the toast to the table.

"She never met her sire and wasn't trained . . . in anything," Victor answered for her, and Elvi felt herself flush when the men all turned to stare at her with combined horror and pity. She felt as embarrassed as if he'd just announced that her skirt was caught in the back of her panties.

"You said that last night, but I never imagined it included not teaching her how to feed herself," Edward commented and moved to take the bag from her before Alessandro did, and instructed, "Open your mouth."

Elvi caught the irritation that flashed across the men's faces at Edward's usurping the chore as she opened her mouth, then gave a start when the bag was popped onto her fangs with a quick sharp move.

Elvi instinctively tried to ask what he was doing, but of course she couldn't talk around the bag in her mouth and gave up the effort when Edward caught her hand and said firmly, "No speaking. This will only take a moment."

Elvi stood still as she waited for the bag to empty, surprised to find the man hadn't been kidding. He was soon tugging the emptied bag from her teeth.

"That's incredible," she said with amazement as he moved to discard the bag.

"Much faster than drinking from the glass, no?" Alessandro took her elbow and steered her around the counter to the table.

"Much," Elvi agreed with a smile, and then turned her attention to the breakfast laid out in front of her as she took her seat. Her eyes widened incredulously at the amount of food on the table. They must have used all three packages of bacon she'd bought. Harper had apparently toasted a whole loaf of bread, and she suspected Victor had put both cartons of eggs and one of the frozen rolls of sausage in the scrambled eggs. It seemed the men had found their appetites.

"Here." Victor began to scoop scrambled eggs on her plate and Elvi's eyes widened with amused horror at the small mountain he served her. Harper immediately began to dump bacon on top of the eggs.

"Toast?" Alessandro asked, holding the plate out for her as Edward poured fresh-squeezed orange juice into her glass.

Wow! If this was what being courted was like, she could learn to like it, Elvi thought and murmured "thank you" to all of them as she took a piece of toast. She was not going to eat all this, but would have fun trying.

"I take it you guys are eating again?" she commented

with amusement as the men claimed their seats around the table and began to fill their own plates. "Over your boredom with food, are you?"

The sudden silence at the table made her glance up curiously from scooping eggs onto her fork. The men were all still and staring at each other.

"What?" she asked curiously. "Did I say something wrong?"

"No," they answered in stereo. Then Victor and Harper turned their attention to their plates, their expressions troubled. Alessandro had a curious expression on his face as he glanced from man to man, and Edward was eyeing everyone with calculation. It was all very odd and Elvi hadn't a clue what these reactions were all about.

They ate in silence for a bit, and then she decided to make another gambit at conversation. She glanced at Alessandro and said curiously, "You said last night that you hadn't eaten in fifty years?"

"Si," he nodded.

"DJ is the only one young enough to still eat . . . prior to this," Victor added uncomfortably, and then forged on with, "I fear the rest of us are too old to be bothered with food most of the time."

"Too old to be bothered with it?" Elvi echoed, glancing around at their faces.

"After a century or two most immortals grow bored with the trouble of eating and refrain from bothering unless it is a social occasion," Harper explained.

"A century or two?" Elvi gasped but had some vague recollection of having heard this before. Probably the night before, either on the way to or during shopping.

Anything told to her then had gone out the window. Her mind had been wholly on food at that point. She glanced from man to man. "How old are you?"

The others all looked to Victor in question. When he shrugged, Edward cleared his throat, drawing her gaze. "I was born in 1004."

While Elvi was sucking in her breath over this, Harper leaned forward and offered, "I was born in 1282."

"Me, I was born in 1794," Alessandro announced. When she glanced his way, he grinned and added, "I am the youngest."

"The youngest?" Elvi murmured faintly. The room suddenly seemed to be spinning. Or perhaps it was her head.

"Actually, DJ is just over a hundred. He's the youngest," Edward corrected him.

Alessandro shrugged. "*Si*. But he is not here right now."

"Yes," Edward conceded, then announced out of the blue, "Victor is the oldest."

Elvi's mind wobbled to a stop and she turned a look full of horror on the British man. "Older than *you*?"

Edward smiled at her expression and nodded.

Elvi turned slowly to peer at Victor. He didn't look a day over thirty and could have passed for twenty-five, but they were telling her he was more than a thousand years old.

Victor shifted under her glance, looking embarrassed and uncomfortable, then muttered, "230."

"That's the year he was born, not his age," Edward explained helpfully.

"230?" Elvi asked with incomprehension. "But that would make you"—she paused to do the math then said—"one thousand, seven hundred and seventy-seven years old?"

Victor pursed his lips and shook his head, but before he could answer, Edward said, "I'm afraid not. Victor was born in 230 *B.C.*"

"B.C.," Elvi echoed, blinking rapidly as her head began to spin again. "Before Christ . . . Oh my," she murmured and began to slide down her seat.

"I think she's waking up."

Elvi fought off the last of sleep's cobwebs at what she felt sure was Harper's voice. The next one was definitely Edward's as he muttered a grim, "Hmm. Finally."

Blinking her eyes open, she found herself staring up at the four men. They all had identical expressions of worry on their faces as they bent over her.

"You're awake," Victor said with relief. "You've been out so long we were starting to worry. Are you all right?"

"What happened?" Elvi murmured with confusion.

"You fainted," Edward announced. "A very Victorian thing to do, if I may say so."

Elvi scowled. "I never faint."

"Apparently you do now," he pointed out.

"How much blood have you had over the last twenty-four hours?" Victor asked.

"One bag last night and the one before breakfast," she murmured, pushing herself up to sit upright. The men backed off a bit to allow her to lean back against the arm of the couch and Elvi glanced around to see that they'd moved her to the couch in the big living room while she was unconscious.

"One yesterday and one this evening?" Victor asked with irritation. "No wonder you fainted. You should have at least two or three bags a day. You'll be sorry if you try going without."

"Yes, I know." Elvi had tried to resist blood when she'd first been turned and had given that up in a hurry when the pain had claimed her. If she didn't eat enough, it physically hurt. In fact, now that she thought about it, the tummy upset and headache she'd been suffering last night had probably been due to not having enough blood rather than being due to the food she'd consumed. Both symptoms had been worse this morning, but had eased the moment she'd consumed the bag of blood. Another bag or two and they'd probably disappear altogether.

"I—" Elvi paused as Victor suddenly stood and moved out of the room. She stared after him with surprise, then swung her feet to the floor and cautiously stood up, waving off the other three men when they reached out to steady her. She was still a bit wobbly, but suspected it had as much to do with what she'd learned earlier about these men as any lack of blood.

Elvi and Mabel had discussed her new, extended life, pondering that she might continue to exist another hundred years or so, but neither of them had considered as much as seven hundred, one thousand, or even two thousand years. This had been shattering news. And she wasn't at all sure she'd classify it as good. The idea of living another hundred years was rather distressing, let alone a thousand or more. Dear God. Everyone she knew, plus their children, their children's children, and so on, would die before her and she'd have to witness it, grieving over each new loss, mourning yet another passing while she stayed there, living in Port Henry, as unchanging as a statue.

Hell, her home and even Port Henry might very well crumble around her and return to dust before she died. What sort of future was that?

"Here."

The men shifted to make a path for Victor as he returned, carrying a bag of blood.

"Thank you." She accepted the offering.

The moment the cold bag rested in her palm, Elvi felt her teeth shift, allowing her fangs to slide out.

When she peered at the bag uncertainly, Victor seemed to understand what was making her hesitate and instructed, "Just pop it firmly to your teeth."

Nodding, Elvi opened her mouth, took a breath, and then popped the bag upward as Edward had done for her earlier. There was a moment's resistance when the bag met her teeth, then a popping sound and it continued upward, until it was fully impaled on her fangs.

"Perfect," Victor praised.

"*Si,* is very good," Alessandro agreed.

Harper nodded. "A natural."

Edward merely grunted.

An amused snort came out muffled around the bag as Elvi stared at them, unable to speak. They were acting like she'd just taken her first ride on a two-wheel bike. All she'd done is stuck a bag on her teeth. Judging by the concern still visible in their faces, she supposed they were worried she'd faint on them again. Men tended to hate things like that. Fainting, crying, and so on seemed to leave them at a loss.

With the four men staring at her as if she might topple over at any moment, the few minutes it took for the bag to empty seemed unbearably long to her. It was with relief she removed the bag when it was empty and moved through them, determined to dispose of it herself and prove she was just fine.

"I brought you two bags," Victor said, following her out of the room and across the foyer to the dining room.

"Oh, thanks." Elvi reached back for the full bag and popped it to her teeth, then continued on to the garbage can in the corner of the kitchen to toss the other. The second was almost empty by then, so she waited there until it too was done and tossed it as well.

When she turned back to the room, the men were all there, crowded around the stove and taking the plates and bowls Victor was retrieving from the oven.

"We put the food in to stay warm when you fainted," Victor explained as he took out the last item.

"Oh." Elvi followed him to the table, and then asked curiously, "Where is DJ?"

"He's at the restaurant with Mabel," Harper said, holding out her chair.

Elvi sat, her eyebrows rising at this news. She was pretty sure Mabel wouldn't have been happy to have the man with her and couldn't imagine why he was. "Why is he at the restaurant?"

When Victor hesitated, Edward announced, "As she was leaving, Mabel said she was going to let you sleep in, but that when you did wake up, we were to tell you not to go to the restaurant tonight, but to pick one of us to spend the evening getting to know."

"*Si.*" Alessandro nodded. "And then DJ said as he wasn't on the list of suitors, he would go to the restaurant in your place and help out."

Elvi blushed at the reminder that these men were in search of a mate . . . and she was the only single female

vamp in town. Clearing her throat, she merely commented, "I don't imagine Mabel was pleased with DJ's
volunteering to take my place."

"Not at all," Victor agreed with amusement, and then
gestured to her plate. "Eat."

Nodding, she turned her attention to the food. The
toast had grown soggy, but otherwise it was all very
good. They fell into a natural silence as they concentrated on their meal, leaving Elvi to consider what she'd
learned before she fainted. The ages these men claimed
to be were rather staggering. She wouldn't have been
so upset if they'd all been two or three hundred years
old like Alessandro and DJ, but the ages of the other
men . . .

Elvi peered from one face to the other now, looking
for any sign of their advanced age, but really none of
them looked their age. Hell, none of them even looked
as old as her own age of sixty-two. But then, neither did
she, she acknowledged.

Her gaze focused on Victor as she recalled that he was
the oldest, born in 230 . . . B.C. Before Christ. She pondered that briefly, realizing it meant he'd been around
when Jesus had walked the earth, and almost asked if
he'd met him, but then thought better of it. They were
soulless after all, thanks to their curse, and soulless be-
ings would hardly go seeking the son of God. Would
they? She frowned as she recalled Mabel saying that
Victor had touched her cross at the restaurant without
an undo reaction. She'd meant to ask him about that,
but had forgotten when they were in the sunroom last
night.

"What are you thinking?" Victor asked suddenly.

Elvi bit her lip, then admitted, "About our being soulless and cursed and yet you touched Mabel's cross and she said nothing happened. I—"

"We aren't soulless," Victor interrupted.

Elvi stilled, her fork held aloft in one hand. "What?"

"We aren't immortals because of some curse that has left us soulless," he said.

Her gaze slid to the other men in question. Each one nodded reassuringly.

"Then how—?"

"Bugs," Alessandro announced eagerly. When Elvi turned to him with disbelief, he nodded excitedly, "*Si.* Truly, is the little bugs. They are in our blood, eating up all the sickness and—"

"They aren't bugs, idiot," Edward interrupted dryly, and then told Elvi, "they are nanos. Our forefathers came from Atlantis. I presume you've heard of it?"

Elvi nodded slowly. *Man from Atlantis* used to be a popular show when she was younger.

"Well, that is where our kind and these nanos originate," Edward informed her. "Really, we're a superior people. Our scientists were well-advanced. They used technology beyond even today's abilities to combine bioengineering and nano technology to create specialized medical nanos that could be introduced to the blood stream of a person with . . . say . . . internal injuries or cancer. These nanos use blood for fuel as they repair whatever damage is present or surround any germs or cancerous cells and kill them. They were created as a way to avoid invasive surgery. Once finished, they would disintegrate and leave the body as all waste does."

"Nanos?" Elvi dropped her fork to her plate and sat back in her seat, her mind racing to take this all in. "So, the nanos . . . they're what made me young again?"

"They see the effects of aging as damage that needs repairing," Victor said quietly.

Edward nodded. "The effects of aging, sunlight . . ." He shrugged. "Anything that affects the body's balance is seen as something they should tend to, and the body is under constant attack from the environment and even just time."

"So the nanos are always busy and never disintegrate and leave the body," Harper explained. "Instead they stay and keep us forever at optimal levels of health, strength, and age."

"But it means the nanos are constantly reproducing, constantly repairing," Victor added. "They use a lot of blood, more than a body can produce and so they evolve our bodies to get what they need to keep us in optimal health."

"The fangs." Elvi ran her tongue over her teeth.

"And the increased strength, speed, hearing, sight, mind control . . ." Victor nodded. "Anything that will improve our ability to get the extra blood."

Nanos, she thought. Not soulless, just nanos. Somehow these nanos had been *"introduced to her blood stream"* as Edward had put it. But how, she wondered. Had she got infected blood after the accident? All she recalled was the accident, then waking up in their hotel room covered in blood, her teeth sunk deep in Mabel's throat.

Elvi shuddered at the memory she most often tried to forget. That episode with the raging, mindless, and uncontrollable hunger that had made her do something she normally never would have done, had assured her she was cursed and soulless.

Although, Elvi thought now, she'd suffered horrible

guilt ever since and perhaps that alone should have re-assured her she still had a soul. Surely soulless demons didn't feel guilty for their crimes?

Wow. She'd had it all wrong. She wasn't soulless. She could eat. What else could she do?

"What about daylight?" Elvi asked suddenly, sitting up in her seat. Please God, she thought desperately, let me see the sun again. Her garden had always been her haven, where she could retire from life's troubles and just relax, digging in the earth with the aroma of flowers and herbs around her. She had missed it terribly.

"Daylight can be a problem," Victor admitted apologetically. "But only in so much as sunlight damages skin, which makes the nanos work harder, which means you must consume more blood."

"But I can go out in it?" she asked, holding her breath.

"Yes, but I wouldn't recommend long periods of exposure and you must increase your blood intake," he said firmly.

Elvi didn't care. She'd drink an ocean of blood just to be able to feel the sun on her face again. What else, she wondered. What else had she given up these last five years because she'd thought vampires had to live a certain way?

"So we can eat, we can go out in sunlight . . ." Elvi peered at Victor and added, "And religious relics don't harm us."

Victor smiled and shook his head. "We can eat, we can go out in sunlight, we can walk in churches and touch crosses and holy water without bursting into flame, we don't sleep in coffins filled with dirt, we have reflections . . ." He paused and glanced to the others. "Is there any other ridiculous myth I've forgotten to address?"

The men all shook their heads, but Elvi wasn't paying much attention, her mind had fixed on the part about not sleeping in coffins.

"We don't sleep in coffins filled with dirt." His words sang in her ears. No coffin. She could sleep in a bed. A big, soft, comfortable bed without sides and a lid on it. With lots of pillows and a huge down-filled comforter and—

Elvi stood up abruptly. "I have to go."

"What?" Victor asked. He and the others stared at her with amazement.

"I have to go," Elvi repeated, her head swinging around, eyes finding the clock. She had thirty minutes before the furniture store closed for the night and she wasn't waiting until tomorrow to buy a bed.

Spinning on her heel, she hurried for the stairs, hardly aware of the screech of wood on ceramic tile as the men all got up from the table. She needed her purse. It had her car keys and wallet. There was a small furniture store just up the block from the restaurant, but it closed early, however there was another on the outskirts of town that was much larger and still open. It was a fifteen-minute drive away, which left her fifteen minutes to shop. She had to move!

"What is happening?" Elvi heard Alessandro ask as she raced up the stairs. No one answered. Instead, there was the pounding of footsteps on the staircase behind her as the men hurried to catch up.

"Elvi," Victor called.

Elvi ignored him and hurried to her room. She charged

inside and raced to her dresser to grab the purse that sat on top, then turned back just as Victor burst into the room, the others hard on his heels.

"What—?" Victor's question died a quick death as his gaze landed on the coffin in the center of the room. He blanched.

Following his gaze, the others stared in horror. There was a moment of silence, then Edward moved forward to examine the casket, saying, "I haven't heard of one of our kind sleeping in one of these since . . . well, for a good hundred years anyway."

Elvi glanced at him with surprise. "You mean vampires really did sleep in these things at one time?" She'd briefly thought that had been completely wrong.

Harper nodded and moved to run a hand over the shiny wood. "Houses used to be large and drafty and not as well put together at times. Some slept in coffins or tombs to ensure they were protected from any sunlight creeping in."

"Why?" she asked with a frown, and then glanced accusingly at Victor. "You said we could go out in sunlight."

"Yes, but I also said it means consuming more blood. Before blood banks that was a risky proposition. The more we had to feed, the more likely the chance of discovery," he explained patiently. "We avoided sunlight at all times and anything else that used more blood."

"Oh," she murmured.

"You have been sleeping in this?" Victor asked, now moving to the coffin as well.

Elvi flushed and nodded.

"For five years?" he asked, lifting the lid to peer inside. She nodded again.

"This is another cheesecake emergency," Alessandro murmured with a shake of the head.

"Yes," Victor agreed, mouth grim as he gently lowered the lid back down. "And it's growing late. The stores will soon close."

"My car is the last one in the driveway," Edward announced, turning for the door. "I'll get my keys."

Recalling how slow he drove, Elvi glanced worriedly toward the digital clock on the dresser. It was only then she remembered that the clock downstairs ran ten minutes slow. And they'd wasted five minutes up here staring at her coffin.

"The store closes in fifteen minutes. We'll never make it in time," she said with despair.

"We will make it," Victor assured her, taking her arm to hurry her out of the room.

"Not if Edward is driving," she moaned.

The British man stopped and turned back indignantly. "I beg your pardon?"

"I'm sorry," she said apologetically. "But you drive like an old man."

"I *am* an old man," Edward said dryly. "We all are."

Elvi bit her lip, at a loss as to what to say now. It was Victor who broke the silence saying, "Alessandro can drive. His car is at the back of the second lane."

"*Si*. I drive fast, and I have my keys," Alessandro announced triumphantly. He started for the stairs and the rest of them followed, but paused again when Harper pointed out, "Alessandro's car only rides two."

"No," the Italian assured them, leading them forward once more. "Is more comfortable for two, but four can fit."

"There are five of us," Edward reminded him and everyone screeched to a halt.

Elvi closed her eyes, feeling the seconds tick away. They weren't going to make it. They may as well—

"Elvi can sit on my lap," Victor announced and the group immediately started forward again, including Elvi, but she was only moving because Victor had her by the arm. Her feet were definitely dragging. Sit on his lap? No way. She hardly knew him. Besides, that was illegal she was sure. And what about seat belts? She was *not* sitting on his lap.

Ten

"Comfortable?"

Elvi heard the muttered question from Victor. She even felt his breath brush against her lobe as he asked, but she didn't stop clutching him and lean back to answer. She stayed where she was, plastered against his chest, head burrowed near his neck, face turned toward the driver's side of the front seat as she stared with a horrified fascination at the car's speedometer.

Glancing sideways, Alessandro caught her eye and beamed. "I drive fast, no?"

Elvi heard what might have been a whimper issue from her lips and returned her eyes to the control panel. The man didn't drive fast, he drove at light speed. She could see the speedometer from where she sat hunched on Victor's lap in the front passenger seat. It was in miles per hour, not the kilometers she was used to. The speedometer went as high as 155 mph and could actually go that fast. She knew this because this was what Alessandro was doing. She'd never before seen telephone poles go by so fast they became a blur.

Elvi turned her face into Victor's shoulder, her hands clutching a little more frantically as they hit a curve in the road and Alessandro took it without slowing. With her mouth pressed into Victor's shoulder, she could now see the two men crammed into the backseat. The car had a backseat of sorts, obviously not intended and certainly not by two such large men. Edward and Harper didn't look very comfortable back there, but Harper did manage a weak smile as he grabbed for anything he could get his hands on to keep from being thrown into Edward's lap by the centrifugal force.

As for Edward, he sat, expression grim, furious eyes burning holes into the back of Alessandro's head.

A flashing light drew her attention to the back window, and Elvi's eyes widened in alarm. "Police!"

She glanced toward Alessandro to see him glancing with unconcern in the rearview mirror. He eased up on the gas, allowing the car to slow and the police car to catch up, then smiled her way.

"No worry. I handle him quick," he assured her, then turned his attention back to the rearview mirror, his gaze becoming concentrated.

Confusion clouding her mind, Elvi glanced back to the road in time to see the police lights suddenly go out and the car turn and head back the way it had come. Alessandro immediately sped up again.

"What did you do?" she asked, turning on him with amazement.

"I just put suggestion in his head, he maybe wanna

go find doughnuts," Alessandro said with a shrug. "Police, they like doughnuts here, no?"

"You—!" Elvi began with dismay, but the berating she would have given him for controlling a member of the police department died in her throat, replaced by a whimper as they hit another curve and she was thrown backward. She would have slammed into the passenger door if Victor hadn't caught her and pulled her swiftly back to his chest.

"Just hang on," he murmured by her ear. "The ride will be over soon."

Elvi swallowed the reprimand she'd wanted to give Alessandro and held on. She inhaled a shaky breath and closed her eyes, then opened them and inhaled again, eyes widening slightly at Victor's tantalizing scent. She didn't know what it was, but it was spicy and really delightful and she found herself pressing closer and inhaling again. It was Harper's raised eyebrows right behind her that made her realize what she was doing and that it had been witnessed.

Flushing, Elvi forced herself to sit up a little, only to be thrown against Victor's chest, then slide down his lap to land tangled in his legs as Alessandro suddenly swerved off the road and slammed on the breaks.

"We are here, no?" the Italian asked, peering down at her cheerfully.

Elvi stared up at him with disbelief, then grasped the dashboard with one hand and Victor's knee with the other and managed to drag herself back up to peer around, relieved to see the big yellow furniture store sign.

"Yes," she breathed, grateful the ride from hell was over.

Victor opened the door, grasped her by the waist, and

lifted her out, handing her to Harper who had hopped out of the back and was waiting to help.

The second vampire set her on her feet beside the car and then held her long enough to be sure she had her feet beneath her before letting go and stepping away as Victor unfolded himself from the car to join them. Elvi muttered a *"thank you"* to both men, then turned and scurried for the store, doing her best to forget that she had to get back into that vehicle later.

Thanks to Alessandro's speeding, they slid through the doors just as the manager approached, no doubt intending to close shop. Elvi offered him an apologetic glance.

"We'll be quick," she promised, making a beeline for the beds. The men followed in her wake.

"Is there something I can help you with?" the manager asked, hustling to catch up to her.

Elvi was about to answer when she felt a hand on her arm and glanced to Victor with surprise at the proprietary move.

"We need a bed," he announced.

"Yes, of course," the manager said. She supposed that was obvious, since they had hurried through the whole store to the beds at the back. "We have some lovely beds. What size are you interested in?

"King," Elvi answered promptly. She could hardly wait to sprawl on one of those huge surfaces again, unrestrained by side panels or a lid, surrounded only by a big soft comforter and luxurious pillows . . . God, her toes tingled at the very idea.

"This is a popular model," the manager said, pointing at the first of the beds.

Elvi stared, taking in the sheer size. To her it was like

an ocean of bed after five years in her cramped coffin.

"Try it," Alessandro suggested. "You must to try before you buy."

"He's right," the manager offered when Elvi hesitated.

Nodding, she handed her purse to Victor, paused to take a breath, and threw herself on the bed. If the men hadn't been standing their watching, she would have rolled and flopped about in her excitement. She could throw out her coffin. She could sleep in an ocean of sheets. . . . ohhhhh. *Silk,* she thought, imagining sliding around in a silk sea . . . or satin.

Blinking her eyes open, she found herself staring at five men all watching her expectantly.

"It's all right," Elvi murmured, forcing herself to get up and straighten her clothes. "I'll take it."

"Don't you think you should try the others as well?" Victor suggested mildly, killing the glee on the manager's face before it had fully formed.

"Yes, definitely you must try them all," Harper said.

"Yes," the manager said on a regretful sigh. "It's better to try at least a couple before picking one."

Elvi turned to peer over the number of beds, her eyes wide.

"We will help," Victor assured her.

"How is that bed?" Harper asked several moments later. "This one seems comfortable."

Elvi sat up on the bed she was presently trying out and which seemed ridiculously hard to her, and glanced over to where Harper sat, bouncing lightly on another model.

"Perhaps I can save you some trouble," the manager said, wincing as Alessandro dove onto yet another bed.

"Do you and your wife prefer a hard or soft bed, sir?"

Elvi glanced over with surprise when he addressed Victor with the question. She had no idea why he would assume they were a couple. Unless it was because she and Victor seemed to keep gravitating toward the same beds, each laying down on opposite sides, Elvi taking the right and Victor the left.

Sitting up beside her on the bed, Victor didn't correct the man's misconception; he merely turned a raised eyebrow her way.

"Soft," she said decisively and stood to move to the bed Harper was now lying on. Elvi sat on the side opposite him, swung her feet up and lay down.

"This is better than the last one," she announced, then added, "I'm not sure though. I might want something softer."

"Let me see." Victor patted her leg to urge her over.

Elvi shifted closer to the center of the bed, making room for him. She watched him lie down, and then turned to peer up at the ceiling overhead; contemplating if this was as comfortable as the bed she'd given up five years ago. In her memories, it had been like lying on a cloud.

"It might be too firm," Victor said.

"We do have softer beds," the manager announced. "The ones you've been trying are at the firmer end of the scale."

"Show us." Elvi skated to the end of the bed on her bottom to get up. She was extremely grateful that she'd thrown on jeans this morning. One of her ridiculous gowns would have been impossible to maneuver in.

"Here we are," the manager announced, leading them

to a bed set off by itself. "This is the best bed we sell. There's no turning necessary and it has a twenty-year warranty."

Elvi climbed on and settled on her back almost in the middle of the bed.

"Oh," she sighed as the bed embraced her. "This is lovely."

Victor and Harper immediately moved up on either side to try it as well, but this time Alessandro also got in, crawling up the middle to squeeze himself between her and Harper.

"Oh yes," Harper murmured.

"Si," Alessandro sighed. "This is nice. I will get one too. Do you ship to Toronto?"

"Yes, we do," the manager said cheerfully, then cautioned. "However, you should really try it in whatever position you normally sleep in. If you prefer to sleep on your side, for instance, it's good to try it that way. How do you normally sleep?"

Elvi grimaced. "I used to sleep on my right side in a bed, but for the last five years I've been stuck in the coff—"

"Everyone roll to your right," Victor barked, cutting her off before she could mention her casket, and she recalled that they weren't in Port Henry where everyone knew what she was. The man would think she was nuts if she started yipping about coffins and vampires.

Grimacing, Elvi rolled to her right even as the men did, and settled down on the bed with her arm under her head in place of a pillow, her eyes on the back of Alessandro's head.

"You know, this reminds me of a movie I once saw,"

Edward murmured, peering down at them thoughtfully. He stood on one side of the bed, the manager on the other.

"What movie is that?" Elvi asked curiously.

"I can't recall the title, but it was x-rated."

Elvi blinked, and then flushed as she realized that she was rolling around in a bed with three men. Brilliant. Flushing, she sat up and scooted off the bed.

"She'll take this one," Victor said as he too got to his feet. He cast a scowl Edward's way once upright.

"Yes, I will." Elvi began to dig in her purse for her wallet.

"Wonderful!" The manager turned to lead the way toward the service counter where a lone woman sat waiting impatiently for them to either buy something or leave.

"Will you be taking it with you or do you need it delivered?" he asked, grabbing an invoice off the counter and beginning to write on it.

"Delivered," Elvi said at once and handed over her credit card. There was no way they were transporting it with Alessandro's little car. Unfortunately, she'd have to sleep in the coffin one more night.

"I'll need your address."

Elvi rattled off her address, her gaze slipping over her shoulder and back toward the bed. It was a beautiful bed and so comfortable . . . She couldn't wait to sleep in it.

"Port Henry?" the manager murmured as he handed back her credit card. "Let's see. We deliver there on Wednesdays. How's this Wednesday?"

Elvi's head whipped back with horror.

"Wednesday?" she squawked. It was a ridiculously

expensive bed and for the price she was paying, Elvi
had hoped to at least be able to get it the next day. She
feared her voice was desperately whiney as she asked,
"Can't they deliver it tomorrow?"

"Tomorrow is Sunday," he pointed out, and then
added with a frown, "we don't deliver on Sunday. And
we only deliver to Port Henry on Wednesdays."

Elvi stared at him nonplussed. She couldn't believe
she was going to have to wait until Wednesday to sleep
in a bed. She couldn't wait until Wednesday. She'd
spent five years in a coffin when she needn't have. One
more night, she might be able to handle. But four was
asking too much.

"You'll deliver the bed tomorrow," Victor said calmly.

Elvi glanced at him in surprise, but her gaze shot
back to the manager as he said, "We'll deliver the bed
tomorrow."

"No," she said sharply as she realized that Victor had
to be somehow controlling the man just as Alessandro
had controlled the police officer and made him stop
pursuing them. There was no way the sales manager
had changed his tune so quickly without some incen-
tive unless Victor had somehow made him. The fact
that the woman behind the counter was gaping at the
man as if he'd suddenly sprouted another head, also
seemed to suggest this wasn't normal. And as badly as
she wanted the bed delivered tomorrow, Elvi wasn't
willing to get it this way.

Catching at Victor's arm, she hissed, "No, Victor."

"You need a bed," he said simply.

"Here you are, all set."

Elvi glanced around to see the manager holding out
her copy of the invoice. "It will be there tomorrow af-

ternoon if I have to deliver it myself. Thank you for shopping here."

"Thank you." Victor took the receipt Elvi refused to accept.

"Victor," she said grimly, but he simply turned her toward the exit.

"You can't do this," Elvi protested as he urged her out of the building.

"Relax," he murmured, steering her toward the car. "You paid for the bed and delivery."

"That's not the point," Elvi snapped, coming to a halt on the parking lot pavement and turning on him. Spotting the other men watching with fascination, she paused, and then glanced around before grabbing Victor's arm and urging him away and around the building out of sight.

Elvi made it a practice never to argue with, or berate, someone in front of others. To her mind it was embarrassing and no matter how angry she got, there was no reason to humiliate someone that way.

Pausing on the grass between the building on one side and the trees on the other, Elvi turned to face him, took a breath for patience and sought her mind for an argument to make him see what he was doing was wrong.

"It's wrong," she blurted finally.

Heaving a deep sigh, Victor shifted his stance and crossed his arms as if his patience was being tested here rather than hers.

"What's wrong about it *exactly*?" he asked. "You bought a bed, you paid for it, you paid for delivery and are getting delivery when you want. It's not like you got the bed for free or anything."

"Yes, but they don't deliver on Sundays."

"Apparently now they do," Victor said mildly.

"No they don't," Elvi said shortly. "You—you influenced him."

He cocked one eyebrow. "Influenced him?"

Elvi made an impatient gesture. "I don't know what it is exactly you people do, but you did something, because they don't deliver on Sundays and only deliver to Port Henry on Wednesdays."

"Elvi, do you really want to wait until Wednesday for the bed?"

She scowled. "Of course not, but that's not the point."

"What *is* the point, then?" he asked growing impatient.

"You made him do something he didn't want to do," she said.

"How do you know? Maybe he really wanted to deliver it for you tomorrow. Besides, what does it matter? No one is hurt by this."

"How do you know?" Elvi shot back. "Maybe whoever he forces to deliver it tomorrow had something else he had to do and can't do now. Maybe it's his daughter's birthday and now he's going to miss it, and his wife will be upset, and it will all end in divorce. Or maybe someone he loves is in hospital and he would have visited them, but won't be able to and the person dies and he missed out on seeing that person one last time."

"Dear God," Victor muttered and shook his head with disbelief. "You think way too much."

Elvi ground her teeth together and said, "So where does it end?"

Confusion crossed over his face. "Where does what end?"

"Are you controlling me too?" she asked.

"Of course not," he waved the idea away as ridiculous.

"No? How do I know?"

"I wouldn't do that," Victor assured her firmly.

"Really? Why not? You controlled him."

"He is mortal."

Elvi stiffened. "Until five years ago I too was mortal," she pointed out coldly, and then glared. "You know what you are? You're a . . a . . . mortalist."

"A mortalist?" Victor echoed. "What the hell is that?"

"It's like a racist only—" Elvi's explanation died in her throat as something suddenly pierced the air in front of her face. Blinking, she stared at the feathered shaft trembling between them, and then followed it to the tip that was buried in the sign on the side of the building beside them.

"What— argh!" Elvi ended with surprise as Victor suddenly pushed her to the ground, coming down on top of her.

Covering her with his own body, he raised his head and peered around, eyes narrowed as he tried to spot the source of the arrow that had just missed them.

"Er . . . Victor?" Elvi pushed at his shoulder ineffectually. Finally, she gasped, "I can't breathe!"

Victor lifted himself slightly and peered down at her with concern. "Are you all right?"

"Of course. A little bruised from being thrown to the ground and jumped on maybe, but otherwise fine," Elvi said dryly. "Can we get up now?"

"No." He glanced around again.

"Why not?" she asked with real bewilderment and he turned his face to stare at her with disbelief.

"Why not? Has it escaped your attention that some-one just shot an arrow at you?"

"Me?" Elvi snorted with disbelief and rolled to the side, knocking his arm out from under him and leaving him collapsing to the ground as she stood and brushed herself down. "If they were shooting at anyone, it would be you. You're the one not from around here. I've lived in this area my whole life without a prob-lem," she pointed out, and then added, "but no one's shooting at us. Why should they? We're immortal and can't die."

Giving up on her clothes, she straightened and eyed him where he was just sitting up on the ground. Hands propped on her hips, Elvi asked, "Didn't you see the business sign next door as we drove past? It's the archery club. Obviously, someone isn't a very good aim."

Shaking her head, she turned and started back around the building.

Victor watched her go, then stood and moved to the trees lining this side of the furniture store. Peering cau-tiously through the branches, he eyed the lot next door. Sure enough it was an archery club, there were huge targets lined up along the back of the property. His gaze slid over the area, but there was no one there now. He presumed whoever had shot the arrow had gone back in the building.

His gaze returned to the targets, and then he turned to peer at the arrow still sticking out of the bottom corner of the large sign on the side of the furniture store. Vic-tor shook his head. Elvi was wrong. This hadn't been an accident. The bull's-eyes were at the back of the archery property, not along the side behind the trees. Someone had shot an arrow at them.

As for Elvi's argument that they were immortal and couldn't die, it reminded him that he still had some things to explain to her, including their laws and the fact that they weren't *completely* immortal.

His gaze slid over the lot next door once more, just to be sure no one was there and he wouldn't get an arrow in the back as he left, then he turned to follow the path Elvi had taken, his mind taken up with two questions. Who had shot at them? And which of them was being shot at?

Elvi turned her gaze away from the fire the men had built on returning home from buying her bed and scowled at Victor. Not that he seemed to notice. He'd been distracted since leaving the furniture store, and hadn't seemed to take note of even one of the dirty looks she'd sent his way. That just irritated her more. He should notice she was annoyed with him and care about it, dammit!

The sound of a car engine drew her attention to the driveway in time to see Mabel park behind Alessandro's sports car. As she watched, her friend threw the car door open, leapt out, and slammed the door closed with more force than was absolutely necessary.

Elvi pursed her lips. Judging by the way Mabel stomped up the sidewalk to the deck and then into the house without even a glance in their direction, she may not be the only one annoyed with a member of the male sex tonight.

The slamming of a second car door drew her attention back to the car as DJ rushed up the sidewalk. However, when he went to follow Mabel inside, it appeared the door was locked.

He jerked at it twice, cursed, then stomped down to throw himself into one of the two empty seats by the fire with a muttered, "Women!"

"What did you do to her?" Harper asked with amusement.

"I was nice," DJ said with disgust.

Elvi bit her lip at this explanation, for some reason believing it. After a moment, she cleared her throat, and asked, "She locked the door?"

DJ didn't even glance her way as he nodded.

"I'll go unlock it," she murmured. Getting to her feet, Elvi headed for the deck. It seemed to her that the men could use a few moments alone to jolly DJ out of his morose mood.

They continued to speak in quiet tones as she crossed to the stairs leading to the sunroom. Elvi entered the house there, passing through her bedroom and out into the hall just in time to see Mabel headed for her own room.

"Mabel?" she asked, moving up the hall toward her. "Are you okay?"

"I'm fine," the gray-haired woman said with forced cheer. "Why would you ask?"

Elvi raised her eyebrows, and then said carefully, "It's just that you seemed a bit upset when you got home."

"Oh. No." Mabel gave a forced laugh as she moved into her room, leaving the door open for Elvi to follow if she wished. "What would give you that idea?"

"Oh, I don't know," she said dryly, trailing her into the room. "Maybe the way you stomped into the house without even a hello to the rest of us by the fire, then locked the door behind you so DJ couldn't enter." When Mabel's only answer was to mutter something unintelligible under her breath, Elvi said, "I thought maybe DJ had done something to upset you?"

Mabel turned with a huff. "Don't even mention the name to me. That man is the most annoying, irritating, exasperating . . . *man*." She said the word as if it were synonymous with poop, and then went on, "He shouldn't even be here! He wasn't invited."

"No," Elvi agreed carefully. "But—"

"Do you know he followed me around *all* day? I couldn't move for tripping over him."

"I think he likes you," Elvi blurted.

"Oh, please! Elvi, look at me." Mabel held her hands out to the side. "I'm an old woman. He's a strapping young man. He is *not* interested in me."

"He isn't as young as you think," Elvi assured her, but Mabel wasn't listening, she was moving into the connecting bathroom.

Elvi followed, watching her bend to close the stopper on the tub, then pour bubble bath in and turn on the water.

Straightening then, Mabel wheeled and continued her rant, "That boy's forever reaching up to grab this for me or hurrying to lift that for me like I'm some useless old woman," she said with disgust, then cried unhappily, "And why does he wear such tight jeans?"

Elvi blinked at the question, wondering if the problem wasn't DJ being attracted to her, but that Mabel was attracted back and distressed by it.

"I told you, I think he likes you," Elvi repeated.

"Stop saying that!" Mabel snapped, spinning on her angrily. "I'm—"

"A beautiful woman," Elvi interrupted before she could insult herself again.

"You're a vampire, Elvi," she said grimly. "You have better eyesight than the rest of us. Now look at me. Look at this wrinkled old face."

"Oh, Mabel, for heaven sakes," she said impatiently. "Yes, you have laugh lines—"

"I have *wrinkles*," Mabel repeated harshly, then added, "everywhere."

Elvi waved that away as unimportant. "So? None of us look the same as we did twenty years ago."

"You do," Mabel pointed out. "Hell, you look *better* than you did twenty years ago; you look like you did *forty* years ago."

"Oh, right." Elvi bit her lip. While she hadn't had a mirror since returning from Mexico, she'd caught a quick glimpse of herself there. She knew she looked young.

"Forget I said that," Mabel said wearily when Elvi just stared at her with helpless guilt, then asked, "How was your night?"

Relieved at the change of topic, Elvi quickly told her about buying a bed and her annoyance with Victor for influencing the manager into delivering it the next day.

"I did call the store when I got home," she announced. "But of course it was closed. I left a message, telling them not to deliver it tomorrow."

"I don't know why you bothered," Mabel said with a shake of the head. "It's not that big a deal. Besides, do you think it will work? I mean, their control must reach beyond simple influence. They must be able to cause some sort of a compulsion in the person. Otherwise, the moment Victor left, the manager would have snapped out of it and cancelled the delivery himself. Don't you think?"

"I hadn't thought of that," Elvi admitted. "I need to find out more about this stuff, I guess."

Silence fell in the room, and then Elvi glanced at the robe and book Mabel had collected and now held loosely in her hands. She turned toward the door. "I guess I should leave you to your bath . . . maybe I'll take one myself."

"Good night," Mabel murmured.

"'Night." Elvi slid back out into the hall, pulling the bedroom door closed behind her, then wandered toward her own room. She'd had a shower that morning, but a nice relaxing bubble bath really did sound lovely.

Nodding to herself, Elvi picked up her pace. She had a lovely new bath set she wanted to try. A vanilla bubble bath with a crème brûlée body lotion to put on after. She gave a little shiver at the very thought. Elvi loved bubble baths. In the past, the tub was often the only place she'd got a moment of peace and privacy. As a mother and wife, there was always some great tragedy like having nothing to wear to the party the next weekend, or being unable to find the cheddar cheese that brought her daughter or husband to knock on the door.

Elvi smiled sadly at the memories of just such interruptions as she ran her bath. If she'd realized then how little time she would have with them, she would have savored those moments at the time.

Shrugging these thoughts away, Elvi closed the bathroom door, retrieved a bath towel and washcloth, then stripped out of her clothes. By then, the water was only a couple of inches from the top of the tub. Elvi bent to turn off the taps, then stepped carefully into the tub and eased herself into the hot bubbly water with a little sigh.

Oh yes, this was nice.

"I thought Elvi said she was going to unlock the door?"

Victor glanced toward Alessandro as the man returned to the group around the fire. He'd been pretending to listen to Harper regale DJ with their latest adventure in shopping with Elvi, but had really been preoccupied with the best way to make Elvi explain this business of being an "accidental vampire." It was obvious from her reaction last night that she didn't really wish to discuss the subject further than to say that, but it was the reason he was here. He didn't wish to upset her or make her recall what were obviously unpleasant memories, but he had to sort this matter out.

Victor knew he should have sat her down and addressed the issue today rather than allow this latest shopping expedition, but found himself too easily distracted by the woman. She was constantly taking him by surprise, flitting this way or that like a hummingbird in a garden. He found himself running to keep up with her, and eagerly doing what he could to aid her in getting what she needed rather than pinning her wings down to attend to his job as enforcer. This wasn't like him at all. It had been a very long time since a woman had fascinated him so, and he had never once been distracted from his duty as enforcer, not since the day he'd taken on the position more than three hundred years ago.

"Hasn't she?" DJ asked, drawing Victor's attention back to the conversation taking place around him.

When Alessandro shook his head, Victor frowned and glanced toward the upper windows of the house. The lights at Elvi's end of the house had come on a good hour ago. From the brief few moments he and the others had been in her room earlier that night, he thought it was the window in her bathroom. It was still on, he saw now.

He opened his mouth to suggest the man try knocking on Elvi's sunroom door, then closed it again and stood. If anyone was going to bother her in her bedroom, it was going to be him, besides, now was as good a time as any for him to get to the bottom of her turning.

"I'll see to it," he murmured, moving away from the fire.

Elvi had left the sunroom door open when she'd entered earlier, only the screen door was closed and it wasn't locked. Victor peered through the screen to the open door between it and the bedroom, frowning when he saw that the room was in darkness.

Raising a hand, he tapped lightly at the door, waited, then tapped a little louder. When there was no answer after a third knock, Victor hesitated, then slid into the sunroom. She obviously wasn't in her room. He'd just slip through her room, go down and unlock the kitchen door, then find her and have the talk he knew he needed to have with her.

Victor was halfway through her room, heading for the door to the hall when a door on his right suddenly opened. His feet froze guiltily and his head whipped toward the sound.

Elvi was coming out of the bathroom, wet hair slicked back from her face and wearing only a towel. A very small towel.

Victor swallowed heavily, all thoughts of talk slipping from his mind as his gaze traveled over every inch of exposed flesh. He started at the top, his eyes dancing over her shoulders, arms, and chest above the towel, before dropping down to slide lovingly over the legs visible beneath. It was short enough to reveal calves, knees, and a good three-quarters of her thighs.

His devoted exploration was interrupted when Elvi apparently spotted him, stopped short, dropped a small bundle she was carrying and let loose a little, startled shriek.

"It's okay," Victor said quickly. "I was just passing through. You forgot to unlock the door downstairs. I knocked, but there was no answer, so I thought I'd just slip through your room to do it."

"Oh," Elvi breathed, her shoulders relaxing. "I—You startled me. I didn't expect . . ." Her voice trailed away and she glanced down at the bundle she'd dropped. Clutching at her towel with one hand, she bent to retrieve the bundle with the other, but something slipped free and wafted back to the floor as she straightened. Victor moved forward at once.

"Here, let me get that." He knelt to pick up the bit of silk, his brain slow to realize they were red silk panties. Recognizing that, he started to raise his face to glance at her apologetically, but his eyes got caught on her naked legs. They were lovely. Pale, but perfect. And there was a drop of water she'd missed while drying. It was at the top inside of her knee and he had the sudden, crazy urge to lean forward and catch it with his tongue.

A small sound from Elvi dragged him back to his senses, and Victor forced himself upright. He held the bit of cloth between them. "Your . . . er . . ."

Flushing, Elvi took the panties from him, murmuring, "Thank you. I'm sorry I forgot to unlock the door."

"Yes," Victor mumbled, his eyes locked on her lips. There was another drop of water just there in the center of her lower lip. It seemed to be taunting him, daring him to capture her lower lip between both of his and suck off the drop.

Her expression was confused and uncertain, but he could also hear her heartbeat and knew it was racing in response to his nearness. As was his own, he realized.

"Victor?" His name was barely a breath of sound, but it was enough to send the water droplet tumbling forward. Before it could roll off, Victor swooped forward, closing his mouth over her lower lip and drawing on it gently, capturing the drop and taking it into his mouth.

Elvi drew in a small gasp of surprise and Victor took full advantage. Shifting, he covered both her lips, allowing his tongue to fill the space between. She tasted sweet and smelled of vanilla, the aroma of home-baked cookies. Victor had an urge to eat her up. It was a reaction he hadn't had since his wife had died and was impossible for him to ignore. Giving into it, he used his tongue to urge her mouth farther open, slid one hand up to her head to tilt it, then deepened the kiss even as his other hand slid around her waist to flatten against her lower spine and urge her body forward.

Elvi moaned into his mouth, her own hands creeping to his arms and clutching as he let the hand at her back drift down to the edge of the towel and slip beneath to close over one firm cheek of her behind.

It was the stomp of feet on the stairs leading to the deck that made him stop. Breaking the kiss, Victor glanced toward the open door to the sunroom, cursing himself for not closing it. He released Elvi with an apology and stepped away, pausing abruptly and bending to catch at her towel as it began to drift to the floor. When his hand closed over it, he found his face directly in front of one round breast, its nipple a puckered rose.

Victor closed his eyes briefly against the temptation, then forced himself upward and wrapped the towel around her. He then placed her hand over it, turned her toward the bathroom and gave her a gentle push back into the room as someone knocked at the sunroom door.

"I'll get that," he murmured, pulling the bathroom door closed behind her. Then Victor took a moment to run his fingers through his hair, gave his head a shake to get it working again, and moved into the sunroom.

Eleven

"Sorry," DJ said when Victor opened the door. "We were starting to get worried. First Elvi went to unlock the door and didn't return, and then you went with the same result. We thought maybe something was wrong."

Alessandro nodded from his position on the step below DJ.

"No. Nothing wrong," Victor assured them. "Elvi just forgot and went to take a bath."

"Ah," DJ murmured, and then raised an eyebrow, obviously expecting an explanation for his own failure to unlock it.

Victor ignored the look. He stood there, solid as stone, waiting.

"Alessandro has to use the facilities and I need a bag

of blood. I haven't eaten all day," DJ announced when Victor remained silent.

"Oh." Victor hesitated, his gaze moving to the closed bathroom door and then he reluctantly stepped back and gestured them in.

"Thank you," Alessandro said as he slipped out through the bedroom door Victor opened a moment later. "I unlock door to kitchen on my way back out."

"Good." Victor nodded, and then glanced to DJ expectantly. Rather than leave, the man turned a serious look his way and said, "Have you fed today?"

Victor scowled. He wasn't a child to be chased after. Besides, the answer was no. He should have slipped out before cooking when he got up, but he'd wanted to be sure that breakfast was ready when Elvi awoke, so hadn't. He hadn't even thought of feeding since then, though now that DJ mentioned it, his stomach was beginning to cramp.

"You haven't, have you?" DJ's voice was full of the "Ah-ha!" factor. "I thought you looked pale."

"I'll see to it," Victor assured him, though there were other things he wanted to see to first.

DJ nodded, "I'll come with you. I can help keep an eye out and we need to talk anyway."

Victor scowled. He didn't want to feed now. He didn't want to talk now. He wanted Elvi. However, it didn't look like he was going to get what he wanted. DJ was waiting expectantly.

Sighing, he cast one regret-filled glance toward the closed bathroom door, and then stepped out in the hall, pulling the door quietly closed behind him.

"Edward mentioned something about an arrow being

shot at you this evening," DJ announced abruptly as they started up the street moments later. He eyed Victor with concern. "What was that all about?"

Victor grimaced and quickly explained what had happened. He also mentioned Elvi's thoughts that it had been an accident, but that if it hadn't been, he had been the most likely target.

"You?" DJ asked with surprise. "Why would she think you were the target?"

Victor turned to the right as they reached Main Street. It was just after two A.M. on a Saturday night, closing time for the bars. The sidewalk was full of people making their way home. Victor's gaze slid predatorily over them as he explained, "She says she's lived in this area her whole life and no one has ever tried to harm her. As the outsider, she thinks I am the more likely victim."

He rolled his eyes at the ridiculous reasoning, but DJ was looking thoughtful.

"Hmm," he said finally.

"Hmm?" Victor echoed with disbelief. "DJ, no one would have any reason to try to kill me."

"Hmm." DJ didn't look convinced, which actually made Victor take pause.

"What are you thinking?" he asked warily, his steps slowing.

DJ shrugged and released a little breath. "Well, I was thinking that if she's never had any trouble with the people of Port Henry or the surrounding area in the five years since she was turned, then it isn't likely they would try to kill her now."

"True, but there's no reason for them to kill me either," Victor said sharply.

"Well . . ." DJ had a sort of wince on his face.

"What?"

"There is that stake bit," he said reluctantly.

"What stake bit?"

"You know. When you thought Elvi was going to bite that Owen kid and you charged through the restaurant to stake her." He shrugged. "Someone may not have believed that baloney about returning the stake as an excuse to see her. They might be trying to protect Elvi from you."

Victor frowned over the possibility. He'd forgotten that little incident. Now, he wondered . . .

"Where were the other men?" DJ asked suddenly.

Victor glanced at him with surprise. "Around in front of the store. Why?"

"They were all there?"

"Yes," Victor said. "Well, no. Edward wasn't there when I first rejoined them."

"Where was he?"

"He'd gone to '*find a handy bush*,'" Victor quoted the man. "He came around the opposite side of the building a moment later, though. Why? What are you thinking?"

DJ shrugged. "It might have been one of them."

Victor's head whipped around. "Why would one of them shoot at me?"

"To eliminate the competition?" he suggested.

Victor stopped walking and stared at him with confusion. "What competition?"

"For Elvi," DJ said patiently.

"Don't be ridiculous," Victor waved it away as ridiculous and started walking again. "They've probably all read her by now and found they can and she isn't their lifemate."

"Then why are they still here?" DJ asked reasonably.

Victor paused to think on that, but finally shook his head, unwilling to even consider that one of the other men was a lifemate to the woman he was lusting after. A feeling he hadn't had in a very, very long time and wasn't willing to ignore for anyone's sake.

"I don't know why they're still here," Victor admitted. "But they can't all be her lifemate."

"No?" DJ asked. "What about that story Harper told us the first night? About his friend and the friend's cousin who both met a woman they couldn't read?"

The reminder of the story made his stomach turn, which in turn reminded him of why they were out there on Port Henry's streets. To feed. As Victor had told Elvi, it was against their laws to feed on a mortal unless it was an emergency. For Victor, it was always an emergency. He'd been born with a genetic anomaly that wouldn't allow him to survive on bagged blood. He could consume all the bagged blood he wanted, but it was useless. He had to feed off the hoof to survive.

They were passing a park between two buildings and Victor glanced into it, noting a couple staggering through the walkway toward the parking lot on the other side. The man was obviously drunk and held no interest for him. Victor didn't wish to be intoxicated himself. The woman on the other hand had consumed a couple drinks but was only at the relaxed stage. She was stumbling under the weight of her much bigger boyfriend as she tried to steer him toward the parking lot ahead.

Victor turned into the park to offer his assistance; he would take only a small bit of blood in return for his aid. It was a fair trade to his mind. DJ followed.

Fifteen minutes and three couples later, Victor led DJ out of the park, headed for Casey Cottage.

"I suppose there is one other possibility," the young immortal said, returning to the topic they'd been discussing earlier as if it had never been interrupted.

"What's that?" Victor asked.

"Her sire."

Victor glanced at him with surprise. "Her sire? What sire? According to Elvi, she doesn't have one."

"Yes, but we know that's not possible," DJ pointed out. "One of our kind had to have given her blood . . . and whoever it is may be trying to kill Elvi. Perhaps he's found out that the council is snooping around. Maybe he'd already turned someone else, she was a second turn, and this would put him in deep trouble with the council. Maybe he's trying to kill Elvi before we can discover who he is."

Victor was silent, not wanting to believe this theory, yet unable to pooh-pooh it as he had the others. Someone had turned Elvi. And they hadn't laid claim to her and trained her as a proper sire should. Even if she wasn't a second turn for this unknown immortal, he would be in trouble for that. Deep trouble. Silencing her could save his neck.

"So we still can't be sure who the arrow was meant for," Victor muttered.

DJ nodded, and then asked, "Can you read her?"

Mouth tightening with irritation, Victor admitted, "I don't know. I haven't tried."

"Why?" DJ asked with surprise.

"I just didn't think of it," Victor admitted, feeling foolish. He should have tried to read her if for no other reason than it would have sped up their work on this case. Why the hell hadn't he thought of reading her? he wondered.

Because she was distracting him with her intoxicating scent every time he was near her, and that damned wide, open, guileless smile and those big beautiful eyes, his mind answered.

"I bet you *can't* read her," DJ said suddenly. "I bet she's just unreadable."

Victor frowned. "Can't you read her?"

"I haven't tried," DJ admitted. "I didn't bother after I found I couldn't read Mabel." His eyes suddenly widened incredulously. "Maybe it's just the whole town. Maybe no one here can be read."

"What?" Victor asked with surprise.

"Yeah," DJ said, suddenly cheering. "Maybe it's something in the water here."

"Don't be ridiculous," Victor muttered.

"No, listen," DJ insisted. "I can't read Mabel, and none of the men can read Elvi."

"They can't?" He glanced at him with alarm. "They've admitted as much to you?"

"Well . . ." DJ shrugged. "Edward claims he can and is only staying because there is so much interesting architecture in Port Henry, and Alessandro says he can, but the women here are so "bella" he decided to stay the whole week, but . . ." He arched his eyebrows dubiously. "Come on, do you believe either story?"

Victor frowned. He hadn't considered that the others might not be able to read her. In his mind, he was slowly claiming Elvi himself. He didn't like the idea that he might have some competition.

"I think if they could read her they'd be gone already," DJ said with certainty. "Neither of them were thrilled about coming here, and the first night they were saying they were out of here the first chance they got if they couldn't read her . . . But they're still here." He shook his head. "They're lying. Neither of them can read her either."

"Why lie?" Victor asked with a frown.

DJ shrugged. "Who knows? Maybe they're waiting to see what happens with the council."

Victor grimaced. At the rate he'd been working, or not working as the case may be, they'd have a long wait to see what happened with the council. Raising his eyebrows in question, he asked, "What about Harper?"

DJ pursed his lips. "I don't know. I haven't had the chance to ask him yet, but I suspect he can't read her either . . . which just proves my point. Have you ever heard of three or four immortals not being able to read someone?" He didn't give Victor a chance to answer, but went on: "It has to be something in the water here. Or the ground or something. It makes the whole damned town unreadable."

Victor blinked in surprise at the suggestion and at the man's pleasure in thinking that Mabel might not be his lifemate, that he simply couldn't read her because the town was unreadable. But then he recalled the hard time the woman had been giving DJ and supposed it might almost be a relief to the man to think he didn't have to woo her around to his side. He was almost sorry to disabuse him of the possibility, but he did anyway, announcing, "I read Teddy Brunswick the first night we were here."

"Oh." DJ looked disappointed, and then brightened and said, "Maybe it just affects the women. Maybe the men are all still wide open, but the women are blocked."

Victor was horrified at this possibility. If so, it might

mean Elvi wasn't his lifemate after all and that all these hopes that had reawakened the last few days might be just empty wishes.

He froze on the sidewalk, his mind in sudden turmoil. *It might mean Elvi wasn't his lifemate after all?* When had he decided she might be his lifemate? Sure, he was eating again, and okay, so he'd nearly had a heart attack when she'd fainted at the breakfast table that night, and, yes, he'd found it thoroughly enjoyable having her perched in his lap in the car, burrowing into him as if he were the only safe port in a storm. He'd also been secretly pleased when the sales manager had recognized that they were a couple. And he wouldn't deny that he was lusting after her, the first woman he'd lusted after for over three hundred years, but . . . a lifemate?

He could still feel her in his arms and taste her on his tongue and he wanted to feel and taste a lot more.

Crap, Victor thought with dismay. He wanted her for a lifemate. And while he hadn't tried, so had no idea if he could read her or not, DJ was suggesting that even if he couldn't, it might just be some town-wide anomaly. The women here might just be unreadable, period. That wouldn't do. It wouldn't do at all.

"Victor?"

DJ's voice startled him from his thoughts and Victor glanced around at the dark street. They were at the corner of Elvi's road. The streets were now empty, not another female resident in sight and he suddenly needed another Port Henry female.

"Mabel," he muttered and started to walk again, moving quickly now.

"What about Mabel? Where are you going?" DJ asked anxiously, hurrying to keep up.

"To find Mabel," Victor said abruptly as he reached the gate to Casey Cottage and tugged it open.

"She's gone to bed," DJ said, following him to the front door of the house.

"Good," he snapped. "Then she'll be easy to find."

"Victor!" he cried with alarm.

When the man rushed after him and tried to catch his arm to stop him, Victor waved him away as if he were an irritating gnat. "I'm sorting this out right now."

"But—"

"There are no buts," he argued. "If the women in this town are unreadable, I want to know it. It affects everything. Unreadables are almost impossible to wipe and this whole damned town needs wiping. And what the hell are we going to do if we can't wipe them? What will the council do?" While it wasn't really his main concern at the moment, it was a concern, and would do to explain his sudden determination.

"What *will* the council do?" DJ asked with dismay.

"I don't know," Victor admitted as he opened the front door of Casey Cottage and led the way inside. "But it won't be good. We can't have a whole town full of people knowing about us. The chance of one of them talking is astronomical. The council won't stand for it."

"Damn," DJ breathed, trailing him up the winding staircase to the second floor.

Stopping at Mabel's door, Victor raised a hand to knock, and then decided against it. If the woman was sleeping, he could slip into her mind and see if he could read it without ever disturbing her. If not, he'd claim he'd thought it was Elvi's room. Nodding to himself, he reached for the doorknob and opened the door.

Mabel wasn't asleep. She was sitting up in bed, glasses perched on her nose, and one of those torrid female romance books in her hands. She glanced up with surprise at the intrusion, and then scowled when she saw Victor standing there with DJ hovering behind.

"Have you ever heard of knocking?" she asked sharply. "What do you want?"

Victor didn't bother to answer; instead he concentrated on her forehead and sent his thoughts out to find hers. Much to his relief, he slipped into her mind like a warm knife through soft butter. His jaw immediately dropped at the thoughts and feelings whirling there.

Mabel wasn't as hard core as she'd have them believe. In fact, she was as soft as a roasted marshmallow. The hard outer casing was just a protective shell she put on to deal with the world. Her husband had been a weak man and she'd been forced to deal with everything the least bit difficult in life, from disciplining their children to handling recalcitrant servicemen and so on. Mabel hadn't been comfortable dealing with everything unsupported and had longed for her husband to be the strong male he'd seemed to be while courting her.

She'd been so unhappy, she might have divorced him, but had been pregnant with their first child by the time she'd learned the weak nature his macho approach had hidden. That hadn't seemed like a good enough reason to break up a family. After all, he wasn't a wife beater or alcoholic, she'd told herself and struggled on, taking on all the hard tasks in life in his stead.

That wasn't what had Victor's jaw dropping, however. That didn't surprise him at all. Her love and concern for Elvi had already told him she wasn't the hard case she liked to project. What made his jaw drop was the small tornado of turmoil she was suffering at their appearance.

There was no confusion in the woman's mind over Victor, his presence just annoyed her, but DJ was another matter. Mabel liked the younger immortal, which didn't bother her as much as the fact that she found him unbearably attractive. His appearance raised all sorts of longings in her and a lust like nothing she'd experienced since she was a teenager. This in turn caused guilt and horror because she thought he was so much younger than her and she thought it was disgusting to have erotic fantasies and dreams about a boy no older than her own son. The woman was finding the whole situation unbearable and heart wrenching.

"Well?" Mabel snapped the word, but he knew that her self-disgust made her tone sharper than she'd intended.

"Victor?" DJ hissed and he didn't need to read the immortal's mind to know what he was asking. Could he read Mabel?

"Yes," Victor said to answer DJ's question and the realization that washed over the man's face as he accepted that she was, indeed, his lifemate was enough to make up his mind on how to answer Mabel. His own situation may be a mess, but DJ's didn't have to be.

"*Hellooo!*" Mabel said with irritation. "Is there a reason you've barged into my room in the middle of the night? Did you want something?"

"I don't, but DJ does. He wants you," Victor answered, collaring the younger immortal and shoving him into the room. Ignoring DJ's embarrassed protestations and Mabel's horrified squawking, Victor started to close the door, then paused. "Despite his looks, he's one hundred and eleven years old, Mabel. An older man, not a young stud. There's no reason you shouldn't enjoy each other. You can stop feeling guilty for lusting after him."

Victor pulled the door closed, but didn't leave; instead he waited and listened, then even stooped to peer through the keyhole when the silence in the room drew out. He would just stay long enough to be sure DJ didn't screw it up and they didn't need further refereeing. By his guess, DJ was either about to land his lifemate, or mess up everything.

"Did he say one hundred and eleven?" Mabel asked in a whisper after several moments of silence.

DJ cleared his throat, then finally looked at Mabel and nodded solemnly. "One hundred and twelve actually. I just had a birthday last week."

Mabel sank back against the headboard, her hands dropping weakly to her lap and taking the book with them. "One hundred and twelve," she murmured faintly, obviously having difficulty wrapping her mind around that and unsure what it meant for her.

DJ was still for so long that Victor nearly opened the door and shouted at him to get to it, but then the man suddenly straightened his shoulders and moved toward the bed. "He was also telling the truth when he said that I want you, Mabel."

"You mean to feed on?" she asked uncertainly.

"No." DJ's voice was strong now and assured as he moved around the bed and approached her. "I want *you*. I find you endlessly fascinating, amusing and exciting. I want you. Your body, your mind, your heart. All of you."

"No, you don't," she said with certainty. "I'm old."

"I'm older, and always will be," DJ countered easily.

"But I *look* old," Mabel shot back, eyes widening as he drew nearer. She began to pull the blankets up to her chin.

"I love the way you look," DJ said simply.

"Then you need glasses," Mabel said grimly. "My face is as wrinkled as a prune."

"Your face is marked with the lines of life, put there by love and laughter, suffering and tears. It's beautiful." DJ paused beside the bed and eased slowly to sit next to her.

"But—"

DJ didn't wait for her to voice more fears. Leaning forward, he kissed first her forehead, then her eyes, forcing her to close them, and then he kissed her on the mouth. It was a hot kiss and Victor had to bite his lip to keep from shouting out "'Atta boy!"

He almost left then, but waited to see whether she'd toss him out, or give in to the inevitable. Women could be difficult in these situations. Immortals knew that once they found a member of the opposite sex they couldn't read, they'd found their lifemate and accepted it as bond. Mortals generally took a little time to come around, fearing rushing into things and making mistakes.

DJ ended the kiss and sat back, giving her a chance to respond; both he, and Victor in the hall, waited with bated breath.

She simply sat there staring at him, her face an expressway with conflicting and confused thoughts flashing past like cars. Finally, she tossed aside the book she'd been reading, and reached for DJ.

"That a girl, Mabel," Victor breathed and started to straighten, then jerked upright at the slam of a door up the hall. Turning with alarm, he found Elvi in front of her door.

Twelve

"It's not what you think," Victor said as he hurried down the stairs after Elvi. "Really. I was just trying to help DJ."

"By playing Peeping Tom on Mabel?" she asked with disbelief, flouncing off the stairs in her blue robe and turning into the dining room. "What? Were you supposed to report back to DJ on what she wears to bed?"

"No, of course not," he said quickly. "Besides he knows. He's in there with her."

Elvi froze and whirled back. "What?"

"That probably wasn't the best way to go about explaining things," Victor muttered.

"What is DJ doing up there?" Anger replaced by concern, Elvi rushed back now, hurrying past him for the stairs, obviously intent on saving Mabel.

Cursing, Victor hurried after her.

"Wait, stop, you'll ruin everything," he hissed, catching up to her and grabbing her arm to stop her outside the bedroom door.

Elvi whirled, mouth open, no doubt to yell at him to let her go, but they both froze at the sudden cry that came through the bedroom door. Mouth snapping closed, she spun back to grab the bedroom door, but froze again as Mabel's voice came loud and clear, gasping, "Oh, DJ! God, yes!"

Blinking, she released the knob as if it had turned into a snake and stared at the closed door as if she'd never seen it before.

A growl—definitely DJ's—sounded, almost drowning out the rhythmic squeaking of the antique bed that left them in no doubt as to what was happening beyond the door.

"He works fast," Victor muttered with surprise, and then shrugged. The first time with a lifemate was always fast and furious, the pent-up longings and flashpoint passions bursting into flames and burning them both up quickly as they fed on each other's desire. If Victor was very lucky, he might get to experience that very thing soon.

Briefly, he added on a sigh. If Elvi was his lifemate, fate couldn't have handed him a worse hand. The last thing he would have hoped for was a lifemate who might very well be executed by the council. It wasn't exactly every immortal's dream woman.

"What are they doing?" Elvi asked uncertainly.

Victor peered at her with disbelief, then caught his hands behind his back and stared at the hall wall, refusing to meet her gaze. He was *not* explaining what was going on in that room. She was old enough to know what it was anyway and was—he was sure—just having difficulty believing that her sturdy, grumpy friend could make sounds like that.

He was rather surprised himself, Victor decided, as Mabel cried, "Harder. Oh yes! Oh, DJ! Oh God, *yes*! Ride me till the cows come home!"

Victor blinked at that, and then asked uncertainly, "Did she grow up on a dairy farm?"

Elvi opened her mouth, closed it again, then threw up her hands and whirled away as Mabel shouted something about stallions and saddles.

Victor's gaze dropped to the keyhole, but he shook his head and turned to follow Elvi. DJ was on his own.

Elvi's back was stiff as she descended the stairs once more.

Victor followed, searching his mind for something to say to ease the situation, but really, this was beyond him so he remained silent as he followed her through the dining room and around the counter into the kitchen. Elvi opened the refrigerator to consider its contents, and Victor glanced out the window to see that the fire was out and the men were now gone. He supposed they'd gone to their rooms while he was out with DJ.

The slam of the refrigerator door drew his startled gaze as Elvi turned on him.

"If he's messing with her feelings I will personally hide him," she warned through gritted teeth.

"He isn't," Victor assured her quickly. "He can't read her."

"And what the hell am I supposed to take that to mean?" she asked with mingled anger and bewilderment.

"It means she's his lifemate," Victor explained. "He won't hurt her."

"His lifemate," Elvi echoed, obviously confused, and he was reminded that she hadn't been taught all the things he'd been taught centuries ago and took for granted.

"Each of us has a lifemate," he explained. "Someone we can't read or control who is our perfect mate. Mabel is DJ's."

"But Mabel isn't a vampire," she said.

"An immortal," he corrected.

"Whatever," Elvi snapped. "She is mortal. How can she be his lifemate?"

"She isn't an immortal *yet*," Victor corrected. "If she agrees to be his lifemate, he will change her."

"He can do that?" she asked with amazement.

"Of course. DJ has never turned anyone, so by our laws is free to turn her if he wishes."

"That makes absolutely no sense to me," Elvi informed him on an unhappy sigh. "But what I meant was . . . Can he actually, physically turn her? I mean, I tried several times to turn Mabel. The books say biting them three times will do it, but I must have bit her a dozen times and she never turned. We kept trying and trying, but—"

"You *tried* to turn Mabel?" Victor asked with horror.

"Well, of course," she said, obviously surprised by his reaction. "We've been friends since childhood and suddenly I was young again and strong and she wanted to be too, and I didn't want to be alone in this."

Victor opened his mouth, thought better of what he'd been about to say, shook his head and instead said, "They have to consume or take in your blood. The sire has to give up their own blood. It carries the nanos. They'll move into the turnee's bloodstream, reproduce themselves, and spread until they infect the whole body."

"Right. Nanos," Elvi muttered to herself. She'd been pondering that while in her bath earlier. Considering what the men had said had left her feeling slightly deflated. As much as she hated to admit it, she was almost sorry to hear she was a vampire because of nanos, not a curse. It was ridiculous, she knew but . . . that was how she felt.

Her dissatisfaction must have shown in her voice. Victor's eyebrows rose and he asked, "What?"

Elvi grimaced, and then shook her head. "It's just so . . . Well, there's no romance in nanos and science and . . . stuff."

"And there *is* in the explanation of the cursed and soulless walking dead?" he asked with disbelief.

She scowled, feeling foolish. "Well, at least the vampire is a tragic hero and not some science experiment."

Victor rolled his eyes. "The Dracula of Bram Stoker's story is not a tragic hero. He's a parasite, feeding on and turning the innocent willynilly, and the man he's based on damned near got us all destroyed back in the day."

"Dracula was based on a real person?" Elvi asked with interest. "Can I meet him?"

"No," Victor snapped. "He's dead."

"How could he be dead?" she asked. "We're immortal."

"No, we're not. I mean, we are mostly, but we can die if we're beheaded or—"

"Staked?" she asked.

"Staked, stabbed, or being shot in the heart can kill us if the implement used is left there. As will being burnt to death."

"Hmm." She considered this news, and then frowned.

"Then why on earth do you keep insisting I call it immortal? We aren't immortal at all. We're vampires."

Before he could respond to that, Elvi said, "So how did this man Dracula was based on nearly get you all destroyed?"

Victor's mouth twisted with irritation. This was a sore spot for him. "By being a bloody, stupid lush who mouthed off to Stoker and told him all about our kind while he was drunk. We had managed to get away with only causing quiet rumors ere that. Once Jean Claude opened his stupid mouth and Stoker published his book, we were hunted. It took decades to convince the majority that it was all fiction and we still have to wipe minds and stop the occasional vampire stalker."

"Immortal stalker," she corrected absently, and then asked, "So Dracula was based on someone named Jean Claude. Who was he?"

"Not exactly based on him, no, and I'm not discussing this," Victor muttered and moved to the refrigerator to retrieve a bag of blood for her. She was looking pale

"So you have to give them your blood," Elvi said, returning to the original point. "Huh. I must have missed that part of the movie."

"What movie?" he asked with confusion as he handed her the bag.

"Dracula. I must have been in the bathroom or something when he fed her his blood. I don't remember seeing that," Elvi explained and popped the bag to her teeth.

"What?" This comment so took him aback, that Victor unthinkingly snatched the bag away from her mouth so that she could answer, and then dropped it in surprise when it began to squirt blood everywhere. He started to bend to pick it up, but then stopped, unable to keep from asking with disbelief, "You researched by watching the movie rather than reading the damned book?"

Tsking at the mess he'd made, Elvi grabbed some paper towels from the roll, snapping, "Well, the book was checked out of the library and I wanted to learn as much as I could as quickly as I could. Movies are faster than books."

Victor rolled his eyes and muttered, "Definitely a child of your times. It used to be that university kids read the crib sheets on books they were supposed to read, now they watch the movie."

Holding the wadded-up paper towel, Elvi narrowed her eyes. "You know, Victor, sometimes you sound as pompous as a horse's ass."

"Mabel wasn't the only one brought up on a farm, I see," he said stiffly, then asked politely, "Are horse's asses really pompous?"

"God! Sometimes you're such a . . . a . . . *man*."

"Good of you to notice," Victor responded with a grin and the irritation slowly faded from her face, replaced with a reluctant smile.

Several moments passed with the two of them simply standing there smiling at each other, and then Victor's eyes focused on her forehead as he thought that he should try to read her and find out exactly where he stood. Before he could, Elvi's tongue slipped out to glide along her lips. It was a nervous action, but as seductive and distracting as could be and he found his gaze shifting to her lips instead. She had the most incredible mouth. Full, red lips that begged to be caressed and kissed and he already knew they were as soft as they appeared. He found himself moving slowly forward, his focus locked on her lips and what they would feel and taste like and nothing else.

"Victor?" Elvi said uncertainly.

"I want to kiss you." It wasn't a request, but an explanation and her answer was a soft puff of air that came out as an "oh."

Taking that as agreement, he closed his lips over hers. They were soft pillows, giving way to his firmer mouth. Victor abruptly slipped his tongue out to urge her lips apart and test her taste.

Sweet, he decided. She'd obviously had chocolate since they last kissed. She must have it stashed somewhere in her room. He liked the taste of chocolate mingled with her, he decided. It was the last almost coherent thought he had, then his brain disengaged, allowing his body's wants and needs to take over the driver's seat.

Elvi stood completely still, almost holding her breath as Victor's mouth pressed gently against hers. She was suffering a definite sense of déjà vu. All the feelings and needs he'd brought to roaring life in her body up in her room, needs that had been forced onto the back burner when they were interrupted, now burst back to raging life. When he suddenly pressed forward, urging her head back as his tongue slid out and invaded, she drew in a gasp and dropped the paper towel she'd gathered to clean up the blood on the floor and caught at his upper arms to steady herself.

For one moment, Elvi felt like an invaded country, overwhelmed and unprepared, but then his tongue rasped over her own, drawing a moan from her throat as he reawakened and pulled passions from her she hadn't felt in years. Her body stretched and arched of its own accord, pressing her breasts against his chest and thrusting her pelvis forward until it met a hard resistance that pressed back.

Elvi groaned, her own tongue coming to life in her mouth and greeting his with an eager, lavish welcome.

She felt the counter against her back, but her attention was on his body pressing against her in front and the hunger it invoked. It had been so long since she'd been held and kissed this way. She was like a flower opening to sunlight after years of night. Her body ached to be touched and ached to touch as well.

Elvi let her hands slide up over his shoulders to his neck, one holding him there and urging him to take the kiss even deeper. The other slid up into his hair, nails scraping across the skin of his scalp as the soft locks caressed her fingers.

Victor growled and obliged the silent request. The kiss was suddenly harder, more demanding, and his hands began to move, sliding first around her waist then down to her behind to urge her closer until her body was plastered against his. Then one slid away, to run up over her hip and side, swiveling around in front as he reached her breast.

Passion had pooled between her legs as he ground into her, but Elvi gave a start in his arms at the excitement that immediately shot through her when his hand closed over her breast through the silk of her robe. Her nipples were immediately hard and aching, thrusting themselves eagerly forward for a caress they hadn't experienced in ages.

"Oh, Victor," she breathed as his mouth left hers and slid to her neck, drawing on the tender skin below her ear. He wasn't biting her, but she almost wished he would. Elvi wanted to bite him and could feel the pressure as her teeth shifted.

Crying out, she tilted her head back to avoid temptation, and stared blindly at the lights overhead as the blood rushed through her, hot with excitement. She wanted him; his kisses, his caresses, his body thrusting into hers, her teeth plunging into him, his sinking into her. Elvi's mind whirled with images and desires that scattered like dry leaves in a fall breeze when he suddenly tugged the neckline of her robe aside and dropped his mouth to latch onto a nipple.

Elvi clutched at his shoulders briefly, then began to tug on the back of his T-shirt, pulling the cloth upward until it bunched at his arms and she could touch the bare skin of his back. It wasn't enough. Growling deep in her throat, she caught her fingers in his hair and urged his head back up. Victor came reluctantly, allowing her nipple to slip from his lips and catching the naked breast in his hand as he raised his head to kiss her again.

Their tongues fought now, battling with their desires as she slid her hands under his T-shirt in front and scraped her nails over his flesh. His chest was hard and wide and muscular, a veritable playground, but her hands barely ran over all that masculine muscle before one dropped of its own accord and slid around to clutch at his behind, urging him harder against her until they were grinding through their clothes.

Victor growled at her aggression and suddenly reached down to catch her behind the thighs and lift her up, balancing her against the countertop as he pulled one leg forward around him. Elvi gasped as he suddenly tugged her robe the rest of the way open, then his hand slid between them, caressing her through her silk panties. The only thing she'd donned under the robe.

Crying out, she arched into the touch, aware that her body was weeping, soaking her panties with her need for him. Everything of any importance in the world suddenly seemed focused on that hot spot between her legs that he was stirring to turbulent life. She was aware that her breathing had become a fast, shallow panting, but it halted abruptly when he slid one finger beneath her lace panties and ran it over her bare flesh. Elvi sucked frantically at his tongue as her body bucked to his touch.

Her hand slid between them now too, finding him through his jeans and squeezing. Victor's reaction was almost violent. He thrust himself into that caress, then suddenly forced her hand away, caught his fingers in the delicate lace of her panties, and tugged sharply, ripping them from her body.

Elvi gasped in startled excitement, and then groaned as his hand returned to caressing her. Unobstructed, he cupped her in his hand and pressed the heel of his palm against the core of her, rubbing aggressively, and then slid one finger inside.

Elvi cried out, her hips shifting to meet the caress, and then cried out again as his mouth slid down her throat to her breast, his teeth grazing her nipple before he closed his mouth and began to suckle, his finger slipping away then thrusting into her again.

Elvi was on the edge of exploding from the pleasure. Her body was as tight as a bow string, her mind a confusion of need, sound was thundering in her ears and then— Victor suddenly jumped away from her like a rat abandoning ship.

Without his support, her trembling legs gave out and Elvi fell to her knees on the kitchen floor, a mass of confusion and frustration.

"There you are, Victor."

Elvi heard Edward Kenric's voice through her own panting and immediately understood that the thundering had been his jogging lightly down the stairs. She also understood why Victor was now standing wide-eyed at the end of the counter, a guilty look on his face. They'd nearly been caught misbehaving in the kitchen. Actually, they still might be caught, Elvi realized, when she spotted her torn panties lying on the floor next to the spilled bag of blood a few feet away.

If Edward came around the counter . . .

"I have a question for you," Kenric continued and much to her horror his voice was moving along the counter toward the end.

Panicking, she scrambled forward on all fours to snatch up her panties.

"Have you— Oh, Elvi."

She'd just stuffed her panties in the pocket of her robe, tied it closed, and snatched up the paper towel she'd dropped earlier when Edward came around the counter to join Victor.

"Hello, Edward." Forcing an innocent smile, Elvi began to swipe at the drying blood on the floor, then paused to snatch up the empty blood bag and toss it up and—she hoped—into the sink, before continuing to clean up the mess on the floor as if that's what she'd been doing all along.

"I didn't realize you were here as well. Can I help you with that?" he asked, moving closer.

"No, no. It's almost done. You go on and talk to Victor. Take him out on the deck if you want privacy," she encouraged. "I'll be done here in just a moment."

"If you're sure," he said politely, then turned to Victor and said, "If you wouldn't mind?"

Victor hesitated, then gave in to the inevitable and led the way out onto the deck.

Elvi sagged where she knelt, feeling as wrung out as a dishcloth. She only allowed herself a moment's respite, however, then quickly finished wiping up the blood on the floor. Once done, she stood and threw out the paper towel, then grabbed the empty blood bag from the sink and tossed it as well before moving to the refrigerator to collect a fresh bag of blood for herself. It was the reason she'd been headed downstairs in the first place, but she'd allowed herself to be distracted.

Her gaze slid to the counter where she'd almost had her first orgasm as a . . . well . . . not dead person.

Elvi took her bag with her and fled the kitchen. Now that the passion had passed she was embarrassed and unsure how to act with Victor. Dear Lord, she barely knew the man and had nearly had sex with him right there on the kitchen counter for anyone to walk in and catch them at it. What was the matter with her?

What's wrong with *us*? Elvi corrected silently as she moved past Mabel's room and heard the sounds coming from inside. She felt a moment's envy and had a brief flash in her mind of her and Victor making love in her . . . coffin, she ended the thought with a grimace as she recalled she didn't yet have a bed, then pushed the image away with a shake of the head.

For God's sake she—and Mabel—were both sixty-two-year-old women, practically senior citizens, both of whom had lived sedate, conservative lives. They

were small-town girls who'd married their childhood
sweethearts. She'd had no other lover other than her
husband and knew the same was true of Mabel, and yet
here they were acting like a couple of tramps.

Elvi managed not to roll her eyes at her own thoughts.
She knew it was an old-fashioned term and that her
thinking, too, was old-fashioned. But that was what she
was, an old-fashioned, small-town girl who suddenly
found herself behaving completely out of character.

Worse yet, while Elvi was aware she should be grateful that Edward had interrupted before things had gone
any further, she really wished the annoying man had
just stuck to his damned room and not interrupted at all.
She'd had a taste of the delights Victor could show her
and wanted more.

"Damn," Elvi muttered. She never should have come
down for a bag of blood before retiring. And what had
happened to the *"I'm not ready to date?"* feelings that
had first attacked her on hearing these men were here.
Now she didn't care about dating, she wanted to sleep
with one of them. She supposed that was a good thing
at least. There was only one she was interested in sleeping with.

A passionate scream drew her gaze back over her
shoulder to Mabel's door as she slid into her own room.
Elvi wished she could talk to the woman, but, of course,
that was impossible right now. It looked like she would
just have to wait until DJ left. In the meantime, she'd
take a cold shower, change into her nightgown, and
probably relive every moment in the kitchen in great
detail. Damn, the man could kiss.

Thirteen

Elvi woke Monday evening with a smile on her face as she stretched luxuriously in her lovely new bed. Sunday had been a great day. She'd woken late and gone below to find that her bed had been delivered. Not willing to disturb her, they'd made the delivery men put it in the foyer to await her rising.

The moment she made an appearance, they'd moved her coffin out and carried her bed up. When asked what she wanted done with the casket, Elvi had grimaced and muttered, "Burn it." The men had taken her at her word. While Victor and Edward had set up the plain metal frame that came with the bed, Alessandro and Harper had taken axes to her coffin, turning it into tinder.

They'd then built a fire, roasting hotdogs over the flaming remains of her casket. When it began to rain later in the evening, Elvi and the men had moved indoors and turned to a deck of cards for their entertainment. On learning that Elvi had never played poker, they'd decided to teach her and they'd spent an enjoyable evening laughing, talking, and taking all her chips.

Elvi stretched again on her lovely new bed and opened her eyes with a little sigh. While Sunday had been nice for the most part, she'd found it a bit stressful as well—as she worked to avoid being alone with Victor. It had been an act of pure cowardice on her part. She didn't know how she should act around him after the episode in the kitchen and so avoided any situation where she couldn't treat him as anything but one of the *"guys."*

Now she had another day of doing that ahead of her.

Making a face at the ceiling, Elvi reluctantly pushed the sheets off and climbed out of her lovely new bed. She'd slept like a dream. Too well actually. Elvi had hoped to get up early enough today to spend some time out in daylight for the first time in five years. She'd hoped to look over her garden and enjoy the sun on her face, but could tell from one glance at the window that the sun had already set.

It was her own fault, Elvi supposed; she'd retired to her room early, but stayed up waiting for Mabel and DJ to get home from the restaurant so she could finally talk to the woman. She'd never got the chance on Saturday night. DJ simply hadn't left Mabel's room, from what she could tell. At least he hadn't by the time she'd given up and fallen asleep. Then Sunday the couple had already been up and gone when she got up. Hopefully, she'd get the chance to talk to her today. Elvi could use some advice on how to deal with Victor. She couldn't avoid him indefinitely.

Elvi didn't bother drying her hair when she got out

of the shower, instead she simply brushed it back and left it to dry on its own, then quickly dressed in a peasant blouse and festive cotton Mexican skirt and headed below. Normally, she'd be heading to the restaurant tonight, but she wasn't sure at this point what would be expected of her. They had houseguests after all. Once she knew what she was doing, she could change accordingly.

When Elvi first made her way downstairs and glanced around, she thought she was the only one there, then the door to the deck opened and Victor stepped inside.

He paused on first spotting her, then murmured a greeting and moved to the refrigerator. Retrieving a bag of blood, he held it out and asked, "How was the new bed?"

Despite her uncertainty, Elvi felt a smile stretch her mouth. "Marvelous."

"Glad to hear it." His smile pulled into a grin as she took the blood.

"Where is everyone?" she asked.

"The men all went to a play at the school with your neighbors . . . Mark and Sharon is it?"

"Mike and Karen," Elvi corrected, not at all surprised the couple had extended an invitation. The Knights were a lovely couple. They were always offering help with things around the house, or inviting her and Mabel places. Elvi wasn't surprised they were generous enough to extend those invitations to include the men. Their generosity and thoughtfulness were part of why they were so popular in town and why their son Owen's birthday celebration had been so well attended.

"And Mabel and DJ are at the restaurant," Victor continued. "She said to tell you you're not expected there tonight. She wanted you to pick one of the men and spend the evening getting to know him."

Elvi blinked. "But you said the guys went to a play."

"Yes. As you weren't up, I made an arbitrary decision for you and told the others tonight you were getting to know me," he announced unapologetically. "I thought that way I could finally tell you our laws and rules."

"Oh." Elvi bit her lip. So much for being able to avoid him.

"Feed," Victor ordered, gesturing to the bag she still held in her hand.

Relieved at the distraction, Elvi allowed her teeth to slip out and popped the bag into her mouth, then avoided Victor's eyes as she tried to sort out what to do. It was her gaze sliding over the fireplace in the living room that did it. It was a very ornate fireplace with ceramic tiles up each side and a carved wooden mantel. There was also a mirror in a beautifully carved frame that belonged above it, but it had been removed and stored in the garage five years ago. Now the empty space gave Elvi an idea.

She waited until she'd finished a second bag of blood, then grabbed her purse and announced, "Well, that's fine, but we'll have to talk while shopping."

"What?" Victor asked with surprise.

"I need to go shopping," Elvi said patiently as she moved toward the garage door.

"Mabel and DJ took the car," Victor announced, bringing her to a halt, and then added, "we'll have to take my car. I had the men move theirs so I could park at the back in case we need it."

Relieved he wasn't arguing, Elvi smiled and continued out of the house.

"So, what are we shopping for this time?" Victor asked as he parked in the local Wal-Mart parking lot several minutes later.

"A mirror," Elvi said. "I haven't been able to use one in five years. It would be nice to be able to see that my hair isn't standing on end, and to do my makeup."

They fell silent as they entered the store and sought out the section they needed. Elvi wanted a full-length mirror. Actually, eventually she wanted a proper bathroom mirror too, as well as to have the mirror in the garage put back over the mantel and so on. But for the moment, a full-length mirror seemed the more sensible buy. Reaching the aisle where the mirrors were displayed, Elvi approached slowly, almost afraid at what she would find, but then she steeled herself and forced herself to walk in front of the first one, only to pause with amazement.

She was staring at a woman with long, vibrant red hair that fell around a lovely face in soft waves. Her complexion was perfect, and so was her figure.

Damn, she was a fox, Elvi realized with amazement. She looked like Casey. How had she never noticed that her daughter had taken so much after her?

Movement in the mirror caught her eye and Elvi managed to tear her gaze from herself to focus on Victor as he stepped up behind her so they stood framed in the mirror, a handsome couple. They seemed to complement each other.

"So," she murmured, forcing her eyes away from him and continuing along the selection of mirrors. "What about these laws?"

Victor frowned at her question. "I don't know if Wal-Mart is quite the right place to be discussing—"

"Why not?" Elvi interrupted with amusement as she

peered over the various mirrors offered. "Everyone in town knows about me, and these are laws you're going to tell me, not the facts of life."

"Yes, but what if someone from out of town is shopping here?" he said grimly.

Elvi shrugged. "Then talk quietly. We're alone in this aisle right now. If someone joins us, stop."

Victor hesitated, then she heard him let out a breath before he said, "Very well." Still, he paused for a moment to glance around before saying uncomfortably, "Well, you know the most important one."

"No biting mortals," Elvi recited, amused by his discomfort. She supposed he was used to keeping everything secret and clandestine and thought she was probably lucky she hadn't had to. When Victor remained silent, she murmured, "So far I like the laws. At least that one, it gives me an excuse to put an end to the Birthday Bite celebrations. They've always been more trouble than anything else, but they were expected and I didn't want to disappoint."

She saw Victor's mouth tighten as he moved past her and wondered what she'd said to upset him. Before she could ask, he was stopping at a mirror. He ran one hand down the dark wood frame, his fingers gliding over intricate carving. "This one would suit the house."

"Yes." Elvi paused to examine the mirror. The carving was very similar to the woodwork in her house. It would suit very well indeed.

Victor watched her walk around the standing mirror, and then continued with the lesson. "One of the other more important laws to you as a woman is that you're allowed to have only one child every hundred years."

Elvi froze, her gaze searching out his face in the mirror. "What?"

Victor's reflection grimaced. "I know it seems harsh, but we need to keep the population down. If we didn't, with our life expectancy we'd quickly outnumber our blood source."

Elvi waved that away impatiently. She couldn't care less about the reasons behind the law. "Are you saying we can have children?"

"Yes." Victor tilted his head, examining her expression.

Elvi bit her lip, then asked more specifically, "What about if we couldn't, or had trouble having them as mortals?"

Victor examined her face, and then murmured, "Brunswick said your daughter died in a car accident. Did you have trouble conceiving her?"

Elvi moved away, pretending to look at another mirror, but in truth she wasn't seeing anything in the store just then. She was seeing the past.

"I always wanted a lot of children," she admitted quietly. "Five or six at least. But I had six miscarriages before Casey was born, and then nearly died giving birth to her. They said no more children."

Elvi didn't hear Victor approach, but he was suddenly there, his hand moving soothingly up and down her back as she continued, "Casey was doubly precious because of that. She was the perfect baby; always good tempered, rarely cried, and she started sleeping through the night almost at once. And she stayed perfect, every parent's dream. She grew into a beautiful young woman, never going wild or breaking curfew. She got good grades, had lots of friends, was a hard worker, and got a scholarship to university."

"Casey," Victor murmured. "You named Casey Cottage after her."

Elvi nodded.

"She's dead," he said quietly.

It wasn't a question, but Elvi treated it as if it were. Nodding, she said, "She used to come home from university on weekends. Usually I picked her up from the train station, but the last time it was Harry, my husband, who went to get her while I stayed home making a special dinner for her." Her hand tightened on the mirror frame. "Halfway home, he suffered a stroke and they crashed. The stroke killed Harry at once they think, but Casey—" Elvi paused and bit her lip when her voice broke, then took a deep breath and, ignoring the tears suddenly veiling her eyes, said, "Casey was trapped in the car. They had to use the Jaws of Life. She was awake and in terrible pain, but lost consciousness by the time they got her out. She died in the hospital that night."

"I'm sorry," Victor murmured. Sliding his arms around her waist from behind, he rested his chin on her head and held her as she wept silently. Then she pulled free and turned to face him.

"Are you saying I might be able to have another child?" A new baby wouldn't replace Casey, but it might help to fill the hole her loss left behind.

Victor nodded solemnly. "If you wish it. You won't have problems conceiving. The nanos will already have seen to it that your reproductive system is in perfect order. And they'll be immortal children."

Elvi closed her eyes as silent sobs shuddered through

her. She'd never imagined she'd ever again hold a baby in her arms. Not her own. Now he was not only telling her she could, but that it would be an immortal baby she wouldn't need fear losing to childhood illness, or drowning, or car accidents.

If only she'd been turned before the accident, Elvi thought suddenly. If only she'd been able to turn her daughter. If only . . .

"Elvi?"

Giving a start of surprise. Elvi blinked her tears away and turned to peer at the woman moving up the aisle toward her. Louise Ascot. She was the same age as Elvi, but an inch or two shorter and thin as a bird with short salt-and-pepper hair and a look of concern on her face.

"Are you all right?" she asked, stopping beside Elvi. "Why are you crying?"

Elvi groaned inwardly. Louise had gone to school with Mabel and Elvi and had been a huge gossip even then. She'd only got worse with age. She was the worst possible person to run into in Wal-Mart while sobbing like a baby. The story would be all over town within fifteen minutes.

"I'm fine, Louise," she said, dashing away the tears and managing a smile.

She obviously didn't believe her and glared at Victor as she said, "Well, okay, but I hope you know that if *someone*"—her glare deepened on Victor—"were bothering you, there isn't a person in Port Henry who would hesitate to take care of him."

"Fortunately, there isn't, though," Elvi assured her, then turned to Victor and said, "I think I'll take the wooden one that suits the house. Shall we go get a cart?"

Victor shook his head. "I can carry it."

He ignored Louise's continued glares and bent to pull one of the boxed mirrors off the shelf, then started back up the aisle with it.

Murmuring *"good-bye,"* Elvi quickly followed.

They waited in line, bought the mirror, and drove home in silence, but by the time they pulled into the driveway, Elvi couldn't stand it anymore and blurted, "I'm sorry."

Victor shut off the engine and turned to her with surprise. "What for?"

"For Louise, and for crying in Wal-Mart."

Victor raised an eyebrow. "You're not responsible for what other people do, and it didn't upset me that you were crying." He frowned. "Well, I mean I was upset that you were upset, but . . . you can cry anywhere you want . . . if you want to," he finished, obviously unused to dealing with such matters.

"Harry didn't like it when I got emotional in public," Elvi said suddenly. "Especially crying. It embarrassed him."

"He was young," Victor said quietly. "After a century or two you learn there is very little worth getting embarrassed about in life. Everyone does foolish things, everyone makes mistakes, no one is perfect."

Elvi smiled faintly over the bit about Harry being young. He'd been the same age as she. Fifty-seven at the time of his death. Hardly young by mortal standards, but a babe to an immortal over two thousand years old.

The brush of Victor's finger along her cheek drew her attention back as he asked, "Are you all right? I didn't mean to bring up sad memories for you."

"I'm okay," Elvi said and gave a shrug. "Life can't always be cheesecake."

Victor grinned and reminded her, "You still haven't eaten that cheesecake you wanted so desperately."

"No." She smiled, and then added with surprise, "In fact, I didn't even think to have breakfast tonight before we left. I guess I've gotten out of the habit."

"Is that what it is?" Victor asked mildly. "I thought maybe you were just trying to avoid being alone with me in the house for fear I'd start kissing you again."

Elvi sucked in a breath, her eyes widening at the challenge in his voice. The air in the car was suddenly supercharged as they stared at each other. She didn't know what to say or do, but couldn't seem to look away from him. Her eyes suddenly had an agenda of their own and were focused on his mouth as she recalled the way they'd felt as they claimed her.

"Would you have?" she asked finally, surprised at how husky her voice sounded.

"Most definitely," Victor growled.

Elvi nodded. "Would you now?"

The words came out of her mouth completely unbidden, startling her so much that she almost bit her own tongue. If someone had told her that Victor had slipped into her mind and influenced her to say the words, she wouldn't have had any trouble at all believing it. In fact, she already half believed it now, but didn't care because it was what she wanted. It's what she'd wanted ever since the episode in the kitchen, which was the real reason she'd been avoiding being alone with him. Elvi had feared jumping him herself and that just wasn't in her nature. However, the man was addictive, he was a drug she was jonesing for, badly.

Much to her relief, Victor took up the invitation. Leaning forward, he unsnapped her seat belt, letting it slip back into its holder as he kissed her. It was not tentative. There was nothing uncertain in his approach. One moment they were seated on opposite sides of the car, the next his mouth was on hers, her seat was dropping back, and he was on top of her as his tongue slid between her lips.

It was as if he were just picking up from where he'd left off the other night. There was no slow buildup, no coaxing. His mouth was hot and desperate, his tongue demanding, and it spurred a similar response in her. Elvi was suddenly on fire. Slipping her arms around his back, she clutched at his shirt, her body pushing upward, eager to press itself against his as she let her own tongue join the fray.

"God, I want you," Victor muttered, tearing his mouth from hers and trailing kisses across her cheek to the pulse point below her ear.

"Yes," Elvi breathed, one hand slipping around to run over his chest through the white T-shirt he wore. "Yes."

"I've never wanted anyone this badly." His teeth grazed against her throat as he spoke and Elvi moaned and tipped her head to the side, and then back as his mouth moved down the long column to her collarbone. She then gasped as he nudged the neckline of her blouse lower and licked the upper curve of one breast.

"Oh yes," Elvi murmured. She was feeling exactly what he claimed to be feeling, but couldn't seem to find the words to say so. "*Yes*" was apparently the only word in her vocabulary at the moment. And she lost the ability to say even that when his hand closed over one breast, squeezing it gently as he lowered his mouth further still to close it over the tip and breathe hot air on it through the cloth covering it.

Unintelligible sounds of pleading slipping from her lips, Elvi arched in the passenger seat, pressing her breasts upward and wishing her clothes weren't in the way, that she could feel his warm mouth without obstruction.

Apparently, it was what Victor wanted too because in the next moment he was tugging impatiently at the blouse and drawing it down to reveal the thin white strapless silk bra beneath. It was a front-fastening bra and took only a quick snap of his finger and thumb to release it.

Elvi gasped and shuddered as the cloth fell away, allowing her breasts to pop up, then cried out as his mouth finally covered one excited nipple. Clutching her fingers in his hair, she held on for dear life as he suckled, her hips gyrating upward as she felt his hand slide under her skirt and move up her thigh. That was when a tap on the window made them both stiffen, then jerk apart.

Elvi quickly pulled her blouse up to cover herself and glanced around, groaning with embarrassment when she recognized Teddy Brunswick's grim face peering in through the driver's window. They'd just been caught parking by the local police. Elvi hadn't even had that happen as a teenager.

"Put on your bra," Victor said calmly, shifting to block Teddy's view.

Elvi tried, but her hands were shaking so badly, she kept fumbling it until Victor brushed her hands aside and did it for her. He also tugged the blouse back into place before getting out of the car to face Brunswick.

Taking a deep breath, Elvi slid out of the passenger side.

"I got a call that someone was upsetting you at Wal-Mart," Teddy announced abruptly as soon as she paused at Victor's side.

"Louise," Elvi said with despair. She'd known the woman would spread the story, but should have realized the first call she made would be to Teddy.

"Yes." His gaze narrowed, taking in her disheveled clothes and swollen lips. "Are you all right?"

"Yes, I'm fine," Elvi said quickly. "Louise misunderstood everything. I was crying because Victor had just told me that I could have babies now, and I . . ." She shrugged helplessly.

Teddy nodded slowly, then said, "So you thought you'd come back here and start right away."

Elvi stiffened in surprise, her face flushing with a combination of shame and anger. Teddy had never before talked to her with such distaste or so coldly and what he said hurt, but when she sensed Victor tensing beside her, she reached to the side and caught his hand.

"That was uncalled for," Victor said quietly, his grip on her hand firm. "I'd like to call you on it, but since I know it's just jealousy talking I won't . . . This time. Don't mistake this for a free pass to hurt Elvi again, though."

"Jealousy?" Elvi echoed, peering at Brunswick with confusion. "Teddy?"

The police captain was silent, his mouth set and expression empty. Without a word, he turned and walked to the patrol car parked behind Victor's BMW and got in.

Victor turned back to the car and lifted the mirror out as she watched Teddy drive away.

"You didn't know he loved you?" Victor asked when she realized he was holding the mirror and hurried to lead the way to the side door of the garage.

"No," Elvi murmured, still not really believing it. She paused at the side door to the garage. Reaching in her purse for her keys, she added, "I still don't know that. We've been friends for years."

"He's loved you for years." Victor stepped inside, and then paused to wait in the narrow space between the wall and Mabel's car as she locked the door behind them. "That's why he never married. No other woman could compete with you. When your husband died, he hoped . . ." Victor shrugged those useless hopes away. "But you were turned."

"And he didn't want me anymore," Elvi guessed wryly as she turned to face him.

"Oh, he wanted you, all right," Victor assured her. "But he thought you wouldn't want an old guy like him, so he set his mind to helping Mabel find you someone else. He loves you that much."

"You read his mind?" she realized.

Victor nodded.

"Can you read mine?" she asked, suddenly horrified at the possibility. The idea of his knowing exactly how he made her feel and just what she wanted to do to him and what she wanted him to do to her was somewhat humiliating.

Victor was silent so long, she began to think he wouldn't answer the question, and then he admitted, "I don't know. I've never tried."

Her eyebrows rose in surprise. "Why not?"

Instead of answering, Victor leaned the mirror against the wall and then peered at her with an expression of concentration.

Elvi waited, knowing he was trying to read her. She wasn't sure if she'd know if he'd read her or not, but nothing seemed to happen. They just stood there while an odd array of expressions flew across his face; concentration, bewilderment, amazement, then doubt. She'd just become sure he must be reading her mind, when he suddenly stepped closer and reached out to touch her arms, holding them in a firm grip as he refocused his concentration.

"I can't," he said at last and Elvi couldn't tell from his expression if it was a good thing or not. He'd gone suddenly pale, but his expression was hard to read. Turning away, he leaned against the car as if suddenly weak, and she felt concern claim her.

"Victor?" She moved to his side, then slipped under his arm to stand between him and the car and peered up into his face. His eyes had been closed, but now opened.

"Are you all right?" Elvi asked uncertainly, reaching up to press a hand to his chest.

Victor covered her hand with his own, pressing it to his heart, then lifted it to his lips and pressed a kiss to it. The gesture was so caring that she found herself holding her breath, and then his tongue dipped out and slid over one finger, sliding along it to the spot where it met her hand.

Elvi felt a shiver run up her back and swallowed thickly as she watched what he was doing with fascination. Heat was pooling in her belly again. When he then drew that finger into his mouth and sucked on it, her whole body seemed to tingle with the caress and she suddenly found herself leaning heavily on the side of the car behind her.

Drawing her hand away, he let her finger pop from his mouth, and then used the hand to pull her into his arms as his mouth claimed hers again. Elvi slipped her arms around his neck, her mouth opening beneath his as she felt the top of her blouse being tugged downward. The snap of the bra being released barely reached her ears, but she gasped as the cool air touched them, then Victor caught her by the waist and lifted her onto the hood of the car.

Moaning into his mouth, Elvi arched as his hands closed over both breasts, the rough skin of his fingers, unimpeded, now caressed and kneaded as his tongue swept through her mouth.

Eager to touch him as well, Elvi slid her hands beneath his cotton T-shirt, urging it up his body until it caught under his arms. She then delighted in running her hands over the naked flesh she'd revealed, catching and gently tweaking his nipples as he was doing to her.

The cloth of her blouse must have been getting in his way, Elvi realized, when he forced her arms to her sides so that he could tug the cloth down and free her hands. She shivered as the light material of the peasant blouse pooled around her waist, leaving her topless, but Victor slid his arms around her at once, warming her with his body, the springy hair on his chest brushing her nipples.

Missing his kisses, Elvi slid a hand into his hair and urged his mouth back to hers, murmuring happily when he thrust his tongue inside. It was a short kiss, however. Pulling free, he dropped his mouth to explore her breasts, kissing a trail around and between them, lavishing them with his tongue, and then finally suckling at one then the other.

Forced backward on the hood to accommodate him, Elvi leaned on one elbow, and ran her other hand over his back and head, her eyes glued to where his mouth was taking first one nipple, and then moving to take the other. Distracted as she was, she didn't miss the feel of his hands gliding up her outer thighs, pushing her skirt before them, before sliding back down toward her knee. The next time they came forward, they burned a trail along the inside of her thighs, and Elvi could feel the muscles of her thighs begin to tremble and her breathing becoming a short, harsh pant the higher they rose. One stopped on her thigh, resting there lightly, but the other continued up to brush along her panties lightly. The teasing touch tore a cry from Elvi's lips and her hips lifted of their own accord, urging him on even as her thighs closed instinctively around his hand like a flower protectively closing its petals at nightfall.

In response, Victor caught her thighs with both hands and forced them apart, then let her nipple slip from his lips and dropped to his haunches beside the car and pressed his mouth to her panties, nuzzling her through the silk.

Elvi cried out and dropped onto her back on the hood of the car, her hands reaching fruitlessly for something to grab hold of as her hips jolted, thrusting her pelvis forward. Then the cloth was suddenly pulled to the side and his tongue rasped over the delicate flesh in an unbearably exciting caress.

She was vaguely aware when he snapped her panties off and thought she'd definitely have to make a trip to the lingerie shop at this rate, but then her mind shut down and she became a moaning, groaning, sobbing idiot as his mouth returned to torment her. Eyes opening and closing and head twisting back and forth, Elvi got snapshot images of the garage ceiling overhead, but she wasn't seeing anything. Her mind was completely taken up with trying to accept the pleasure flooding her. She'd never experienced anything like it. There was the pleasure, then endless echoes of the pleasure vibrating through her brain as if the sensations she was experiencing were some weird boomerang that she was sending out, only to have them return bigger somehow, amplified, almost overwhelming.

Elvi was close to exploding, but she wanted to feel him inside her when she did. Forcing herself to sit up, she reached to tangle her fingers in his hair, relieved when he began to straighten.

Stepping between her legs, Victor took her in his arms and pressed kisses to her throat and face as she reached between them for the button of his jeans. She managed the button and zipper, and then slid her hand inside to find him, nipping his ear lightly with her teeth as she drew him out of his pants.

Muttering something incoherent by her ear, Victor clasped her by the bottom and lifted her slightly as she directed his hard length into her.

Elvi bit her lip and groaned as he filled her, her body expanding eagerly to except him. Pressing her heels against the side of the car, she clutched his bottom as he began to withdraw and drive himself into her in the age-old dance.

It was a short dance. Already well primed, Victor had barely thrust into her half a dozen times when Elvi's body suddenly stiffened, then convulsed, her hands clutching desperately at him as the world shattered around her. She was vaguely aware of Victor shouting out with his own release, but the sound seemed far away as she lost her grip on consciousness and fainted.

Fourteen

Elvi woke to find herself in bed once again. Confusion clouding her mind, she peered around, then slowly turned onto her back to peer at the other side of the bed.

Victor was lying on top of the sheets next to her, contemplating the ceiling overhead with a smile on his face. A glance upward proved there was nothing on the ceiling to cause the expression so Elvi supposed it must be his thoughts he was smiling about. When she turned her eyes back, she found his head turned her way, his smile curved into a grin.

"I fainted," she said.

Victor nodded.

"And you carried me up here?"

"Yes."

Elvi shook her head. "I'm sorry. I had two bags of

blood this morning, I don't know why I fainted. I—" She stopped abruptly as his chest began to shake with silent laughter. "What's funny here? I'm starting to get concerned. I never faint."

"There's nothing wrong," he assured her, turning on his side to run one hand up her arm. "Fainting is common for the first year when . . . two immortals get together."

"For the first year?" she asked with disbelief, and then her eyes narrowed. "Did you faint?"

"I briefly lost consciousness, yes," Victor acknowledged.

Elvi rolled her eyes. Leave it to a guy. For her it was fainting, for him, it was briefly losing consciousness. She didn't care, he could call it what he wanted. She felt marvelous. Her body felt marvelous. Her bed was marvelous. Life was just plain marvelous at the moment.

"Is that you and your daughter?"

Elvi followed his gaze to the photo on her dresser. It was she and Casey at the town fair the summer before she died.

"Yes," she murmured quietly.

"And that's your late husband?"

Elvi nodded as her gaze slid over the picture on the other side of the dresser. Harry had been a handsome man. Tall, silver-haired and distinguished looking. Elvi stared at the picture for a minute, and then glanced at Victor curiously. "Why have you never married? Two thousand years is a long time to remain single."

Victor rolled onto his back and closed his eyes and then admitted, "I did marry. Once. Her name was Marion. She was burnt at the stake in 1695. I was away in London at the time. If I'd been home—"

"You may have been burnt at the stake too," Elvi interrupted and was extremely glad he hadn't been home.

"No," he assured her solemnly. "There were too many for Marion to handle alone, but had I been there . . ." He let the sentence trail away on a weary sigh.

The memory obviously upset him. Elvi left the subject alone and asked instead, "Did you have any children?"

He opened his eyes to stare at the ceiling. "One. Vincent. He was born in 1590. He is four hundred and seventeen years old."

Elvi winced. Even the man's son was old. "Where is he?"

"He lives in California," Victor said quietly, then blurted, "I don't see him much."

"Well, he's older," she excused. "Once kids grow up and get a life of their own, parents never see them."

"My not seeing him is by choice."

"You don't want to see him?" she asked uncertainly, finding it difficult to even imagine such a thing. If Casey had survived the crash and only Harry had died, the poor girl would no doubt have been complaining to all and sundry because Elvi visited too much. "I don't understand. Why don't you see him?"

Victor closed his eyes again, a little sigh escaping him, "It's difficult to explain. Marion was . . . my lifemate. I waited so long for her, and was so lonely before she came into my life . . ." He paused and frowned, then glanced her way, repeating, "It's difficult to explain."

"Try," Elvi urged, really wanting to understand.

Victor looked away and then said, "Without training, I'm sure you haven't learned to read thoughts yet?"

Elvi shook her head. "Will I?"

"Yes. It's one of the extra abilities the nanos give us. You must have noticed that you were more intuitive?"

"Very," she admitted. Elvi had found she was extra-sensitive to feelings and could sense emotions.

He nodded. "Then you have the ability and just need the training to use it."

"I'm not sure I want to," Elvi murmured. "It seems an intrusion."

"You need to learn to do it to avoid doing it," Victor said with confusing logic, and Elvi blinked at him stupidly.

"What?"

He glanced her way to ask, "Do you suffer a lot of headaches?"

"Yes," she said with surprise. Elvi hadn't thought anything of it, she'd had headaches a lot before the turning and had just assumed they were continuing, but now she thought about it and realized, "They come every time I go to the restaurant or any of the local events. They aren't so bad when I'm home alone."

"And yet you continue to go to the restaurant and these local events," Victor murmured.

Elvi shrugged. "It's expected."

Victor looked as if he wanted to say something, but then glanced away. "The headaches are because you're picking up the thoughts of the people around you. They're worse at the restaurant and social events because there are more people there bombarding you."

Elvi shook her head. "I'm sure I don't pick up thoughts. My head just hurts, there are no thoughts with it."

"That's because there are too many," Victor explained. "You haven't been trained to control and focus so you're picking up everyone's thoughts. It becomes like static on a radio or white noise on a television. That's why you suffer headaches when you're around others but not when you're alone. Once you learn to focus, it will be better, but that's draining as well. You'll have to be constantly on guard, constantly blocking thoughts and protecting your own. It's wearying. Most immortals withdraw from society as much as possible because of that, but it leaves us alone all the time. A lifemate eases the loneliness. You don't have to guard your thoughts around them. Or block them. Your lifemate becomes your only safe haven, a cool and soothing breeze on a hot day."

"And Marion was that for you," Elvi murmured quietly.

"Yes . . . And much more," he admitted. "When she died . . . I was lost at first, not wanting to see anyone, do anything or go anywhere. I just wanted to curl into a ball and lick my wounds." He smiled suddenly and said with affection, "It was my pain-in-the-ass brother, Lucian, who pulled me out of that. He dragged me back into the world kicking and screaming and gave me a purpose."

"What purpose?" Elvi asked with a smile.

Victor paused and then admitted, "An enforcer for the council."

"What is an enforcer?"

"We hunt rogue immortals. Those who have gone bad and are breaking our laws," he explained.

Elvi nodded. "How did he get you to do it? I doubt asking nicely worked."

"No." Victor laughed. "Lucian came to my house one day with a family portrait; a huge painting of a family;

a beautiful woman, a smiling man, and two happy children. The painting immediately infuriated me because my lovely family had been torn asunder. Then Lucian took out his epee and sliced the woman out of the picture and while I sat there, shocked, he told me she'd been taken by a rogue, her family was as devastated as I at the loss of Marion, but I could help stop it from happening to another family."

Victor gave a short laugh. "I pointed out it was mortals who took my Marion so why should I care if they suffered, and he asked if I would blame all for what one church official did? If so, didn't it mean that her family had every right to blame me and everyone of our kind for the loss of their mother and wife."

He shrugged. "I went hunting with him for this rogue, then another and another . . . It's been my only real purpose since then."

"And your son?" Elvi asked, wondering where he came in.

Victor sighed. "After the first hunt, I went to see Vincent. I hadn't seen him or anyone else but Lucian since Marion's death." Remembered pain flashed briefly in his eyes. "Vincent looks so like his mother. He has my coloring and build but her smile and eyes and . . . I couldn't bear to look at him. It hurt too much," he admitted, then added shamefaced, "I left as soon as I could and have seen him as little as possible since."

"You must have loved her deeply," Elvi murmured.

"She saved my soul," Victor said simply. "The loneliness was maddening and I was very close to going rogue myself when we met. Her arrival in my life was a blessing." He turned to stare deep into her eyes and added, "As is yours."

Elvi pulled back slightly on the bed, feeling blind-sided by his words. "Mine?"

Victor nodded. "Some are never so lucky even once. I never thought I would be lucky enough to be blessed twice. But Elvi, you too are my lifemate."

"Calm down," Mabel said firmly. "Elvi, you have to calm down."

"But he thinks I'm his lifemate," Elvi squawked, pacing from one end of the restaurant office to the other. "We hardly know each other and he's talking about forever and— I'm not ready for this," she cried with dismay.

"You looked pretty ready to me in the car," Teddy commented and Elvi turned a glare on her old friend.

After Victor had made his announcement that she was his lifemate, she'd just lain there staring at him for the longest time, then she got up without a word and left the room.

The moment the door closed behind her, she'd broken into a run, flying down the stairs and out of the house in her wrinkled skirt and blouse, headed straight for Bella Black's and Mabel. She was halfway to the restaurant when Teddy's cruiser pulled into a driveway in front of her, forcing her to a halt. Seeing her running down the street *"like a mad thing"* as he'd put it, he'd stopped to be sure she was all right, but when all he could get out of her was incoherent ranting about lifemates, Teddy had done the sensible thing. He'd ushered her into his car and drove her to the restaurant. Mabel had taken one look at Elvi's face and ushered her into the office, only to be followed there by both Teddy and DJ.

"Listen to me," Mabel took her by the arms and

turned her physically away from their old friend. "DJ has explained this all to me. I can help."

Elvi nodded. "Help."

"Yes," she said calmly, then took a breath and said, "Immortals can read everyone, often even other immortals unless they're much more powerful. They can also be read by other older and stronger immortals."

"Victor explained all that," Elvi muttered. "But how does that make me his lifemate?"

"He must not be able to read you," Mabel said simply.

Elvi just stared at her, her mind returning to the garage and his concentrating on her, attempting to read her. He'd said he couldn't. He'd also said the night she caught him outside Mabel's door that Mabel was DJ's lifemate because he couldn't read her. Elvi simply hadn't put the two things together.

"Marion was his lifemate," Elvi protested. "He loves her."

"And Harry was your husband and you love him," Mabel said reasonably. "So what? The human heart is big enough to love more than one in a lifetime."

That was true enough, she supposed, but . . . "What if it's just a fluke that he can't read me?"

"There are other signs too," Mabel assured her. "Like the fact that he's eating again."

Elvi waved that away as ridiculous. "They're all eating. Even DJ."

The sandy-haired man swallowed the bite of chimichanga in his mouth and said, "That's because Mabel's my lifemate."

"Well, what about the others?" Elvi asked. "Edward, Harper, and Alessandro are all eating too."

"Yes," DJ admitted. "We're a bit concerned about that. And they're all still here as well, which suggests they can't read you either or they'd have left by now."

"Are you saying she could be a lifemate for any one of those four men?" Teddy asked with amazement, and then turned an impressed gaze Mabel's way. "Damn, you're good, Mabel. Care to find me a woman?"

"This isn't funny, Teddy," Elvi snapped.

"Do you see me laughing?" he asked.

Turning away from him, she said, "So you're saying that all four of them could be my lifemate? What am I supposed to do?"

"Choose one," Mabel said reasonably. "I'd guess since you've slept with Victor, he'd be the wisest choice."

"How do you know that?" Elvi squawked with amazement as her face flushed with embarrassment.

"Elvi, your lips are swollen, your hair's a mess, you aren't wearing a bra and you look like a woman who's been well satisfied," Mabel said dryly.

"And we were at the house," DJ added. "Mabel forgot the work schedules for the week and we'd come back for them. When we started into the garage to head back, you and Victor were using the car. We decided to wait until you were finished."

"DJ!" Mabel snapped.

"Well, it's true," he said defensively.

"Oh God," Elvi mumbled, lowering her face into her hands. The car. Why hadn't it occurred to her that the car was there? They did it right there on the damned thing.

"Look, honey," Mabel rubbed a hand up and down her arm. "There's nothing to be embarrassed about. We're all adults here."

When Teddy snorted at the comment, Mabel turned a glare his way.

"Don't get mad at me," he said raising his hands. "I'm not the one acting like an idiot teenager."

Elvi lifted her head. "Are you saying I am?"

"Well, if the shoe fits, Ellen."

Her eyes widened at the use of her real name. Teddy hadn't called her that since the turning. No one had. She often bemoaned the fact, but now it sounded like an insult.

"Teddy," Mabel said in warning.

"Well, it's true," Teddy said in the same defensive tone DJ had used moments ago. Crossing his arms, he glared at Elvi. "You like the guy. He likes you. You have great sex in the garage and rather than pull some love 'em and leave 'em stunt, he wants a future with you. And what do you do?" he asked. "You run hell for leather up the street to the restaurant all in a panic asking what you should do."

"What does that expression mean exactly, hell for leather?" DJ asked in the silence that followed Brunswick's words. "And where does it come from?"

Teddy blinked at the immortal, and then said with exasperation, "How the hell should I know. People just use it all the damned time."

"I always thought it meant crazy fast," Mabel commented. "Though, I don't know why. It doesn't make sense when you think about it."

"Not now, but it's an old expression and we used to wear leather shoes rather than rubber soled," DJ murmured thoughtfully. "Maybe that's where it comes from, going fast or hard and being hell on the leather shoes."

"Oh, I never thought of that," Mabel said with surprise, then beamed. "You're so smart, love."

Shaking his head with disgust as the pair began to kiss, Teddy caught Elvi's arm and urged her toward the door. "Come on. You won't get any sense out of those two now. They'll be locking the office door in about three minutes."

Elvi allowed him to lead her out of the restaurant, but tried to pull free as they neared his car. "I can walk."

"Yes, but then I couldn't talk to you and I have some wisdom I'd like to impart," he snapped. Opening the passenger door, he ushered her in, slammed it, and then walked around to his side.

Elvi was silent as Teddy started the car, and left him to get to the point in his own time. It didn't take long.

"Mabel and I arranged this week to find you a mate," he started as he steered out of the parking lot. "We don't like the idea of leaving you here on your own."

"Yes, I know. She told me."

Teddy nodded. "Well, it seems we did good. Out of all the vampires in the world, she picked the four who would be suitable lifemates." He paused, and concentrated on driving for a minute before saying, "Elvi, if you love this guy, don't let fear keep you from him. You'll regret it. Trust me, I know," he added solemnly, and then said, "You're home. Get out."

Elvi glanced around with surprise to see that they were indeed in her driveway, and then turned an incredulous gaze back to Teddy.

"That's it?" she asked with disbelief. "Don't let fear stop me. We're home, now get out? That's your wisdom?"

"The best advice is often the simplest," he said with

a shrug, then softened slightly and added, "Elvi, you're scared. I understand that. I've been there. I let it stop me once from asking someone to a high school dance, someone else asked her and she ended up marrying him. Forty years later I still regret it, but my life is almost over. You have a hell of a lot longer to regret it than me."

Elvi recalled Victor's saying Teddy loved her and had for a long time. She suspected she was the girl he hadn't asked to the dance, and wanted to say something to make it better for him, but there wasn't really anything to say.

"Now, do me a favor and get out of the car before Tall-boy tries to beat my brains in. I'd hate to have to deal with the paperwork of arresting him tonight."

Elvi glanced out to see Victor stomping up the sidewalk toward them. Sighing, she opened the car door, and then leaned over to give Teddy a kiss on the cheek before sliding out of the car.

"Where—" Victor began the moment she started up the sidewalk, but Elvi interrupted him quickly.

"Sorry I took so long. I should have let you know where I was going before I took off, but I suddenly remembered something I had to tell Mabel," she lied cheerfully, moving past him on the sidewalk and heading for the door to the house.

Scowling, Victor turned to follow her. "You—"

"Gosh, all that running around did me in and I'm famished. Do you want a bag of blood? Or maybe a steak or something? I could start the barbecue."

Aware that he was following her, Elvi kept up a lively chatter as she led him to the kitchen and began to poke around the refrigerator. Mostly to keep him from asking questions or saying something they might both regret. She wasn't ready to answer questions. She needed to think. She needed time to adjust to all this.

It was all well and good for Teddy to tell her not to let fear stop her, but Elvi wasn't jumping into anything either. She'd only known Victor a couple of days. It was too soon to love him. She wasn't committing herself to anything until she was ready.

The men returned while they were eating and regaled them with their thoughts on the play. For the most part, they seemed to have enjoyed themselves despite its being an obviously amateur event. They'd also enjoyed the company and praised her for having *"quite civil and entertaining"* neighbors. Elvi suspected this was high praise from these men.

"We were talking about building another fire on the way back," Harper announced as he claimed a seat at the table and snatched a bit of salad from Elvi's plate. "But it's started to rain."

Elvi glanced toward the window to see that this was true and wondered to herself how she was going to entertain these men. She was considering suggesting another game of poker when Victor spoke up.

"I haven't quite finished telling Elvi all our laws yet. We're going to take coffee up to the sunroom and finish it."

Elvi shrugged when the men glanced her way. Victor was telling the truth. She'd only learned one more law today and was sure there must be more than that. It would probably be good to learn them all so she didn't inadvertently break one.

"There are movies in the cupboard in the living room if you want to watch something," she suggested as

Victor picked up his empty plate and carried it to the kitchen. "I'm sure we won't be long."

She was being optimistic, Elvi knew, but really, there couldn't be that many laws and if they would just stop getting distracted, they might get through them quickly, Elvi thought as she carried her own plate out and collected two cups for the coffee.

The men were silent at first, but by the time she'd poured the coffee and started to lead Victor out of the room, they'd begun to discuss their options when it came to entertainment.

Elvi led Victor up to the sunroom, and moved to open a couple of windows to allow the cool night breeze in as Victor settled in one of the wicker chairs. Once done, she settled on the wicker sofa adjacent to him and raised her eyebrows expectantly. "So, no biting, only one child every hundred years, and . . . ?"

"And you can only turn one mortal in a lifetime," Victor said. "Those are the top three."

"You can only turn one?" Elvi asked with surprise.

"I told you, it's all to keep the population down."

"Yes," she murmured.

"Most immortals save that turn for their lifemate."

"Yes, I guess they would," Elvi said, but was frowning. "Then who turned me and why would they waste their one turning, turning me?"

"DJ and I were wondering about that," Victor admitted, then set his coffee cup down and leaned forward, resting his elbows on his knees. "Elvi, would you tell me exactly what you remember about your turning? Maybe we can sort it out from that."

"I can try," she said unhappily. "But it's all pretty blurry."

"Just close your eyes, relax, and take yourself back there," he suggested.

Elvi smiled faintly. "You sound like a hypnotist."

"I wish I was," Victor admitted, then added, "If I could read your mind I could pull the memory from you myself, but—" He paused, eyebrows rising. "DJ might be able to. We can wait for him and—"

"No," Elvi interrupted quickly. The last thing she wanted was someone poking around in her brain. Besides, no one else seemed to be able to read her, what if DJ couldn't either? That was a complication she didn't need, especially not with Mabel so obviously head over heels for the man.

"Okay, we'll do it the hard way, then," he said wryly. "Sit back, close your eyes, relax and just let yourself go back to that day. You said you were in Mexico . . ."

"Yes," Elvi murmured. "Mabel and I were supposed to stay in a resort, but when we arrived we found there was a problem with their water. Everyone was being moved to other resorts. They'd made arrangements for us too and we got out of our taxi just to be ushered into a van."

"Were there others in this van?" Victor asked.

Elvi nodded. "Three couples and four individuals."

"Describe them," Victor suggested.

"Two of the couples were our age," Elvi said, her brow drawing together as she tried to picture the people in the van. "They were near the front of the van. The other couple was younger. In their forties I think. They were right behind the driver."

"And the other four?" Victor prompted when she paused.

"Three were young women, university students,

I think," she began, and then grimaced. "They were seated at the back and complaining about the lack of "*action*" at the resort and hoping the next one was better." Her voice was surprised as she said that. She'd forgotten all about it, but then she'd spent the better part of the last five years trying to forget that trip.

"And the last person?" Victor asked.

Elvi squinted her eyes more tightly closed, searching her memory for the last man. For some reason, her mind seemed to shy away from him.

"He was seated across the aisle from Mabel and me," she said slowly. "I can't . . . I have a vague recollection of jeans and a dress shirt. Average looks. He was quiet. The rest of us talked some, but he seemed to want to keep mostly to himself."

"How old would you say he was?" Victor asked, sounding tense.

"Mid to late twenties," she said and opened her eyes with realization. All five of the men in her home this week looked to be in that age range. For that matter so did she.

Victor nodded, and then suggested, "Okay, now tell me about the trip itself."

Elvi closed her eyes again. "They told us it would be a five-hour drive. It started out fine. Mabel and I were tired from the flight and napped for the first hour or so. When I woke up, Mabel was chatting with the German couple in front of us. They were a nice couple," she added sadly. Mabel told her afterward that they both died in the crash.

"So, you were chatting with this other couple . . ." Victor prompted.

"The accident happened about an hour after I woke

up." She paused and frowned. "We were on a narrow mountain road. I think the driver swerved to miss something. The next thing I knew we were rolling. Everyone was screaming and the world was topsy-turvy, baggage was flying everywhere.

"The van ended up on its side, on the side Mabel and I were on. I must've been knocked out; I remember waking up to find I was lying on Mabel. I heard her moan and was afraid I may be crushing her, but when I tried to move, pain shot through my head and I think I passed out again."

"And the next time you awoke?"

"That was in the hotel. We were apparently transported there after we were found," Elvi said reluctantly, then ground her teeth together and admitted, "I woke up to find I had fangs and they were sunk in Mabel's throat while she struggled weakly." She opened her eyes to see Victor was wincing at these words and nodded grimly. "Yes. I damn near killed her."

"To be frank, I'm surprised you didn't. It takes a lot of blood for a turning. More than one mortal could supply." Victor frowned with sudden curiosity. "Where *did* you get the blood?"

"Mabel bribed one of the maids. The woman's brother worked at a blood bank. She paid a lot of money for it."

Victor raised his eyebrows. "Well, at least she didn't follow the story of Dracula and think you could only drink from the source. Was your biting her the first clue to your having been turned? And how did you end up at the hotel? The turning makes a mortal very sick. Why didn't you end up in a hospital?"

"I think regaining consciousness after the accident

to find me with my head in a cooler, lapping up spilled blood from burst blood bags was really her first clue," Elvi said dryly.

Victor stiffened. "You didn't mention that."

"Well, it's not really a clear memory," Elvi explained. "And you said to tell you the next thing I remember. Mostly the blood bag episode at the crash site seems like a dream to me and I'm only sure it happened because Mabel said it did."

Victor frowned. "Tell me your memory of it, dreamlike or not."

Elvi paused to collect the memory, and then said, "Well, as I say, it's kind of blurry. I remember waking up and smelling something that . . ." She hesitated, unsure how to describe what she'd felt. She'd been in terrible pain, every inch of her body aching, and that smell had driven her into a frenzy. She'd been desperate to get to it.

"I understand," Victor said. "You must have been amazed when you realized it was blood drawing you so."

"Maybe. I don't remember feeling anything at all except relief. I'd caught the scent, struggled to get free of my seat belt, crawled over Mabel, trailing the smell and there was an open cooler there. It must have been in with the luggage that fell everywhere. The lid was off and one of the bags had burst open. And . . ."

"And you lapped it up, then went after the unburst bags," Victor guessed.

Elvi nodded. "I didn't have anything to open them with, not even fangs at that point, so I was tearing them open with my teeth, getting more blood on me than in me when Mabel woke up and spotted what I was doing. I have a vague recollection of her yelling at me, and then I think I passed out again."

"She said I was already starting to look younger when she found me and that I had a bad gash on my forehead, but an hour later it was gone and I looked younger still. She knew right away something was wrong," Elvi offered. "When someone came across the accident scene and the authorities showed up, they wanted me to go to hospital, but she wouldn't let them take me. She bribed them to take us on to the resort."

Victor was silent for a minute, and then asked, "Are there any other dreamlike memories, prior to that one, that you haven't mentioned?"

"One," Elvi admitted. "But I know that one's a dream."

"Tell me," he insisted.

She closed her eyes, trying to place herself back in the van so that she would remember more clearly. Finally, she said, "The first thing I remember is it was raining."

"Raining?" Victor echoed with bewilderment.

Elvi nodded. "Yes. My mouth was open and filling with water."

"In the bus?" he asked doubtfully.

She nodded. "It tasted funny when I swallowed it. Tinny."

"Like blood," Victor suggested.

Elvi kept her eyes closed. Now that she was examining the memory, it was clearer than it had ever been before. She could actually recall the slow drip, drip, as the liquid hit her tongue and slid down her throat.

"I opened my eyes, and . . . the lone man in his twenties was hanging over me."

She sensed Victor leaning further forward, his body tense. "Hanging over you?"

"The bus was on its side," she reminded him. "His seat belt had kept him in the seat, but he was dangling over us." Elvi could see him there now and cringed. "He'd been injured in the accident." She opened her eyes, banishing the image. "That's how I knew it was a dream. Mabel said she saw him after the accident and he was just fine. Uninjured."

"Forget about that," Victor instructed. "I want you to close your eyes and picture the scene again. What exactly did you see?"

Elvi reluctantly closed her eyes. She allowed the memory to blossom in her mind despite its unpleasantness. "His eyes were closed. I thought he was dead. There was a large, sharp triangle of glass in his stomach, and another in his upper shoulder. It had pretty much sliced his arm off and there was blood running down his dangling arm and dripping . . ."

"Into your mouth," Victor said with triumph.

Elvi opened her eyes with amazement. "Yes."

"You really are an accidental vampire," he said with a grin that then faded. "I'm surprised he didn't realize what had happened when he woke up and saw you jonesing for blood."

"I don't think he did," Elvi said with a frown. "Mabel says she got me out of the van and away from the others when she realized something was wrong with me."

"That was very brave of her," Victor said solemnly. "Especially if she suspected what you had become."

"Yes," Elvi agreed. "She's a good friend. She got me to the hotel, arranged for blood for me, and then called Teddy and had him overnight Casey's passport to us in Mexico."

"Your daughter's?"

"Yes. Mabel wanted to fly me home right away, but my passport picture showed me with graying hair and wrinkles . . ."

"And you didn't look like that anymore," he murmured.

Elvi nodded. "I don't think I would have survived if Mabel hadn't been there to take care of everything. She kept me alive, got me home, talked to Teddy and some others and smoothed it over so they didn't come after me with stakes." She grinned. "Somehow she presented it to the town as a really cool adventure rather than a horror story, and I was the tragic hero rather than a monster."

"But to yourself, you were a monster," Victor guessed quietly.

Elvi eyed him solemnly. "I nearly killed her."

"You were out of your head, Elvi. She knows that. If the situation had been reversed and Mabel had been the one turned that day, or if it had been Casey, how would you feel?"

Elvi released a shaky sigh. She'd carried the guilt of that episode in her heart for five years and it wasn't going to wash away that easily. And she didn't want to think about it. It was time for a change of subject, she decided.

"Are you ready to talk about what happened earlier between us yet?" Victor asked suddenly, and Elvi glanced at him with alarm. This was not the topic change she'd wanted. She was not ready to talk about the possibility of their being lifemates.

When a brief, panicked search of her mind didn't turn up any ideas for another topic change, Elvi simply leaned forward and kissed him. In her experience, that was always a good way to silence a man. At least, it had always worked with her husband.

It worked well with Victor too, she realized when he caught her by the waist and drew her off the sofa to settle on his lap in the wicker chair.

Smiling against his mouth, Elvi slid her arms around his shoulders, and then stiffened when a sudden sharp pain exploded between her shoulder blades and vibrated outward, stealing her breath and consciousness.

"Elvi?" Victor murmured uncertainly when she went limp in his arms.

Pulling back, he used a hand to catch her face by the chin and tilt it back, frowning when he saw her closed eyes and pale, slack face. Concern immediately claimed him. It was one thing for her to faint at the climax of their lovemaking, that was normal for immortals on first joining, but they'd hardly started here.

"Elvi?" he said again and gently slapped her cheek. When he got no response, Victor started to move the hand at her back, intending to lift her and set her on the sofa so he could go get a wet cloth or something, but he froze when his hand brushed something hard.

Tugging her forward against his chest, Victor peered over her shoulder and down, his heart stopping at the sight of the arrow protruding from her back.

Fifteen

"I guess this means the first arrow wasn't an accident, and answers the question of who the target is," DJ murmured as he watched Victor pop another bag of blood to Elvi's teeth.

Victor grunted. In truth, he'd rather have been the target himself than see Elvi like this. He'd been frantic when he realized she'd been shot. Standing with her clasped against his chest, he'd crossed the sunroom, glancing out at the dark yard beyond as he passed the window. He hadn't seen anyone below, but the shooter could have been hiding in the shadows.

Leaving the hunt for her shooter for later, Victor had carried Elvi into her room to tend her, grateful that DJ and Mabel had chosen that moment to return home and that the younger immortal had come in search of him.

DJ had taken one look at Elvi on the bed with the

arrow in her back, and promptly yelled for Mabel to bring blood up at once. He'd then slipped into Elvi's bathroom for some towels, and settled on the opposite side of the bed, offering support and encouragement as Victor began the incredibly delicate task of removing the arrow without causing further damage.

Mabel had arrived with blood just as Victor finished pulling the arrow. Much to his relief, Mabel hadn't gone into hysterics. She'd been upset and demanded to know what had happened, but hadn't gone about shrieking or fainting or anything of that ilk. Modern women, it seemed, were a sturdy bunch.

"Her wound is healing," Victor muttered as he switched blood bags. He'd already given her four bags and her wound was obviously closing. At least it certainly looked smaller to him, still she wasn't showing any sign of waking yet, but there would no doubt be internal damage to be repaired as well.

"The men are wondering what's going on," Mabel announced, returning from another blood run. "My bringing up all this blood has tipped them to the fact that something is going on."

"What did you tell them?" Victor asked, taking the blood from her and setting it on the side of the bed.

"Nothing, I just waved away their questions, and came back up here."

"They'll follow her up then," DJ said with a frown.

"They already have," Edward announced from the now crowded doorway.

Elvi heard the murmur of voices and wondered fuzzily who was standing outside her coffin talking. It was only when she opened her eyes that she recalled she no longer slept in a coffin. She was on her stomach in her bed, and her room was full of people. Victor, Mabel, DJ, Harper, Alessandro, and Edward were all there from the voices she could hear.

"Who would want to hurt Elvi?" Harper was asking with dismay.

"I don't know, but I intend to find out," Victor said grimly.

Elvi frowned, trying to understand what they were talking about. Hurt her? Had someone hurt her? She'd barely asked herself the question when she spotted the bloody arrow on the side of the bed and recalled sitting on Victor's lap in the sunroom and a sharp pain in the back.

So that had been the source of the pain. She stared at the bloody arrow and recalled the one that had narrowly missed them at the furniture store. Elvi had been sure then that it was an accident and, if not, then it had been meant for Victor. She'd lived in Port Henry her entire life. No one here would harm her, she'd thought. And still thought that.

Elvi briefly struggled with what had happened, trying to make sense of it, and then stiffened as an idea struck her. She turned cautiously onto her back, relieved when there was no pain. It seemed she was healed.

"We must find who did this," Alessandro said furiously. "They can not hurt the Elvi. She is good woman, so bella, so sweet."

"Yes, and we will have to guard her until we do," Harper murmured.

"Then you'll be guarding the wrong person," Elvi announced, drawing their attention as she managed to sit up. While there was no pain, she was feeling a bit weak and suspected she needed more blood to replace that used up in the healing.

"Elvi." Victor hurried to the bed, concern on his face. "You shouldn't be moving around yet."

"I'm fine," she assured him, but was frowning at the weakness hampering her and asked, "Is there more blood?"

"I'll go get more," Mabel assured her and rushed from the room as the men moved to surround the bed.

"How are you feeling?" Harper asked, his face lined with concern.

"Fine," she repeated, then admitted, "A little weak maybe, but fine."

"What did you mean we'd be protecting the wrong person if we guarded you?" Edward asked curiously.

"I wasn't the target," Elvi announced.

"Elvi," Victor said, shaking his head. "You were shot in the back. You had to be the target."

"I don't think I was," she argued pleasantly.

"Well, I doubt I was. They'd hardly shoot through you to get to me."

"No, but—" Elvi fell silent and smiled at Mabel as she rushed in with four more bags of blood. Murmuring a *"thank you,"* she accepted the bag Mabel held out and slapped it to her teeth, giving herself the time to try to find a way to explain what she was thinking. By the second bag, she'd decided that showing would be more effective than trying to explain and slid her feet off the bed to stand up.

"What are you doing?" Victor asked, sounding alarmed. "You shouldn't be up yet. Allow your body time to—"

"I feel fine," Elvi said with exasperation as she took the second empty bag away. "I'm not suffering any pain, and most of the weakness is gone thanks to the blood."

"Yes, but a little rest wouldn't go amiss," Harper said, cutting off whatever Victor had opened his mouth to say. Judging from his expression, it hadn't been as diplomatic as Harper's words and she suspected he'd done the man a favor by cutting him off.

"Probably," Elvi said agreeably as she accepted a third bag from Mabel, then added firmly, "and I will after I make one trip downstairs."

There was rumbling all around at this announcement, but Elvi ignored the men and leaned to whisper in Mabel's ear. When she'd straightened and her friend nodded, Elvi turned to the men.

"Come with me and I'll prove I wasn't the target," she said, then slapped the latest bag to her teeth and headed for the door.

The men followed, protesting the whole way, but Elvi ignored them, merely glancing back to see that DJ wasn't one of them following. She smiled around the bag in her mouth when Mabel caught the man's arm and urged him the other way, toward the door to the sunroom.

"Elvi, this is ridiculous," Victor said impatiently as he followed her downstairs and into the kitchen. "You should be resting and recuperating, not— You aren't going outside!" he exclaimed, catching her arm to draw her to a halt when he realized she was heading for the door.

"It's perfectly safe . . . for me. Maybe you should wait here, though," she suggested with sudden concern, but really wanted him to see this too. Her gaze slid to the others. "Do you think you could position yourselves around Victor in case the archer is still here? I don't think he'll shoot if he can't get a clear shot."

"Don't be ridiculous," Victor snapped when the men voiced their agreement. "I'm not the target—Wait for me," he snapped when she turned to head out of the house.

Much to her annoyance, the men decided it was better safe than sorry and surrounded both she and Victor the moment they were outside. Shaking her head, Elvi merely directed them off the deck and to the back of her property. Once there the whole group turned to peer up through the sunroom windows.

"What do you see?" she asked.

"Is that the DJ in the sunroom?" Alessandro asked with surprise, obviously not having noticed he hadn't come out with them.

"Yes," Elvi said, noting that only his upper body was visible from this angle, then repeated, "What do you see?"

There was a moment of silence as the men cast perplexed looks her way, then Harper said, "DJ sitting in the sunroom."

"No, you don't," Elvi argued.

"Si, we do," Alessandro assured her.

"No. You see the silhouette of DJ sitting in the sunroom," she pointed out. "The light is behind the chair and prevents you from distinguishing features."

"True," Edward acknowledged. "But—"

"Okay!" Elvi called out to the house and the dark shape of DJ began to shift, mutating and then separating into a seated DJ and a standing woman as Mabel repositioned herself beside the chair.

"What just happened?" Alessandro asked with confusion. "Is that the Mabel?"

"Yes," Elvi said. "She was sitting on DJ's lap, just as I was sitting on Victor's when I was hit by the arrow."

"They wouldn't have seen you," Harper said with realization. "Just his silhouette."

Elvi turned to Victor. "They were aiming for you. I just got in the way."

When he didn't argue, but stood frowning at the couple in the sunroom, she added, "I'll call Teddy about this in the morning and see what he can do. In the meantime, it might be better if you stay in the house . . . and away from windows."

Elvi found herself harassed back into bed after this little exercise. She didn't argue. The little jaunt had exhausted her. She obviously wasn't fully recovered yet. Leaving Mabel and the men to debate what they should do about the unknown assailant who seemed to be after Victor, Elvi trudged upstairs to her bed and fell asleep almost at once.

Of course, going to sleep so early had her waking early and Elvi opened her eyes to a treat she hadn't enjoyed for a long time; sunlight was backlighting the dark red blinds of her room, not getting in, but lightening them to a rose color. Smiling at the sight, she glanced toward the digital clock and caught her breath. It wasn't even noon yet. She could go out and work in the garden.

Pushing the sheets aside, Elvi hopped out of bed and rushed into the bathroom. She was in and out of the shower and dressed in record time, and then flew from her room.

"Good morning," Mabel greeted her with surprise

as she came around the corner into the kitchen–dining area. "You're up early."

"So are you." Elvi smiled at the woman. Mabel had started out working the day shift in the restaurant, but had found herself staying up later and later to keep Elvi company through the long lonely hours of the night when nothing in their small town was open. The woman had eventually adjusted to a later shift as well.

"DJ and I went to bed right after you," she murmured. The blush that rose up to cover her cheeks seemed to suggest they hadn't spent the entire time sleeping.

Turning her face away to hide a grin, Elvi moved to the refrigerator and retrieved a bag of blood. She had the first bag while standing there with the fridge door open, then grabbed a second bag and slapped it to her teeth, closed the door and walked over to deposit the empty bag in the garbage can. Elvi then walked over to peer out the window while she waited for the second bag to disappear.

A little sigh slid around the bag in her mouth as she peered out at the sunlit yard. Maple trees, spruce trees and lilac trees lined the sides and back, interspersed with irises, rose bushes, climbing clematis and various other flowers. A birdbath sat near the back right corner by a white bower and as Elvi pulled the now empty bag from her teeth, she chuckled at the sight of two birds splashing and flapping around in it.

"Maybe you shouldn't be so close to the window," Mabel said with concern.

"Victor said I could go out in sunlight," Elvi reminded her as she threw out the second bag.

"Yes, but it will weaken you," Mabel told her. "You want to avoid it as much as possible."

Elvi snorted at the suggestion. Far from wanting to avoid it, she wanted to run out there and roll around naked in it. God, she'd missed the sun.

"Mabel's right," DJ announced coming into the kitchen from the foyer. "The more exposure you get, the more blood you will need."

"But I want to go outside in the garden," Elvi said and frowned at the childlike whine in her own voice. She turned to peer out at the yard, feeling like a penniless child staring through the window of a sweetshop, mouth watering over the sight of all those lovely treats, but knowing she couldn't have them.

"You can go out, but you need to be careful," DJ said soothingly. "You'll have to wear long sleeves and a hat and gloves, and stay in the shade as much as possible. And you'll have to double up on blood."

Elvi frowned guiltily. She survived on blood the townspeople donated and didn't want to burden them any more than she had, but she so wanted to go out in the garden.

"Go on," DJ said quietly. "Go put on a long-sleeved shirt and find a hat with a big brim. And switch those capri pants for long-legged slacks."

Elvi didn't have to be told twice, turning on her heel; she jogged back upstairs to change. She would restrict her forays into daylight, but she was definitely going out today.

By the time she was finished changing, Elvi's room looked like a small tornado had hit it. She'd tossed her clothes off, throwing them willy-nilly and leaving them where they landed, hopping back to the door as she was still pulling on a pair of dark slacks. Elvi did up the buttons of her blouse in the hall on the way to the stairs and arrived downstairs lacking only a hat and gloves.

Fortunately, Mabel had those for her. She also had sunscreen, and under DJ's instruction, slathered it on so thick that it was a series of white streaks on her skin.

Elvi suffered all this uncomplaining, knowing the pair were just trying to look after her, but the moment they decided they'd done the best they could to protect her and stepped out of the way, Elvi was off like a racehorse leaving its stall. Charging forward, she slammed through the kitchen door and out onto the back deck, only to pause there and stand frozen, shaking with excitement and a little fear under the midday sun.

She didn't burst into flames, which was a relief, and while the sun felt lovely warm on her skin, it wasn't burning hot or anything. It felt quite lovely. Elvi let loose a little sigh of mingled relief and pleasure, then walked to the edge of the deck, and paused again, her gaze moving over her garden, taking in everything.

Before the turn, Elvi had spent hours everyday in her garden; weeding, planting, pruning, watering. She used to keep feeders with seed for birds and used to leave out peanuts for the squirrels, chipmunks, and blue jays, and bread for the finches. Every day she spent some time just relaxing and watching the animals come for their fare. That all ended when she was turned.

The bird feeders now sat empty and neglected, most of them in poor repair. The birdbath had water in it, but only because it had rained last night. It was in desperate need of cleaning. As for the garden itself, it had grown wild over the last five years. One day wasn't going to be enough to repair the damage time had done. Two weeks of working from dawn to dusk wouldn't have been enough time, and Elvi felt her shoulders slump with disappointment.

By moonlight, the garden hadn't looked nearly this bad. It seemed obvious that she was going to need help with this project. She'd have to hire landscapers or something to do most of it, Elvi realized. She'd look into that next week, once the men were gone, but for now she could at least do some of it herself and see what was left of the garden she'd tended so lovingly before the turn.

"Elvi?"

It took a moment for her to realize where the voice came from. She actually glanced back toward the house before thinking to glance toward her neighbor's backyard. There was a privacy fence between her property and Mike and Karen Knight's, but the deck was raised a good two and a half feet, allowing her a view into their backyard. Elvi used to stop and talk to them over the fence before the turn, but between not thinking she could go out during the day and her evenings being taken up with the restaurant, she hadn't had a chat over the fence since the turn.

A smile curved her lips when she spotted Karen standing beside a basket of laundry on the other side of the fence. The woman was gaping at her.

"Surprise, huh?" Elvi asked wryly. Of course, as far as everyone knew, she couldn't go out in daylight. There would be a lot of surprised people in the near future. Karen wasn't a gossip, so the news of her being out in daylight wouldn't go far until someone else saw her.

Closing her mouth, Karen abandoned her laundry and approached the fence. "What are you doing out during the day? Should you be? And are you all right? You look awfully pale."

"I'm fine. The white is just suntan lotion," Elvi assured her with a laugh. "And, yes, I can be out here as long as I'm careful. Isn't it wonderful?"

"That's marvelous," Karen grinned, but there was still worry on her face and Elvi knew everyone would worry at first. They were used to her hiding from sunlight, it would take time for them to adjust.

"Is Owen working today?" Elvi asked to distract the woman from her concern. Summer would soon be over and school starting again. She knew Owen would be going back for one more year to pick up some extra credits, but in the meantime he had a couple of part-time jobs in the summer. However, rather than distract the woman from her worry, the question backfired, making the concern deepen.

"No." Karen glanced toward the house with a small frown. "He doesn't work until later in the day. He's still sleeping right now."

"Still?" Elvi asked with surprise. It was nearing noon.

"Yes, it's all he seems to do lately," Karen murmured with a troubled expression, then forced a little laugh and said, "Teenagers!"

"Yes." Elvi smiled faintly. Even Casey had gone through a period where she slept a lot.

"Well." Karen managed a more natural smile. "Does this mean we can expect you at the fair earlier in the day than you usually come?"

"The fair?" Elvi asked blankly.

"For the Abused Kids' Shelter," Karen reminded her and laughed teasingly. "All those men in the house didn't make you forget, did they? I hope not. Your booth makes loads of money."

Elvi's mind slowly recalled what she was talking about. The end-of-summer fair. It started Thursday and ran through to Sunday. Elvi usually had a biting booth and also baked—

"And your pies, of course. They always sell like hot-cakes," Karen added. She made a face. "I wish I could make crust as flaky as yours. You know Mike will insist I buy at least six and freeze four for later."

"Pies!" Elvi finished her thought aloud in a panicked voice, then catching Karen's surprised face, explained, "I forgot all about it. Oh, damn! I have to go!"

Whirling on her heel, Elvi raced for the house.

It was late when Victor woke up. He'd spent the better part of the night and morning watching over Elvi while she slept. The men seemed just as convinced as Elvi that no one would try to harm her and he must be the target. Edward had even gone so far as to suggest that perhaps he shouldn't spend time around her since it seemed to be putting her in harm's way. The hell of it was, Edward was right. If he was the target, then her being too close to him had got her hurt last night.

Sighing, he rolled on his back and stared at the ceiling. He'd been leaning heavily toward Edward being behind the attacks directly after Elvi was hurt. The fact that the immortal had been missing from the parking lot in front of the furniture store when the first arrow had been launched, not to mention that the men had been home last night when the second arrow was shot had made him briefly suspect him, but after thinking about it last night, it just didn't make sense.

Any immortal would know an arrow wouldn't kill another immortal, even if lodged in the heart. So long as the arrow was removed, the nanos would heal the wound, set the heart pumping again, and the immortal would be fine . . . unless their head was cut off or something while they were down.

No, the use of the arrow suggested a mortal to him. It was basically a wooden stake with flights and a metal tip and mortals might think it would work if shot through the heart. As far as Victor knew, he hadn't pissed off any mortals lately in Port Henry. He'd only been here a matter of days.

Besides, what if the archer had seen Elvi move onto his lap and saw their silhouettes merge into one? The arrow had hit soon enough after they'd started to kiss for that to be more than possible. Which meant they were back to his not knowing who the target was and fretting over Elvi, which was why he'd stood guard over her while she slept, watching over her until he heard stirring from Mabel's room and had realized he was dozing off in the chair he'd placed next to her bed.

Sure she was safe with Mabel and DJ up and about, Victor finally took himself off to feed and then to bed. He'd briefly considered sleeping in her room, but hadn't wanted to do so without getting her permission first and hadn't been willing to wake her to get it. But now he wished he had. It would have been nice to wake with her lying beside him, to be able to roll over and slip his arms around her, pull her close and press his nose to her neck and inhale the scent of her. Their coming together had been explosive and he'd had trouble keeping it out of his thoughts ever since . . . until he'd seen the arrow protruding from her back. That had been a bucket of ice water on such thoughts, leaving him sick with concern and fury, a fury he hadn't been able to vent, but had been forced to push down and ignore.

Now he felt it tugging at his emotions again and resolutely got out of bed. Anger wouldn't help them in this matter. It would simply cloud his judgment and possibly slow his reactions. He needed a clear head to handle the situation and keep Elvi safe. Unfortunately, he already knew that a clear head would be hard to maintain around Elvi. She was his lifemate. Whether the other men could read her or not, in his mind she had made her choice by making love with him. She was his. His mind had already accepted that and was running on overdrive, putting thoughts and ideas and plans for the future in his head. A future they wouldn't have if she got killed.

It seemed to him that the best way to deal with the matter was to try to keep his distance as Edward had suggested. Keeping an eye on her, but not staying close enough to put her in harm's way, and giving himself some distance in the hopes that his brain would be able to function seemed the best way to proceed. He wasn't happy with this bit of logic. His whole being was crying out to be close to her, but he was going to have to ignore that to keep her safe.

It was going to be a struggle.

After showering and dressing, Victor made his way to Elvi's room, fully expecting her to be lying peacefully in bed, getting the sleep he felt sure her body needed. Instead, he found himself staring at an empty, unmade bed and a floor with clothes lying strewn about.

Pulling the door closed with a snap, Victor turned and hurried downstairs, rushing into the kitchen only to jerk to a halt in amazement.

Elvi was alive and well and presently covered with a fine dusting of flour as she worked frantically at something on the dining room table. So were Edward, Alessandro, and Harper.

"Is this better, Elvi?" Alessandro held up what appeared to be a pie of some sort.

"Much, Alessandro." Elvi beamed at the man. "Definitely a seller. Put it over with the others to be filled."

"My crust keeps breaking," Edward growled impatiently, dipping his fingers in a bowl of some liquid and then rubbing them over a crack that had appeared in the crust he was working with.

"You're doing fine," Elvi assured him. "They always crack."

Edward muttered something under his breath, but repaired the crack and carefully lifted the shell into a foil pie plate, releasing a small breath of relief when he managed to do so without the shell falling apart in his hands.

"Well done," Elvi encouraged, patting his arm briefly before her gaze slipped to Harper's efforts. The German didn't appear to be having any trouble at all with his own pie. If anything, he was wielding the rolling pin and handling the crust with the finesse of a professional. And Victor wasn't the only one to notice.

"You're very good at this, Harper," Elvi said curiously. "I take it you've done this before?"

"Hmm. I was the personal chef for emperor-elect Maximilian I when I was younger," Harper informed her.

"Emperor-elect Maximilian I?" Elvi asked uncertainly.

"The easiest way to explain it is to say he was like a king to the eastern Franks," the man explained with a shrug.

Victor didn't think Elvi was too sure she understood, but rather than ask for a history lesson, she nodded and turned her attention back to her own pie, deftly lifting the crust into an aluminum pie plate.

"Does someone want to tell me why the four of you are playing Betty Crocker?" Victor asked finally. His gaze then slid to the counter where some twenty pie crusts sat waiting to be filled and he added, "And who the hell are all these pies for?"

Elvi raised her head and offered a surprised smile. "Oh, good morning, Victor."

Spotting the smudge of flour on her cheek and nose, Victor found himself smiling back. She was so adorable.

"The pies are for the end of summer fair," she explained, answering the last question first. "The proceeds will go to help the Abused Kids' Shelter. I'm afraid I'd quite forgotten all about it what with your arrival and everything. Fortunately, the men were kind enough to offer their help."

"Harper volunteered us," Edward corrected with a grimace.

"It's only fair. We are here for free, eating the food and consuming the blood. Is little enough to make some pies," Alessandro said with a shrug.

Edward muttered something under his breath, but the fact that he was there helping suggested he agreed. He wasn't someone who did things he didn't want to, so it seemed obvious he was willing to help. Victor supposed the grumbling was purely to ensure his machismo wasn't affected by participating in this womanly chore.

He watched them work for another moment, then heaved a sigh and moved toward the table. "So, what can I do to help?"

Sixteen

"There." Elvi sealed the lid on the last pie and stepped back with a relieved sigh. It had been a hectic two days, but they'd done it. One hundred pies. They'd finished more than half of them yesterday before staggering off to their various beds, then Elvi had woken before the others again today and set right back to work, grateful when the men had joined her again as they woke.

Elvi peered over the results with weary satisfaction. At least the visible results, most of the pies were already baked and sitting on shelves in the cupboard room between the garage and kitchen. There were also a dozen down in the cold room, waiting for their turn in the oven, and these last six here in the kitchen that she and the men had just finished with.

All she had to do was bake the eighteen left and

box them and they were all set for tomorrow. And she couldn't have done it without the men. Alessandro had tried to rush, messing up more than he'd made at first, and Edward was a very slow, meticulous worker, but Harper had been a dream and Victor had proven to be a skilled pie maker once shown how to do it. So, shortly after Victor had joined their efforts, Elvi had set Alessandro and Edward to peeling apples and cooking the cherries for the fillings, and that had worked well.

"These look done," Victor announced from where he stood bent over, peering into the oven. "Should I take them out and switch them for three more?"

"Yes, please." Elvi picked up two of the pies from the table, smiling when Harper hurried over and picked up a third with his free hand. His other was holding a bag of blood to his mouth. As each man had finished their last pie, they'd moved to the fridge in search of sustenance. All except Victor, who had moved to the oven to inspect the pies presently baking.

Come to think of it, Elvi realized, she'd never seen Victor feed. It made her wonder if he had to feed less because of his age, or if he was just shy about feeding in front of others. She pondered the matter as she waited for Victor to lift out the last of the three pies in the oven. Once he'd removed the last one, Elvi slid in both of the pies she carried, and then turned to take the last one from Harper. When she straightened from placing it on the oven shelf, she closed the door and turned away to find Victor at her side, holding out a bag of blood.

"Thank you." Elvi took it, and then asked, "Aren't you going to have one?"

The sudden silence in the room was startling. All eyes

had turned to Victor with an odd, expectant silence, but he merely shrugged and turned away, muttering, "Not right now."

Elvi frowned, noting that the men were all now evading her eyes and concentrating on feeding or throwing out the bag they'd just finished, depending on where they were in the process. Elvi glanced from one man to the other, then to Victor again and commented, "I don't remember you having any when you got up."

Each man had headed to the refrigerator for a bag of blood or two on entering the kitchen, fed, and then disposed of the bags before joining her at the table. All of them except Victor. He'd walked straight to the table without detouring to feed.

"We have refrigerators in our room," he reminded her, and then said, "I'll take these pies down to the cold room."

He collected two of the pies they'd just finished making and headed for the door to the basement. Harper grabbed the last pie, stepped forward to open the door, then followed him down and pulled it closed behind them.

"So, what are we going to do now?" Edward asked ending the silence in the room once the two men were gone. "Bake brownies or some other entertaining pastime?"

Elvi smiled faintly at his sarcasm. The man really needed some social skills. It was no wonder the other men disliked him, but they'd been wrong about his playing nice with her. She was the brunt of his sarcastic comments as often as the others. He really didn't seem to like others much. If he ever wished to get himself a lifemate, he really needed to work on that.

"Actually, I was thinking that I would take you gentlemen out for supper and drinks as a thank-you for all your help with this," Elvi informed him.

"Where?" Edward asked doubtfully.

Elvi shrugged, "Well, we could go to Bella Black's for dinner, or—"

"No, thank you," he said at once.

Elvi bit her lip, wondering if he'd just insulted her restaurant. "Well, as I was going to say before I was so rudely interrupted, or there are a couple other restaurants in town that—"

"Elvi, my dear," Edward interrupted. "I wasn't slagging your restaurant when I said no. I'm sure the food there is wonderful, it certainly smelled delicious while we were there. However, while you may be content to be the local pet, I'd rather not be stared and whispered over all night," the man said dryly, then added, "Eating or drinking anywhere in this town is hardly relaxing."

"*'Pet'*?" Elvi echoed.

"I'm afraid the Edward he is right," Alessandro said gently. "Is not so comfortable here with everyone doing the staring and whispering. At the play with the Knights, we watch the show, but everyone else, they watch us. Is better we go elsewhere I think."

Elvi let her breath out on a little sigh, dropping her contention with Edward's use of the term pet . . . for now. She did understand what the men were saying. It had been the same when she'd first returned, but had eased with time. Now that the men were here, it had started all over again.

"Well, we could go into the city," she suggested.

"The city?" Alessandro asked with interest, but Edward said, "Carousing with a bunch of drunken mortals isn't exactly an alternative we'd be interested in."

"Well, I'm afraid there isn't much choice," Elvi said with exasperation. "As far as I know, most people are mortals. You're the first vampires I've met in five years around here."

"That you know of," Edward pointed out. "Unfortunately, lacking in training as you are, I don't think you'd recognize an *immortal* unless they bit you . . . which of course they wouldn't do because *they'd* know you were an immortal and so your blood would be useless to them."

Elvi scowled with irritation, wondering why he was still here. If he hadn't just spent the last two days helping her make pies, she'd have asked him outright to leave. He really had no chance with her as a lifemate. Even if she weren't already involved with Victor, Edward was just too annoying to suit her.

"Toronto is only two or three hours away," Alessandro piped up. "We could go to the Night Club."

Elvi opened her mouth to ask what the night club was when the door to the garage opened and Mabel led DJ into the house. Forgetting about the night club for the moment, she eyed the pair with surprise. "You're home early."

Mabel shrugged. "I left Pedro in charge. DJ and I wanted some time alone."

"Oh." Elvi was surprised, but supposed she shouldn't have been. While Mabel had intended on taking over all responsibility for the restaurant while Elvi got to know her "dates," she hadn't counted on falling in love with DJ, and that's what she'd done. By her guess, it wouldn't be long before the issue of turning came up and Elvi was hoping she'd agree.

"What are you guys doing? Going out anywhere?"

DJ looked hopeful. It seemed obvious he was hoping for some time alone with Mabel.

"We are thinking to go to the Night Club," Alessandro announced.

"What's the Night Club?" Mabel asked the question their entrance had stopped Elvi from asking, and then shifted out of the way as the door to the basement opened and Victor and Harper rejoined them.

"It is the Night Club," Alessandro said with a shrug. "Is bar, where immortals go at night."

"Of course, it keeps longer hours than mortal bars and clubs, and the beverages are more to our liking," Edward added.

"Hmm." Elvi was curious. The idea of a bar filled with immortals was tantalizing. She might meet other female immortals who could help her with things that a male immortal wouldn't even think of addressing. But her eyes slid to the clock on the stove and she felt disappointment claim her.

"Three hours there, three hours back, and I'd have to shower and change," she shook her head unhappily. "I don't think—"

"We can do it," Harper interrupted firmly. "I'll have my helicopter collect us. We'll be there in a trice. You get ready. I shall arrange everything."

"A helicopter? Really?" Elvi asked with amazement. She'd known from their cars that these men were well off, but a personal helicopter? Holy! The guy must be loaded. Her gaze slid to Victor then and she frowned when she saw that he was looking less than pleased at the idea of the outing.

"Yes, really." Harper gave her a gentle push. "Go on. Get ready."

"But what about the pies?" Elvi said reluctantly.

"I'll bake them for you," Mabel announced, catching Elvi's arm and urging her toward the stairs. "Come on. I'll help you get ready. You can wear that red dress with the slit up the side."

Elvi allowed herself to be hurried upstairs. It bothered her that Victor didn't seem pleased with the idea of the outing, but she was too curious to see this club for immortals to let it stop her. Mabel got out the red dress she'd mentioned while Elvi showered, then helped with her hair and makeup and accessories before helping her dress.

Elvi smiled as she peered down at the deep red cocktail dress with its short skirt and halter top. She'd never expected to get the chance to wear it when she'd bought it. All she ever wore was black at the restaurant and events, but she hadn't been able to help herself when she saw it in the store. Now she was glad she hadn't.

Once finished zipping her up, Mabel stepped back and grinned.

"You are so going to turn on Victor in that," she chuckled and urged her to the door. "Come on. You guys have been working like crazy to get those pies done the last two days, and I know you haven't got a chance to repeat the garage scene with Victor. Have fun tonight. You never have fun anymore, and you deserve it. So promise me you'll try to relax and have fun."

"I promise," Elvi laughed, her anticipation for the night ahead suddenly increasing exponentially. She and Victor hadn't even kissed the last two days since the arrow incident. There simply hadn't been an opportunity with all of the men working on the pies. While Elvi had known that, she'd still felt slightly bereft that he hadn't even tried to sneak a kiss or something here or there. Or slid into her room at night to rouse her with kisses and caresses. Without the real thing, Elvi had found herself suffering—or enjoying, depending on how you looked at it—some pretty erotic dreams. Dreams that had seemed incredibly real and left her waking panting and dripping with sweat among other things.

Not that she was complaining, it was better than the nightmares she normally had about her husband and daughter's death and her own accident in Mexico. Still, the real thing would have been more reassuring. Elvi was starting to doubt his interest in her and knew that was silly. He was the one who had claimed she was his lifemate.

"Ah, *bella,* you are perfection on the legs," Alessandro proclaimed coming up the hall as Mabel joined her outside her bedroom door.

"Does that mean the rest of me is okay but my legs are ugly?" Elvi asked with amusement.

"No!" Alessandro looked horrified that she might think so. "No, *bella.* You have the beautiful legs; so slender, so shapely, every man's dream."

"Oh, Alessandro, you're such a flirt." Elvi laughed, shaking her head as she led the way to the stairs.

"This is a bad thing?" Alessandro asked, sounding concerned.

"Not at all," she assured him lightly. "It's just that I suspect you're just as effusive with every woman you meet, and it makes it difficult to take you seriously."

"That is bad," he said on an unhappy sigh. "The Canadians, they are so sensible, much like the British. As are the Americans. You have no soul, no romance in you. Not like we Italians. To us love is everything and beauty is something to be celebrated. Women should be kissed and told they are *bella*."

"How long have you been in Canada?" Elvi asked with a sudden curiosity.

"Ten years."

"Why did you come?"

"Why not?" he asked with a shrug. "We try not to stay too long in the one place. Ten years, maybe. We no age. Stay too long, it brings the questions. So we go. Another place, then another, and maybe twenty . . . thirty years we go home as a cousin, the son, or someone else. By then, those who knew us they have moved, or aged, or died, or simply do not remember us and we are safe for another ten years before we must move again."

"How awful," Elvi said with real sympathy. "I can't imagine having to live like that."

"Ah, but you don't have to," he pointed out. "You have the good setup here. Your people, they love you, and protect you from needing to do this."

"Yes," Elvi agreed quietly. While her life wasn't perfect, she did have a home she didn't have to leave and didn't have to constantly worry about hiding what she was, which allowed her to enjoy the love and support of her friends and neighbors.

"There you are!" Edward said with annoyance when they came around the corner into the kitchen. "We've been waiting—"

"But you are surely worth every minute of the wait," Harper interrupted gallantly, crossing the room to take her hand and press a kiss to the back of her fingers.

Flushing with embarrassment, Elvi glanced over his bowed head to Victor. He leaned against the low wall, his expression unreadable. She wasn't sure how he felt about Harper's gallant greeting, but he wasn't making an effort to approach her himself.

"Your chariot awaits, my lady." Harper settled her hand on his arm and urged her to the door leading out onto the deck.

Elvi had thought they'd have to drive to the nearest airport where his helicopter would be waiting. She'd thought wrong. With the other men following, Harper escorted her across the deck and down the sidewalk to the driveway, but then continued past the cars parked there.

"What—" Elvi began with confusion, only to pause as she spotted the helicopter in the school yard across the street.

"My pilot is one of the best," Harper informed her with pride. "He can land this contraption anywhere."

"So I see," Elvi said with a laugh as they started across the street.

"Have you ever been in a helicopter before?" he asked, eyes shining. When Elvi shook her head, he grinned. "Then this shall be a treat."

Elvi didn't know about a treat, but it certainly was an experience. One she wasn't entirely sure she enjoyed. It was quick, though, quicker than driving would have been, and it wasn't long before they were setting down on a helipad on the rooftop of a building in downtown Toronto.

"What did you think?" Harper asked expectantly as they rode down to ground level in a rather luxurious elevator.

"I think I need a drink," Elvi said honestly. The men all laughed as if she was joking, but Elvi was pretty sure she'd left her stomach behind in the school yard.

"The Night Club is several blocks from here. Will you be able to manage in those shoes?" Victor asked, speaking for the first time since her arrival in the kitchen.

"I think so," Elvi said, and was sure it was true. Part of her outfit each night at the restaurant included high-heeled black shoes. She was quite used to walking and standing in the items.

Victor nodded, and immediately returned to his previous silence, even stepping back for Harper to escort her as the elevator doors opened. She felt like a football passed off to the other man in a game and couldn't help resenting it. Where had his interest gone? The other night he was claiming she was his lifemate and now he seemed to be staying as far away from her as possible.

Hurt, Elvi felt her lip tremble, then bit it viciously and raised her chin as Harper escorted her out of the building. If he wasn't interested anymore, fine. She had three other suitors to take his place. Her heart cried out that none of those three men were Victor, but Elvi's pride insisted it would have to be enough.

Slipping off her shoes under the table, Elvi peered around the Night Club. She wasn't at all sure what she'd expected, but this wasn't it. With its loud music, flashing lights, and tables crowded around a dance floor, it could have been any mortal nightclub in any city in the world. Not that she'd thought there would be coffins for tables or upside-down crosses on the walls, but really, had she wandered in here by mistake, she was sure there was no way she would know it wasn't a mortal nightclub.

"What can I get you folks?"

Elvi glanced to their waitress. Short, blond, and cute, the girl was no more than twenty-two or twenty-three. *Obviously a university student earning her way through school*— Elvi barely finished the thought when the woman burst out laughing

"You must be a newbie. Honey, I haven't seen twenty-three for over a century," the waitress said, obviously having read her mind. Softening her words with a smile, she added, "The first drinks are on the house for newbies. And it's a Virgin Mary."

"Virgin Mary?" Elvi asked. She wasn't sure, but suspected it wasn't the drink she thought it would be.

"Blood of virgins," the woman informed her. "Very rare, very expensive, and very delicious."

"Oh. Thank you." Elvi managed a smile. She'd noticed a difference in the taste of blood over the years, some were sweeter, some were more robust, some slightly bitter, some thin and almost watery tasting. But it had never occurred to her that the blood of a virgin would taste different than a non-virgin. It made her wonder what the blood of a virgin would taste like. She'd probably had it at least once in five years, but wouldn't know by the flavor. Elvi supposed she'd find out soon enough, though, then frowned as she noted the way the woman was raising her eyebrows at Victor.

"Well, hello Mr. Argeneau. You're running a little late, aren't you?"

"Am I?" he asked with apparent confusion.

"Well, the rest of the tribe got here an hour ago," the waitress explained.

Elsie saw the panic cross Victor's face, but he asked carefully, "The tribe?"

"Etienne and Rachel, Lissianna and Greg, Thomas,

and Lucian, and some girl I've never seen before that they called Leigh." She shrugged and continued, "But if you were expecting to meet up with them, I'm afraid you're too late. They already left."

"What a shame," he murmured, but Elvi got the distinct impression he wasn't sorry to hear this at all.

"So, what would you have to drink?" the waitress asked when he didn't comment further.

"Most of the people she mentioned are relatives of Victor's, his niece and nephews and their mates," Harper murmured as Victor gave his order. "I don't know who this Leigh is, but Lucian is head of the council and Victor's older brother."

"His *older* brother?" Elvi asked with disbelief, finding it hard to believe there was anyone older than Victor.

"He is one of the oldest," Harper said with a nod. "Lucian and his twin brother Jean Claude were among the very few survivors who fled Atlantis."

"Atlantis. Right," Elvi murmured, recalling their explanation of the nanos and where they originated.

"Would you care to dance while we wait for our drinks?" Harper asked once the waitress had finished taking their orders and left the table.

For some reason, Elvi's gaze shifted to Victor before she answered. His expression was completely indifferent and she was reminded that he had apparently lost interest in her. Forcing a bright smile, she nodded and got to her feet. "I'd like that."

Elvi had always loved to dance, fast dancing, slow dancing; she loved it all and hadn't done it in ages. That and the fact that Victor was completely ignoring her, his attention seeming always to be on another table or just moving around the club, encouraged her to avoid the table and dance most of the night away. As long as she was on the dance floor, she didn't have to feel hurt that he was being so distant with her. And could pretend she didn't notice when he slipped away for half an hour.

Elvi danced with all the men but Victor. Edward was very good at salsa. Alessandro was the best of them at fast dancing. Harper was efficient at them all, but it was Victor she really wanted to dance with and the only one who didn't ask her.

Despite her wounded feelings, Elvi had a good time, but she was also relieved when Harper caught her yawning and decided it was time to go. It was only two A.M., but she'd been up early again that day, rising at ten A.M. to work on the pies.

Aside from that, her feet were aching, her body weary, and she'd definitely had too much to drink. The Virgin Mary had only been the first of many. Every time Elvi had sat down, it seemed one of the men had a new drink for her to try. She'd had High Times, Wino Reds, and various other drinks she later found out were supplied by donors on some high or other.

Personally, Elvi would've preferred to stick to Sweet Tooths and drinks of that ilk. She didn't care for the woozy feeling the other beverages gave her and was just glad she was dancing the worst of the effects away . . . or so she'd thought. However, when she stood to leave after finishing her last drink at the end of the night, Elvi found herself a little unsteady on her feet.

The walk back to the helicopter seemed farther than the walk from it had been, but Elvi got there all right and settled between Harper and Victor with a little sigh of relief. It seemed they'd barely taken off when her eyes began to droop from a combination of overfeeding and the substances in the drinks. She soon let her eyes droop closed, and relaxed in her seat.

"She's asleep," Harper murmured when the helicopter landed and Elvi didn't stir from where she'd slumped back against the seat.

"Yes." Victor lifted her into his arms. He knew he shouldn't. He'd determined to try to keep some distance from her while they sorted out who was gunning for him . . . or her, but while he'd stood aside and let Harper, Edward, and Alessandro hang over her all evening, it had been a sort of hell to do so . . . made worse by the fact that Elvi hadn't even seemed to care.

He'd originally intended to take her aside and explain what he was doing, but hadn't got the chance before leaving, and then she'd just seemed so okay with it, his wounded pride had refused to allow him to do it, reminding him that while he couldn't read her, neither could the rest of the men. Any of them would suit her as a lifemate and she apparently had her choice. Despite having slept with him, she may not have committed herself. After all, Victor had reminded himself, she'd fled the house after his announcing that she was his lifemate. Perhaps that was her way of telling him something.

Despite all of that, Victor would be damned if he was leaving her to be carried to the house by one of the others. As far as he was concerned he'd shown enough restraint for a lifetime standing idly by while she danced with them when his very blood had cried out with rage at the very idea. As for the drinks they'd talked her into trying, Victor would have liked to wring Edward and Alessandro's necks for suggesting them. And hers for trying them without asking what they were.

Elvi was far too trusting and was just fortunate the four of them were there, acting as a restraint on each other. He wouldn't like to think of her alone with Alessandro insisting she drink this or that and not telling her what the contents were until after she'd imbibed it. The man was a Cassanova, and though he was behaving himself so far, Victor suspected that was only due to the presence of the others.

As for Edward . . . Victor frowned. He had no idea what the Brit was up to. He wasn't the sort to try to get a lady drunk and take advantage of her, but he'd suggested an intoxicating drink or two that night. Although, that was only at the beginning of the evening and may have been an attempt to make her relax a little and enjoy herself. Elvi had been slightly tense and wound up at first.

They were nearly to the gate leading out of the school yard when the helicopter started its rotor whirling. Pressing Elvi closer to his chest to protect her from the flying debris it kicked up, Victor scowled over his shoulder at the bloody machine. Elvi had been obviously impressed that Harper had his own personal whirlybird. He didn't know why. Hell, he could have a helicopter if he wanted one but he hated the damned things. He flew in them often enough as an enforcer and always felt like his stomach got left behind and took hours to catch up.

"You're back!" DJ came running down the driveway as they started up it, his expression and tone panicked. "Thank God!"

"What is it?" Victor asked, automatically picking up his steps and moving more quickly.

"Mabel," DJ gasped, turning and hurrying back toward the house. "I think something's wrong."

"Mabel?" Elvi asked sleepily as DJ disappeared into the house, not waiting for them or even bothering to explain.

Victor glanced down as he crossed the deck.

Elvi was stirring in his arms, rubbing her hands over her face in an effort to wake up. She glanced around with confusion. "Are we back?"

"Yes," he muttered, stepping through the door Harper held open, and then all hell broke loose. Mabel's shrieks could be heard the moment they were in the house, the sound filled with desperate agony. It turned Elvi into a scalded cat in his arms. The only thing missing was the hissing as she suddenly thrashed around to free herself. Afraid she would hurt herself, Victor set her down, and then gave chase when she raced for the stairs.

"Mabel!" Elvi shouted as the woman's screams clawed down her back, leaving icy trails in their wake. She mounted the stairs at a run, hearing the thunder of the men following her, but uncaring what they did.

She burst into Mabel's bedroom at speed. Spotting the woman thrashing in the bed despite DJ's attempts to restrain her, she hurried to the bedside to help.

"What happened?!" Elsie yelled, trying to hold down Mabel's shoulders. She was a thing in motion, head whipping, body convulsing, and Elvi couldn't see her properly to tell where she was hurting. Much to her relief, on hearing her voice Mabel's screams dropped to quiet moans. She continued to thrash, though, and Elvi repeated, "What happened?"

"I was trying to turn her," DJ said anxiously and shook his head. "But something's gone wrong. She's . . ." He let the words drop away and caught at one of Mabel's hands as she slammed it into the bed headboard.

"Oh, for Christ's sake, DJ!" Victor stomped to the side of the bed with the other men following. "Why the hell didn't you tell me you were going to turn her? I could have helped. There's no need for her to go through this. There are drugs and things we could have done to ease her through it."

"I didn't know!" DJ explained. "It wasn't planned. We were talking and she said she wanted to, and to do it now before she changed her mind. So I . . . did," he said helplessly. "I've never seen a turning before. I didn't know it would be so . . . Help her!" he cried as Mabel's shrieks increased in volume again.

Victor shook his head with exasperation, and then took charge, sending Alessandro to find some rope to tie her down, Harper to the nearest twenty-four-hour drugstore to make the pharmacist give him the drugs that would help her through it, and sending Edward to fetch more blood.

"How long ago did you give her your blood?" Victor asked as soon as the three men had left to search out what he'd sent them for.

"I . . ." DJ looked uncertain. "It seems like days. I thought you'd never get back."

"What time?" Victor insisted.

"Maybe an hour after you guys left," DJ said finally.

"How much blood have you given her?" Victor asked.

"I—" He shook his head. "None. She hasn't got fangs yet."

DJ had barely said the words when Mabel proved him wrong. Elvi was kneeling on the top corner of the bed, leaning over Mabel trying to hold her shoulders down. She also had her head turned away, glancing toward the men as Victor asked his questions. She never saw it coming when Mabel suddenly reared up and ripped into her throat with a frenzied snarl. She sure felt it though . . . and there were definitely fangs there. Elvi managed a strangled scream that got the men's attention. They both immediately moved to help her.

Seventeen

Victor let the towel drop back down over Elvi's throat with a soft curse. "She damned near ripped your head off."

"She didn't mean to," Elvi reminded him for the third time since he'd bundled her into her room and settled her in his lap on the bed to pop bag after bag of blood to her fangs. Her voice, she noticed, was getting better, less a broken hiss and more her old voice. It must be nearly healed.

"Don't talk," Victor said, also for the third time, and slapped another bag of blood to her teeth. He was scowling, but the expression actually soothed her. The man had been cold and distant all night, but there was nothing cold or distant about him now. He definitely cared about her. He was furious and worried and all the things a man who loved her should be when she was so badly injured.

It was just a darned shame she had to get her throat ripped open to see his caring again, Elvi thought, and scowled at him over the bag in her mouth. Really, the man blew hot and cold like an air conditioner with a broken thermostat.

"How is she?" Harper asked, drawing their attention to the door.

"Fine," Elvi assured him, pulling the empty bag from her teeth. "How is Mabel?"

"She's doing better," he said cautiously. "It's going to be a long one, though. She's older and there's a lot to repair. We're going to need more blood."

"I'll call Teddy. He'll pick up some from the blood bank and bring it by," Elvi assured him. "Do we have enough to last a couple more hours? I'd rather not wake him up at"—she paused to glance at the clock, then finished—"four-thirty in the morning."

Harper considered the matter before saying, "Barring her ripping out someone else's throat, I think the blood will last until midmorning."

Elvi nodded. "I'll call him first thing in the morning, then. He'll be upset when he hears what's happened and it would be better if she was further along in the turning."

Nodding, Harper backed out of the room, assuring them he'd keep them posted as he pulled the door closed.

"I don't know how you can be so calm about all this," Victor muttered, taking the empty blood bag from her and tossing it in the garbage can he'd moved beside the bed.

"She didn't do it on purpose," Elvi repeated as he reached for a fresh bag.

"Yes, but— Hell, you seem almost cheerful about it," Victor said with bewilderment.

"Well," Elvi said, a smile curving her lips, "I sort of am."

"Why, for Christ's sake?" he asked with exasperation.

"Because now I don't have to feel guilty about my biting her when I was turning in Mexico," she pointed out and then added more seriously, "I've suffered horrible guilt about that over the years. Horrible, horrible guilt," Elvi said with a sigh, and then shrugged. "But now I don't have to. She's bitten me back, so we're even."

"Women," Victor muttered with disgust. "Your reasoning never fails to bewilder me."

Elvi narrowed her eyes and muttered, "We're no worse than you men. None of you make sense either, and you're the worst, as changeable as the wind."

"What?" Victor asked with surprise, but she'd already slapped the blood bag to her teeth and he had to wait while it drained.

"What do you mean I'm as changeable as the wind?" Victor asked again once the bag was empty and she'd removed it from her mouth.

"Nothing," Elvi said, too tired to be bothered arguing with him at this point.

Sitting up, she removed the towel from her throat and got to her feet, then walked to the mirror to peer at her wound. She'd been woozy from blood loss when Victor had brought her in here, but aware enough that she understood what the men said as they kept Victor updated with what was going on. She knew the men had tied Mabel down, fed her several bags of blood, and given her the drugs Harper had fetched back. They'd kicked in quickly and Mabel's screams had soon become nothing but a memory.

The throat wound Elvi had sustained had been almost healed by then, yet Victor kept pressing blood on her. Now she looked in the mirror to see it was completely closed and merely an angry, jagged scar on her throat that she knew would soon be gone.

Her gaze shifted to Victor as he appeared behind her in the mirror. His hands settled on her shoulders and he met her gaze in the reflection. "You should be in bed."

Elvi felt her body respond to the huskiness in his voice and stood very still as his eyes slid over her reflection. The silver had flared in his eyes, burning away the blue of his irises and leaving them a hot, hungry current of electricity that she could almost feel caressing her body. She knew she should suggest he leave, or at least demand an explanation for his distant behavior that night, but her body had other ideas and simply leaned into him, melting to fit his form.

Elvi's breath left her on a small sigh as his hands slid around her waist then up to close over her breasts in the red halter of her dress. She covered them with her own, squeezing them as they squeezed her, her own eyes flaring golden as her body automatically arched, pressing her breasts more firmly into the caress while pressing her bottom back against him.

When Victor bent his head to gently kiss her injured throat, her eyes drooped. She watched through slits as he gave up his caresses to undo the catch that held the halter in place. The deep red cloth immediately dropped away to hang down in front of the skirt, leaving her breasts on display.

"Beautiful," Victor whispered, his gaze sliding over her in the mirror. Just the word breathed by her ear made tingles slide through Elvi and she stretched like a cat, one hand slipping behind her to seek his hip, the other rising to slide around his neck making her back arch further and lifting her erect nipples in a plea for his touch.

Victor obliged at once, his hands covering them both. Elvi moaned at the erotic feel as well as the sight of his touching her. She'd never thought of herself as an exhibitionist, but seeing their entwined reflection and watching him do what he was doing was having an incredible effect on her. When one of his hands drifted down over the skirt of the red dress to cup her between the legs, Elvi groaned and arched further.

Her weariness was suddenly forgotten, but there was still no chance they would be discussing anything. Conversation was the last thing on her mind now.

Elvi turned in his arms. The men had all changed when she had and Victor had chosen a casual blue cotton shirt with jeans. She promptly began to tug it out of his jeans, and then turned her attention to the buttons, undoing them blind as Victor bent his head to kiss her, obscuring her view.

She had half the buttons undone when his hands slid under her skirt to clasp her bottom. He only squeezed and kneaded at first, but the moment Elvi had his shirt undone and began pushing it off his shoulders, he lifted her by his hold on her bottom, urging her firmly against the erection straining his jeans.

Elvi stopped pushing at the shirt and instead clutched at it, sucking desperately at his tongue as they ground together. Easing her back to stand on her feet again, Victor quickly undid the zipper at the waist of her dress. She shivered against his chest as the light cloth slid down to pool around her feet, her panties quickly followed, leaving her standing in only a pair of red high heels.

Victor broke the kiss and raised his head, then stilled, and she glanced curiously over her shoulder to see what had his attention. She caught their reflection—the sight had his eyes swirling with silver, but all it did for Elvi was make her decide one of them was overdressed. Turning back, she finished pushing his shirt off, and then reached for the snap of his jeans to undo it. The zipper quickly followed, then Elvi knelt to drag his jeans down his legs, noting how strong and muscular they were and the fact that he'd gone commando.

When his erection popped free of the blue cloth, Elvi leaned forward and pressed a kiss to it as she continued pushing his jeans down. She gave up on the jeans, however, when she reached his ankles, and instead reached for his erection, and then leaned forward to draw him into her mouth and run her lips his length.

Victor immediately groaned and tangled his hand in her hair, but she was only peripherally aware of that, her mind was swirling with a sudden infusion of pleasure. As she caressed him, her mind filled with the sensations he was enjoying, her body reacting as if it were being pleasured. She didn't know how it was happening, but she seemed to be experiencing what he was experiencing. It was an incredible sensation, letting her know exactly what felt best and how much pressure to apply, and she wondered vaguely if Victor had been experiencing this in the garage the other day. Was this how he'd known exactly what would drive her wild and when to stop and make love to her?

Just when she thought she would explode with the

pleasure overwhelming her, Victor caught her by the upper arms and forced her back to her feet. He covered her mouth with his own, and drove his tongue inside as he caught her behind the thighs and lifted her to wrap her legs around his hips. Holding her in place, he kissed her thoroughly and continued to do so as he turned toward the bed, apparently sufficiently distracted to forget about the jeans still caught around his ankles. With the first step, they were both reminded of it when he suddenly lost his balance and started to fall forward.

Elvi cried out and squeezed her eyes closed, arms tightening desperately around him as she waited for a pain that never came. Releasing her, Victor reached out with his hands, stopping them before her back touched the floor. They both released a relieved breath, and then he peered down at her as she eased her hold on him and allowed herself to ease down to lie on the floor beneath him.

"Are you all right?" he asked with concern.

Elvi started to nod, then froze, her head jerking toward the door at the sound of feet pounding up the hall.

"Victor! Elvi!"

"Stop!" Victor roared, kicking out with his feet to hold the door closed as the knob started to turn. When it stopped turning and silence erupted outside the door, Victor released a breath and lowered his forehead to hers briefly, his eyes closing.

"Is everything all right?" Harper asked, his voice muffled through the door. "We heard Elvi scream."

Victor raised his head and peered at her as he said, "She's fine. She . . . er . . . I was carrying her back to the bed and tripped."

"Carrying her *back*?" Edward asked sharply. "What on

earth was she doing up in the first place? She shouldn't be up."

"Yes, I agree thoroughly . . . and shall endeavor to keep her there," Victor spoke solemnly, but there was sudden devilment in his eyes as his gaze met Elvi's.

She started to smile in response, and then sucked in a breath as he shifted, his erection rubbing against her. The silver in Victor's eyes burned hotter and he deliberately shifted once more, caressing her with his body. Elvi's hands clutched at his shoulders as her own body pressed into the caress.

"Well, I should hope so," Edward muttered. "The woman doesn't know enough to give her body time to recuperate when necessary. She's forever rushing about right after sustaining serious injuries. She needs a damned keeper."

"I'll keep her," Victor breathed by her ear, rubbing against her again, his erection slick with her excitement.

"What was that?" Edward asked sharply. "I couldn't hear you."

"I said I'll be her keeper," Victor lied, his voice almost covering the sound of her moan as they ground together once more. Almost.

"Are you sure she's all right?" Harper asked with concern. "I thought I heard her moan."

"Are you all right, Elvi?" Victor murmured, pressing a kiss to the point below her ear as he shifted to the side and ran one hand down to slip between her legs.

"Yes," Elvi groaned, arching her hips into the caress. She started to groan again, but Victor bent his head to catch the sound in his mouth as his fingers slid over her slick flesh.

"Are you sure?" Harper asked and she could hear the

frown in his voice, knew he was concerned, but just wished he'd go away.

"I'm fine," Elvi gasped the moment Victor lifted his head. The words were faint and breathy, her breathing reduced to short pants by what he was doing to her. In the hopes of getting rid of the annoying men outside the door, she added a breathless, "Really. You can stop worrying. I'm going to sleep now."

"I sincerely hope not," Victor breathed into her ear, and then lowered his head to catch one nipple lightly between his teeth and nip it gently.

"Elvi?" Harper asked.

"Yes?" Elvi breathed, sucking in her stomach with alarm as Victor released her nipple and suddenly began to slide down her body until his face was between her legs. She immediately tried to close them to keep him from doing what she suspected he was going to do, but Victor simply caught her legs and pressed them open again, exposing the core of her to his view.

"Elvi?" Harper repeated and she realized there had been no voice behind her first response.

"Yes," Elvi tried again and this time it came out a near squeal as Victor chose that moment to rasp his tongue over her quivering flesh. Trying for a more normal voice, she panted, "What is it?"

There was an uncertain pause from outside the door and Elvi lifted her head to peer down at Victor, then caught at his hair and tugged, hissing, "Stop that."

At first, she thought he would obey the half-plea, half-command. He rose up slightly between her legs, but merely grinned at Elvi evilly and slid a finger into her. Elvi bucked like a wild horse, her body uncaring that there were men outside the door. Then his mouth found her again and Elvi pressed a hand to her own mouth to stifle a whimper. She closed her eyes as he set to work in earnest.

He was hitting just the right spots with just the right pressure so that her head began to twist frantically back and forth.

Victor must be experiencing the same thing, Elvi thought suddenly, amazed at what he was doing to her. There was no way he could—

"You won't forget to call Brunswick in the morning? About the blood?" Harper finally asked, interrupting her thoughts and bringing her eyes abruptly open.

Elvi had actually forgotten the bloody men were outside the door. How could she forget that? Easy, she realized as Victor caressed her more determinedly.

"Yes!" Elvi cried, hips thrusting. Lights were starting to dance on the periphery of her eyes and she felt ready to explode, but this time Victor was showing no mercy.

"You will?" Harper asked with confusion.

Elvi blinked, wondering what the man was nattering on about. She'd quite forgotten the question. She hadn't been talking to him anyway. *Had she talked?* She might have said something. *What had it been?* She thought it might have been yes or something of that ilk. Since that was apparently the wrong answer, she tried, "No!"

"Oh, good, thanks," Harper murmured. "I'm off to bed, then. Alessandro has already retired, but Edward is going to stay up with DJ for a while, to help watch over Mabel. Just shout if you need anything."

Elvi didn't bother to respond, she hadn't really heard anything he was saying, or perhaps it was more correct to say she'd heard it but hadn't comprehended any of it. Her brain didn't have the capacity at the moment when it was being hit by wave after growing wave of pleasure from what Victor was doing to her. The man was turning her into a mass of raw sensation and she was sure she was going to explode.

The moment footsteps outside the door announced that the men were leaving Victor reared up and scooped her into his arms. Apparently he'd managed to kick his jeans off before doing so because this time they made it to the bed without falling.

Once there he simply turned his back to it and dropped onto the bed with her in his arms. Elvi landed on his chest with a gasp, then quickly took advantage of their position and sat up before he could try to shift her beneath him. She wasn't having anymore torture. She knew what she wanted and would have it. Victor reached for her, but Elvi scrambled backward and shifted to straddle his hips, her hand finding his erection and guiding him into her as she came to rest on his hips.

They both went still, their gazes meeting as he filled her, then Victor suddenly sat up, catching her by the back of the head and drawing her forward to meet him as his mouth covered hers.

Elvi moaned and caught one arm around his shoulders to keep her balance. Her other hand slid into his hair to run over his scalp as his tongue filled her as well. He was in and around her, enveloping her and it still wasn't enough. She couldn't move in this position and she so wanted to move. Elvi moaned a plea into his mouth, her hips shifting the slight bit they could in frustration, then Victor twisted them both on the bed, laying her on her back and coming down on top.

Elvi sighed into his mouth as his body covered hers, and then gasped as he withdrew, only to surge back in.

As he withdrew and plunged forward again, she dug her nails in, clawing at his back and urging him on, but then cried out in protest when Victor caught her wrists and lifted them over her head, holding them there. He immediately covered her mouth again, thrusting his tongue between her lips as his body surged forward.

Elvi struggled to free her hands for a moment, then gave it up and concentrated on using her body to meet his thrusts as the pleasure swirling in her brain became a tornado, wiping out every other thought. It was only one more thrust before the pleasure exploded between them. Elvi tore her mouth from his and bit into his shoulder to keep from screaming out and drawing the others again, then allowed herself to drop into the darkness that waited beyond the fire they'd created.

Elvi woke several times over the next few hours, finding herself wrapped in Victor's arms all but once. She rose up sleepily in the bed that time, and peered around but didn't see him. Thinking he'd gone to his own room, she dropped back to sleep with a disappointed sigh, only to find him there again when next she woke. The last time she opened her eyes it was after nine in the morning. Recalling she was supposed to phone Teddy, she eased carefully out of Victor's embrace and slipped from the bed. A quick shower later, she dressed and crept from her room so as not to disturb Victor.

The house was silent as she made her way up the hall. Elvi paused at Mabel's room and eased the door carefully open. When she saw Mabel sleeping peacefully and both Edward and DJ asleep in their chairs, she eased the door closed and made her way downstairs. She didn't think Mabel's turning was over yet, but it appeared the worst of it was done.

In the kitchen, Elvi placed her call to Teddy. He was understandably surprised to hear they already needed more blood. He and Mabel had laid in a lot before the men arrived. It was only then that Elvi realized she hadn't informed him of the attacks on Victor and her resulting injury. She'd meant to call him, but found she was uncomfortable around him since the day she'd learned he cared for her. He'd been so short with her since then that it had been easy to allow the pie making to distract her.

She didn't tell him now, thinking it better to tell him in person, and was glad she hadn't after his reaction to the news of Mabel's turning. Teddy was cursing up a storm as he hung up. He wasn't pleased.

Making a face as she hung up, Elvi moved to turn on the stove to allow it to heat, and then grabbed a tray from the cupboard over the refrigerator and headed downstairs to see how many pies left in the cold room needed baking. She wasn't surprised to find that there were still fifteen pies on the shelf. DJ had given blood to Mabel an hour after they'd left last night and there was no way he would have been baking pies while Mabel thrashed and screamed upstairs.

Setting three pies on the tray, Elvi carried them back up to the kitchen and set them on the counter. Leaving them there for the moment, she retrieved one of the few bags of blood remaining in the fridge, slapped it to her teeth, and moved to peer out the window while she waited for it to drain. Her gaze slid over the garden with longing as she fed. Elvi had never got to work on it as she'd hoped. She hadn't even made it past the deck in sunlight yet. Perhaps she could do some work while the pies were baking.

Turning away, she tossed the empty bag in the garbage, then moved into the cupboard room and retrieved her hat and the long-sleeved shirt she'd hung there the other day. She donned both, then found the suntan lotion and quickly slathered some on. Satisfied that she'd taken the necessary precautions, Elvi then put the pies in the oven and set the timer before grabbing her gloves and slipping outside.

A smile curled Elvi's lips as she started across the deck. Birds were singing and flapping around in the birdbath, butterflies were dancing among the flowers, and there was a squirrel digging in the garden, no doubt in search of a walnut it had buried there.

"Good morning, Elvi!"

Pausing at the edge of the deck, she glanced over and smiled at Mike Knight. The man was dressed in shorts and a short-sleeved shirt, busily running a fine net over the surface of his pool to remove the leaves that had fallen during the night.

"Good morning, Mike. Not working today?"

He shook his head. "My day off. I arranged the schedule that way so I could help out at the fair."

Elvi nodded. As fire department chief he had that freedom and often took advantage of it. Mike was as involved in local charities as she had been before her turning.

"How are the pies coming?" Mike asked. "Karen said you'd forgotten all about them."

"Yes, thank goodness she reminded me. I *had* forgotten," she admitted. "They're mostly done, though. I'm just baking the last of them now, but I thought I'd come out and see how much work there is to do in the gardens."

"We'll see you out here more often, then." Mike smiled. "Good. We've missed our chats over the fence."

"So have I," Elvi said solemnly, and it was true. That was one of many things she'd missed over the last five years.

"Do you want some help with the garden?" Mike asked, pausing in his scooping to peer at her. "I'd be happy to help get it back in shape. Karen probably would too. In fact, I've had to hold her back from doing so before now. She was so upset to see all your lovely work go to seed these last five years."

Elvi chuckled at the claim, not doubting it for a moment. Karen and Mike kept a beautiful home and yard and could always be found outside mowing, raking, or working in the garden. Their yard was never less than impeccable and she knew the house wasn't either. It must have driven the poor woman mad to see Elvi's own garden slowly go to ruin. Mabel had hired Owen to mow the lawn and such, but had let the garden go.

"No, that's okay," she said as Mike moved to hang up his net. "I'm just looking today to see how bad it is. I'm thinking I might hire a landscaper to get it back in shape if there's too much work. Actually, I might have to have them redo it so that there's less maintenance. I can come out now, but it's better if I'm not out too much I guess. It means I have to have more blood."

"Oh. I'm sorry to hear that," Mike said, his expression concerned.

"I suppose it's better than nothing," Elvi murmured and turned to head toward the stairs leading down into the yard.

"Elvi?" Mike called, bringing her to a halt. When she turned back, he hesitated, and then asked, "Are you happier?"

She blinked in confusion at the question. "Happier?"

"Yes." Mike moved toward the fence. "Mabel once said that you wished you'd never gone to Mexico and never turned into a . . . er . . . vampire. She said you were miserable."

"Yes, I did say that. Many times," Elvi admitted quietly, and it had been how she'd felt then. But then she'd thought she couldn't eat, had slept in a coffin, and avoided daylight like the plague. Things had gotten much better since the arrival of Victor and the others in her life. She supposed that was what everyone was hoping for and why the men had been invited.

"I'm sorry."

Elvi tore herself from her thoughts and peered at him with surprise. "What for?"

"For helping to pressure you into going to Mexico when you didn't want to," he explained. "The lot of us have felt horrible about it ever since Mabel explained what had happened at the town meeting Teddy called when you guys got back. We never would have pressured you so if we'd known—"

"Don't be silly, Mike. I know that," Elvi interrupted. She'd known for years that the reason everyone had been so accepting of her new status was because many of them had felt bad for talking her into taking that trip when she hadn't wanted to. Elvi had intended to cancel the trip to Mexico after the accident, but everyone from Teddy, Mabel, the Knights . . . even Dawn, the grocery store clerk, had all insisted she should go.

"We were hoping that Mabel's plan with the single's ad would help make things better."

Elvi smiled faintly and opened her mouth to tell him it had, then paused and glanced toward the driveway as the sound of a car engine caught her ear.

"Oh, Teddy's here," she said. "I'll talk to you later."

Giving him a wave, Elvi moved to the end of the deck and descended the stairs to greet Teddy as he got out of the car and retrieved a cooler from the trunk.

"How is she?" Teddy asked grimly as he stomped up the sidewalk toward her.

"She was sleeping when I checked on her," Elvi said, hurrying ahead of him to open the door. Teddy carried the cooler inside, slammed it on the counter, and whirled to face her.

"How could you let this happen? After all she's done for you?" he asked furiously.

"I didn't let anything happen," Elvi said quickly. "I wasn't even here. DJ turned her and—"

"Well, you *should* have been here," he interrupted with a snarl. "After the way she's looked after you for five years, doing all those things you couldn't anymore, you could have spent a little time looking after her for a change." He gave a snort of disgust. "But I suppose you couldn't tear yourself away from that damned Argeneau character long enough to be bothered."

"I—" Elvi began, only to be interrupted as Teddy's eyes narrowed.

"DJ did this to her?" he asked suddenly, apparently that part of the conversation just having made it through his anger. Mouth tightening, he snarled, "I'll stake him out like—"

"You will not!" Elvi interrupted sharply. "Mabel loves him, and he was only doing what she asked him to do."

"We'll see about that. I'm checking on her. Alone," he announced in a tone of voice that suggested she not argue.

Elvi watched him head determinedly upstairs, then shook her head and turned to head right back outside. She wasn't interfering. DJ could handle him. If he still wanted to yell at her after that, then he could just come find her, she thought furiously as she crossed the deck to the yard.

Elvi couldn't believe the man had turned on her like that, blaming her for Mabel's turning as if it were her fault. As if she'd been a bad friend and *let* it happen. The truth was if she'd known Mabel wanted it, Elvi would have stood by her decision. And Teddy had no right to stand in judgment, she thought as she stomped around the garden glaring at the damage done by time. That was all she'd intended to do today, but Elvi was so wound up and agitated by her run-in with Teddy that she decided she needed some physical exertion to help get rid of it.

Crossing to the shed at the back of the yard, she dragged the door open, and stepped inside. All her gardening tools were still there; hanging from their hooks and racks, in perfect shape, but covered with a fine coat of dust.

Muttering under her breath, Elvi walked along the implements, trying to decide what she'd need. She wanted to do something that took a lot of hitting or something. *Something like cutting wood would be good*, she thought. Unfortunately, she didn't have any wood to cut. They bought it all corded and split.

Muttering about the stupidity of men, Elvi picked up the shovel, thinking that slamming it in the ground a couple hundred times and jumping up and down on it to dig it into the earth would be good.

She'd started back toward the door when it suddenly

slammed shut. Pausing, she blinked in the darkness. There was no light in the shed, no window even to allow natural light in, not even enough light for *her* eyes to use. Something she'd found annoying on other occasions, but which was almost scary now. It had been years since she'd been in the shed and where—at one time—she would have known exactly where everything was and been able to move through it easily enough, now she couldn't and there were several dangerous items in the shed. There were sharp items everywhere; on the floor to trip over and fall on . . . against the wall for her to walk into. Elvi wasn't at all sure she could find the door without skewering herself.

She should have leaned something against the door to keep it open before entering, Elvi realized, and berated herself briefly for not thinking of that before the wind had blown the door closed. And then she paused to sniff the air as something wafted past her nose.

Was that smoke? Elvi sniffed more deeply, frowning when she got a good nose full of the scent. It *was* smoke.

Aware of creeping light in the back corner, she turned slowly and stared at the flames licking their way up the back wall.

"Well, hell," Elvi muttered.

Eighteen

The sound of shouting made Victor scowl as he opened Elvi's bedroom door. DJ and Teddy Brunswick's arguing had woken him earlier and he'd crawled out of bed to break it up. It had taken several minutes for him to convince Brunswick that Mabel was fine and DJ hadn't done anything she hadn't wished. By the time the officer had finally left, Victor had been wide awake. Knowing it would be useless to go back to bed, he'd headed off to take a shower. Now he was dressed and ready to face the day, but the shouting had started up again.

Victor's immediate reaction was irritation, but that turned into surprise and then concern as he stepped into the hall and realized it wasn't DJ and a returned Teddy doing the yelling, but Harper. Just then, the German came crashing down the stairs from the third floor, and charged by shouting about something being on fire in the backyard.

Victor stared after the man with amazement . . . until his brain digested what the man was yelling about.

Something on fire? In the backyard?

"Where's Elvi?!" Victor roared with sudden panic, and immediately chased after Harper. He was positive that if there was trouble, that was where he'd find Elvi.

He raced out onto the deck, pausing at the sight of the small shed at the back of the yard on fire. One whole side was a wall of flames. He heard a muffled shout and several thuds and felt his blood run cold. Someone was inside the burning shack. It didn't take two guesses to know who it must be.

Not bothering with the stairs, Victor left Harper to wrestle with the garden hose and charged, leaping up and over the railing that ran around the deck. He was at the shed door in barely more than a heartbeat. There was a shovel jammed against the handle, blocking it closed. Victor kicked it aside with his foot even as he reached for the handle.

He pulled the door open and started to step in, only to grunt and stumble back as a smoking bundle crashed into his chest. It appeared Elvi had decided to rush the door just as he opened it. Unprepared, Victor lurched several steps backward, his arms closing around her even as he did. They both cried out as he crashed into the birdbath and sent it tumbling as they crashed to the ground.

Victor grunted as his back slammed into the dirt, cursed in pain as Elvi came down, her knee landing bull's-eye on his groin, then simply whimpered like a baby when she realized what had happened and quickly slid off him, only to have the still flipping birdbath finish its own fall by allowing the base to take her place, crushing his testicles.

"Victor?" Elvi's anxious voice sounded by his ear. "Are you all right?"

Stars exploding behind his eyes and body racked with pain that radiated out from his groin, Victor lay completely still and merely groaned, amazed that he was able to do so. He followed that with a moan when water began to pour over him.

"No, Harper!" Elvi cried by his ear. "You have to set it to jet! It isn't reaching the shed! You're getting us! Set it to jet!"

"What the hell happened here?"

Victor recognized Teddy Brunswick's voice, but didn't bother to open his eyes or look around. He just lay where he was, waiting for his body to stop protesting the abuse it had received.

"Victor?" DJ's voice sounded anxious as it neared. "Are you all right?"

"What happened?" Edward asked.

"Was anyone hurt?" Alessandro's question almost had Victor opening his eyes in disbelief, but it seemed like too much effort, so he stayed as he was.

"I've got it! Out of the way!" That voice belonged to Mike Knight, the fire chief and Elvi's neighbor. Recognizing it, Victor didn't immediately open his eyes. It wasn't until he heard the hissing sound that followed the man's authoritative shout that Victor popped his eyes open to see Elvi's mortal neighbor was the only one who had been sensible enough to bring a fire extinguisher to the party.

A disappointed sigh to his side drew Victor's gaze

to Harper to see the immortal standing, shoulders slumped, the dripping garden hose in his hands. The hose itself was a tangled mass straggling between the deck and where he stood. It seemed in his rush to be of assistance, he'd somehow tangled up the hose and hadn't been able to reach the back of the yard with the spray.

That explained the small shower he'd got, Victor supposed.

A rustle at his side drew his gaze to Elvi as she sat up beside him to watch Mike finish putting out the fire. Her face was streaked with soot, and her hat and clothing a bit singed, but she appeared all right otherwise. However, he'd already expected as much. Her voice had been strong both times she'd spoken since their crash landing.

His gaze shifted to the birdbath still lying on top of him and Victor grimaced. It had done some real damage. If he were mortal, there would be some question as to whether he would ever have more children. Fortunately, he wasn't mortal. Victor reached down and pushed the birdbath off.

Elvi immediately turned to peer at him. Managing a worried smile, she leaned over and placed one hand on his cheek as she asked, "How are you? Are you all right? I think you got the wind knocked out of you."

Before Victor could respond, Teddy appeared behind her, his wrinkled face grim as he peered down at them. "What happened?"

"What are you dong here?" Victor asked instead of answering. "You left a good fifteen minutes ago."

Brunswick's eyebrows rose at the question, but he answered calmly enough. "I was almost back to the station when I realized I left the blood bank cooler here. So I turned back and saw the smoke about two blocks away. I hit the siren, radioed the fire department, put my foot down and pulled up just in time to see you and Elvi crash over the birdbath."

Victor narrowed his eyes, concentrating on the man's thoughts, but relaxed when he found Brunswick was telling the truth. He wasn't the mortal who had set the fire. That left—

"It's out," Mike Knight announced, approaching the small group gathered around Victor and Elvi. "It's still hot, though. I'll have the men give her a spray down when they get here just to be sure she doesn't start back up. There they are now," he added, glancing toward the driveway as a red fire truck pulled in, siren blaring.

Victor didn't glance toward the driveway. His attention was now focused on Mike's thoughts, sifting through his memories of the last few minutes to find that Elvi's neighbor had been inside changing his clothes after spilling weed spray on himself when his wife had yelled from the kitchen that Elvi's shed was on fire. The fire chief had tugged on a T-shirt as he ran from the room, stopping only to grab the fire extinguisher before running around the two fenced properties to get to the backyard and the burning shed. He hadn't set the fire either.

Victor relaxed back where he lay, frowning over who it could have been, but stilled when he saw the way Elvi was eyeing him.

"Why don't you go find Father O'Flaherty and read his mind too?" she asked sarcastically, obviously guessing what he'd been doing. "The church is just up the street."

When Victor's eyes sharpened with interest at this news, she threw her hands up with disgust and hissed, "It was an accident."

"It wasn't a damned accident," Victor snapped.

"Of course it was," she insisted. "No one in Port Henry would want to hurt me."

"She's right, son," Brunswick informed him. "Everyone here loves Elvi."

"See?" Elvi said with a smile for Teddy for backing her up.

Victor merely scowled and turned his gaze to the fire chief. "Knight?"

"Well, I'm sure no one would want to hurt Elvi," he agreed, and then shifted uncomfortably. "But I smelled gasoline while I was putting it out."

"Gasoline?" Elvi asked with dismay. Apparently, she hadn't noticed the pungent scent, but then she'd probably been a bit distracted with trying to get out, he acknowledged.

"I'm afraid so, Elvi," Mike said, and then muttered that he had to speak to his men and hurried toward the driveway as several uniformed firefighters jumped from their trucks and began to unravel their hoses.

"Now will you admit that someone is out to get you?" Victor asked wearily.

"But no one would want to hurt me," Elvi protested. "It had to be an accident."

Victor's eyes popped back open. Incensed by her continued denial, he roared, "Goddammit woman! Someone doesn't jam a shovel against the shed door to lock you in, pour gasoline down the side wall, and strike a match by accident. Someone is trying to kill you."

Elvi's eyes widened at the explanation for why she

hadn't been able to open the door, but before she could say anything, he went on, "And you can stop glaring at me for reading your friends. Of course I suspect them. It's a mortal attacking you."

Elvi's mouth tightened. "You don't know that for sure."

"Yes, I do," he snarled. "Only a mortal would try to kill you by shooting an arrow through your back. *And,* only an idiot mortal could fail at killing someone who was so eager to throw herself into danger."

Elvi stiffened. "Some of my best friends are mortals, Victor, and they are not idiots. Besides, coming out to work in the garden is hardly throwing myself into danger."

"The hell it isn't!" he snapped, and then added, "You shouldn't have been out here in the first place. You should have been in bed. Mabel nearly took your head off last night. You had a terrible wound and lost a lot of blood. *And* you took an arrow in the back not long before that! You shouldn't be doing anything but recuperating. But are you? No, not Elvi Black. You have to hop out of bed and rush out here and try to get yourself killed *again*!"

"Now just a cotton pickin' minute here." Brunswick glanced from Victor to Elvi and back before settling on Elvi as he asked, "Mabel ripped your throat out? Someone shot you in the back? What the hell has been going on around here, Ellen Stone?"

"Ellen Stone?" Harper echoed with confusion.

"It's her real name," DJ explained, obviously having learned this from Mabel. "She was born Ellen Black, took her husband's name Stone when they married, then reverted to her maiden name after the turning."

"Then why does everyone call her Elvi?" Edward asked.

"I'm asking the questions right now," Brunswick barked, and then raised an eyebrow at Elvi. "Why the hell didn't you tell me what was going on? I'm the police captain here. You should have told me."

"She should have stayed in bed where she was safe," Victor snapped as Mike rejoined them.

"I'm afraid I have to agree with Victor, *Ellen*," Edward said, emphasizing the name. "You have a dreadful tendency to get yourself into trouble. I really think the best place for you is indoors until we men solve this matter."

"There is no *we*," Brunswick said coldly. "I'm the cop. This is my town. You're just visitors here. I'll solve it . . . *Now that I know it's happening*," he added with another glare at Elvi.

"If you'd at least told *me* what was happening, Elvi, I could have kept an eye out for anyone skulking around," Mike added.

Elvi peered at the angry male faces surrounding her for a moment and then stood up and pushed her way through them, muttering, "I have some pies in the oven I need to check on."

"Well done, gentlemen," Harper murmured as they watched her make her way into the house, her posture defeated. "Attacking the victim is always very effective."

Victor glanced at the German sharply, and then let his head drop back to the ground with a sigh as he realized that was exactly what he'd done. Worse yet, he hadn't just attacked her, he'd blamed her. He hadn't meant to, but the whole thing had terrified the hell out of him. When he'd realized that Elvi was trapped in the burning shed it had been Marion all over again. Victor hadn't been there to witness his first wife's death, but he'd heard about it and had nightmares ever since. He couldn't lose Elvi to fire too. He couldn't lose her at all. She had become the most important thing in his life. He *wouldn't* lose her now.

"Well, hell!" Brunswick ran an agitated hand through his thinning hair. "I suppose we owe her an apology."

"I'd say so," Harper agreed.

"Well, come on then, Argeneau," he said, turning away. "We may as well get it over with before she gets herself upset enough to start crying or some other female thing. I hate a crying woman. Elvi isn't usually like that, but she's been through a lot lately and . . ." Brunswick paused and turned back as he realized no one had followed him. Victor still lay on the ground and the rest of the men were staring at him silently.

"What is it? Can't you get up?" Brunswick returned to join the circle of men.

"Not at the moment, no," Victor admitted calmly.

"Well, why didn't you say so?" He dropped to his haunches at his side. "Where are you hurt? Let me have a look."

"I don't think so," Victor said dryly.

"I think the birdbath, she landed on his . . ." Alessandro glanced to Harper and Edward for help. "How you say? Bowls?"

"The birdbath landed on his groin," Edward said with exasperation.

"Oh." Brunswick pulled back, obviously no more willing to look at the wound than Victor was to have him look.

"Si." Alessandro nodded. "I hear something pop when she hit. I think he be very sorely hurt."

"Thank you, Alessandro," Victor said dryly.

"What do we do?" Mike Knight asked.

"We wait," Harper said with a shrug. "It will heal itself. It just takes time. He probably won't feel much like moving until it does, though."

"And he'll need to feed," Edward murmured.

"It's a good thing I brought more blood, then," Brunswick commented.

The immortals merely exchanged glances and then turned to peer toward the firemen. They had finished spraying down the shed and were now putting away their equipment.

"Mike," Harper said suddenly. "I think you should take Teddy over to examine the shed for evidence."

Mike glanced at him with surprise. "I . . . Yes," he said suddenly, his face going slack. Turning he walked to the shed and stood facing it. When Harper then turned his gaze on Brunswick, the police captain followed. The two men stood silent and still, staring at the burnt shed in silence.

"I shall fetch your dinner," Edward said, turning to head for the firemen.

"I'll help." Alessandro hurried after him.

"Thanks," Victor breathed, closing his eyes.

Elvi scowled out her sunroom window at the men still congregated in her backyard. She'd come inside, switched the cooked pies in the oven for three uncooked ones, then come upstairs to shower. A glance out the bathroom window while she waited for the water temperature to warm up had shown Teddy and Mike standing staring at the shed while the rest of the men, including the firemen, stood in a circle around Victor. One of the firemen had been kneeling beside him, checking him over, Elvi supposed.

She'd actually worried for an instant that he'd been more seriously injured than she'd realized, but had refused to go find out just to get yelled at again. Instead, she'd got into the shower to wash away the smoke and soot, telling herself he was fine.

But he was still out there, lying on the ground. Though, Elvi noted, the firemen were now gone and Teddy and Mike had rejoined the smaller circle of men. As she watched, Victor sat up slowly, and then accepted the hand DJ held out to help him rise. He got cautiously to his feet, and stayed bent over for a minute, but she didn't see blood anywhere to suggest he'd had anything but the wind knocked out of him as she'd first supposed.

Sighing, she turned away from the window and passed through her room to the hall. Mabel had been left alone a long time. She should check to be sure she was all right.

Mabel was in the process of trying to get up when Elvi entered her room.

"No, no, no," she said at once, rushing forward. "You shouldn't get up."

"I need to go to the bathroom," Mabel announced with exasperation, waving her away as she stood.

"I'll help y—" Elvi froze as Mabel straightened and she got a good look at her. She'd only seen Mabel twice since the turning started. When they'd first arrived back from the Night Club, and then this morning on her way downstairs. Last night, Mabel had been thrashing so violently, Elvi hadn't paid attention to anything but helping to keep her from hurting herself, then of course, she'd been bitten. This morning, she'd merely peered in from the door and Mabel had been sleeping with her head turned away, the sheets tangled around her body and partially concealing her head.

She wasn't concealed now and Elvi just stood and gaped at the change. Mabel didn't look a day over twenty-two. Her face was peaches-and-cream perfection, her eyes were pure gold, her figure slender and lithe, and her hair a halo of shiny, glossy golden waves around her face.

Elvi shook her head in wonder. Mabel didn't look like she had when she was younger, she looked better. Unfortunately, the blonde had suffered a terrible case of acne as a teen and her complexion had forever after been pockmarked because of it. She'd also been too thin and flat-chested until she hit her mid-forties when she'd taken on a good forty pounds. Mabel was neither too thin now, nor overweight. The turning had removed at least twenty pounds, redistributing what it left behind to give her a healthy, curvy shape. She was gorgeous and had the added confidence of age to add to that beauty. It made Elvi wonder what the woman's life might have been like had she looked like this back then.

"You look almost as poleaxed as Teddy was when he saw me. Is it that bad?" Mabel asked warily, noting her expression.

Elvi managed to close her mouth, but then she just shook her head, took her by the arm, and led her over to stand in front of the full-length mirror at the foot of the bed.

"Jesus, Mary, and Joseph," Mabel breathed, staring at her reflection with stunned golden eyes.

Elvi grinned at her flummoxed expression, and then laughed as Mabel began to poke herself in various places as if to see if her new body was real. When she then opened her mouth and began to prod around in search of her canines, Elvi moved to the refrigerator to fetch a bag of blood. All she had to do was carry it back to her. The moment Mabel spotted the blood, her teeth began to shift and Mabel covered her mouth with dismay then whirled back to the mirror to look at them.

"Come on," Elvi said after letting her examine herself for a few more minutes. "You should get back in bed and feed."

"I don't want to get back in bed," Mabel said impatiently, but she did take the bag of blood. "Do I just . . ."

"Just open your mouth and pop it to your teeth," Elvi instructed, then watched her do it and smiled. "See? Easy. Now, at least sit on the bed while you feed."

Mabel followed reluctantly and sat on the bed as Elvi retrieved several more bags of blood from the refrigerator. The small mini fridge had originally been in DJ and Victor's room, but the men had moved it over last night.

While Mabel fed, Elvi regaled her with all that had happened since she and the men had left the house the day before. She told her about their trip to the club and Victor's coldness, then arriving back to find DJ in a state and her mid-turn.

Mabel flushed guiltily and interrupted her then to admit she remembered biting her the night before. When she started to apologize for it, Elvi waved it away.

"I bit you in Mexico. We're even," she said lightly, and then went on to tell her about Victor's sudden about-face last night, and, finally, the incident in the garden shed.

Mabel listened with eyes that grew wider as Elvi told

her how both Teddy and Victor and even Edward had pretty much blamed her for nearly getting killed, as if it were her fault.

"Men!" Mabel snorted with disgust as she removed the last bag, then stood and headed for the bathroom door, saying, "Now, I *really* have to pee."

Chuckling, Elvi stood and followed to wait outside the door in case she suddenly became weak or passed out, but when the sound of the toilet flushing was followed by the shower turning on, she reached for the doorknob.

"Mabel, I don't think you ought to shower yet. What if you pass out or something?" she asked, opening the door.

"I won't. I feel fine," Mabel assured her, retrieving a towel and washcloth from the cupboard. "Besides, it's been almost twenty-four hours. You were up and around after twenty-four hours."

Elvi glanced at her wristwatch, startled to see that it was late-afternoon. She'd been up here for quite a while.

"What's wrong?" Mabel asked, catching her expression.

Elvi grimaced. "I'm just wondering what the men are doing."

"Who cares?" Mabel said with a snort.

"I do," Elvi admitted. "And you should too. Why hasn't DJ come up to check on you?"

"He did," Mabel announced. "He opened the door and stuck his head in while you were telling me about the Night Club. When he saw I was sitting up in bed, fine, and you were with me, he blew me a kiss and backed out."

"Oh," Elvi murmured, but began worrying her lip. DJ had been hanging over Mabel ever since he got to Port Henry, more so since the turning, and now he was suddenly downstairs with the men. . . . It made her suspect that they were up to something.

She pondered what that could be while Mabel showered, and then stiffened where she leaned against the bathroom counter when there was a tap on the bedroom door.

Mabel stuck her head out of the shower to ask with a frown, "Was that the door?"

Elvi nodded.

"DJ wouldn't knock," Mabel said the obvious.

Nodding again, Elvi stared out at the bedroom door as if it were a snake, only relaxing when a second knock came, followed by a female voice calling, "Hello?"

"Karen," she said with relief. "I'll get it. Shout if you have a problem."

"I'm done, I'm getting out," Mabel announced and ducked back into the shower. Elvi heard the water shut off as she left the room.

"There you are," Karen smiled when Elvi opened the door, and then asked anxiously, "I didn't wake Mabel, did I? DJ said she was awake and you two were talking when he last checked, so I thought it would be okay to come up."

"Of course it's okay, and no you didn't wake Mabel," Elvi assured her, stepping aside to let her in. "She's in the shower."

"Oh, good. She's feeling better, then, is she?" Karen asked as she entered.

Elvi nodded and closed the door. "Much."

"Well, I came looking for Mike when he didn't come

back after the fire and found the men in your dining room having a powwow. They say you've been having some trouble?"

"A little," Elvi admitted with a grimace. "But I'm sure it's nothing."

"Oh," Karen hesitated, and then told her, "well, the men said you and Mabel weren't going to the fair tonight so I thought I'd come up and see if you wanted me to take the pies and—"

"They said what?" Elvi asked sharply.

Eyes wide at Elvi's tone of voice, Karen said uncertainly, "You aren't going to the fair?"

"Who said that? Victor?" she asked, her temper rearing its head.

"Well, actually, I think it was Teddy who said it first, but they all seemed to be in agreement."

"Teddy's still here too?" she asked with surprise.

"Yes. He and Mike have been here since the fire."

Elvi let her breath out slowly. She'd known they were up to something.

"I can take the pies for you," Karen repeated. "I mean, if you're in danger, maybe it *is* best if you stay here."

Elvi frowned. "I forgot about the pies. I still have another dozen to bake I think."

Karen shook her head. "The men did them. They're all done and the last three are cooling."

"Oh." Elvi stared at the wall, wondering how men could be so wonderful and so annoying at the same time. On the one hand, they'd helped make the pies, and now helped bake them, which was really sweet, but on the other hand, they were plotting to keep her from taking them to the fair to be sold.

"So I'll take the pies for you?"

"No, that's okay," Elvi said. "I'll take them."

Karen bit her lip, and then admitted, "I don't think they're going to let you out of the house, Elvi. They were plotting how to keep you here when I started upstairs."

"Oh, they were, were they?" Mabel said and both women turned to find her standing in the bathroom door, still damp from her shower and wrapped in a bath towel. She'd obviously heard everything.

"Mabel?" Karen gasped, staring at her with amazement. "You—You—"

"Not bad for an old broad, huh?" Mabel asked with amusement when Karen couldn't seem to find the words she was looking for.

Karen sank to sit on the side of the bed and just stared.

"I gather the men didn't mention that Mabel had turned?" Elvi asked gently.

Karen just shook her head, apparently dumbstruck.

Elvi patted her shoulder, and then glanced to Mabel as the woman crossed the room with determined strides.

"So the men are plotting, are they?" Mabel muttered as she moved to her closet and began to rifle through her clothes. "Well, they're about to have a fight on their hands. Mabel Allen and Ellen Stone do not lie down for anyone to step on. We—" She paused suddenly, alarm on her face, and then cried, "I don't have a thing that will fit me anymore!"

"I have clothes you can wear," Elvi said quickly, and then added, "And I have a plan too; one that doesn't include the need for confrontation."

"No confrontation?" Mabel asked, sounding almost disappointed. She always had been a fighter.

"Mabel, there are more of them and they're bigger than us," Elvi pointed out. "In a confrontation, they'd win. Brains are better here."

"Brains." Mabel nodded. "We've got them beat already, then."

Elvi smiled and turned toward the door. "Come on. Let's go find you something to wear. You too, Karen. We're definitely going to need your help."

"This isn't going to get me into trouble, is it?" Karen asked as she stood to follow.

"Trouble?" Elvi asked with surprise. "No, of course not. We're just going to the fair. It's not like we're going to do something illegal."

Nineteen

"I'm sure they didn't steal your car, Teddy. Elvi said they weren't going to do anything illegal."

Victor exchanged a glance with DJ as Karen Knight tried to soothe the outraged police captain. Teddy Brunswick hadn't taken it at all well when—after DJ had returned from checking on Mabel to announce that the women were gone—they'd all rushed out to the driveway to find his patrol car missing. He'd cursed a blue streak as they'd piled into Victor and Harper's cars and raced to the park where the fair was being held.

Karen had the unfortunate luck of returning to her car in the parking lot for another box of pies as they pulled in. Spotting her, Teddy had leapt out of Victor's car and charged over, practically foaming at the mouth.

"They were just going to come to the fair," Karen went on. "The plan was they were going to sneak out through Elvi's sunroom and ride over in *my* car, but there wasn't enough room, with all the pies in it. I wasn't sure what to do, but they said to go ahead, they'd find another way to get here."

"And then they stole my car," Teddy Brunswick said furiously.

"I'm sure they didn't. Elvi said they wouldn't do anything illegal," Karen repeated anxiously.

"Well, then she lied," Teddy snapped.

"That's kind of harsh, Teddy," Mike said with a frown, slipping a supportive arm around his wife. "Elvi and Mabel aren't the sort to lie and steal. They probably just borrowed it. They would have brought it back after the fair."

Seeing that Brunswick was winding up for another rant, Victor interceded. "Where are they now, Karen? I presume they got here, all right? The patrol car is here."

"Oh, yes, of course." She smiled at him with relief, apparently grateful to turn away from Teddy. "They're manning the booth."

"What booth?" DJ asked fretfully. "Mabel shouldn't be out of bed."

"Mabel was supposed to man the pie booth, but there was so much demand at Elvi's booth, she ended up helping her over there and I took over the pie booth," Karen explained. "They're really racking it up too, I can tell you."

"What and where is Elvi's booth?" Victor asked patiently.

"It's the Biting Booth, only it isn't the—" Karen broke off as Victor turned and headed off into the park, the other men hard on his heels.

"I can't believe she's still biting when she knows

it's against our laws," Harper said with dismay as they hurried through the crowd in search of the Biting Booth. "And Mabel too. Surely you told her it's not allowed, DJ?"

"Yes," DJ bit off the word.

"The Biting Booth is usually in the back right corner," Brunswick announced, hurrying to keep up with them.

"Show us," Victor said, and allowed him to take the lead as they made their way through the crowded grounds.

Victor was concentrating on keeping Brunswick in his sights in the busy area, so wasn't looking around much, but when Edward suddenly gave a bark of laughter, he glanced around curiously.

"What—?" Victor broke off the question as he spotted the booth Edward was looking at. The booth itself and its occupants were impossible to see for the crowd gathered in front of it, but the sign was clearly visible overhead. It did read Biting Booth, but the Biting had a black line through it and Kissing had been written above it.

"Well," Edward said mildly, "I suppose we can at least stop worrying about the ladies losing their heads over this."

"The hell we can," Victor muttered and strode past Brunswick to make his way through the crowd. He pushed his way to the front of the crowd of men, ignoring the complaints and mutters it caused, but came to an abrupt halt as he arrived at the booth.

Mabel was at the counter, checking off items on a clipboard as she asked questions of the man at the front of the line. He heard DJ's sigh of relief as he reached his side and spotted his lifemate with her clipboard, but Victor didn't comment as his eyes sought out and found Elvi.

She was at the back of the booth, busy removing a needle from the arm of a leering young man. As they watched, she gave him a cookie, a small glass of juice, then a quick peck on the lips, before moving to the man seated in the next of three chairs.

Growling, Victor started around to the entrance to the booth, only to find Mabel suddenly in his way.

"Sorry, Victor, you don't qualify," she said brightly. "We can't take your blood. No blood, no kiss. Off you go now. We're busy here."

"Mabel." DJ caught her arm and drew her to the side to begin whispering frantically. He wasn't as angry as Victor now that he saw Mabel wasn't actually kissing anyone, but Victor was furious.

"There you go," Elvi was saying cheerfully as she removed the needle on the second man and put a wad of cotton over the hole where the needle had been. "Just hold that firmly for a minute while I get you a Band-Aid."

She turned then, only to come to a halt to keep from crashing into Victor.

"Oh!" she said with alarmed surprise. "Victor. What are you doing here?"

"I think the more important question would be what are *you* doing here?" he said grimly, and then took her arm to move her away from the three men seated in the chairs at the back of the booth.

"I'm working," she answered shortly, then glanced nervously around. "Teddy isn't here, is he? Does he know—?"

"That you stole his car?" he finished dryly. "Yes, he does and he's pretty angry."

"We didn't steal it," Elvi said quickly. "We just borrowed it."

"I don't think he sees it that way," Victor muttered. "He's not happy, and neither am I."

"Well, that hardly matters, since you weren't happy with me before," she said impatiently. "From what you were shouting, it's obvious you think I'm a brainless twit."

"I do not," Victor denied at once, cursing himself for yelling at her earlier. In the next moment he was frowning in confusion, wondering how he'd suddenly become the one in the wrong. Before he could sort it out, Brunswick came rushing up with the others.

"Ellen Stone," he said, yanking out his handcuffs. "You're under arrest for grand theft auto."

"Why is it you only call me by my proper name when you're angry at me?" Elvi asked smartly, not seeming too concerned by the handcuffs he was waving angrily around. "And put those silly things away. You can't arrest me."

"I can and I'm going to," Teddy assured her.

"Then you'll just have to charge yourself with conspiracy to kidnap," she said calmly. When Teddy drew himself up in shock, she went on, "Oh, don't try to deny it. We heard everything from the upstairs landing on the way to my room." Making a stern face, she imitated him in a deep growl, "'We'll just tell them they can't go to the fair, and if they give us any trouble we'll lock them in the cold room.'" She arched one eyebrow and said, "If it isn't kidnapping, it's at least unlawful confinement."

"But we *didn't* get the chance to lock you in," he argued quickly.

"And I *didn't* steal your car, I borrowed it. Here are your keys." She dug a set of keys out of her pocket and dropped them into his hand. "Thanks for leaving them in the car for me. It's in the parking lot."

"You left the keys in the ignition?" Victor asked with disbelief.

"The shed was on fire," Teddy muttered, with embarrassment. "I don't even remember turning off the engine. I just slammed the car into park and jumped out to run over." He grimaced. "I didn't even think of them again until the car was missing."

"That ought to look good in the report," Mabel commented, drawing their attention to her and DJ. The couple stood arm in arm. Victor supposed that meant they'd patched things up. It was what he really wanted to do with Elvi, patch things up and get her back to the house where she would be safe. And yelling at her obviously wasn't going to achieve that, he acknowledged. He supposed he'd best try reason.

"Elvi," he began calmly, "DJ can help Mabel with the booth. Please come home with me."

It almost seemed to work. Her stance and expression softened, but then she shook her head and said apologetically, "I can't, Victor. I'm expected to be here."

Victor snorted with irritation. "From what I've heard this last week, you're expected at *every* town event. It won't kill you to leave this *one* event early."

"Actually, it very well might kill me," she said coldly, her own temper returning. "In case you haven't noticed, it isn't money they're donating here."

"You shouldn't have to sing for your supper like

some sort of town pet," Victor said sharply and knew at once that it had been the wrong thing to say. Elvi had started to turn away, but paused and spun back at his words. Curiously, her gaze shot to Edward first and then to him.

"Town pet?" she asked in a very quiet voice.

Victor's mouth tightened, and he pointed out, "That's how it seems to be. They supply you blood and you come when they call like a well-trained dog. They have plays and fairs and displays, and you show up and perform like a trained bear."

Victor saw the blood drain from her face and was sorry he'd said that, but couldn't take back the words. Besides, they were true. He'd caught glimpses of it everywhere in her life. She hated the name Elvi, but didn't demand people stop using it because she didn't want to upset them. She'd admitted that she hated the costumes she wore to the restaurant and these events—like the sleek black gowns she and Mabel both had on now—but wore them because it was expected. The Birthday Bite business was a pain, but she'd continued with it rather than disappoint anyone. And then there was her panic about the pies for the fair, as if should she not participate in this one event it would be cataclysmic. He'd got the impression that she feared they'd stop donating if she didn't make these appearances.

Still, his choice of words could have been more diplomatic, Victor realized as he saw the cool expression now replacing the hurt on her face. He braced himself for a telling off, instead she nodded abruptly and said in icy tones, "It's good to know what you really think of me."

"Elvi," he reached for her hand, but she jerked it away.

"No. You've made your opinion perfectly clear. You may not be able to read me and that might suggest I'm your lifemate, but I don't think I am. You don't think much of me, Victor. You think I'm stupid and in need of a keeper. I don't want to be anyone's pet. Not even yours. Now, if you'll excuse me, I have work to do."

Turning away, she moved back to her charges in the donation chairs, leaving Victor staring helplessly after her, knowing he'd screwed up royally, but unsure how to fix it.

"I can't believe you!" Mabel snapped, suddenly in his face. "You're supposed to be her lifemate, but you call her the town pet and a trained bear?"

"Mabel," DJ murmured, reaching for her arm, but she shook him off with a sharp "no" and glared at Victor. "For your information, this particular fair is all because of you."

"What?" Victor asked with surprise.

"Mabel's right," Teddy announced wearily, most of his anger with Elvi appearing gone. "We arranged this fair to bring in more donors . . . because of you and the men."

When they began to protest, he raised a hand for silence and explained, "There are five of you here that we're giving blood to for a week. That's five weeks of Elvi's supply gone like that." He snapped his thumb and finger together.

"Actually," Mabel added. "It's probably more than five weeks since you men seem to drink more than she does. We have to replace that blood so she doesn't suffer for your visit."

Teddy nodded. "We realized that when we made the plans for you to come here and arranged the fair to try to build up the blood supply. Though, of course, we didn't tell Elvi that at the time. She just thought it was yet another of the endless Fairs we have each summer. There are so many she loses track. But that was the reasoning behind it . . . to make sure we had the blood to support this week."

"Yes," Mabel said grimly. "So, perhaps instead of insulting her, you men could be more supportive. It's not like we expect *you* to sing for your supper. Elvi and I are willing to do it for you. Although," she added grimly, "perhaps you *should*. Maybe if you had to sing for your supper for a change you'd understand Elvi better and wouldn't be so damned judgmental." Turning on her heel, she stalked off to join Elvi.

"Elvi isn't a pet," Brunswick said quietly, watching the two women work. "She's well loved and cared for in Port Henry. She's one of us. And that's why she comes to these events, not because she's some trained animal expected to perform."

Victor hesitated, knowing that's the way he and everyone else in this town saw it, but they weren't seeing everything. Finally he asked, "Do you really think she wants to attend and volunteer at every single event this town holds?"

"Well, why wouldn't she?" Brunswick asked with surprise. "I do."

"That's your job, Brunswick. To make sure there's no trouble. Her job is the restaurant and bed-and-breakfast, not making an appearance as Elvi the town vampire and running a Biting Booth or whatever else she's done these last five years. When does she get to just sit back and relax and read a book by the fire? Or anything like that?"

Brunswick looked uncertain. "She could say no if she didn't —"

"How could she possibly say no?" Victor asked. "Look, most immortals get their blood from the Argeneau Blood Bank. The donors are completely anonymous. They're faceless, nameless mortals an immortal never has to encounter. It's even delivered like groceries, leaving us to consume it guilt free.

"Elvi, on the other hand, *lives and walks* among her donors. Almost every mortal in this town has donated to her survival, which is kind and giving and really quite marvelous of you, but it's also guilt-inducing for her. How could she possibly feel she can say *'No, I don't feel like attending this or that'* to people she feels she owes her very life to?"

DJ nodded and said, "Her life would have been much easier these last five years if she'd been able to simply order her blood as we do."

"We didn't know she could order blood," Brunswick said defensively, and then added, "And, hell, she's got nothing to feel guilty for. We're the ones who insisted she take that damned trip. We all pressured her into it. If we hadn't, she never would have come back a vampire and wouldn't have needed the blood in the first place. Why the hell do you think everyone gives blood so willingly? Normally, trying to get blood donors is like pulling teeth, but mention Elvi needs more blood and everyone from Dawn down at the grocery store to Jimmy at the garage is lining up to donate because everyone pushed her to take that damned trip. She couldn't go to the corner store that fall without the cashier telling her she should go. So, we feel we owe it to her. And she's one of our own and we take care of our own."

"And I'm sure she's grateful for it," Victor assured him. "I know I am. You kept her alive for me to find. But you need to see that in saving her life, you also took it. Her life is no longer her own. She spends her time running from the restaurant where she's expected to make appearances, to rushing to event after event to pay back for the blood she needs. . . . To the point where now she's putting her life at risk by attending this fair so no one's disappointed. That's wrong, Teddy."

Brunswick frowned unhappily and turned to watch the two women work.

"Damn," DJ muttered, his gaze shifting over the mortal men all crowding around Elvi and Mabel, eager to give blood to please them. "Why don't we just call Bastien and have a year's worth of blood sent down? Then they wouldn't have an excuse to be here."

"We can't call Bastien," Victor said.

"Why?"

Victor turned a grim look on the younger immortal and pointed out, "Bastien reports to Lucian."

"Right," DJ said with defeat.

It appeared the others didn't understand, however. They all looked curious, but it was Harper who asked, "So?"

"The first question out of Bastien's mouth would be *'How is the case going?'* he explained, and then added, "I don't want to answer that question."

"Just what case would that be, and why wouldn't you want to answer the question?" Brunswick asked, reminding them of his presence.

Victor frowned, hesitant to admit his original purpose in coming here, but in the end he didn't have to, Edward did it for him.

"I believe Victor is referring to his job as enforcer for our council."

"His job as enforcer?" Teddy raised his eyebrows, and asked with interest, "Is that like a vampire cop?"

"Basically," Edward agreed. "He is sent out to hunt down rogue immortals."

"Rogue immortals?" Teddy's eyes narrowed. "Like ones who go around biting mortals and such?"

Victor grimaced.

"Yes," Edward answered when he didn't. "Of course, his case was complicated when he got here and found he couldn't read Elvi and she is his lifemate."

"Lifemate, lifemate, lifemate. What the hell is a lifemate?" Teddy asked with irritation. "Everyone keeps throwing that word around. Mabel is DJ's lifemate, Elvi is—or according to her isn't—Victor's lifemate. What the hell does it mean?"

"It is what it sounds like," Victor said simply. "Our other half. The rare woman who would be a proper mate. A woman we can neither read nor control and who balances out our shortcomings."

"She completes us," Harper said quietly. "And fills up the emptiness our existence forces upon us."

Brunswick chewed that over, and then asked, "And Elvi's that for you?"

Victor frowned, his gaze sliding over the other men before he admitted, "It seems she may be that for all of us."

"Yeah, DJ was saying as much the other day," Teddy said with a grimace. "Does this mean that instead of a mate, we've found Elvi a harem?"

"No," Edward assured him. "It does rarely happen

where two immortals can't read and would suit one of the opposite sex, but it is very rare, and not the case here. At least," he added, glancing around the men, "I can read her. She is not my lifemate."

"Well, why the hell are you still here, then?" Victor asked with annoyance. "Why didn't you leave the minute you knew you could read her?"

"It was a free week away," Edward said with a shrug. "Besides, I was curious to see how it would turn out. It's like one of those movies-of-the-week. The big tough council enforcer sent to bring in a rogue vampire, only she's not what he thinks she is, *and* she's his lifemate. What will he do?" He shrugged. "Besides, this town is just . . . and she's so . . . and then there are other interests here," he finished with a shrug.

Victor just gaped at the man, unsure how to respond. He then turned a disbelieving glance DJ's way when the younger immortal commented, "Well, at least there's one less man in the running."

"Actually, is two less men," Alessandro announced, drawing their attention his way. He gave a shrug and said, "I too can read *bella* Elvi."

"You stayed for the free week too?" DJ suggested with amusement.

Alessandro shrugged again. "And other things."

"That leaves you, Harper," Teddy announced pointedly, turning Victor's attention the German's way. "I suppose you can read her too and were just hanging out for the free blood all week and to see what would happen."

"Actually, no," Harper said, and then admitted, "I haven't tried to read her."

Victor frowned. "You haven't?"

"No," Harper said calmly. "I didn't bother to try after finding I couldn't read Jenny Harper."

Teddy Brunswick stiffened. "Jenny Harper, our mail-woman?"

"Yes. The first night at the restaurant I went to thank her party for switching tables with us, if you'll recall?"

When the men all nodded, he said, "Well, the coincidence of her last name being Harper as is my first name, started a conversation and . . ." He shrugged.

"But you've been courting Elvi," Victor pointed out. "Why—"

"I wasn't exactly courting her, Victor. But I was here at her invitation—or Mabel's as the case may be—and it did seem polite to keep company with her until the week is over. It also seemed a good opportunity to allow Jenny to get used to me before I tell her she's mine," he said simply. "Besides, you did seem to need the help keeping an eye on her with someone out to kill her."

"Which is still the case," Edward pointed out. "Although now there is the added problem of keeping you from losing her. And then keeping the council from demanding her head." He smiled with mild amusement. "For a two-thousand-year-old vampire your lack of finesse in dealing with women is rather appalling."

"What are you going to do about this council?" Brunswick asked before Victor could react to Edward's words.

Victor sighed, his shoulders slumping as he admitted, "I don't know what the hell to do about the council. I've been trying to sort that out all week, but got distracted by . . . things," he ended lamely. Most of the distraction was due to Elvi herself. Truly, an immortal was useless when he first found his lifemate.

"Well"—Teddy shifted unhappily—"what exactly is it they're sore about?"

"We were sent here originally because of the ad in the paper and the rumors in Toronto," Victor said.

Brunswick scowled at the accusation in his face. "Don't get all pissy with me. If it weren't for the ad, you never would have met her. Besides, they can't punish her for either thing. You already know that the rumors around the clubs are because of me and Barney, and the ad was placed by Mabel. They can't blame her for that."

"Surely, he's right, Victor," Harper said. "They can hardly blame and punish her for something others did."

"No," Victor agreed. "But they can blame her for other things. She isn't exactly living quietly and doing her best to evade notice here. She's a celebrity, if only in this small town, which they won't like at all. And she was biting mortals, and that's worse, that's breaking our laws."

"She didn't know it was against your laws, surely they'd take that into account?" Teddy argued.

Victor arched an eyebrow. "So you let go every mortal who claims they didn't know they were going over the speed limit, or didn't know what they were doing was against a law?"

"Damn," Teddy muttered, dropping his eyes.

"We'll figure something out," DJ assured the man quietly. "Victor's smart and powerful and his brother is the head of the council. He'll sort it out."

Victor managed not to wince at this claim. He didn't have a single idea as to what to do about it all. And Lucian may be his brother, but it didn't mean the man would show mercy here. Lucian Argeneau had a reputation for being one of the most cold-blooded bastards on the continent, and with good reason. Victor's instincts were shouting at him to grab Elvi and flee, hide, move to Europe maybe where the council might not follow.

"Anyway," DJ commented, "that's why Victor doesn't want to order blood in. He's trying to avoid any contact with the council or anyone close to the council until he sorts out the safest way to present this matter to them."

"Yes, I understand now." Harper looked thoughtful. "So, we too are now forced to depend on the goodness of these townspeople for our sustenance."

"And Elvi and Mabel," Edward pointed out. "Unless we'd care to get off our high horses and help, Elvi and Mabel are the ones who will be singing for our supper . . . or kissing for it as the case may be."

"No," Alessandro said indignantly. "They will not sing. I allow no woman to prostitution herself for me. I will do the prostitution for my own blood."

"And I," Harper murmured.

Victor glanced at Teddy. "So? What can we do to help?"

Brunswick hesitated, his gaze sliding around the fairgrounds, and then turned away. "Come with me. We'll go find Karen and Mike. They're on the committee for this thing."

Victor started to follow, slowing when Edward appeared at his side to murmur, "Once we've settled the issue of helping out, I think we should discuss how best

to help you win the fair Elvi. You don't seem to be doing very well on your own."

"He's right," Harper said from his other side. "We'll
put our heads together and come up with something.
Don't you worry."

For some reason, their assurances only made him
worry more.

Twenty

"Teddy just told me the men are running the pie booth," Mabel murmured, handing her a bandage for the latest donor.

Elvi glanced at her with surprise. "I thought Karen was running the pie booth?"

Mabel shook her head. "Teddy says Karen and Mike are still out in the parking lot, arguing about something. So the men took over the booth and are offering women a kiss if they return with a bandage showing they've given blood."

Elvi's eyebrows rose. That explained the increase in women donors. It was usually mostly men at her booth, the women sticking to going to the blood bank, but she'd noticed several women in the line the last couple of times she'd glanced that way.

"Who gets to kiss them?" Elvi asked as she bent to

apply the bandage to John Dorsey's arm, and then gave him a quick peck on the lips, a glass of juice, and a cookie.

"That was my first question too," Mabel said with a laugh. "I gather Victor and DJ are only doing the selling part, the women have their choice of Edward, Harper, or Alessandro. And," she added dryly, "apparently they volunteered for it. It seems their appetite for food isn't the only thing that has been reawakened on this trip. Which is kind of weird when you think about it . . . or not," she added mysteriously.

"What have you heard?" Elvi demanded at once.

"Well, there *is* some gossip running around," she admitted.

"About?"

"Well . . . did you notice that Edward kept volunteering to go to the grocery store for you to get more flour, then more butter, then apples and so on while you guys were making the pies?"

"Yes," Elvi nodded. The man had taken forever on those trips, but she'd just put it down to his slow driving.

"Well, it seems every single time he went to Dawn's till, and spent a good deal of time chatting her up and laughing with her," Mabel announced.

"Laughing? Edward?" she asked with disbelief.

"I knowwwww," Mabel said with a nod. "Maybe she's his lifemate."

"Dawn? No way," Elvi said, but wondered.

"And then there's Alessandro."

"What about Alessandro?" Elvi asked, eyes widening.

"Well, Louise Ascot says he's been over sitting on

Mrs. Ricci's front porch every morning this week while she's out doing her embroidering by sunlight."

"In the morning? While the rest of us are sleeping?" Elvi considered that and supposed it explained why the man was always the last one up.

"Apparently he sits there until almost noon," Mabel went on. "Just talking to her and helping her thread her needle and so on. And Louise says this morning they went inside and he didn't come out for hours . . . and he was grinning like an idiot when he did."

"Mrs. Ricci?" Elvi gasped. "She's eighty-four!"

Mabel snorted. "Well, I'm sixty-two and that didn't stop DJ."

"Yes, but . . . DJ is sweet and intelligent, and Alessandro is so immature and . . ." She paused to ask, "I don't suppose you've heard anything about Harper?"

She nodded. "Karen says that at the play she and Mike took them to, Harper chose their seats and he settled down right beside our mailwoman, Jenny, and he spent the whole play talking to her."

"Well . . . I guess I can stop worrying about how to let them down easy," she said with a grin, and then muttered, "I suppose now I just have to worry about dealing with Victor."

"Yes." Mabel bit her lip, and then said, "Elvi, don't be too hard on him. I don't think he thinks you're an idiot or any of that stuff. And as for the *'pet'* deal . . ." She sighed unhappily. "Honey, he's seen and understood more in a week than this whole town has in five years, including me, your supposed best friend who lives with you." She shook her head. "I'm sorry I didn't realize how you were feeling. It never occurred to me that you might feel guilted into doing these things."

"Mabel, it's OK," Elvi said quickly.

"No, it's not. I'm seeing things different now that I'm immortal too. For instance, these costumes are damned uncomfortable and just plain ridiculous. How the hell have you stood it these last five— Oh my God, DJ shaved and cut his hair!"

Elvi glanced over her shoulder to see Victor and DJ approaching, both of them must have visited Irene's booth. The hairdresser was cutting hair at the fair, the donations all going to the Abused Kids' Shelter as was the money from Elvi's pies.

"I like the shave," Mabel announced, then added, "but I liked his hair longer."

"So did I," Elvi murmured, her gaze on Victor's short, conservative cut. He was still gorgeous, but there was just something about a man with longer hair. She stared at him silently until Mabel touched her arm, drawing her attention.

"Listen, Elv— Ellie," Mabel corrected herself, reverting to her old nickname with an apologetic smile. "Look, just listen to Victor, okay? From everything I've seen and everything DJ has said, I think Victor really does love you."

"He thinks I'm an idiot," Elvi muttered.

"Don't be ridiculous. Anyone with half a brain could tell you're no idiot," she argued. "Just let him talk, okay?"

"I thought you were mad at him too for what he said," she asked with a frown.

"Well, I was, but I've been thinking he was right. We didn't mean to, but we were treating you like a pet or something. None of us considered that you might want to do something besides perform for everyone all the time, and—" She broke off and shook her head. "There isn't time, just let him talk. I'll take over the booth; you two just take your time."

Elvi watched her hurry off to the back of the booth, and then turned to see DJ break off to join the blonde. Victor continued on until he stood directly in front of her. "I don't think you're an idiot," he blurted. "I have the greatest respect for your intelligence. I think you're charming, and beautiful and sexy, and sharp-witted and sexy and sweet and kind and sexy and— Ah hell." Giving up his verbal attempt to explain himself, Victor grabbed her by the shoulders and dragged her against his chest to kiss her thoroughly.

Elvi was gasping for breath by the time he released her, but still heard him say softly, "I love you, Ellen Stone."

Letting her breath out on a little sigh, she leaned her head against his chest and whispered, "I'm not an idiot."

"I know," he assured her, rubbing her back.

"I don't run heedlessly into danger."

"No . . . well . . ." Victor paused when Elvi lifted narrowed eyes. Grimacing, he said, "You have a frightening tendency to rush about doing things without thinking first."

"Like what?" she challenged sharply.

"Like the cheesecake emergency," he pointed out. "The minute you knew you could eat food you were off like a shot, desperate to get to the A&P, and woe and betide anyone who got in your way."

"I wanted food," Elvi said in her own defense. "It had been five years, Victor."

"Yes, I know," he said soothingly and pressed her

head back to his chest, but added, "And then there was the bed business. The minute you realized you could sleep in one, you were up and running for the door."

Elvi jerked back again to exclaim, "I was sleeping in a coffin!"

"Yes," Victor nodded, rubbing her back, and pressing her head against his shoulder once more before continuing, "but you don't stop to plan things, you just rush ahead . . . And it scared the hell out of me when I realized you were in that burning shed. That's why I yelled at you . . . And you're far too trusting."

"Too trusting? I don't think—"

"Just recall how you were trying all those drinks Edward and Alessandro were pushing on you at the Night Club. Things like that make me worried sick that you're going to trust the wrong person and get hurt, Elvi . . . er . . . Ellie . . . Ellen. What do you want to be called?" he asked with frustration.

Elvi remained where he'd pressed her, her upset slipping away to be replaced by soft chuckles.

"Are you laughing or crying?" Victor asked warily.

"Laughing," she assured him softly.

"Right," he murmured, pressing a kiss to the top of her head. Then he asked, "Is laughing a good thing or bad?"

Smiling, Elvi pulled back and leaned up on her tiptoes to kiss him and then whispered, "It's good."

"Oh." Victor smiled.

"Why did you cut your hair?"

His expression turned wary when she blurted the question. "Don't you like it?"

"Well . . ."

"You don't like it," he said with disappointment. "DJ

was upset about the men hanging all over Mabel over here now that she's turned and decided he was getting a shave and haircut to please her and I thought you might like—"

Elvi covered his mouth with her hand to silence him, and said, "I don't dislike it. It's just different and I fell in love with you with long hair. I'll adjust."

"You love me?" Victor echoed with a grin.

"Victor! Down!"

Elvi started to glance around to see what DJ was shouting about, but all she saw was him flying toward them from the back of the booth. He crashed into them even as Victor instinctively started dragging her to the ground. The three of them landed in a tangle of arms and legs.

"Jesus, DJ," Victor muttered, struggling to sit up. "What the hell—"

Curious about his sudden silence, Elvi followed his gaze to see an arrow sticking out of the counter right where she'd been standing before DJ's shout.

"It was Mike Knight," DJ gasped breathlessly, sitting up beside him.

Victor turned on the younger immortal sharply. "Mike Knight? Are you sure?"

DJ nodded.

"It couldn't have been," Elvi said positively. "He and Karen have been my neighbors for sixteen years. I watched their kids grow up. He would never hurt me."

She started to rise even as she said the words, but barely got her chin above counter level before Victor grabbed her arm and dragged her back down. She'd seen enough, however. Eyes wide with shock, she breathed, "It *is* Mike."

Elvi could hardly believe what she'd seen. Mike Knight, her friend and neighbor, had been standing a good twenty feet from the booth, legs spread in a shooter's stance and a crossbow in hand that he'd been reloading.

"Mike?" Victor shook his head with confusion. "That makes no sense. I read him after the fire in the shed. He didn't set it."

Elvi didn't comment, her mind was still grappling with the fact that her neighbor, Mike, whom she'd known and been friends with for years, was trying to kill her. Thinking of friends reminded her of Mabel, and Elvi glanced toward the back of the booth to see that the blonde and three donors had flattened themselves on the ground, though Mabel was now crawling over to join them.

"Hi," she said as she reached them. "What are we doing?"

"Hiding," Elvi answered.

"Devising a plan," DJ corrected with a scowl, then raised an eyebrow at Victor. "Any ideas?"

Victor shrugged. "We could jump over the counter from opposite ends and rush him from different sides. He can only hit one of us."

"What?" Elvi asked with dismay. "That's not a plan, that's madness! You—"

"Er . . . Elvi?" Mike's voice called tentatively from the other side of the counter. "Do you think you could stand up? This will only take a minute."

Elvi turned wide eyes to Mabel. "Is he serious?"

"He's lost his mind," Mabel announced with a sad shake of the head.

Victor ignored them and suddenly stood up.

Elvi grabbed at his hand with alarm, trying to pull him down as she hissed, "Victor! Get back down here."

He just shook her hand away, and turned, apparently, to face Mike. "What's this all about, Knight? Why are you trying to kill Elvi?"

"Er . . . well, it's kind of between Elvi and us if you don't mind, Victor," Mike said politely.

"I'm afraid anything involving Elvi involves me now, Mike," Victor answered equally politely.

Scowling, Elvi stood up beside him. If he was brave enough to do it, she could too . . . or so she thought. The moment he noticed she was getting to her feet, Victor stepped in front of her, a protective wall. When Elvi tried to step to the side, it was only to find DJ on his feet beside her, blocking the way.

"Don't even think about it," Mabel muttered, standing on her other side so that she was protected from every angle but the back of the booth.

Making a face, Elvi gave up trying to step out in the open and simply craned her neck to see around Victor's arm. Mike and Karen stood on the other side. Mike held the crossbow cocked at waist level and Karen stood at his side, expression grim.

"Was it Karen who set the shed on fire?" Victor asked when the silence drew out.

Mike grimaced and tossed his wife a heavy look, but admitted, "Yes. She did it behind my back. She knew I wouldn't approve. The fire could have easily spread to the neighbor's house, or ours. I didn't realize she'd done it until she told me after you guys went off in search of the Kissing Booth tonight."

"And the arrow at the furniture store?" Victor asked. "You or her?"

"Me," he admitted. "That was an accident, though. I was heading out to get some practice when Bob, the owner of the archery club, yelled at me that Karen was on the phone. I swung back and somehow released the arrow as I turned." He shrugged. "Sorry about that. I didn't even realize there was anyone over there until I saw you and Elvi appear at the edge of the trees, and by then I was inside on the phone. I saw you through the window. You were gone by the time I got off and went over to make sure no one was hurt. But that's where Karen got the idea of how to kill you. She figured an arrow was as good as a stake."

"So you shot Elvi in the sunroom."

Mike nodded. "Or tried to. I was sure I got her too, but obviously I missed the heart. I won't miss at this distance, though, Elvi," he assured her, meeting her gaze with a solemn expression. "It will be quick, I promise."

"Michael Knight have you lost your mind?" Mabel shouted suddenly. "What does it being fast or slow have to do with anything? She doesn't want to die."

He looked startled by this news. "But you told Karen she was miserable as a vampire and wished she'd just died in that car accident rather than become a vampire."

"That was four years ago. She's happy now," Mabel snapped, then turned to Elvi and said, "Tell him."

"Actually, she's right, Mike. I really have no desire to die."

Mike glanced to his wife who moved to his side and whispered furiously. When he sighed and turned back to face them, Karen took a step toward the booth and said, "I'm sorry, Elvi. You know we love you, but he's our son."

"Owen?" Elvi stood on her tiptoes to get a better look

at them as she asked, "What on earth does Owen have to do with this?"

Her obvious confusion just seemed to infuriate the woman. Propping her hands on her hips, Karen yelled, "You know what he has to do with this, you . . . you *vamp*!"

The way Karen had said *vamp* seemed to suggest it was synonymous with hussy, but Elvi merely said, "No, actually, I don't know."

"You *bit* him!" Karen exclaimed as if it were obvious.

Elvi's eyes widened incredulously at the venom in those words, but rather than admit she hadn't bit him, she said, "You brought him there to be bit."

Karen's shoulders sagged unhappily. "It was his birthday, it's what he wanted. Besides, I didn't want him to go through with it in the first place." She glared at her husband. "I told you we shouldn't allow him to do it, but oh no, you wouldn't listen to me. I was being a silly woman. Now we have a vampire for a son when if you'd just listened to me, just this once—"

"What!" Elvi interrupted with disbelief. "A vampire?"

"Now, now," Brunswick interrupted, stepping out of the gathered crowd to make his presence known. Someone had obviously gone running to fetch him when the disturbance broke out. Now he moved between the Knights and the booth, while Edward, Harper, and Alessandro began to slip along the edge of the crowd to surround the couple.

"I'm sure Elvi didn't mean to do it," Teddy said soothingly. "It was all just an accident. She's been biting the boys in this town for five years and nothing's gone wrong. How was she to know this time the bite would take?"

"I don't care if it was an accident. I want my baby back," Karen cried. "Mike, do something!"

When Mike looked uncertain, her eyes narrowed suspiciously. "Don't tell me you would rather our son was a vampire?"

"Well, hell," he muttered. "It's not like its hurt Elvi any, and she needs a husband. Better someone from here than—"

"Jesus Christ, the woman is the same age as my mother!" Karen interrupted with disgust. "She's sixty-two years old."

Mike's eyes slid to Elvi where she was peering around Victor's arm. He pursed his lips. "She looks damn fine for sixty-two. And Owen could look just as good forever. Just think, Karen, you won't have to worry about him getting hurt in football anymore."

Karen wasn't impressed. "Michael Knight if you don't kill this woman and let our son go back to being just a boy you're going to find yourself in divorce court and I *will* take the house, the boat, the cottage, the—"

"All right, all right," he said with defeat, and then turned to Elvi and the others and said apologetically, "I'm sorry. I tried, but you can see what I have to deal with here. The woman just isn't reasonable when it comes to her boy."

"Now, Mike . . ." Brunswick took another step, blocking Elvi's view. "What is killing Elvi going to solve?"

"Oh, for heaven's sake, Teddy! Don't you know anything?" Karen said with exasperation. Rushing forward, she caught his arm and managed to tug him a couple of steps to the side so that Elvi could see again as she explained, "The only way to turn Owen back is to kill the vampire who turned him. So, we have to kill Elvi. We don't want to do it. We'll probably end up with horrible neighbors with her gone and Mabel off in Toronto with DJ, but I want my son back, dammit!"

"You'd rather have your husband in jail for killing Elvi than have your son be a vampire?" Mabel asked with disbelief.

"Jail?" Mike said with alarm.

"You won't go to jail," Karen assured him quickly. "You can't be charged with killing her, because she's already dead. You're just putting her to rest. Go on honey, get it over with. Sorry, Elvi," she added in an apologetic mutter.

Mike gave a long-suffering sigh, offered an apologetic glance, raised the crossbow, and said, "I'd prefer it if you moved, Victor, but I'll shoot you to get to her if I have to."

Taking the men by surprise, Elvi managed to squeeze between them and throw herself in front of Victor as she blurted, "I didn't bite Owen."

"Damn, Elvi," Teddy said with disgust as he shook off Karen's hold and moved back between Mike and the booth. "That's not going to work. We all know you bit him. It was his birthday."

"Did you see me bite him?" she asked grimly.

"No, you took him in the back room, but we saw the bite mark when he came back out," Karen said.

Shaking her head urgently, Elvi corrected, "You saw a Band-Aid on his neck. There was no bite. We put the bandage on to make it look like he'd been bitten so his friends wouldn't make fun of him, but the truth is he backed out."

"Oh now, that's just bad form," Mike complained.

"It's just wrong to try to make my son look like a coward to save your own life."

Elvi rolled her eyes. "He isn't a coward. Most of the boys back out. I *didn't* bite him."

When Mike looked uncertain, Karen scowled and asked, "Then why is he turning into a vampire?"

"He's not turning into a vampire," Elvi assured her.

"He sleeps all day, is up all night, and won't eat anything or—"

"Oh, you mean he's being a typical teenager," Elvi interrupted her list of attributes. "I was a mother once too, Karen. Trust me, sleeping late, staying up late, and not eating his veggies, but instead going out and eating junk food with friends is standard procedure."

"He has the fangs," Karen said grimly.

Elvi snorted with disbelief. There was no way Owen could be a vampire. She hadn't bit him. Besides, according to Victor, it wasn't biting them that would do it anyway, it was sharing your blood. And she hadn't shared her blood with anyone.

"He does," Karen insisted, obviously infuriated at her disbelief. Straightening, she craned her neck to try to peer over the crowd surrounding them. A look of satisfaction crossed her face when she spotted her son. "Owen! Get over here and show Elvi your fangs."

Elvi followed her gaze and spotted the teenager shaking his head wildly as he tried to duck behind Mr. Albrecht, the high school principal.

Eyes narrowing, Elvi said, "Owen Knight, get over here now, please."

Owen peered out from behind Mr. Albrecht, eyes wide with panic. He shook his head again.

"Don't make me send Victor over there," she threatened. That had the effect she'd hoped and after a brief hesitation, the boy slunk out from behind the principal and started reluctantly forward, weaving through the crowd toward the booth.

"Gee, thanks. Make me the heavy," Victor said by her ear, his hands settling heavily on her shoulder.

"I'm sorry," Elvi murmured. "But you're scarier than I am."

"And I always will be," Victor agreed. "Besides, there's no need to apologize. This is all very informative. It tells me that '*Wait 'til your father gets home*' will be something our children hear a lot of."

Elvi glanced at him with a start. "Children? Is that your idea of a proposal?"

Rather than answer, Victor gestured in front of her. "Owen has arrived."

Setting aside the subject of their future, Elvi turned to peer at the teenage boy. A small frown plucked at her eyebrows when she saw how pale he looked. Part of it was his fear, but another part wasn't, she decided, as she noted a streak in the white by his eyebrow. Mouth tightening, she leaned over the counter and ran a finger over his cheek. When she took it away, the tip of the finger was covered with white face makeup.

"Teenagers," Victor muttered with amusement.

Elvi let a little sigh slip through her lips and turned her disappointed gaze to meet Owen's. "Let's see these fangs."

Owen closed his mouth more tightly and shook his head again.

"Owen," she growled, "open."

His anxious gaze slid to Victor. Whatever he saw there, made him promptly open his mouth.

Elvi gaped at the canine teeth revealed, and then cast her glare out to encompass the three men who had been creeping up on Mike and Karen. "Edward. Harper. Alessandro . . . get over here!"

The three immortals glanced at each other, then shook their heads and gave up their positions to approach the booth. Rather than walk around to the side entrance, Edward simply swung the hinged countertop up to lean against the frame, then entered followed by Harper and Alessandro.

"What is it?" Edward asked as soon as he was standing in front of Elvi.

Elvi propped her hands on her hips and demanded, "Which one of you turned him?"

"Er . . ." Mike moved forward to stand beside his son to remind her, "You did, Elvi, when you bit him on his birthday."

Elvi turned her gaze to him with exasperation. "You can't turn someone by biting them, you have to—"

Her mouth snapped shut when Victor grabbed her arm and tugged her backward behind Mabel and DJ.

"I think it might be a good idea if we keep the *hows* of a turn to ourselves," he murmured as the other immortals closed in around them.

"Why?" Elvi asked with surprise.

"Because I don't think you want someone sneaking up on you while you're sleeping to get some of your blood."

Elvi relaxed and even chuckled at the possibility. "No one would do that! These are my friends."

"Friends?" Edward arched an eyebrow and asked drolly, "Does that include the guy with the crossbow and arrow aimed at your heart?"

Elvi cast a glare the Brit's way, and snapped, "He's looking out for his son. Besides, you'll notice he hasn't used it yet!"

"God, you're right, Victor. She *is* terribly naive for her age," Harper murmured with dismay and Elvi didn't know who to glare at: Victor for apparently saying such a thing at some point, or Harper for agreeing with him.

"I'm not naive," she informed them grimly. "I've spent my whole life in this town and I *know* these people. Unlike you five." She scowled at them and demanded, "Now which of you turned Owen?"

"My dear Ellen," Edward said with disgust. "We are allowed only one turn in our lives. You can hardly believe any of us would waste it on that young lad?"

Elvi frowned, knowing he was right. They would save it for their lifemate if needed, not fritter it away on a boy who had apparently got over his fear and decided to become a vampire. Sighing unhappily, she said, "Well, someone turned him."

"Ellen," Victor murmured patiently. "Did you see his teeth?"

"Of course, I did. And I want to know who gave them to him."

"My guess would be the costume shop in the city," he said dryly, and then asked with exasperation, "Have you even seen your own teeth?"

Elvi scowled. "Yes. Once."

"Once?" he asked with disbelief.

"Once," Elvi insisted. "In Mexico right after the turn."

She grimaced. "They were kind of scary looking as I recall, so I haven't bothered looking since we bought the mirror."

"I forgot you haven't had mirrors until recently," Victor muttered and shook his head, then said, "Look, his teeth . . . our teeth . . ."

Elvi waited patiently when he paused and frowned, and then Victor gave up trying to explain. Stepping through the men, he reached out to put a hand to the back of Owen's neck and dragged him into the booth. He must have squeezed his neck painfully then, because the boy squealed with surprised pain. Quick as a whip Victor reached into his open mouth with his free hand and snatched out one of the fangs.

"Oww!" Owen cried, covering his abused mouth. "That was glued in."

"Glued?" Victor asked with surprise.

He nodded. "The bonding stuff didn't work very well, so I used crazy glue."

"Idiot," Victor muttered, but simply walked to Elvi and held out his hand. The tooth lay in the middle of his palm, nothing more than a cap. "They're fake."

"What?" Mike lowered his crossbow and crowded into the booth, Karen rushing up behind him. The couple stared down at the fake tooth as Elvi did, then peered at each other, then back to the tooth, then to their son.

"Owen Knight," Karen snapped, moving toward her son. "How could you do something so stupid? Your father nearly killed Elvi because of this stunt!"

"I didn't mean to get Elvi killed," Owen squawked, backing away. "I was just— Bev thought vampires were cool, so I thought . . ." His explanation faded away as he ducked behind the other immortals, doing a side maneuver to avoid his irate mother.

"Ah," Victor said wisely, drawing Elvi's curious gaze.

"Ah what?"

"A female. It explains everything. Mortal males do incredibly stupid things to try to impress females."

"You mean like cutting your hair?" she asked archly.

Victor grinned. "Yes. Just like that."

Shaking her head, Elvi slid through the men and stepped between Owen and his mother. "It's all right, Karen. All's well that ends well and no one got hurt."

"What?" Victor squawked. "You were nearly killed *three* times!"

"Yes, well she knows we didn't mean anything by it," Mike assured him. "We really like Elvi. She's the best neighbor we've ever had. I was really torn by the idea of having to kill her."

A burst of laughter from Edward is the only thing that kept Victor from grabbing the man and snapping his neck. The short, harsh sound drew his vexation instead and he turned on the Brit with fury. "What the hell are you laughing at?"

"You," he said easily, and added, "And this whole situation. I don't envy you having to deal with this town. It will make for an interesting—but no doubt exasperating and exhausting—life."

Victor just grimaced, he suspected the man was right.

"I'm sorry I called you a vamp like that," Karen was saying now.

"Don't be silly, I *am* one," Elvi assured her.

"Yes, but it's not your fault. Besides I made it sound

like a bad thing and it isn't really. You're a lovely vampire," the blonde assured her. "And we really do love having you as a neighbor. We were just so upset about Owen being a vampire and didn't know what to do. I'm sorry I made Mike try to kill you. I hope this doesn't ruin our friendship?"

"Of course not," Elvi gave her a hug. "If I'd been you I would have done the same thing."

Victor shook his head with bewilderment at how women's minds functioned . . . if they functioned at all.

"Well," Mabel said mildly, drawing his attention, "I guess that resolves everything."

Victor gave a snort of disbelief. They may have solved the mystery of who was trying to kill her and brought an end to it, but there was still a long way to go before everything was resolved. They needed to talk, and then there was still the town and the council to worry about.

"Oh, oh," DJ muttered, drawing Victor's questioning gaze. The younger immortal nodded to the side and Victor glanced over to see his brother, Lucian Argeneau, head of the council, standing at the edge of the crowd around the booth. It seemed those other issues were going to be dealt with now, Victor thought with a curse under his breath.

Twenty-one

"Shit," Victor muttered, wondering how long Lucian had been there. "Elvi, come here."

"What is it, Victor?" she asked, returning to his side, concern marring her face. No doubt a response to the panic in his voice. "Is something wrong?"

"My brother is here," he said grimly, his gaze locking with the blond immortal's eyes.

"Oh," Elvi said. "How nice, I'll get to meet your brother."

"Yes," Victor groaned. He could have waited a long time for this meeting. At least until he figured out how to present the situation here in Port Henry in the least damaging light.

"You say that like it's a bad thing for me to meet him," Elvi said with concern. "Is something wrong?"

"No, no," Victor assured her dryly. "Other than the

fact that we're dead once he finds out what's been going on here, everything's fine."

"Oh, you." She chuckled and gave his arm a slap, obviously thinking he was joking or exaggerating, then turned to glance out at the crowd milling around the booth. "He must be the blond who looks so like you."

Victor wasn't surprised she knew which one was Lucian. He was the only stranger to her in the crowd.

"Who is the pretty brunette with him?"

Victor turned his gaze to the petite woman in white pants and a red silk top.

"I don't know," he admitted slowly.

"How do I look, Mabel?"

Victor glanced down to see Elvi peering down at the dress she wore with alarm.

"Damn," she said unhappily. "I wish we hadn't worn these stupid Elvira dresses. Do you think I should run home and change?"

"You're always lovely," Karen assured her. "Both of you could wear potato sacks and look lovely."

"I don't know," Elvi muttered, her gaze returning to the couple now moving toward the booth. She stared at the woman's elegant clothes and then back to herself, bit her lip, and then threw her hands in the air. "I need to change!"

"If you are, I am too," Mabel announced.

"I'll drive!" Karen offered.

Victor's mouth tightened. "Elvi."

She paused and glanced back. "What?"

"You don't have time to change," he said quietly. "Besides, I want you at my side for this."

Her eyes widened slightly, and Victor took her hand in his and gave it a squeeze.

"It will be all right," she assured him soothingly, squeezing him back, and he glanced at her sharply to find her giving him a reassuring look. *Sweet Jesus.* She thought he was the one who needed comfort when it was her he was worried about, and he wasn't at all sure it would be all right at all.

"Just how bad is this?" Brunswick asked, a frown of concern wrinkling his forehead as his gaze slid from Victor's stiffening form to DJ's grim expression.

"Bad," DJ assured him.

"It will be fine," Elvi assured him, scowling at DJ.

Victor shook his head at her optimism and told the police captain, "Lucian is the head of the council and Elvi's broken at least two of our laws."

"The biting and the rest of us knowing about her being a vampire," Brunswick said with a nod, and explained to Mike, "According to Mabel, that's against their rules."

"Laws," Victor corrected. "Laws Elvi could be sentenced to death for breaking."

"Hmmph." Mike scowled at the approaching couple. "Maybe you should take this."

Victor stared at the crossbow that was now being offered, his mind boggling. Minutes ago the man was aiming it at Elvi, and now he was offering it in her defense. This had to be the craziest town—

"Should I go get the rifle Dad got me for my birthday?" Owen asked worriedly, reminding him of his presence. "I could take the car. I'd be back in minutes."

Victor scowled at the lad who had nearly got Elvi killed and said firmly, "No."

"Mr. Argeneau's right, son"—Karen patted his arm—"Leave this to us adults."

"Don't worry, Owen," Brunswick said firmly. "Nothing will happen so long as I'm here."

Victor rolled his eyes. Brunswick still didn't get it. Badge or no badge, he had no sway here. His authority and even his gun would be useless against Lucian's position and abilities. He didn't say as much, however, but simply pushed away the crossbow Mike was still holding out and hissed, "Put that away."

"It's tempting, though, isn't it?" DJ muttered and he didn't deny it. He loved his brother, but would kill him in a heartbeat to save Elvi. And he knew DJ was feeling the same way about Mabel.

"Victor," Lucian said in greeting as he and the woman reached the other side of the counter.

"Lucian," he said warily, his gaze curious as he noted the smile on the man's face and the affectionate way he now slid his arm around the brunette's shoulder.

"Hello, what's this," DJ murmured under his breath. "I've *never* seen Lucian smile. And who's the squeeze?"

"I don't know," Victor repeated as Lucian urged the woman forward into the booth before him.

They fell silent, waiting, and Victor tried desperately not to think about how bad this could be.

"You cut your hair," Lucian said with a grin.

Before Victor could respond, he found himself pulled into a quick hug. His eyes widened incredulously and he was a tad slow in responding to the greeting, his hands belatedly rising to weakly pat Lucian's back as he released him. His oldest brother hadn't been one to show affection in all the time he'd known him, though Victor had been told the man had been openly affectionate before the fall of Atlantis and the loss of his wife, Luna, and their daughters. It seemed that man was back.

As Lucian turned his attention to greeting DJ, Victor found his gaze sliding to the petite brunette at his brother's side, sure she was the reason for Lucian's softening.

"Brother . . ." Lucian stepped back to slip his arm around the brunette again and draw her forward. "I'd like you to meet my lifemate, Leigh Gerard, soon to be Argeneau."

"Lifemate?" DJ gasped incredulously. "Well, hello dragon slayer."

"Dragon slayer?" Leigh laughed as she shook the hand the immortal offered.

"Hmm. You must be a dragon slayer to have claimed this guy's rock-hard heart," DJ explained as he stepped back to make way for Victor to greet her. However, when Victor offered her his hand, she merely used it to pull him forward for a hug.

"It's a pleasure to meet you, Victor," she said. "Lucian's told me a lot about you."

"Welcome to the family," he murmured, hugging her back. He then stepped back, squeezing Elvi's hand when she slipped it into his. He almost introduced her then, but put it off by asking, "When did this happen? The last I heard you were headed to Kansas to deal with Morgan."

"A lot's happened since I last talked to you," Lucian said with a grin, then added more seriously, "I'd have told you all about it over the phone but I couldn't get you on your cell."

"I forgot the charger and the battery ran out," Victor muttered, hoping his brother didn't read him and learn that he was lying through his teeth. The truth was that he'd shut the damned thing off once he'd realized he was attracted to Elvi. He hadn't wanted to have to report what was going on here until he figured out the best way to do so. He knew DJ had done the same in an effort to protect both Elvi and Mabel.

"Hmm." Lucian nodded and glanced to DJ. "And you? I couldn't get through on your number either. I suppose you forgot your charger too?"

"Oh, no, I have my charger," DJ said honestly, and then added the lie, "I forgot my phone."

Lucian's eyes narrowed. "Right."

The three of them fell silent, Victor ignoring the light tugs Elvi was giving his hand. He knew she was expecting him to introduce her, but was still hesitant to do so, so stood there silently, doing his best not to fidget under his brother's narrow gaze.

It was Elvi herself who finally ended the silence. Letting out an annoyed little cluck, she tugged her hand free of his and stepped forward, offering it to Lucian. "I'm Ellen Stone. Welcome to Port Henry."

"Hello, Ellen," Lucian said politely, accepting and shaking her hand even as he turned a questioning gaze to Victor.

"She's my lifemate," Victor growled in response to the look, and wasn't the only one to notice that he sounded less than pleased to say as much.

Elvi frowned at him, then forced a laugh and said, "Don't mind him. I think Victor's afraid you're going to want to kill me, but I'm sure you won't once we explain everything. This is my friend, Mabel. She's DJ's lifemate and this is—"

"Excuse me," Lucian said over Victor's groan when

she dropped that bomb and then tried to jump right into the introductions he'd neglected. "Why would Victor think I'd want to kill you?"

"Because I've bitten mortals and everyone knows I'm a vampire," she explained.

Victor groaned again.

"Now, now," Brunswick said, stepping nervously to her other side. "You'll have the man thinking you're some rogue or something. She's not a rogue," he added firmly to Lucian.

Lucian raised an eyebrow. "Who are you?"

"I'm Captain Teddy Brunswick," he introduced himself, offering a hand. When Lucian automatically took it, he added, "I'm head of the police force here in Port Henry so you can believe me when I say you needn't fear Elvi breaking your laws now that she knows them. I've known her all my life. She's a good God-fearing, law-abiding citizen of this town. She hasn't broken a law ever in her life. Not even jaywalking . . ." He paused and pursed his lips, then added reluctantly, "Well, except for when she stole my patrol car tonight. But it wasn't really stealing, it was borrowing. I mean we *were* threatening to lock them in the cold room and I did leave the keys in the car, so it was more like borrowing than stealing if you see what I mean."

When Victor groaned again, Mike stepped nervously forward and tried to help matters.

"Teddy's right," he said firmly. "It wasn't stealing really. And Elvi didn't know she wasn't supposed to bite us, none of us did or she never would have bitten all the boys as they turned eighteen. Besides, she only ever bit the willing."

"Well, except for when she bit Mabel while she was sick with the turning," Karen interjected, then quickly added, "but Mabel forgave her and they're still friends and Mabel bit her back during her own turn so it kind of cancels it out, right?"

"Who are these mortals?" Lucian asked Victor with bewilderment.

"Oh, I'm sorry," Mike held out his hand, "Michael Knight, fire chief for Port Henry. And this is my lovely wife, Karen."

"I thought they didn't want to kill you anymore, Elvi," DJ muttered under his breath. "And I didn't realize Brunswick had it in for you too."

Sighing, Victor decided it was time to intercede, but before he could, Harper said, "She didn't put the ad in the single's column, and has never been to Toronto. She isn't the source of the rumors going around the clubs."

"I put the ad in," Mabel admitted.

"And the rumors around Toronto were caused by Brunswick hitting the club scene there in search of other vampires," Edward announced.

"*Si,*" Alessandro nodded. "They were looking for the mate for the Elvi."

"We didn't know we were doing anything wrong," Teddy assured him. "We won't do it again."

When Lucian turned his way, Victor ran a weary hand through his hair and said, "Look Lucian, there's a lot to explain here. Maybe we should head back to the house and discuss this."

"You aren't going without me, son," Brunswick announced firmly. "I'm the law in this town and no one's hurting Elvi."

"We'll just follow you over," Mike announced, making it obvious he was backing the police captain.

Karen glanced toward the crowd still gathered around the booth and said, "I think we should all go."

A rumble of agreement began among the crowd. Before it could grow too loud, Lucian snapped, "Enough."

Victor waited tensely as Lucian's gaze slid over the crowd of people who had closed in on the booth. He couldn't help noticing that they had that same lynch-mob look they'd had in the restaurant that first night when he rushed up, stake in hand, threatening Elvi. If Lucian noticed it, he didn't look concerned, though he did shift himself closer to Leigh in a protective manner.

Finally, he turned his attention to Elvi and asked, "Elvi Black?"

"No . . . well, yes, but no," she said quickly, and explained, "My name is really Ellen Stone, but everyone calls me Elvi Black. Black is my maiden name, you see, and Elvi is . . . well, a nickname."

Lucian stared at Elvi for a minute, then nodded and turned to first Brunswick, then Mike, his wife, each of the other immortals, and finally to Victor.

Victor didn't resist or try to block Lucian when he felt the ruffling in his mind, knowing that his brother had already read Elvi's thoughts as well as those of Brunswick, the Knights', the other immortals, and probably half the crowd outside the booth if not all of them. It was the quickest and easiest way to get to the truth of the matter and probably the only way to sort this one out.

Apparently finished, Lucian relaxed and glanced at

Leigh. "I believe Bastien is going to have to rent a bigger hall. We'll be adding several more names to the guest list for our wedding."

Victor let his breath out in a slow hiss, his shoulders relaxing, but stilled when Lucian turned back to him.

"Just for the record, Victor," he said, "you couldn't take me in a fight. I'd have slaughtered you. But I understand the reason you would have tried. She's quite special. Almost as special as my Leigh."

"I'm still surprised that I'm not going to get called before the council or receive any kind of punishment," Elvi murmured, leaning her back into Victor's chest and resting her arms on his as they watched Lucian's car pull out of her driveway several hours later. "I expected some small punishment at least."

"Lucian *is* the council, or at least the head of it. What he decides is usually law," Victor explained, then laughed and added, "and he considers making us live here to keep an eye on the people of Port Henry to ensure they don't tell anyone as punishment."

"He does not," Elvi laughed, slapping his arm lightly.

"He does, he said so," Victor assured her with a grin.

Elvi just shook her head. "I really like him and Leigh. It's a shame they couldn't stay the day. They could have taken the room you and DJ used to have."

"They like you too," Victor assured her, hugging her closer and pressing a kiss to the top of her head. "But they have a plane in Toronto waiting to take them down to Kansas to take care of a few things at Leigh's restaurant before they head to Europe. Lucian's worried about our sister-in-law and wants to check on her."

"Marguerite," Elvi murmured with a nod. "Leigh explained that they can't reach her and her daughter's had a baby."

"Yes." He hugged her close, his eyes searching the sky. Mention of Lissianna's baby reminded him of a last issue he had to cover before he could be sure there were no obstacles to their future.

"Love, I know you want to have children, but . . ."

"But?" she asked and he could hear the frown in her voice.

Victor opened his mouth to speak, then hesitated and unwound his arms from her waist to catch her hand and draw her to a deck chair. Settling himself in it, he pulled her down onto his lap, cocooning her in his arms before he spoke.

"My son, Vincent, can't survive on bagged blood," he announced.

Elvi glanced up at him with surprise. "He can't?"

Victor shook his head. "He has a genetic anomaly that won't allow it. On a diet of bagged blood, he'd starve to death."

Elvi frowned. "I thought the nanos fixed things and made us perfect."

"Not perfect, better. Stronger, faster, healthier . . ." He shrugged. "They apparently don't see this anomaly as something that needs to be repaired."

"Oh," Elvi murmured thoughtfully, then asked, "How does he survive, then?"

"He has to feed directly from the source," Victor answered.

"He has to bite people," she clarified.

"Yes."

She was silent for several heartbeats and then asked, "He inherited it from you?"

Victor sucked in a breath, he'd known he'd have to tell her, but hadn't imagined she'd guess. "How did you—?"

"You've been here a week, Victor, and never once fed in front of me," she said solemnly. "Besides, I overheard DJ offering to cover for you that first night. And another time. I didn't understand then why, but this explains everything." She tilted her head to ask, "Is that why you disappeared for a bit when we were at the Night Club?"

"Yes," he acknowledged warily, but she just nodded and leaned into him again.

"Do you mind?" he asked after a moment of silence.

"Mind what?" she asked, sounding confused.

"About my having to bite other women?"

"Well, you could bite men too," she pointed out with amusement.

"Yes, and I will, but there will be times when it's a woman who will be most handy," he said quietly.

Elvi shrugged. "Why should I mind? If it's the only way for you to feed. . . ." She shrugged again.

"Marion minded," he murmured.

"Marion died before there were blood banks, she must have had to feed by biting as well. Why would it bother her?"

"She was afraid I'd find the women attractive, I think," he admitted.

Elvi gave a laugh. "Then maybe there was something wrong with Marion. It's hard to find someone attractive when you're thinking of them as dinner. At least, it was for me. I certainly didn't find any of those eighteen-year-old boys attractive."

She peered at him solemnly. "Victor, even if you found them attractive, I know you wouldn't do anything with them. I'm your lifemate. I doubt you're likely to run into another woman you can't read while out feeding. I'm not insecure enough to fret over that." She tilted her head. "Is that why you haven't told me until now?"

"That and I worried that you might be upset at the idea of having children who would have to feed that way as well. Bastien says the chances might be fifty-fifty as to whether they are or not, it depends on whether they take after the mother or the father. It's something of a stigma among our people."

"Well, then, I guess we'll have to hope they take after me," she said reasonably. "But if they don't we'll deal with it. We can deal with anything together. I love you."

"I love you too," he breathed, hugging her close. "How did I get lucky enough to find you?"

"Mabel put an ad in the single's column," she reminded him teasingly and Victor laughed and hugged her close, and then stood with her in his arms and started up the stairs to the sunroom.

"I was thinking we might like to take a trip in the near future," he murmured as he paused at the top of the stairs.

"Oh?" Elvi asked, pulling the sunroom door open so that he could carry her in.

"Yes. To California. To see my son."

Elvi glanced at him sharply. "Really?"

"Really," he said softly. "It's time. And somehow I don't think it will be painful anymore."

"I love you, Victor Argeneau," she whispered, hugging him tightly as he carried her through to the bedroom.

"I love you, Ellen Elvi Black Stone. . . . But I can't wait to change your name to Argeneau so I know what to call you."

"Just call me *'Love,'*" she whispered and kissed him as he lowered them both to the bed.

Turn the page for a sneak peek at the next
novel in the Argeneau Vampire series,
Vampires are Forever

"Thanks, just set it there on the table," Thomas said as the bellhop followed him into the suite's sitting room. When the man did and then turned, mouth opening to inform him of all the amenities on offer, he waved him to silence.

"I'm good, thanks," Thomas assured him. Offering the man a tip for seeing him to his suite and carrying the knapsack, Thomas urged him toward the door.

"Thank you, sir," the bellhop's mouth spread into a grin that he quickly softened into a more businesslike smile. "Just ring the desk if you need anything. Ask for Jimmy and I'll get you whatever you need."

"I will. Thanks again," Thomas murmured.

Closing the door behind the bellhop, he then turned and stepped back into the sitting room of his suite. Classy, luxurious, tasteful . . . Nothing less than he'd expect. Aunt Marguerite always had shown good taste.

Moving forward, Thomas collected his knapsack and headed for the door leading into the rest of the suite, intending to place it in the bedroom. The ring of his cell phone made him pause, however.

Dropping the knapsack back on the table, he pulled the phone from his back pocket and flipped it open as he dropped onto one of the love seats.

"Yo?" he said lightly, already knowing who it would be.

"You arrived all right, then?" Bastien asked.

"Of course, dude. The flight was smooth sailing."

"And Inez had no problem finding you at the airport?"

Thomas's eyebrows rose. "Inez?"

"Yes. I called her to meet your plane and take you into the city."

Thomas could hear the frown in Bastien's voice, but ignored it, his mind on his arrival in Heathrow as he suddenly recalled a little dark-haired woman running through the airport, waving. Thomas had noticed her, but Etienne hadn't mentioned there being anyone to meet him so had just assumed she was there to collect someone behind him and kept walking. Now that Bastien mentioned Inez, however, he recalled the pristine and tucked-up little miss he'd met some months ago in his cousin's office and knew she was who had been waving so frantically. She'd been less than pristine and tucked-up at the airport that morning. That woman had looked like she'd just rolled out of bed.

"Thomas?" Bastien said impatiently. "Did she not show up?"

"Yes. She was there," he answered truthfully, a knock drawing his gaze to the door of the suite. Standing, he moved to answer it.

"Good," Bastien was saying as Thomas opened the door. "She's very efficient as a rule, but I did wake her up at five in the morning to collect you and I worried that she hadn't made it there in time."

"Yes, she—" Thomas stopped abruptly as he recognized the woman at his door. His gaze slid over her limp dark curls, her slightly wrinkled clothes, and her makeup-free face with its irritated scowl. Inez Urso. A very angry Inez Urso, he added noting the fire flashing in her eyes.

When her mouth opened, Thomas instinctively slammed the cell phone to his chest to prevent Bastien's hearing the tirade he suspected was coming. He wasn't wrong. The phone had barely hit his chest when a barrage of words shot from her full, luscious mouth and poured over him. Unfortunately, very little of it was in English. Portuguese would have been his guess. He gathered that was her mother tongue and the language she slipped into when upset, and Inez Urso was definitely upset.

When she began to move forward, Thomas automatically backed up, allowing her into the room. He was too distracted to do otherwise, finding it fascinating how a woman who had looked perfectly plain on first sight could become almost beautiful as she berated him. Her eyes were flashing, her cheeks were flushed with anger, her lips flapping so rapidly they were almost a blur. She was also waving a finger angrily under his nose as she backed him up, something he normally found vastly annoying if the women in his family tried it. But coming from this short woman, he found it kind of cute and couldn't help the smile that tugged at his mouth.

Big mistake, Thomas realized at once. Inez Urso did not like his amusement and her rant took on some real energy. Unfortunately, that's when he became aware of the chittering coming from the phone.

Thomas scowled down at it, then glanced toward the

door closing behind the little barracuda still lecturing him, judging whether he could get her back out of the room long enough for him to deal with Bastien. It didn't seem very possible, at least not without being rude, and Aunt Marguerite had raised him better than that.

Giving up on the door, he glanced toward the one leading to the rest of the suite and back to the woman and then held up a hand for silence. Surprisingly—she obeyed the directive, her tirade ending at once, but then he supposed she'd been close to winding down. At least, her eyes had lost some of their heat, becoming more subdued. Inez was still breathing rapidly from her anger, though, and Thomas found his eyes falling to her slightly heaving chest, noting that with every inhalation, her blouse was stretched tight, almost seeming to threaten to pop a button.

A sharp inhalation drew his gaze back up to her face. Her dark brown eyes were flashing again, her mouth opening to go at him once more. Thomas didn't blame her at all . . . really . . . it was perfectly rude to stare at a woman's chest. Aunt Marguerite would be pissed at him too. Still, he didn't really have time to apologize properly, or let her vent with Bastien's voice still squawking into his chest, so Thomas raised his hand again for silence and said, "Hold that thought."

Inez blinked at the order, but closed her mouth and Thomas gave her an approving smile before whirling away and rushing from the room. He hurried through the small dining area in the next room, judged it too close, and continued on into a small hallway with two doors leading off of it. The first led into a spacious marble bathroom, the second a bedroom. Knowing the bathroom would have a lock, Thomas slid inside, closed and then locked it for good measure lest the woman follow to finish her lecture. He then took a breath and raised the phone back to his ear. "Bastien?"

"What the hell was that about?" his cousin growled.

"Oh, I . . . er . . . sat on the remote control and accidentally turned on the television. Some foreign film was playing and I couldn't figure out how to shut it off," Thomas lied blithely.

"Right," Bastien said with open disbelief. "What was the name of this movie?"

"The name?" Thomas echoed and then scowled. "How the hell would I know?"

"I don't know, Thomas. I thought maybe you caught it before you turned it off. It sounded terribly interesting. I quite enjoyed it when the woman called the man an idiot for making her drag her butt out of bed at five o'clock in the morning and haul herself down to the airport without either tea, or a shower, only to have him ignore her and march out to get in a taxi and take off to the Dorchester Hotel."

Thomas closed his eyes on a sigh as he recalled Bastien spoke several languages, including Portuguese.

"Hmm," Bastien said suddenly. "That's the same hotel I booked you into. What a coincidence."

"All right, all right, so it wasn't the television," Thomas muttered irritably and then asked, "Did she really call me an idiot?"

An exasperated sigh came through the line. "How could you walk right past her, Thomas? *Why* would you? For Christ's sake, I called her to make things easier for you, and you just—"

"You didn't mention that anyone was picking me up at the airport," Thomas interrupted grimly. "Neither did

Etienne. He said you had a plane waiting at the airport and had booked a room at the Dorchester. That's it. There was no mention of anyone waiting for me at the airport, so I just hopped in a taxi."

"Well, when you saw Inez—"

"Bastien, I met the woman once for about three minutes in your office almost six months ago," Thomas pointed out dryly and then acknowledged, "I *did* see her waving and rushing toward me at the airport, but didn't recognize her. I thought she was there for someone else. How was I to know otherwise when *no one told me she would be meeting me*," he ended, emphasizing every word.

"All right, I get the point. You didn't know," Bastien said.

"Right," Thomas sighed.

"Okay." A moment of silence passed and then a sigh slid from the phone and Bastien said, "I should have contacted you myself and told you she would meet you rather than counting on Etienne. You'll have to apologize to her for me."

"Are you sure you told Etienne?" Thomas asked.

"What?" Bastien asked, his voice short. "Of course I did."

"Of course you did, because you wouldn't ever make a mistake. Those are for lesser immortals like Etienne and me."

"Thomas," Bastien said wearily.

"Yes?" he asked sweetly.

"Never mind. Look, she's there to help you. Let her. She knows London and she's a damned efficient woman. One of our best employees. She gets things done, that's why I decided to have her help you."

"You mean that's why you decided to have her baby-sit me, don't you?" Thomas asked dryly.

There was a brief silence on the other end of the line, then Bastien took a breath, but before he could speak, Thomas said, "Don't worry about it. I know you think I'm useless. Me, Etienne, and anyone under four hundred years old. So don't worry about it. I'll apologize to her for you and let her help me."

He pushed the off button on the phone before Bastien could respond and tossed it irritably on the marble counter as he headed for the door. He'd grasped the doorknob when a thought made him pause. Releasing the doorknob, Thomas turned back to briefly pace the room.

He didn't want another berating by Bastien's underling. While it was cute and he'd found it fascinating to watch the fire dance in her eyes as she'd spat words rapid fire at him, it would have been more entertaining had he understood some of it. Besides, he didn't know London and this woman obviously did and while he'd like to be able to find his aunt all by himself and be the hero of the moment, the main concern was *finding* Aunt Marguerite. Common sense said he would probably get farther faster with help, and Inez was the only help on offer. But she was no doubt in a really rotten mood right now and he couldn't blame her. Bastien might owe her an apology, but Thomas felt he owed her something too. He might not have known she was coming to collect him, but the woman had gone out of her way to do so and been ignored and left behind for her trouble. He wished to offer his own apology as well.

After pacing the room twice, Thomas reached for the hotel phone on the bathroom's marble counter.

He punched the button for room service and quickly placed an order, then hung up and moved to the tub. His cell phone rang as he pushed the button to drop the tub's stopper into place, but—knowing it would be Bastien with more orders and instructions—he ignored it and grabbed the bottle of bubble bath off the counter. Thomas dumped a generous amount of the liquid in and turned on the taps, then sat down on the side of the tub to wait for it to fill.

Inez dropped wearily to sit on one of the love seats situated on either side of the fireplace and scowled at the knapsack on the table in front of her. The man couldn't even bother with proper luggage. He was staying in a five-star hotel and checked in with a knapsack. It was the only article of luggage in the room and the only thing he'd been carrying when she'd seen him at the airport.

She glared at the offending article and then realized what she was doing and shook her head, her eyes closing in dismay. She was losing it. Inez never lost her temper, yet here she was not just glaring at luggage, but having greeted her boss's cousin by berating him like a harridan and cursing him in two different languages. Her boss's cousin!

Dear God, she hadn't just lost her mind but probably her job too, once Bastien heard about this. Thomas Argeneau was probably on the phone in the other room right now complaining to him.